Benita Brown was born an  er
English mother, the you nd
her Indian father, who can ne
and fell in love with the pl ng
her husband at drama school in London, Benita returned
to her home town and worked as a teacher and broadcaster
before becoming a full-time writer. Her previous novels are
published by Headline.

Praise for Benita Brown:

'A romantic tale of rivalry and deceit' *Newcastle Upon Tyne Journal*

'A delightfully interwoven story of passion, love and loss' *Sunderland Echo*

'I didn't want to put it down . . . A must for Catherine Cookson lovers' *Coventry Telegraph*

'[A] powerful and moving tale of love and survival' *Lancashire Evening Post*

Benita BROWN

Dreaming Out Loud

headline

First published in Great Britain in 2013
by HEADLINE PUBLISHING GROUP

First published in paperback in Great Britain in 2013
by HEADLINE PUBLISHING GROUP

1

Cataloguing in Publication Data is available from the British Library

ISBN 978 0 7553 8471 6

Typeset in Bembo by Avon DataSet Ltd, Bidford-on-Avon, Warwickshire

Printed and bound in Great Britain by Clays Ltd, St Ives plc

Headline's policy is to use papers that are natural, renewable and
recyclable products and made from wood grown in sustainable
forests. The logging and manufacturing processes are expected
to conform to the environmental regulations of the country of origin.

HEADLINE PUBLISHING GROUP
An Hachette UK Company
338 Euston Road
London NW1 3BH

www.headline.co.uk
www.hachette.co.uk

To my darling husband, Norman

Part One

London, 1935

The audience were on their feet. They clapped and whistled and shouted her name. Her co-star, Robert Spencer, tall and impossibly suave in his evening clothes, stood slightly aside and smiled good-naturedly. In his early forties, he was firmly established in the hearts of theatre goers and was generous enough to allow his co-star, Lana Fontaine, to enjoy her well-deserved ovation. The final act of *Just Good Friends* took place at a ball, so Lana, too, was in evening dress: a floor-length, crimson taffeta sheath which enhanced her slim but womanly figure.

When the rest of the cast had withdrawn, Robert and Lana had stepped forward so that the curtains could close behind them. The pair were encircled by a spotlight – a magic circle, Violet thought, although she knew no magic spells had been required to ensure Lana's success. Her friend from days gone by was blessed with supreme talent and had been prepared to work hard to gain her exalted place in the world of entertainment.

The fire curtain began its slow descent and the audience groaned. Robert Spencer and Lana started to walk towards the wings. They smiled and waved until they vanished from sight. It took a while for the audience to accept that their darlings were not coming back and then there was the usual disorganised exit, accompanied by excited comment. In their seats in the front row of the dress circle, for which they'd paid the staggering sum of three and sixpence each, Violet turned to Eve and said, 'Stay here. We don't want to be crushed or trampled on. Let them all go.'

Eve looked worried. 'But don't you want to go to the stage door and say hello?'

'Don't worry. They'll be a while yet. They have to take their make-up off and change their clothes. Remember?'

Eve looked downcast. 'I do. Do you think we'll ever get to tread the boards again?'

'I fully intend to,' Violet said. 'But are you sure that's what you really want? I mean, what about that gent in the pinstripe suit who makes eyes at you over the luncheon menu?'

Eve flushed and looked away. 'There's nothing in it. Don't tease.'

'I won't. But I'm not convinced.'

'Can we go now?'

Violet glanced round at the gradually emptying aisles. 'Yes, let's go.'

There was an excited crowd of fans in the narrow street behind the theatre. They clutched their programmes or their autograph books, and thrust them at any member of the cast who emerged from the stage door. So far there was no sign of the two stars.

'Do you think we've missed them after all?' Eve asked.

'No, I think they're waiting to let the lesser mortals make their exits.'

She had hardly finished her sentence before the crowd around them cheered and Lana Fontaine and Robert Spencer appeared together standing beneath the old-fashioned lantern above the door. It was impossible to get near them so Violet and Eve just had to wait their turn to approach them.

4

'We should have left the theatre when I wanted to,' Eve said.

Just then a taxi arrived and Robert Spencer turned to Lana and said, 'It's time to go.'

'Lana!' Eve shouted. 'Wait!'

In her excitement she pushed a solid-looking woman aside and Lana turned to look at her just as the woman began to complain loudly. 'Take your turn,' she said to Eve. 'I've been here longer than you have.'

To everyone's surprise Lana began to walk towards them. 'Eve . . . Is that you? And Violet as well? How wonderful!' She turned her head and said, 'Robert, come and meet two of my old friends.'

The crowd parted for the two stars and then listened avidly as Lana introduced Robert to her friends.

'Did you come to see the play tonight?' Lana asked.

'We did,' Eve said. 'It was wonderful. You were wonderful!'

'I'm glad you enjoyed it. But Violet, what about you?'

'I thought you were marvellous. And I'm sorry that I was so beastly to you the last time I saw you.'

'Were you? I don't remember that. But now, what are you both doing? Have you come to join a show in London?'

'No such luck,' Violet said. We're working as Nippies at the Strand Corner House.'

'Oh, I'm sorry. I know times are hard.'

'It's not a bad sort of job,' Violet said. 'Although our uniform makes us look like housemaids in a French farce.'

'Oh, but the skirts are longer and much more stylish,' Eve interjected. 'And did you know hundreds, absolutely *hundreds*, of Nippies have married customers. Some of them real gentlemen!'

Lana smiled and then Robert stepped forward. 'We'd better go, darling. The party won't get going without us.'

'Yes, I know. Well, you two, it was so good to see you. I might just pop into the Corner House for an afternoon tea one day.'

Robert Spencer smiled at Violet and Eve, then put his arm around Lana and, to the disappointment of the remaining fans, guided her towards the taxi.

'He called her darling,' Eve said. 'Do you think . . . ?'

'No. That's just the way they talk. There was no kind of electricity between them. I think they're just good friends, like the title of the play.'

'Do you think she'll pop in to the Corner House to see us?'

'I believe she fully intends to. But in any case, by the time she gets around to it, I'll be treading the boards again and you will have walked down the aisle with your pinstriped gentleman.'

Chapter One

Northridge Bay, October 1949

Kay glanced out of the window and saw dark clouds gathering over the sea. The restless swell of the water matched her troubled mood.

'I don't think the sun is going to shine today,' Miss Bennet said. 'Now take your coat off and sit down while I make a pot of tea. There's my order on the table.'

The elderly lady left the room, straight-backed but walking somewhat stiffly. Kay picked up the list. The handwriting, in old-fashioned copperplate style, was as neat as Miss Bennet herself and Kay had no problem reading and copying the items into her order book. It didn't take long.

When Miss Bennet returned with her best tea set on a tray Kay looked up and smiled. 'Is this everything?' she asked.

'Yes, that's all. Unless you have any nice broken biscuits.'

'We have. Shortbread no less.'

'Then I'll have half a pound. And I think I may have enough points for a jar of jam. If that's the case I would prefer strawberry.'

'I'll pack your box myself,' Kay said. She slipped the order book and pencil into her shoulder bag.

'You're a good girl,' Miss Bennet said. 'I'll miss you when you're gone.'

Kay concentrated on stirring a spoonful of sugar into her tea.

'You *are* going, aren't you?' Miss Bennet asked.

Kay sipped her tea before she answered. 'I haven't decided yet.'

'For goodness' sake. What on earth is stopping you?'

'My mother . . . my sister . . . Tony . . .'

'Ah, yes, Tony Chalmers DFC, our very own war hero,' Miss Bennet said dryly. 'Good-looking, dashing, and the heir to a successful light engineering business. But you're not actually engaged, are you?'

'I don't suppose so.'

'Don't suppose so? Has he asked you to marry him or hasn't he?'

'Not in so many words.'

'And what does that mean?'

'Well . . . I think he just assumes that we will marry one day.'

Miss Bennet shook her head. 'That's not good enough. It sounds to me as if he is just playing with your affections.'

Kay burst out laughing.

'What has amused you?'

'Playing with my affections! That sounds like something from a Victorian novel.'

Miss Bennet's eyes widened and then she shook her head and smiled. 'I know. I suppose to you I'm just an old fogey, someone left over from a former age. But, my dear, my sentiments are genuine. I don't want you to be hurt.' She paused. 'Have you told him your news yet?'

'No.'

'Kay, you did me the honour of confiding in me, so I assume you won't mind if I offer my advice?'

'Of course not.'

Miss Bennet picked up the teapot and topped up both

their cups; her slim hand trembling slightly with the effort. 'I realise what a big step leaving home would be for you,' she said, 'but you know how disappointed I was when your mother took you away from school. You were one of my most promising pupils. I cannot bear the thought of your working in a shop while your younger sister goes to college. And now a trick of fate has offered you new opportunities. Please don't let them slip by.'

'You keep asking me if I'm going,' Kay said, 'but where exactly do you think I should go?'

'Well, first of all London. That's obvious. You have matters you have to sort out there, haven't you? Then you could move on. Go abroad, even. Or stay in London and get a proper job.'

'What do you mean by a proper job?'

'One with training of some sort.'

'Isn't it a bit late for that?'

'You are only twenty-two, and you are an intelligent young woman with a good speaking voice. No doubt you inherited that from your father.'

Kay smiled reminiscently. 'We used to read aloud together. He enjoyed teaching me to speak clearly – and my sister too. We used to make up little plays and perform them for our parents, but Julie didn't enjoy doing that as much as I did. She was happier making tea parties for her dolls.'

'Your father gave you a great gift,' Miss Bennet said. 'I'm sure you would have no difficulty finding an occupation more suitable than working in a grocery shop.'

'I quite like working at Sampson's. And I meet such interesting people when I'm out collecting the orders.'

Miss Bennet tutted impatiently. 'You work long hours. You've told me yourself that you don't have much time to socialise with your old school friends. Surely you must be aware that you could do much better for yourself?'

'It depends what you mean by better.'

'Are you deliberately trying my patience?'

'No, I'm being serious. I need to think very carefully about what I should do if I am to leave home.'

'Kay, don't you have any dreams?'

'Dreams?'

'Do you never dream about making a different life for yourself? Don't you have any ambitions? If you have you keep them all to yourself.'

'Perhaps I have but only in the sense that no matter how much I enjoy my job at Sampson's, I dream that somewhere, somehow there may be a different kind of life. I'm not being very clear, am I?' She paused. 'I'm sorry.'

Miss Bennet relented. 'Don't be sorry, Kay. I know you well enough to be confident that you will make the right decision, and until then, I promise you that I won't ask you again. I'll wait until you are ready to tell me what you have decided. And, of course, your secret remains safe with me.'

'My secret . . .'

'You're smiling.'

'Well, it is rather wonderful, isn't it? Again, it's like a novel. The poor but honest girl and the inheritance that changes her life.'

Kay and Miss Bennet looked at each other and laughed.

'What a dear girl you are,' Miss Bennet said. 'But now,' she glanced round at the clock on the mantelshelf. 'We've spent so much time talking I wonder if you have time to do me the usual favour?' She placed a hand on the folded copy of the local newspaper which lay on the table.

'Yes, of course I have.'

'I don't want to cause trouble for you by making you late back for work.'

'I won't be late. I whizzed round collecting my other orders in record time so I could have more time with you.'

Miss Bennet laughed. 'Honestly, Kay, I don't know how you manage it.'

'What do you mean?'

'Well . . . oh dear, I wish I hadn't started this but now I must finish. I mean cycling so vigorously when . . .'

'When one of my legs is shorter than the other one? No, please don't be embarrassed. My leg was injured when I was very small. I grew up learning to cope with it. I can't remember what it was like not to have a limp.'

'Well, you cope very well.' Miss Bennet paused then smiled broadly. 'The way you zip around on that old bicycle reminds me of Miss Gulch in *The Wizard of Oz*. You know, when she's pedalling furiously on her way to collect Toto.'

Kay hunched her shoulders and raised her hands, her fingers hooked like claws. 'I'll get you my pretty,' she croaked, 'and your little dog, too!'

Miss Bennet shook her head. 'Amazing. You sound just like her.'

Kay laughed. 'Well I hope you don't think I look like her.'

'Oh, no. Your face isn't at all green.'

'Thank you very much!' Kay laughed again.

Miss Bennet paused and looked at Kay thoughtfully. 'In fact you are very beautiful. But that's enough. I have no wish to turn your head.'

Kay reached for the newspaper. It had been opened and then folded at the usual page. 'A TRIP TO YESTERYEAR', the headline promised and then a sub-headline read, somewhat unnecessarily: 'Our Town in Years Gone By'. Four photographs were arranged around the text, which was too small for Miss Bennet to read easily.

'It's not just a matter of getting new spectacles,' she had informed Kay when she had first mentioned her problem and asked if Kay had time to read something from the local paper to her. 'It's more complicated than that. I have no problem with the photographs, but even with my spectacles on I can't manage to read print properly. I've tried using a magnifying glass but I've never mastered the way you have to squint through it. If I read for too long I end up with a headache. I depend on the wireless for news and information but that particular feature in the *Chronicle* is one I enjoy.'

Ever since Miss Bennet had confided in Kay about her poor eyesight, Kay had made sure that she always arrived in time to read the newspaper feature to her. Thursday, the day the *Seaside Chronicle* was published, was also the day that Kay visited Sampson's regular customers in their own homes, the ones who were elderly or infirm and could not get to the shop themselves, and did not have a telephone. Kay took their orders which would then be delivered by Mr Sampson, himself, the following day.

Kay and Miss Bennet had fallen into the habit of having a cosy gossip over tea and biscuits and they had become so at ease with each other that when the letter had arrived which could potentially change her life, Kay had found it quite natural to confide in her elderly friend even though the only other person who knew was her mother.

'Kay?'

Miss Bennet was looking at her enquiringly, and Kay brought her mind back to the task in hand. She examined the newspaper and was delighted to see that the subject this week was the Pavilion Theatre; her father had been an actor-manager at the Pavilion. She started reading eagerly.

The building of the railway station at the turn of the century brought many visitors to Northridge Bay. These visitors liked to take the sea air, promenading along the seafront and then dining at the Waverly Hotel, Roberto's Italian restaurant, or one of the excellent fish and chip establishments. Local businessman Mr George Waugh saw the opportunity to boost the local economy even more by providing entertainment for the visitors. He lost no time in having the Pavilion Theatre built on the new lower promenade.

The Pavilion opened in time for the summer season of 1910 and Mr Waugh let it be known that the famous child impersonator, Lily Elsie, known on the stage as Little Elsie, would be taking to the boards on opening night. Unfortunately for Mr Waugh, one gentleman in the audience had recently seen the real Lily Elsie on the stage in London, and he rose from his seat and shouted, 'Imposter! Get off the stage!'

The hapless woman was indeed an imposter and was, in fact, Mr Waugh's own daughter, who had theatrical ambitions. However, the audience was in a good mood and soon forgave her. The first night was an outstanding success and the Pavilion went on to stage first class variety shows for season after season.

Henry Payne led a small resident orchestra, handing on his baton to his son Cyril when he retired, and many top artists appeared there over the years, including such household names as George Formby and Arthur Askey.

During the Great War the theatre never closed, cheering the spirits not only of the local population but also of the wounded servicemen from the nearby convalescent home. Perhaps the theatre had its greatest success during the years between the wars, when Mr Jack Lockwood was the actor–manager there. However, at the start of World War II, when the beaches were closed, the government saw fit to close the Pavilion, and sadly it has never reopened.

When Kay had finished reading, Miss Bennet suggested that they look at the photographs together, and Kay moved her chair round and spread the paper out on the table.

The first photograph was an exterior shot of the Pavilion in its glory days. An elaborate façade gave it the appearance of a pagoda, and a couple of dragons sat on their haunches facing each other above the entrance.

'I wish these photographs could have been in colour,' Miss Bennet said. 'The outside of the theatre was painted green and red and the dragons were gold.'

'Yes, I think I can remember that,' Kay said. 'Although I was only a child when my father worked there.'

'I believe he was working there before you were even born,' Miss Bennet told her.

The next three photographs had all been taken inside the theatre. One was of George Formby on stage, smiling and playing his ukulele, captioned: 'A famous star makes a guest appearance in Northridge Bay!' Another photograph was of a line of girls in frilly blouses and short skirts, arms linked and smiling brightly as they kicked their heights. The caption underneath informed: 'The Dolly Girls. An ever popular local dancing troupe'.

The final photograph had been taken from the stage looking into the auditorium and showed that every seat was occupied and everyone was smiling. No matter that they were on holiday by the sea, the men and women in the audience were smartly dressed; their clothes almost formal. Kay wondered out loud if they always dressed like that when they were going to a seaside variety show, or whether they had known that they were going to have their photograph taken and that they would become part of the history of the Pavilion Theatre.

'People did dress more smartly then,' Miss Bennet said.

'No matter what your station in life, a night at the theatre was an occasion to look your best. When was the photograph taken?'

Kay peered at the caption: 'Full House at the Pavilion'. 'It doesn't give a date,' she said. 'But from what I can see of the women's dresses and hairstyles, I guess it could be sometime in the nineteen-twenties.'

'Then, just think, your father was probably there the night this photograph was taken. His troupe played several summer seasons at the Pavilion and he must have liked the place so much that he decided to settle here. He fell in love with your mother, of course. Does she ever tell you about those days?'

'Never.'

There was an awkward pause and Miss Bennet, sensing that Kay was reluctant to talk about her parents, changed the subject slightly.

'Of course, Lana Fontaine would have been there at the time. Do you remember her at all?'

'Yes I do.'

'But she was just a chorus girl at the time,' Miss Bennet continued. 'Then look what happened: she went on to be a film star leaving her old friends at the Pavilion far behind. But, obviously, she never forgot them. Particularly you. Your father was very talented, but he was content to stay here. He must have loved your mother very much. I know you've told me about your reading together, but what else do you remember about your father, Kay? No! Don't answer that. I'm being personal again.' Miss Bennet looked embarrassed.

'I don't mind answering you. I remember quite a lot about him. He was tall and handsome, and such good fun. The house was always a happier place with him around. My mother and Julie and I all adored him.'

'How sad for you that that happy time was all too short.'

'I don't think my mother has ever recovered.' Suddenly Kay felt awkward. Her mother was a very private person and Kay knew she had revealed too much. She smiled at Miss Bennet, 'But now, sadly, I really do have to go.'

'And you'll be coming for my order as usual next week?

'Of course I will – why shouldn't I?'

'There are two possible reasons. Firstly because I have annoyed you with my gossiping.'

'Of course you haven't.'

'And secondly, you may decide to leave your job at Sampson's and begin to enjoy your inheritance.'

Kay stuffed her shoulder bag into the basket on the handlebars and turned up her coat collar before setting off. She couldn't make up her mind whether it was raining or whether the spots of moisture landing on her face were part of the hazy mist that was rolling in from the sea. As she cycled along the seafront the tyres made swishing noises on the damp surface of the road. She turned and made her way to the town centre, up through avenues of respectable semi-detached houses, passing the house where she lived with her mother and sister on the way.

She saw the glimmer of a fire in the front parlour and imagined her mother sitting by the hearth with her lunch tray and the local paper. Kay wondered if Thelma had read the feature about the Pavilion Theatre. If she had, would it have brought back happy memories? Whether it had or not, Kay would never know, because her mother never talked about the past.

The sea fret turned into light rain, and by the time Kay got back to Sampson's, her shoulder-length dark hair had twisted into damp ringlets and her face was gleaming wetly.

She put her bicycle in the shed in the yard behind the shop, took her bag and hurried in through the back door. She hung her coat up on a peg in the dimly lit corridor and went into the shabby but comfortably furnished room where the staff took their tea breaks and ate whatever they had brought from home when the shop closed at lunchtime.

Thomas Sampson and his wife Rhoda retired to their roomy flat above the double-fronted shop to take their lunch, but Kay and Beryl boiled a kettle in this little back room and ate their lunch whilst savouring the aromas of cheese, cooked meats and coffee which had seeped into the very fabric of the building.

Kay and Beryl Walker had been in the same class at school. They had never been best friends but had always got on well together. Kay had always been at the centre of a lively group and Beryl had been content to watch them admiringly. Often Kay would find some way of drawing her into the group, not wanting her to feel left out. Beryl had been a plumply pretty child and now she was an overweight but still nice-looking young woman.

She looked up when Kay entered. 'You look like something the cat dragged in,' she said.

'Thank you very much!' Kay pretended to be offended and they both laughed.

'You'd better sit by the fire and dry off a bit.' Beryl began to heave herself up from the only comfortable chair.

'No, it's all right. You stay there. I'd rather sit at the table.'

'Thanks, you're a pal.'

Beryl looked relieved as she sank back gratefully. She propped her legs up on the ancient padded fender seat, far too near to the fire, but she didn't seem to mind the heat marks on her legs, as long as she could raise her feet from the draughty floor.

'What've you got, then?' Beryl asked, glancing curiously over to the table as Kay sat down and took a greaseproof packet from her shoulder bag.

'Sandwiches.'

'I can see that! What's in them?'

'Carrot and mayonnaise.'

'Ugh!'

'No, honestly, they're not bad. And better for you than the chips you eat day after day.'

'Chips are lovely and anyway, I read that fish and chips are good for you.'

'Perhaps they are, but you don't have the fish, and you're not supposed to eat chips every day.'

'Slipping round the corner to the chip shop is better than getting up early to make sandwiches. Want a chip?' Beryl grinned as she held her newspaper-wrapped bundle out towards Kay. 'Isn't that hot vinegary smell lovely? There's some batter in there. You can have some as long as you don't take too much.'

Kay took a couple of chips and a little bit of batter. 'Thanks, Beryl. Would you like one of my sandwiches?'

'Not on your life. Be a pal and make the tea, will you?'

Kay obliged, and soon they were sitting quietly in the dimly lit room enjoying their respective meals while rain slid down the soot-stained window and the clock ticked on the mantel shelf.

When Beryl had finished her chips she rolled the newspaper into a tight ball and stuffed it into the already bulging wastepaper basket. It sat there for a moment and then toppled over onto the floor. Beryl ignored the mess and sighed as she rose and reached for the cinder guard.

'Back to work, then,' she said wearily. 'Give me the order book and I'll start on the boxes, shall I? You know, sometimes I think I'll be here at Sampson's until they put me in my own box and deliver me to the graveyard.'

'Don't talk like that, Beryl.'

The other girl straightened up and turned to smile sadly. 'No, seriously, I'm resigned to the fact that I'll be here all my working life. Haven't you noticed there's a shortage of good men in this town? We can't all be as lucky as you are.'

'What do you mean?'

'Come off it, Kay. Tony Chalmers, that's who I mean. As soon as he pops the question you'll be out of here, and the next thing we know you'll be phoning in your order – "just the usual, plus a few little exotic extras, Beryl" – and Mr Sampson will be delivering it to a posh house overlooking the golf course.'

'Is that what you think?'

'Of course it is. Doesn't everyone? And when you're Mrs Tony Chalmers that'll be one up on that stuck-up sister of yours.'

'Beryl, please don't talk about Julie like that.'

'I'm sorry, but she does put on airs and graces, doesn't she? Oh, all right, I know you won't have a word said against her, but just wait until you walk down the aisle with the best catch in town; she won't be able to act so superior then.'

'And what if I don't?'

'What do you mean?'

'What if I don't marry Tony?'

'I'd say you were crazy. But you're kidding me, aren't you? You wouldn't be so stupid as to let an opportunity like that slip by.' Beryl didn't expect an answer. She made sure the cinder guard was in place and headed for the door. 'I can hear Mr Sampson coming down the stairs. Come on; it's time to get back to work.'

The girls grabbed their overalls from the row of hooks by the door and put them on, then Kay followed Beryl along the passage to the shop.

Beryl was the second person that day to tell her not to let an opportunity slip by. Kay wondered what the older girl would say if she knew that marrying Tony Chalmers might not be the only opportunity she had to change her life.

Chapter Two

Thelma Lockwood's tea had grown cold and her sandwiches remained untouched. She stared moodily into the fire. It had been bad enough when the letter from a solicitor in London had arrived. After the first shock and surge of resentment, Thelma had managed to come up with a plan that she thought would be fair to everyone; to Kay, to Julie and to Thelma herself. She was pretty sure that Kay would agree once she'd had time to consider it.

This had enabled her to suppress her outrage until today, when a photograph in the newspaper had succeeded in reviving it. She stared at the line of chorus girls, their smiling faces, their shapely limbs, their arms linked securely as they performed a high-kicking synchronised dance routine. She remembered how they always smiled no matter how long they had been rehearsing, no matter how hard Jack had driven them, no matter how exhausted and nearer to tears than laughter they had been. Once the curtain went up and the music started, they pinned on their smiles then tapped and kicked their way across the stage and back to the appreciative applause of the summer visitors, whose night out at the Pavilion Theatre was the highlight of their holiday.

And nobody worked as hard or smiled as brightly as Lana did. Thelma studied the picture closely. Lana, with her lovely long legs, was slightly taller than the other girls and Thelma was fairly certain that she could identify her in the centre of the line-up. Lana Fontaine . . .

Thelma clutched the newspaper tightly then, giving way to rage, tore the page from the paper, crushed it into a ball and hurled it on the fire. She gripped the arms of her chair and watched as the paper turned brown, then caught fire, blazing briefly before collapsing into ash. One or two burnt flakes escaped and drifted out to land on the hearth. Habit made Thelma rise from her seat, take hold of the fire irons, and kneel down to sweep the hearth clean.

When she had done it she sat back on her heels and stared at the glowing coals. This was how Jack had found her that fateful day all those years ago. The day it began. Not in this room, of course, but in the room directly above. The room he was renting for the summer season. It had been a cold, rainy summer and Thelma's mother had agreed to light the fires in her lodgers' bedrooms so long as they were prepared to pay extra for the coal. It had been Thelma's job to keep the fires burning.

'So it's you who makes sure that my room is as warm as toast,' Jack had said when he came home after the show one evening.

Thelma stood up and wiped her hands down her pinafore. 'Who did you think it would be?' she asked. 'There's only me and my mother here, and surely you don't imagine she would see to the fires?' She smiled at Jack. She knew that the paying guests, even Jack, were a little in awe of her mother and her overbearing manner.

'Of course not,' Jack said. 'Nor does she wait on table or, I imagine, wash the dishes, or clean the house.'

Wanting to be fair, Thelma said, 'She does all the cooking.'

'Nevertheless, I've seen how hard you work, Thelma.'

'Have you?'

'Why do you look so surprised?'

Thelma felt herself blushing. 'Well . . . I mean, why should you notice me?'

'Are you fishing for compliments?'

'Of course not!'

'Now I've annoyed you when I only meant to be kind.'

'Do you know how patronising that sounds?'

Jack looked at her in surprise. Then he laughed. 'Guilty as charged. The suave, debonair Jack Lockwood putting on his usual act to charm the impressionable little help, and instead finding an intelligent young woman who is not at all impressed and is prepared to put him in his place.'

Thelma was appalled. She had not meant to talk back to him the way she had, and she could just imagine what her mother would say if Mr Lockwood complained to her. 'Have I been rude?' she asked him. 'I have, haven't I? I'm sorry.'

'Please don't back down, Thelma. I haven't found you rude. In fact I find you utterly charming.'

'Oh.'

'No, I mean it. You must know how pretty you are. I noticed that the minute I walked into this house. Your blonde curls, your blue eyes and your pink and white complexion. A delightful English rose, I thought to myself. I have an eye for pretty girls, you know, and I know how to charm them. Well, most of them. But not you, apparently, and the fact that you can see right through me makes you all the more attractive.' Then while she was desperately trying to work out how she should respond to such extravagant and probably insincere praise, he hurried on. 'I tell you what, why don't you make me a cup of cocoa?'

Now thoroughly confused, Thelma could only stare at him. He laughed.

'In fact, why don't you make two cups of cocoa? One for me and one for you. And if you can find a toasting fork and

23

cut us some slices of bread, we'll sit here by the fire and have a sort of midnight feast. Would you like that?'

There was nothing Thelma would have liked more. Jack Lockwood was very handsome: only a little taller than average, but somehow commanding. He had dark, wavy hair and film-star good looks. She thought he looked a little like Ronald Coleman. She didn't know whether he was telling the truth about having noticed her and thinking her pretty the moment he came to stay here, but she had certainly noticed him.

'Thelma, don't keep me in suspense like this.' He placed one hand, fingers spread, on his chest and raised the other arm in a theatrical gesture of supplication. 'No, don't laugh. Am I to enjoy a midnight feast with you or not?' Despite his playful teasing, there was something in his eyes that made her believe he really wanted her to stay.

'Yes . . . I mean, no. I mean, my mother . . .'

'Where is she?'

'In bed.'

'And no doubt fast asleep?'

'I suppose so.'

'There you are, then.'

'Why do you want me to stay and talk to you?'

'Because you're different. It would be good to forget about the theatre for a while and talk to a normal person.'

'Normal person?'

'Yes.'

'I'm not sure what you mean.'

'You don't suppose all those poor souls singing and dancing their hearts out in a little seaside entertainment are anywhere near normal, do you? I mean, they would probably kill to be top of the bill.'

'*You* are top of the bill. And in the programmes and on the posters your name is bigger than any other name.'

He laughed. 'Which is all the more reason why I would like to leave that Jack Lockwood behind for a while. Wipe off all pretensions with my make-up and shed all affectations along with my stage costumes. Can you understand that, Thelma?'

'I can, but I think you would find it very difficult.'

Jack's smile vanished and he looked at her quite coolly. Immediately she regretted what she had said. She wanted him to smile at her again. Her distress was so great that she actually felt a lump of misery rising in her throat.

After a long pause when she could hear the clock ticking on the mantel shelf and the crackle of the coals in the grate, he smiled again and she almost fainted with relief.

'My goodness,' he said. 'A prickly little rose.'

'Are you angry with me?'

'Would that upset you?'

'Very much.'

'I'm not angry and I would like us to be friends. We can find out about each other over a cup of cocoa and a couple of slices of toast – with butter, not margarine.'

'Butter? I'm not so sure about that.'

'Does your mother keep it under lock and key?'

She smiled. 'I think I can find some.'

Thelma made the cocoa and found the butter. They sat on the hearth rug and made toast. Jack insisted on wielding the toasting fork. When they had eaten, he leaned towards her and, in a curiously intimate gesture, he brushed the crumbs from her lips with a clean white handkerchief. For a moment Thelma found it difficult to breathe.

When the rain began to beat on the window panes, Jack rose and switched off the light. Taking her hand, he pulled her up then drew her towards the bed. She resisted as she knew she should, but not for long. That night became the first of many that she spent in his arms, only leaving him when the grey light of dawn had crept around the edges of the floral curtains.

Had he loved her? All these years later, this was a question that Thelma could not answer with any certainty. Would he have married her if her mother had not found them in bed together? Probably not. But he had done the honourable thing, and he had never been unkind to her. And at first she had been happy, deliriously so. Even now she could recall the delight she had taken in being Jack Lockwood's wife.

Thelma rose to her feet, picked up the tray containing her sandwiches and her cold cup of tea, and went through to the kitchen. Her daughters would be home for their meal soon, and so would Miss Pearson and Miss Elkin. Neither of her paying guests caused much trouble. They went to work at the Ministry of Pensions early in the morning, and after their evening meal they sat with their knitting as they listened to the wireless.

Both always expressed extravagant gratitude for the tray of tea and home-made cake she provided just before they went to bed. They were model guests. But even so, Thelma was heartily sick of not being able to call her home her own. Surely Kay would do the right thing if she could convince her that it would mean a better life for all of them.

'Oh dear, Kay. I wish you wouldn't bring guests into the kitchen.'

Thelma had just taken the dish of macaroni cheese from the oven when Kay arrived home with Tony Chalmers in tow. Even though she was flustered, Thelma smiled at Tony. As ever, it was hard not to.

'Please don't mind me, Mrs Lockwood,' he said. 'I met Kay after work, and I wanted to ask you if it would be all right for me to take her to the flicks tonight.'

'Of course it is. Will you stay and have some tea with us before you go? I'm afraid there's nothing very exciting on the menu.'

'I'd love to.' Tony wrinkled his nose and sniffed the air like one of the Bisto kids. 'Anything you have made is bound to be delicious.'

'Flatterer!' Thelma dished up two plates of macaroni cheese. 'Kay, when you've taken your coat off, would you take this tray through to the dining room?'

Kay took her own coat and Tony's and hung them up in the hall, then she returned for the tray bearing their paying guests' evening meal.

'When you've taken that in, come back for this sponge cake.'

'Allow me,' Tony said. 'Is that teapot for the ladies? Pop it all on a tray and I'll take it through.'

'Oh, no, Tony!' Thelma protested. 'I can't have you waiting on my guests.'

'I don't see why not. Kay is.'

Not giving her time to say any more, Tony placed everything on a tray and followed Kay along to the dining room, leaving Thelma thoroughly vexed.

Without shedding his charming manner, Tony had managed to imply that she was treating Kay badly. And of course she wasn't. It was only natural to expect Kay to help in the house. Thelma had helped her own mother, hadn't she? In fact, she had done much more than Kay had ever done, because Kay was out at work all day.

There wasn't much macaroni cheese left. Thelma always gave her lodgers generous portions; she didn't want to be thought of as miserly, as her mother had been. It was just as well that she had thought to make an egg and bacon tart and an apple pie while she had the oven on.

When Tony and Kay returned, she shepherded them into

the breakfast room and told Kay to set the table. 'Just two places,' Thelma told her. 'I'll wait and have my meal with Julie when she gets back from college.'

After she had carried the food through for them – she didn't ask Kay to help; in fact, she stopped her from doing so – Thelma shut the kitchen door, made herself a cup of tea and sat down. For the second time that day she let a cup of tea grow cold. She had wanted to talk to Kay about her inheritance and what she proposed to do with it – but she could hardly have refused to allow her to go to the pictures with her boyfriend. Kay was twenty-two years old. The fact that Tony had asked her was a mere formality. She supposed she could wait up and talk to Kay when she got home, but that would be ten o'clock or later, not the ideal time to start a serious discussion.

Then, to increase her vexation, Tony insisted on clearing the table while Kay went up to get ready. After they had gone, Thelma wondered if Kay had told him about Lana's will. Probably not, she decided. Kay was not exactly secretive, but she had always been rather reticent. *Like me*, Thelma thought, and smiled for the first time that day. *I don't see the point in letting people know all your business, or how you feel about things; whereas Julie takes after Jack – cheerfully chatty and never stopping to think whether people really need to know what's happening in your life.*

But at least Jack had been able to keep a secret when he had to. Julie would have found it totally impossible not to tell her friends that her sister had inherited a small fortune. That was why Thelma had advised Kay not to tell her. At least until she had decided what to do.

Thelma rose from the table and emptied her cup into the sink. Julie would be home any minute now, and she would be hungry. She worked hard at college and she deserved a bit of pampering. As well as the remains of the egg and bacon pie and the apple tart, there was another dish of macaroni cheese keeping warm in the oven, made just for Julie. But best of all, there was a chocolate cake in the pantry.

Tony stood in the doorway and looked up at the dark clouds. 'I think you'd better bring an umbrella, Kay. There've been showers on and off all day, and now it's begun to rain in earnest.'

'There's one in the scullery. I'll get it.'

Just as Kay left him, the gate opened and Julie hurried up the path. 'Hello, Tony.' She stopped and smiled teasingly. 'Waiting for me?'

'You know I'm not. Come in before you get soaked.'

'Thanks for caring.'

He didn't reply but stood well back to allow her to enter. Nevertheless, she managed to brush against him. She turned and looked up at him. 'Ah, well,' she said. 'I'm sure you'll come to your senses one day.'

'Meaning?'

'You know what I mean.' And although she was aware that Kay was hurrying along the passage towards them, she smiled flirtatiously.

Tony sighed. 'Pack it in, Julie. You know I'm not interested.'

'More's the pity.' She shook her head as if she couldn't believe he was being so stupid, and turned to face Kay. 'Going somewhere nice?'

Kay's response was equable. 'We're going to the pictures.'

'Ooh, can I come with you?'

'That's up to Tony.'

Tony reached over and took the umbrella from Kay. He turned round to put it up. 'Then the answer is no.'

Julie pouted. 'Rotten spoilsports.'

'In any case, your tea's ready,' Kay told her.

'Come on, Kay,' Tony said. 'There's bound to be a queue, and I don't fancy standing for too long in this weather.'

'Bye, then,' Julie said.

Ignoring her, Tony took Kay's arm and hurried her down the path and out of the gate. Kay must have sensed his irritation.

'Don't be cross with her,' she said. 'She just likes to tease.'

'I know, but she's not a kid any more. She's in her last year at college and old enough to know better.'

Tony was surprised that the usually perspicacious Kay could not see that Julie's teasing was far from innocent. He supposed that Kay, being so thoroughly decent herself, could not imagine that her younger sister was trying to steal her boyfriend.

Am I her boyfriend? he mused. Everyone seemed to think so. He loved being with her; she was attractive, well-spoken, intelligent and self-confident. Maybe that was the problem. When he had come home from the war, he had dreamed of domestic bliss, of settling down with a more compliant kind of girl. Someone who would accept that he was the senior partner in the marriage. Kay would never do that; she would see herself as an equal partner, and much as he cared for her, he wasn't sure if he could accept that.

When they reached the Essoldo, the queue was round the block. Even people without umbrellas were willing to wait in the rain to see *The Glass Mountain*.

'What do you think?' Tony asked. 'It doesn't look as if we'll get in in time to see much of the second feature.'

'That doesn't matter,' Kay replied. 'I don't mind, if you don't.'

'We might have more luck at the Playhouse. They're showing *The Interrupted Journey*. Apparently it's a great movie, but for some reason not quite as popular as *The Glass Mountain*.

Tony smiled down at her and Kay was reminded of how handsome he was. Tall and broad-shouldered, with fair hair and grey eyes, he looked every inch the sort of man an officer in the RAF – fondly known as the Brylcreem Boys – would be. Somehow she had forgotten this during the last few days of wondering what she should do. Not that being handsome should have anything to do with her decision. Tony Chalmers was considerate and kind, and during his wartime service as a flying officer he had been truly brave.

Kay wasn't quite sure why he had chosen her, nor, having done so, why he had never seemed to want to take their relationship further. He had told her he loved her often enough but had never proposed to her. Kay had a sneaking feeling it might be something to do with his parents. After all, the Chalmers were further up the social scale than the Lockwoods. Perhaps they didn't want their only son to marry the daughter of a seaside landlady.

She hoped she was wrong about this, but then if she was, why was Tony waiting? It was this puzzling state of affairs that made Kay unwilling to tell Tony about her inheritance.

'Kay? Sorry to hurry you, but it's raining harder than ever. Do we stay here, huddled under your umbrella, or do we make a dash for the Playhouse? As far as the film is concerned, it's a choice between a plane crash or a train crash. What do you think?'

'Oh, the train crash.'

'Righto. Grab my arm.'

The way Tony guided her through the wet streets would have looked normal to any passer-by. Only Kay realised he was giving her extra support because of her limp.

Tony bought tickets for the circle, and as they settled into their seats just before the film started, Kay imagined she could see the steam rising from the stalls below as people's coats dried off in the comforting warmth. She and Tony wriggled out of their coats and slipped them over the seat backs, then Tony reached for her hand and held it throughout the performance. He always did this, although Kay often wished he would put his arm around her.

'Did you enjoy that?' he asked her when the film came to an end.

'Very much. But I thought it was a bit of a cheat to say it was all a dream.'

'I agree.' Tony helped her into her coat. The lights came up and Kay saw that he was looking at her quite seriously. 'We agree about a lot of things, don't we?'

'I suppose so.' Kay waited for him to say something more, but he didn't.

The feeling of frustration when he behaved like this was becoming all too familiar. Usually when he walked her home she would invite him in for a hot drink and whatever cakes her mother had been baking. Tonight she didn't. Far too polite to take the invitation for granted, he kissed her lightly on the forehead and walked away. Kay wondered if he was hurt – or whether he had sensed that something about their relationship had just changed.

Chapter Three

Thelma switched off the light then stood by her bedroom window and looked out into the darkened street. Soon echoing footsteps told her they were coming, and a moment later Kay and Tony entered the misty circle of light shed by a nearby street lamp. Their arms were linked.

Tony never stayed long when he brought her home – maybe half an hour at the most – and Thelma had decided to go downstairs after all, and talk to Kay the moment he had gone. The letter telling Kay of her inheritance had arrived a week ago. Surely she had made her mind up by now. Thelma reckoned she had been very patient, but that piece in the *Chronicle* today had thoroughly unsettled her, and anyway, a daughter owed it to her mother to tell her of her intentions, didn't she?

Thelma decided to go back to bed until she heard Tony taking his leave. But just before she let the curtain fall, she saw his tall figure walk away again. It crossed her mind briefly that this was unusual, but spurred on by her determination to talk to Kay, she didn't give it a second thought. She pulled on her robe and opened her door carefully – she didn't want to disturb Julie – then walked quietly along the corridor and hurried downstairs.

Kay was in the kitchen warming up some milk when her mother walked in and surprised her.

'Can't you sleep?' Kay asked.

'No, and you know why.'

'Do I?'

'Don't pretend you don't . . . I mean . . . Oh, Kay . . .' Kay watched as her mother sought to control her impatience.

She knew she was at fault and tried to make amends. 'Would you like a hot drink?' she asked, and when her mother pursed her lips and nodded speechlessly she added, 'Cocoa? Ovaltine?'

'Whatever you're having.'

'Cocoa it is, then. Where would you like to sit? Here at the kitchen table, or shall we see if there's any life left in the fire in the front parlour?'

A short while later Kay put aside the cinder guard in the parlour and they pulled the armchairs closer to the hearth. Kay knew she owed her mother an apology. 'Look, I'm sorry, Mum. I must have been trying your patience, but I truly couldn't decide what to do.'

Thelma Lockwood's struggle to be reasonable was visible. 'Well, of course, such a surprise . . . so much money . . . I mean, *two thousand* pounds.' Then her patience snapped. 'I can't believe she left it all to you.'

'She was my godmother.'

'The last time she saw you, you were eight years old!'

Kay saw the frustration and anger in her mother's face but decided to ask the question anyway. 'You were such good friends.' Her mother's look suddenly became guarded, but Kay pressed on, 'Did you quarrel?'

There was a long silence, and Kay had almost decided that the conversation was over when her mother replied tersely, 'No, we didn't.' Suddenly Thelma couldn't meet her daughter's eyes. 'Kay, do you remember her at all? I mean, you were only a little girl.'

'Yes, I remember her. She was full of fun. She was kind

34

to Julie and me. She brought us treats.' Kay heard her mother sniff disparagingly and hurried on. 'She was as dark as you were fair. Father used to joke that you two were like Snow White and Rose Red in the fairy tale, remember?'

'Your father was full of fairy tales.'

Kay was surprised by the sarcasm, but she continued. 'He liked to tell us the story. Both little girls were beautiful, but Rose Red was outspoken and cheerful and liked to play outside, whereas Snow White was quiet and shy and preferred reading and doing housework.'

'You remember that?'

'Mmm. And there was a wicked dwarf and a bear who was really a prince, and I think in the end it was Snow White who married the Prince. But the two little girls loved each other very much.' Kay glanced at her mother to find that her eyes were closed. She looked so distraught that Kay ventured, 'You did quarrel, didn't you?'

Her mother opened her eyes and looked at Kay thoughtfully. 'No, nothing like that. We didn't exactly quarrel. I don't want to make you sad, but it was at the time your father died. Lana's visits just stopped. It seems she wasn't interested in the rest of us. Not even her own god-daughter.'

'It doesn't make sense, does it?'

'What do you mean?'

'Well, if she lost interest in us . . . in me, why would she leave me all this money?'

'Just to be spiteful, I should imagine.'

'That's crazy. I don't understand what you mean.'

Her mother sighed. 'And it's no use you ever trying to understand Lana Fontaine, believe me. So, now that she's upset the applecart, all we have to do is decide what we're going to do.'

'Don't you mean what *I* am going to do?'

Her mother's head turned sharply towards her. 'Oh, so it's like that, is it?'

'Yes, Mum. It's like that. Ever since the letter arrived you've made it plain that we have to come to some sort of joint decision, and although I'll certainly listen to what you have to say, in the end it's up to me. That's why I've been taking so long. I'm sorry.'

That's the second time today I've apologised to someone for not having made a decision yet, Kay thought. *First to Miss Bennet, who only has my interests at heart, and now to my mother, who I'm pretty sure has her own and Julie's interests quite high on the list of priorities.*

Suddenly ashamed of the direction her thoughts had taken, Kay said impulsively, 'Of course I'll listen to you. I wouldn't dream of not doing something for my mother and my sister; it's just that I want to make my own plans.'

Her mother glanced at the clock on the mantel shelf and sighed wearily. 'My goodness, it's nearly midnight. You've got to go to work in the morning and I have to make the ladies' breakfasts. I suppose we'd better go to bed.'

She half rose, but Kay saw her reluctance and made a gesture to stop her. 'Stay there. I'm sure we can both stand one late night. You've let your drink go cold. I'll warm it up and we'll thrash this out. I know it's important to you, and I admit I've been selfish.'

When Kay returned she also brought two slices of chocolate cake.

'What's this?' Her mother looked up sharply. 'I hope you've left sufficient for Julie's lunch box.'

'Of course I have. I wouldn't dream of making my little sister go without.'

'Are you being sarcastic?'

'No, I'm being irritated. There's quite enough for Julie unless she requires gargantuan portions. Now take your cake and let's have a midnight feast. Wouldn't that be cosy?'

'I suppose so.'

Kay was taken aback by her mother's lassitude but she decided the only thing to do was press on. 'Go on then. Tell me what you think I should do. But don't let that cocoa go cold again.' She tried a cheerful smile, but it was wasted on her mother.

Thelma sipped her cocoa and took several small bites of chocolate cake. Kay guessed she was deliberately keeping her waiting, paying her back − if that wasn't too childish a term to use for a grown woman with two grown-up daughters. When she did speak her mother sounded businesslike.

'Two thousand pounds is a lot of money,' she began. 'I mean, a lot of money for one young woman. I have two daughters; Lana knew that. I consider it unfair that she should have left it all to you.' Kay waited for her mother to go on. 'I don't want you to think that what I'm going to suggest is unreasonable. You must admit that over the years I've done the best I could for both you and Julie.'

Kay couldn't help herself. 'The best?'

Thelma bridled. 'Yes, the best.'

'Oh, yes,' Kay said, 'I remember. You took me away from school so that I could bring some money in to help you save up to send Julie to commercial college as soon as she was old enough. Of course, you made sure that I got a job in the best grocery shop in town.'

Thelma was silent. Was it too much to hope that she was ashamed? Apparently it was. 'Julie showed great promise,' she said. 'It was obvious that she would do well.'

'As a clerk in an office?'

'A secretary.'

'Of course. Whereas I . . .'

'You were such a daydreamer. Even your friend Miss

37

Bennet said that she wasn't sure what your strengths would be.'

'However, she didn't say I was stupid or that you ought to take me away from school.'

'I couldn't afford to keep you on at school. I earn little enough from taking in paying guests. And most of the money you give me is for your own keep, which is only right and proper.'

'And what about Julie's keep?'

'You can't expect her to contribute when she isn't working.'

'Some students take Saturday jobs, not to mention working in the summer holidays. There are plenty of waitressing jobs during the holiday season.'

'Julie has homework to do in the holidays.'

'That doesn't stop her going out with her friends. I've often thought she could take a little job, if only to earn enough to buy her own clothes.'

'I had no idea you felt like this. So angry – so resentful. You've never complained until now.'

'I knew no better. And, of course, I trusted my mother to do her best for me!'

'I've already told you; I have done my best.'

'By sticking me behind a shop counter. You probably didn't think I was capable of doing anything else!'

There was a shocked silence in which they stared at each other, wide-eyed. It was Kay who broke the silence. 'Mum, I'm truly, truly sorry. I shouldn't have said any of that. I'm glad Julie has a chance to do well for herself and I've been happy working at Sampson's. I don't know what came over me.'

'I do. Just see how Lana's money has set us quarrelling. She must be laughing from her grave!'

Kay was aghast. She was furious with herself for letting

her long suppressed feelings of hurt and resentment get the better of her. This was the first time she had actually voiced them. And what about her mother? Kay sensed that now they had stopped, she was frightened she had gone too far. After all, she was going to ask for something, wasn't she?

She had been expecting her mother to propose an allowance for Julie, perhaps, and a lump sum for herself. Kay knew how hard her mother had worked over the years, and it would be nice if she could relax and not have to take in lodgers any more. However, the request, when it came, took her breath away. She had not expected her mother to ask her to buy her a house.

After a shocked silence Kay asked, 'But why would you want to move? This is a lovely house.'

'Maybe it is,' her mother replied, 'but it doesn't belong to me, does it? No matter how hard I've worked and how well I've looked after it, and my mother before me, it's rented property. I want a house of my own.'

'And you think I should buy one for you?'

'I do. You can certainly afford to.'

Kay remained silent and her mother, taking this for assent, hurried on. 'Two thousand pounds is a lot of money. I don't know what you intend to do with it, but surely you could spare eight hundred pounds for your own mother.'

'Eight hundred pounds! That would buy you a mansion.'

'Don't exaggerate, Kay. I've been looking at the Houses for Sale column in the *Chronicle* and there are some lovely houses along the seafront by the lighthouse, or overlooking the dene and the golf course. They fall between six and seven hundred pounds, but most of them need some work doing to update them. Eight hundred pounds would mean I could have any work done and furnish the house properly, too.'

'Furnish it?'

'You wouldn't expect me to take this old stuff, would you?'

'I don't know what I would expect. And what about me? Do you plan to take me along to live with you?'

'Of course I do. For as long as you want to. Although I expect you'll be getting married soon enough, once Tony sees you living in a better part of town.'

Kay was stung by that but she let it go. 'And Miss Pearson and Miss Elkin? What would happen to them? Would they come and live in a better part of town, too?'

'Don't be silly. It's easy enough to find other lodgings, but I don't suppose they would have to. Whoever takes this house on after me would probably want lodgers, too. I could manage without taking lodgers – so long as you played fair.'

'You mean as well as buying you a house I should give you some money?'

Her mother's eyes flashed. 'Don't make it sound like charity, Kay. I should think you would want to help your mother without being asked.'

'Of course I do.'

'Then I won't make any apologies. But as a matter of fact my little pension, meagre as it is, would be enough to keep me going quite comfortably.' She paused then shook her head disapprovingly. 'I knew Lana Fontaine when she was just a chorus girl,' she said. 'She didn't have two pennies to rub together. I helped her when she was in dire need. Then off she went to become a film star. Rich and famous. Forgot about her old friends, didn't she? No one knows why she retired when she did, but she must have made a packet. And for some reason she leaves all this money to you. Poor Julie. It just isn't fair.'

'Oh, yes, Julie. I imagine you'll want me to do something for her.'

'Of course I do. Your own sister! A nice little lump sum. I'll leave it to your conscience to decide how much, but I was thinking two hundred pounds would be about right. Goodnight, Kay.'

Thelma rose swiftly and left the room without another word, leaving Kay completely dumbfounded. She was shocked by the strength of her mother's anger and resentment, although she thought she could understand it. And then she thought how squalid it was to be quarrelling over money like this. She remembered her mother's words: *Just see how Lana's money has set us quarrelling. She must be laughing from her grave!'*

Kay rinsed the cups and plates and left them to drain on the wooden bench; then she went to bed, but sleep evaded her. Eventually she reached for the bedside lamp, switched it on and took the letter from the drawer. Lana's letter. The one that had been in the envelope along with the letter from the solicitor, but which she had not shown her mother. Her mother had called Lana's will an act of spite. Was this the letter of a spiteful woman?

My darling girl,

I wonder if you remember me. You were such a little scrap when I last saw you. You must have been seven or eight years old, but you were small for your age, and so slim. A willowy little thing. You were so unlike Julie, who, shall I say, was somewhat podgy. No, that's cruel of me. Julie was an altogether more robust child, and there's no denying she was a pretty little poppet with her big blue eyes and Shirley Temple curls.

So how old are you now, my sweet? You see, although I know how old you are as I write, I have no idea when you will receive this letter. I intend to give it to my solicitor to give to you when I have passed away. Passed away . . . What an amusing expression. Deceased, departed, dead. Why can't we be more forthright?

In any case, it was your birthday today that inspired me to write this letter. Your fifteenth birthday. Why should it be so special? Because it was on my own fifteenth birthday that I ran away from home. I loved my parents and I may have broken their hearts. But young as I was, I was also fiercely ambitious. My father had worked hard to send me to a good school, where I did well, and I think he had hopes of my going to university.

However, my parents had also paid for elocution and dancing lessons. I loved them. I decided that I would rather go on the stage. Of course they were horrified, so all I could do was save up my pocket money – they gave me a generous weekly sum – and I am ashamed to tell you that I also stole from my mother's purse – and off I went.

I never saw my parents again. I did write to them more than once over the years, but my letters were returned unread. And now I never will see them. They were killed in an air raid.

I won't tell you about the years that followed my running away, except to say that I worked damned hard and my ambition never faded. I wasn't an over-night success, and by the time I fetched up in a seaside show at the Pavilion Theatre in Northridge Bay I was almost resigned to being a chorus girl for the rest of my life. However, just like in a movie about show business, I was spotted and yanked from the chorus line, changing my life forever. Ironically, it wasn't only my beautiful speaking voice or my high-kicking dancing skills that opened the door to fame and fortune;

it was my looks. And why should I be ashamed of that?

What do you look like at fifteen, I wonder? Leggy? Coltish? Are you already promising to be a slim, beautiful young woman? And what of your poor damaged leg? Do you still walk with a limp? I fear you do.

Your father telephoned to tell me what had happened and I came straight away. I offered to take you to the best specialist we could find, you know. I would have paid for the treatment, but your mother refused my offer. Should I have insisted? Should I have enlisted your father to the cause? That would only have caused trouble.

Do you remember the accident, my darling? You were only a toddler, so it's very unlikely. It was a summer day and your mother put you in your pram and left you in the garden to enjoy the sunshine while she went indoors to feed your baby sister. You were asleep when she put you out, so she didn't use the harness to clip you in. No one knows how long you slept, or when you sat up and tried to clamber out, but thank goodness your mother came out of the house just as you were about to topple out of the pram.

Your mother had Julie in her arms, so she did the only thing she could do. She reached out with one arm and clutched at you, managing to catch one leg just as you began to fall. She screamed for a neighbour and I can only imagine the pain you must have been in, dangling over the side like that. That image haunted me for years.

The neighbour had a telephone and she called for the doctor. Old Dr Davidson. Tweed-suited and pipe-smoking. I remember him well, a kindly man, although he didn't approve of me, or any of the young women who worked at the Pavilion! Anyway, he came immediately and I think he said you had a greenstick fracture and that it would heal itself in time. I seem to remember he put a cast on and you bore that with fortitude.

Now I'm getting sentimental. Forgive me. It is a fault of mine. Maybe it's because I spend my working days in a heightened state of emotion. If the part I am playing is dramatic I find it very difficult to 'wind down' when I come home. If the film is a comedy it is just as difficult. My poor driver must often have been startled to hear me sob or laugh out loud, apparently at nothing, when I am sitting alone in the back of the car on the way home from the studios or the theatre.

Do you like going to the pictures, Kay? Have you seen *Bambi* or *Casablanca*? They both made me cry. But as I have no intention of 'passing away' just yet there will be other wonderful films that you and I could have discussed. Have you seen any of my own films?

It's late, I'm tired, my defences are down and the questions come flooding in: How old are you, now? Have you left school? Are you working? Are you in love? Maybe you are married? Do you have children?

Oh, I know it's pointless to ask these questions when I cannot hear your answers, but sitting here, late at night, I can even imagine that we are together. I have said too much. I should tear this letter into little pieces and toss them on the fire. But I won't. I shall allow my heart to rule my head. I shall fold the letter and place it in an envelope which I shall seal and then ask my solicitor to keep safely until I have departed this life – shuffled off this mortal coil – you see, Lana Fontaine, erstwhile chorus girl and light-weight leading lady in many successful British films, can actually quote Shakespeare.

Goodnight, my darling girl. I shall make you my heir, of course.

Love from,

Your errant godmother

Kay folded Lana Fontaine's letter and put it back in the envelope. Both the sheets of notepaper and the envelope they came in were a faded pink. Kay held the envelope to her nose and imagined she could smell the scent of roses. *It can't be*, she thought. The notepaper might have been perfumed once, but surely after seven years the scent would have faded. Seven years. Lana Fontaine had written the letter seven years ago, not knowing how long it would be before Kay would read it.

Certain that she would not be able to settle, Kay now gave up all thought of sleep. What a strange mix of memories and sentiment the letter was. The writing was so vivid that it was almost like painting pictures. Kay could see herself as a small child hanging over the pram and probably screaming, although her godmother had not added that detail. And Lana, a rebellious teenager, packing her case and running away from the parents she loved but who did not understand her. Then there were glimpses of Lana's working life which made Kay want to know more.

Lana had wanted to ask her questions – well, that desire was mutual. Kay, too, wished she could have been there the night Lana sat down to write the letter. She wished they could have talked, got to know each other. Well, that was impossible now, and that fact made Kay very sad.

It seemed that Lana had loved her, and yet she did not explain why one day she had cut off all contact. Another thing that needed explaining was the reason why Lana had made Kay her heir. *I shall make you my heir, of course.* Almost a throwaway line at the very end of the letter.

Two thousand pounds. It was certainly enough to change her life – if only she knew what she wanted to do. Of course she would help her mother and Julie, although she had been shocked when her mother told her how much she needed to buy a house. Kay turned over restlessly. Her thoughts had come full circle. Her mother had called Lana's will an act of spite, but nothing in the letter suggested she was a spiteful woman. Enigmatic? Perhaps. Self-absorbed? Certainly. Spiteful? Kay didn't think so. But then there was so much that Lana had not chosen to reveal about herself or what had happened in the past.

Kay made her way to the bathroom and washed in cold water. She had made up her mind. She wanted to know more about Lana Fontaine. And as far as she could see, there was only one way to find out.

Chapter Four

Her collar turned up against the cold and her hands stuffed deep into her pockets, Kay stared at the faded posters on each side of the double doors of the theatre. They had been there since the theatre closed in September 1939. Protected by a sheet of glass, the print was still visible. One of them proclaimed:

Victor Emery
Singing Star of Stage, Screen and Radio
Solo Danseuse Donna Capri
Leading female impressionist Joan Seaton
Illusionist Teddy Fields and his assistant Betty
That Dotty Duo Melville and Farrell
(You Have To Laugh!)
The Truly Twinkling Twinkletoes

Kay wondered what had become of these people. Had any of them gone into the forces, and, if so, had they survived the war?

The golden dragons which faced each other above the entrance to the theatre were now a dirty yellow colour. The curling tongue of one of them had snapped off, and Kay thought that they looked more forlorn than ferocious. She tried to imagine what the scene here on the lower promenade would have been when Lana Fontaine was a chorus girl at the Pavilion and Kay's father, Jack, had been the actor-manager.

It was early afternoon, so maybe the dancers would be rehearsing a new routine for the first house. Kay closed her eyes and strained to hear the rhythm of the chorus girls tap-dancing to the piano accompaniment – but all she could hear was the call of a lone seagull tossed high above the bay. The wind was coming in from the sea, and loose sand began to sting Kay's cheeks. She brushed at it impatiently and made for the steps that would take her to the upper promenade. A short walk brought her to her destination.

When Miss Bennet opened the door she looked surprised. 'Kay! How nice to see you. But what's the problem? Is there something wrong with my ration book?'

'There's no problem. I just want to see you.'

Miss Bennet looked faintly puzzled. 'Shouldn't you be at work?'

'It's half-day closing.'

'Of course it is, and I am being impolite as well as forgetful. Come in at once before you get blown away!'

Miss Bennet led her young guest to the small front parlour, where Kay was pleased to see there was a cheerful fire.

Kay took her coat off and they sat at each side of the hearth. 'You've made up your mind, haven't you?' Miss Bennet said. 'That's why you're here.'

'Yes.'

'Go on then, tell me what you're going to do.'

'I'm not sure what I'm going to do in the long run. But first I must go to London.'

'Do you want to tell me what you will do there?'

'As you know, Lana Fontaine left me some money.'

Miss Bennet nodded.

'Well, she also left me what she called her "goods and chattels".'

'What exactly did she mean by that?'

'Everything she owned.'

'Including her house?'

'No. She never owned a house. The house she lived in was rented. She had been there for many years, and according to her solicitor, I should go and sort things out before the landlady's patience snaps and she sends it all to auction.'

'Can she do that?'

'I'm not sure. Luckily the rent is paid until the New Year. The solicitor thinks I should do the job myself, although, if I don't want to, he has offered to take care of things and send me the proceeds. He would take some sort of commission.'

'Do you trust him?'

'I have no reason not to.'

'I wonder why Miss Fontaine did not itemise things. Her jewellery, at least. She must have had some good pieces. I mean, she was a film star, after all. I remember photographs of her in magazines where she absolutely dripped with diamonds.'

'It's puzzling, isn't it? But it's not so much the financial value of whatever she might have left me; it's just that I can't bear the thought of strangers picking over her belongings. Do you know what I mean?'

'I do, my dear, although as far as I know, you were a stranger to her. Didn't you tell me that she hadn't visited you since you were a small child?'

'That's true. I can't explain why I feel this way.'

Kay found that she didn't want to tell anyone about the personal letter Lana Fontaine had sent her; not even kindly Miss Bennet. The letter had reached out to her on a very deep level, so that even though she had not seen her godmother for years, she felt as though they had always been close.

'Don't worry. I think I understand how you feel. Also I

think I understand Miss Fontaine's motive in making you her heir.'

'Do you?'

'She was a beautiful woman who never married. She pursued her career at the expense of a personal life. I mean marriage and children. Well, your mother was her friend and it's natural that when you were born Miss Fontaine should have become attached to you. I think you became the child she never had.' Miss Bennet laughed. 'Or maybe I have read too many sentimental novels.' She paused then said, 'So you're off to London.'

'Yes.'

'Where will you stay?'

'I shall ask the solicitor to recommend a respectable guest house.'

'Why not treat yourself to a first-class hotel?'

'Oh, no. I could hardly dress the part, could I? I mean, the other guests would take one look at me and cry impostor!'

'Then before you go you must refurbish your wardrobe. Now that clothes rationing is over there is so much to choose from. We could go into Newcastle and have a lovely time in Fenwick's or Bainbridge's. I would so much like to see you dress the way you deserve to be dressed. Off with the sensible and on with the fashionable. Oh, Kay, you will look marvellous.' Miss Bennet paused and her smile faded. 'But I can see by your expression that you don't intend to buy any new clothes.'

'Oh, I do! And I will. But not yet. I don't think I need anything special to wear while I'm clearing out a house. Do you?'

Miss Bennet sighed. 'I suppose not.'

'All I will need is a couple of warm sweaters and a pair of dungarees.' Her old friend looked so disappointed that Kay relented a little. 'Well, I should at least get a decent winter coat, I suppose. Will you come into town with me and help me choose one?'

'I'd love to. But only if you also buy a hat. I have a weakness for hats.'

'Oh, of course a hat, and shoes and gloves, too. And how about some fully fashioned silk stockings! Kayser, of course.'

'Oh, of course.'

They smiled fondly at each other, then to Kay's surprise she saw that Miss Bennet was trying hard not to cry. 'What is it?' she asked.

'I'm so happy for you.'

'You don't look happy.'

'That's because I've just realised how much I will miss you.'

'You're assuming that I won't be coming back.'

'I'm hoping that you won't. I know you don't like me to criticise your mother – quite rightly – and you won't hear a word said against that flighty young miss, your sister, but . . .'

'No, please don't say anything. Why don't I make a pot of tea and we can talk about the new fashions? I know you like to look at them in your weekly magazine.'

'I'm like a child with a new picture book.' Miss Bennet smiled. 'How wise you are, Kay. But at least let me tell you that you mustn't let anyone – *anyone* – take advantage of you.'

'I won't.' Kay opened her shoulder bag and reached inside. 'And now, to celebrate, how about helping me eat these chocolate biscuits?'

'What are we celebrating?'

Kay smiled. 'I gave my notice in to Sampson's today.'

★ ★ ★

'Where have you been?' Thelma looked up from the kitchen table where she was sitting alone. 'I had your lunch ready. Home-made barley broth.' She pursed her lips crossly.

'I'm sorry, Mum, but I just had to go for a walk.'

'*Had* to?'

'To sort things out – in my head, I mean. You see, I've given notice and I've decided to go to London to deal with Lana's things myself.'

Her mother's eyes widened for a moment and then she said, 'I see. Well, take your coat off and sit down. The broth's easy enough to warm up.'

Kay decided it was probably better not to tell her mother that she had been to Miss Bennet's, where she and her old friend had indulged themselves with chocolate biscuits and sherry. Miss Bennet had insisted on opening the sherry, although it had been intended for Christmas when her widowed sister came to stay.

'If we just have one glass each there will be plenty left for Sarah and me,' Miss Bennet had said as she had poured the wine into fine, flute-like glasses. Suddenly she had stopped and looked at Kay anxiously. 'You're not on your bicycle, are you? I mean, I don't know if there are any rules about drinking alcohol when riding a bicycle.'

Kay had assured her that she had walked and they had both collapsed into laughter which was tinged with sadness.

'I think you've probably done the right thing, Kay.'

Kay looked up in surprise as her mother set an appetising bowl of broth before her.

'Do you?'

'Not because you've decided to go to London, but in leaving Sampson's. You couldn't go on working there once it became known that you had money. I mean, it would be depriving some other poor girl of a job, wouldn't it?'

'Would people have to know about the money?'

'Of course they would. How else would we explain the new house?'

'Oh yes, the house. We could say you had inherited the money.'

'That would be a lie, and even if Lana had left the money to me, people would hardly expect me to let you go on working in a grocery shop.'

'You've been happy enough for me to work there all these years. Remember, you did your best for me.'

'Don't, Kay. Don't let's quarrel. It's just like I said. Lana knew this would set us against each other.'

'I'm sorry, Mum. This broth smells good.'

'Then don't just smell it – eat it! And tell me exactly what you're going to do.'

A few minutes later Kay and her mother faced each other across the table. 'I can't tell you exactly what my plans are,' Kay said. 'I don't know myself. However, as soon as it's possible I shall go to London and sort through Lana's belongings.'

'I wish you wouldn't.'

'Why not?'

Her mother didn't answer the question directly. 'It was such a strange thing to do, don't you think?' she said. 'Leaving you to decide what to do with everything?'

'It seems as though she didn't have anyone else.'

'Well, that was her own fault.'

Thelma's tone was bitter and Kay was curious. 'Why do you say that?'

Her mother sighed. 'She didn't treat people very well. Oh, she was friendly and sympathetic – when she could be bothered. She would take you up and make you believe you were important to her, and you would be only too pleased to help her out if needs be. But she never let anything or anyone – I want you to remember this, Kay – come in the way of her ambition. And where did that get her?'

'I don't understand.'

'Oh, she was talented, I can't deny that. And she did well for herself. Acting on the London stage and in all those films. She even made a handful of films in Hollywood. And then one day it seems she just gave up.' Her mother reached across the table for Kay's hand. 'Don't go, Kay. Let the solicitor deal with everything. They're used to that sort of thing.'

'Then what do you expect me to do?'

'What do you mean?'

'With my inheritance.'

Her sensible mother's next words took her by surprise. 'First of all have a holiday. Find a nice hotel for Christmas. People do that, you know. We could all go. You and me and Julie. We would be waited on hand and foot, and then when we're nice and relaxed we can decide what we're going to do with the money.'

Kay nearly snapped, 'With *my* money,' but she stopped herself in time. However, she couldn't help saying, 'You mean, with the money I have left after I've bought you a house.' And that was just as bad.

Her mother stared at her angrily and Kay suddenly felt near to tears. *What are you doing to us, Lana?* she asked silently. *Do you want my mother and me to quarrel? Are you really laughing at us from the grave?*

'I'll ignore that remark,' her mother said at last. 'But remember, Kay, you're only twenty-two. I should think it's natural that you should want my advice.'

'Of course I'll ask your advice,' Kay said, but her heart sank. She knew very well that she and her mother were unlikely to agree about anything. 'But you can't make me change my mind about going to London.'

'Very well. And what do you want me to tell Julie?'

'She has to know sooner or later. So just tell her the truth.'

And on that rather unsatisfactory note their conversation ended.

'I'm sorry, Mr Chalmers, but your usual table is taken.'

'I phoned to reserve it. There was no mention of a problem.' Tony's charm did not desert him but his voice was cool.

'Your message must have been mislaid.'

Tony glanced at the middle-aged couple sitting at one of the tables near the window. They were looking at the menu. 'I suppose I could ask them to move,' the head waiter said doubtfully.

'No, please don't,' Kay said. 'There are other tables overlooking the bay.'

'But none of them give such a good view of the two lighthouses,' Tony said.

'Erm . . . shall I . . . ?' the head waiter began, and Kay pressed Tony's arm.

'No, don't,' Tony said. 'The view isn't as important as a good meal and a bottle of fine wine. And, of course, the company you keep,' he said, smiling at Kay as he placed a hand in the small of her back and guided her to another table.

Luis beckoned one of the waitresses to take their coats and left them with the menus. 'Grilled steak, don't you think?' Tony asked. 'Could you manage that?'

Kay nodded distractedly. Her mind was taken up with what she was going to say later. She had decided she must tell him tonight before he heard the news from Julie.

Tony ordered their steaks and a bottle of wine. When Luis brought the wine he said, 'On the house, Mr Chalmers. To make up for your disappointment over the table.'

'Very kind of you,' Tony said politely.

Kay noticed that several of the other diners were looking

their way. Tony Chalmers was not only the son of an influential and wealthy businessman but had also demonstrated great bravery and piloting skills during the war. On one occasion he had brought his badly damaged Lancaster bomber back from a mission and made a crash landing in Kent, thus saving the lives of his crew. He could have ordered them to bail out over occupied Holland, but he chose to bring them home. It was this that had gained him his Distinguished Flying Cross.

Tony waited until Luis had poured the wine and then he looked straight at Kay and said, 'So you've given notice at Sampson's?'

'Yes. But how did you know that?'

'Don't look so surprised. This is a small town. Word gets round. I suppose you did plan to tell me?'

'Of course. Tonight, as a matter of fact.'

'So that's why you weren't concentrating before. I could have said we'll have fried toad's legs and you would have agreed. But this is good news, Kay. I never liked the idea of your working in a grocery shop. You are far too intelligent. I often felt like telling your mother that it was you she should have sent to college, not Julie.'

'Julie is very bright.'

'Maybe so, but she hasn't got the same – how shall I put it? – style, class, elegance as you have.'

'Elegance? You go too far.'

Kay smiled but Tony shook his head. 'I don't think I do. Even when you go whizzing round town on that old bicycle, you display ladylike qualities that your younger sister could never aspire to. Why are you laughing?'

'Oh, Tony, I love the compliments, but you do sound a trifle pompous.'

'Do I? Good grief. Am I turning into my father? Or worse still, my mother?' He turned to look at his reflection in the window, pretended to study it closely, then shook his head. 'No, there's still time to save me. Promise me you'll save me.'

Kay hesitated. 'I'm not sure what you mean. Tell me how I can save you.'

Here it comes, she thought. One of those moments that in a romantic novel or a film would lead to a proposal. She looked across the table, but Tony must have changed his mind. He was leaning back and smiling at the young waitress who had arrived with their meal.

'Ah, here we are,' he said. 'The fried toad's legs.'

The girl looked at him nervously. 'No, sir, it's steaks. One well done, one medium rare. I don't think we do toad's legs.'

Kay smiled up at her. 'He's teasing,' she said. 'The steaks are exactly what we want, thank you.'

Tony topped up their glasses, and while they ate their meal the conversation was entirely inconsequential. It wasn't until they had finished their peach Melbas and were drinking their coffee that Tony asked, quite straightforwardly, 'So what are you going to do now that you've left Sampson's? Have you found another job?'

'Not exactly.' He looked puzzled and she hurried on. 'I mean, I shall do something eventually, but first I have to go to London to sort out the affairs of an old friend of my mother's.'

How clumsy that sounds, she thought. *And why couldn't I have told him the truth straight away?*

Tony looked dumbfounded. 'I don't know where to begin,' he said. 'But it sounds as though this old friend of your mother's might have passed away.'

His words reminded Kay of Lana's letter, and she smiled sadly. 'Yes, she has, and she's left a houseful of stuff that must be sorted.'

'Junk?'

'I won't know until I get there.'

Tony leaned back in his chair and stared at her. 'Why can't your mother go?'

'Because Lana – her friend – asked specifically for me.' The name had slipped out, but Kay realised that it meant nothing to Tony.

'Kay, why aren't you telling me the truth?'

'I am.'

'The whole truth. You're lying by omission. I'm not stupid. There's obviously a will involved.'

'Yes.'

'The old girl has left you this houseful of junk, hasn't she?'

'She wasn't that old and it might not be junk.'

'And you've given up your job. The old friend has also left a sum of money.'

'Two thousand pounds.'

'To your mother.'

'No. To me. You see, she was my godmother.'

Tony stared at her uncomprehendingly for a moment and then asked, 'Did you intend to tell me?'

'Yes. Tonight. I didn't know how.'

Suddenly he seemed to pull himself together and he smiled reassuringly. 'Don't worry, Kay. I understand. It must have been a huge shock for you. And now, shall we order a fresh pot of coffee and go through to the hotel lounge to be entertained by Mitzi and Minna?'

Mitzi and Minna might or might not have been sisters, but they dressed identically in black evening gowns and wore the same pageboy hairstyle in shining ash blonde. They were so skilfully made up that it was hard to tell how old they were. Minna played the piano and Mitzi the violin. And every night in the lounge of the Grand Hotel they played their way through an enormous repertoire of popular music – everything from light classical to numbers from the Hit

Parade. Tonight they were playing a medley of songs from popular Broadway musicals.

Tony led the way to an empty table and they settled on the crimson padded chairs. They didn't have to wait long before their waitress brought a tray of coffee and a dish of almond biscuits.

'It's all rather faded, isn't it?' Tony said when the waitress had retreated.

'You mean the hotel?'

'I do. If you look at the old photographs displayed on the walls in the foyer, it was once rather grand.' He smiled. 'The Grand Hotel lived up to its name. But it's lived through two wars and now it needs some tender care.' Abruptly he changed the subject. 'I suppose you'll be staying in a good hotel while you're in London?'

Kay concentrated on pouring the coffee into the two small cups and simply nodded her head.

'And I hope it won't be too long before you come home again.'

'Well, I'm not sure how long it will take.' *Evasion*, Kay thought. *I'm avoiding telling Tony that I don't know whether I want to come home. That I haven't a clue what I want to do.*

If she felt guilty about that, his next words made her feel even worse. 'Kay, I'm so happy for you.'

'Are you?'

'Of course. If anyone deserves a stroke of luck like this, it's you. You know, I couldn't believe it when I walked into Sampson's that day and found you serving behind the counter. My mother had run out of her special brand of ground coffee, and by the time I got to the shop I'd entirely forgotten what it was. You saved my bacon.'

Kay laughed. 'That wasn't hard. Your mother had been buying the same coffee ever since I started work there.'

'And as I sat on that high stool by the counter and waited

while you ground the coffee beans, I wondered how on earth a girl like you was working in a grocery store.'

'Do you know how snobbish that sounds?'

'Does it? Oh, God, I'm sorry. First you tell me I'm pompous and now I'm being snobbish. It's a good job I have you to keep me on the right path.'

And this time it was Kay who withdrew and couldn't quite meet his eyes. Tony took up the white porcelain coffee jug and refilled his cup. She watched as he used the silver tongs to pick up two tiny brown sugar cubes.

He couldn't help it, she thought. It was the way he'd been brought up. But joining the air force when he was only just twenty had opened his eyes to a different world, a different way of life. He was brave and generous – he had brought his crew home when it would have been so much easier to order them to bail out and let them take their chances. The two of them had fun when they went out together, they seldom quarrelled, and yet they hadn't truly become close. People assumed that they would get married, but Tony always held back. And now that she had money, would that make things any different? She wished that thought hadn't even crossed her mind.

'What are you thinking?' Tony asked, and Kay realised that he had been watching her.

'Oh, nothing very much.'

'Well, going by the look on your face, "nothing very much" seemed to be causing you some concern.'

'No, really. It's just that I have so much to do before I go to London.'

'If you say so. But when you get there, don't stay away too long, will you?'

Kay's answer was a shake of her head and a smile.

'I'll take that as a no,' Tony said. 'But now shall we sit back and listen to the music? I think it's from *Carousel*.'

'Mmm. It is.'

Mitzi and Minna were playing 'If I loved you'.

It was nearly midnight when Tony walked her home. Usually, when they had been out together, Kay would invite him in for a cup of coffee, but tonight she had too much to think about. She needed to be alone. Tony, always the gentleman, waited for the invitation, but when it didn't come he drew her into his arms and bade her goodnight. His kiss was more fervent than usual, and Kay wondered if the thought of her leaving had prompted him to be more demonstrative.

Fleetingly she wondered if he would beg her to stay, tell her that he could not bear to be without her no matter how short the time was. She had no time to decide what her answer might be before he gave her a friendly hug and walked away.

The house was quiet. Kay closed the door noiselessly and breathed in the usual comforting smells of lavender polish and her mother's home baking. She left her coat on the hallstand and made her way upstairs in the dark.

A thin sliver of light falling across the carpet on the landing told her that her sister's bedroom door was ajar. As she walked past it, Julie pulled the door wide open and stood there staring at her. She was wearing a baby-pink quilted dressing gown that, despite her womanly figure, made her look like a precocious schoolgirl, and an Alice band kept her shoulder-length chestnut-coloured hair back from her face. The whole image contrasted oddly with the unlit cigarette held between two fingers.

Kay couldn't stop herself from saying, 'Mum doesn't like you to smoke upstairs.'

'Then don't tell her,' Julie replied.

'You know I wouldn't. But she'll smell the smoke.'

'Not if I keep the door closed and sit by the open window.'

Kay shrugged. 'Did you want to speak to me?' she asked.

'Why else would I be waiting here? Oh, come on in, Kay, before we wake Mum with our chattering.'

The room was cold. Kay guessed her sister must have had the window open for some time. 'Can't you sleep?' she asked.

'It's not that.'

'What is it then?'

Julie didn't answer. Taking a box of matches from her pocket, she lit her cigarette and went to sit on a pink velvet button-backed bedroom chair which was placed by the window. Kay noticed the half-full ashtray on the window sill. She sat on the bed and waited for Julie to begin.

'Why didn't you tell me yourself?' Julie said at last. A spasm of annoyance marred her pretty face. 'Why did you leave it to Mum to tell me that Lana Fontaine has left you a fortune?'

'It's not a fortune, Julie. But you're right. I should have told you and I'm sorry. It's just that I've been thinking what I should do.'

'And have you made your mind up?'

'I think so.'

'Why didn't you ask me to help you?'

Kay was surprised by the question. 'Perhaps I should have done. I'm sorry.'

'Don't keep apologising. But I'd really like to know why you kept it such a secret. I'm your sister. I should have thought that you would want to confide in me.' Julie frowned and turned to waft the smoke from her cigarette out of the window, then turned back to face Kay and sighed. 'But we're not very close, are we, you and I?'

Kay shook her head. She couldn't deny it.

'I'm not sure if we even like each other.' For a moment Julie looked and sounded like a lost child.

'Oh, Julie, of course we do!'

'It doesn't seem so sometimes. Do you know, there are some days when we barely speak to each other. You've gone to work before I get up in the morning and when we get back you're always dashing off to see Tony.'

Kay smiled. 'That's an exaggeration. I don't go out every night, but sometimes when I stay in you are out with your college friends.'

'That's true,' Julie said grudgingly. Then she looked at Kay wide-eyed and asked, 'Are we quarrelling, Kay?'

'No, we're not. At least, I don't want a quarrel. You know, I think the problem is that we are very different people.'

'You mean because I go to college and you work in a shop?'

Kay had to suppress a sudden spurt of anger. Inwardly she acknowledged that there was probably some truth in her sister's comment, but she simply replied, 'Well, we have different interests, don't we?'

They looked at each other and Julie's bedside clock ticked away the lengthening silence. Eventually Julie turned to close the window. Kay wondered what her sister would do with the incriminating cigarette ash.

When Julie turned back, Kay smiled and said, 'We'd better get to bed.'

'So you're not going to tell me then?'

'Tell you what?'

'What you're going to do with the money.'

'Don't worry, Julie. You'll get your share.'

'I didn't mean that!'

'Oh?'

'Well, not in that sense. I was just curious. That's all.'

63

Julie looked genuinely miserable and Kay relented. 'Don't worry. When everything is sorted out we'll have a cosy gossip and I'll tell you anything you want to know. Will that please you?'

Julie didn't reply. She simply nodded despondently, and Kay went off to bed feeling thoroughly unsettled. She knew in her heart that the reason Julie and she could never be comfortable with each other was because their mother treated each of them so differently.

Chapter Five

London, late October

Kay had expected something rather grand – a dignified building with marble floors and Corinthian pillars, perhaps. Instead she was bemused to find that the solicitor's office was a few rooms above a grocery shop. The sleeper train from Newcastle had arrived at King's Cross at six o'clock that morning, and Kay had breakfasted on tea and a roll and butter in her cabin. This was all she could manage, although the menu offered a much greater choice. When she had booked the ticket Miss Bennet had gone with her to the Central Station and had persuaded her to travel first class.

'You will need a good night's sleep,' her old friend had told her.

However, no matter how comfortable the cabin was, Kay, nerves taut with excitement, had hardly slept a wink.

When she emerged from the train a porter appeared from nowhere and hefted her suitcase on to his trolley. The platform seemed never-ending as she followed him to the taxi stand. He stowed her suitcase into the next waiting cab, and smiled broadly and touched his cap when she handed him a tip of a shilling. It was probably too much, she thought, and immediately began to worry about the size of tip she should give to the taxi driver.

She had shown him the address on the letterhead and he had smiled. Kay thought this was because her destination in Wood Green was some distance from the station, so he would be receiving a good payment. When they arrived, she quickly worked out ten per cent of the fare and hoped that was correct. Perhaps it wasn't, because the cab driver had been completely unsmiling when he pocketed it. He didn't help her with her suitcase.

Feeling tired and deflated, Kay stood on the pavement outside a grocer's shop in a suburban high street staring up at the gold letters on the window of the first floor: Charles A. Butler, Solicitor. That was where she had to go. But how to get there?

'Move along, will you?' a large, unfriendly woman said. 'Folks has to get by.'

'Oh, I'm sorry . . .' Kay began, but the woman had disappeared amongst the early-morning crowd.

People were hurrying because it was cold. Despite her new woollen coat, Kay was shivering. The soles of her new fashionable court shoes did little to protect her toes from the cold pavement.

'If you want the solicitor, the door's right there,' a young lad told her. He was wheeling a bicycle with a basket full of groceries on the front handlebars. He nodded towards a door at one side of the shop.

'Oh, thank you.'

The door pushed open easily and Kay lugged her suitcase up the worn lino-covered stairs. A familiar smell of smoked bacon, cheese and coffee seeped through the walls from the shop, and Kay, light-headed from lack of sleep, almost imagined herself back at Sampson's. As she neared the top, she heard the clattering of a typewriter, and someone with an educated and melodious voice called out, 'Is that you, Miss Lockwood? Do come in.' A door with a frosted glass window was ajar. This was where the voice came from.

Kay entered as she was instructed, and a tall woman rose from her desk. 'It is Miss Lockwood, isn't it?' she asked.

'Yes.'

'I'm Moira. Moira Davies. Pleased to meet you. Do sit down.' She waved an elegant arm in the direction of an armchair. 'I'm just going to finish these letters,' she said, 'but if you've been carrying that bulging suitcase around it will give you time to get your breath back.'

The chair was comfortable and Kay felt her eyes closing. If it hadn't been for the clattering of the typewriter, she might have fallen asleep. Instead she forced herself to look around the room. Miss Davies' office was like any other office, she imagined, with a desk, bookcases and filing cabinets. In the wall on the right there was another door. Kay decided that Mr Butler must be in there.

She looked covertly at the woman behind the desk. The secretary's greying hair was swept back into a French pleat, which made her look more austere than her welcoming manner had suggested. She was carefully made-up, and her black and white checked costume with its slim skirt and boxy jacket was extremely stylish.

In the face of such up to the minute fashion, Kay was glad that she had allowed Miss Bennet to talk her into buying the cherry-red coat with its nipped-in waist and long, full skirt. And although she hardly ever wore a hat, she was thankful that she had remembered to pin on the little saucer-sized Juliet cap before she left the train.

'Won't be long,' the secretary called out. 'Then I'll make us a cup of tea.'

Kay began to wonder where Mr Butler was. This was all so strange. Had she come on the right day? Yes, it was obvious that she had been expected. The noise of the typewriter stopped and Moira Davies began to shuffle papers.

The room was warm and Kay was tired. She wriggled her poor numbed toes to restore the circulation, then she closed her eyes.

'Milk and sugar, Miss Lockwood?'

Kay awoke with a start to find Miss Davies standing over her.

'Oh, I'm sorry. I didn't mean to fall asleep.'

'Don't worry, dear. It gave me time to pop out and post the letters and then to make a pot of tea.' She made one of those graceful gestures again, this time in the direction of her desk, where there was now a tray with a teapot, a milk jug, a sugar bowl and two cups. Kay looked at them and smiled in recognition.

'You've noticed my Royal Albert?' Miss Davies looked pleased.

'They're very pretty. I know someone, an old friend, who has the same set.'

'Old Country Roses. I like nice things. Just because I work in a dreary office doesn't mean that I can't have a bit of luxury to cheer my day. As a matter of fact, this set was a gift from Lana – your godmother. She said I deserved it for putting up with her for so long.'

'Putting up with her?'

'Mr Butler has been her solicitor for many years.' The secretary paused as if there was something else she could have said. This left Kay a little puzzled. 'Now, milk and sugar?'

'Yes, please.'

Miss Davies poured the tea, and after giving Kay her cup she took her own and sat down behind her typewriter. 'I've booked you into a respectable guest house as you requested. I think that was very wise of you, and it's just in the next street to where we will be going. May I suggest that you go to the guest house now? I'll give you directions. Have a rest, then I'll meet you for a late lunch at Domino's and take you along to the house this afternoon.'

'Don't I have to see Mr Butler?'

'No, dear. Mr Butler is in court this morning, but in any case, he's happy to leave this sort of thing to me. He'll be in the office after lunch if there's anything you want to ask him. Do you know, I'm trying to think who you remind me of . . . you have dark hair and yet your eyes are blue . . . no, it escapes me. Wait . . . I know – the red coat . . . Scarlet O'Hara, that's it! Or I should say, Vivien Leigh. Has anyone ever told you, you look like the film star Vivien Leigh?'

Kay smiled. 'No, not Vivien Leigh.'

'You say that as though there is someone else you remind people of.'

'Not people. Just one person in particular.'

'Who, then?'

'Miss Gulch.'

Miss Davies frowned. 'A film star?'

'A character in a film.'

'A well-known film?'

'Very.'

The secretary's eyes widened as light dawned. '*The Wizard of Oz*! Miss Gulch, the Wicked Witch of the West! How cruel. You don't look anything like her and—'

'My face isn't green!'

Kay laughed and Miss Davies looked at her uncomprehendingly. 'Whoever it was, was teasing you, yes?'

'Yes. And she's a very dear friend.'

'How can she be when she thinks you look like Miss Gulch?'

'She doesn't think I look like her. It's the shop's bicycle. The way I ride the bicycle when I'm in a hurry. I'm sorry; it isn't a bit funny if you don't know the circumstances.' To her dismay Kay felt her laughter turn to tears.

69

'No, dear, it isn't. Do you need this?'

Miss Davies opened a drawer in the desk and took out a clean white handkerchief. She held it out but Kay shook her head.

'No, it's all right. I've got one in my handbag . . . somewhere.' Kay fumbled in her shoulder bag, and as she encountered biscuit crumbs and torn grocery lists she wished that either she had cleaned it out, or better still, bought a new bag to match her new shoes. 'I'm sorry,' she said as she dabbed at her eyes and wondered whether the mascara she had applied so hastily that morning was holding up to the challenge.

'Don't worry, Kay. May I call you Kay?'

'Please do.'

'And you must call me Moira. I remember when I first left home and came up to London. I was only seventeen and I'd never been away from home before.' Miss Davies sat back in her chair and closed her eyes for a moment, lost in thought. Then, suddenly, she opened her eyes and stood up. 'Here you are,' she said, holding out a piece of paper. 'I've drawn you a little map to show you how to get to Brook Lodge. They're expecting you. I'll meet you at Domino's. I've marked it on the map – you'll pass it on the way to the guest house.'

Kay took the map and was disconcerted to see how quickly Miss Davies got back to work. She felt as though she had been in to see the headmistress and had now been dismissed. For a short while she had been bathed in friendship and made to feel welcome, but now it was as though a light had been turned off and she was alone in the cold and dark again.

Don't be so melodramatic, she told herself crossly as she manoeuvred the heavy suitcase down the narrow stairway, trying not to bang her shins. *I chose to come to London. I could have stayed at home and simply let Mr Butler deal with everything, although his way of dealing with it would probably have been to hand everything over to Miss Davies.* The thought made Kay smile. Once outside, she found the warm tea had fortified her against the cold, and her heart lifted when she saw the frost sparkling cheerily on the pavements.

Brook Lodge was pretty much what Kay had expected: a respectable Edwardian family home which at some time had been converted into a guest house. It was like one of the smarter guest houses at home in Northridge Bay. The tiny black-clad woman behind the reception desk welcomed her, introduced herself as Mamie Price, and then looked at Kay appraisingly.

'Nice coat, dear,' she said. 'I like those pleats in the back. Dior New Look, is it?'

'Yes, it is.'

'Buy it here in London, did you?'

'No, at home in Newcastle.'

The woman raised her eyebrows. 'In Newcastle? Well, well.'

'We have some very good shops there,' loyalty prompted Kay to say.

'Well, well,' the woman repeated and shook her head as if astonished. 'Now, here's your keys. One for the front door, one for your room. First-floor back overlooking the garden and no traffic noise – although I must say this is a very quiet street.'

She seemed to be waiting for some sort of response so Kay said, 'I'm sure it is.'

'Got your ration book, have you?'

'Oh, yes,' Kay rummaged in her shoulder bag again. 'Here you are.'

'That Miss Davies didn't know how long you'd be staying.' She put her head on one side like a little bright-eyed bird while she waited for an answer.

'That's right. I'm afraid I can't tell you yet.'

'Business or holiday?'

Taken aback by the question, Kay said, 'Business, I suppose. But, if you don't mind, I'm a little tired and I'd like to go up to my room now.'

Mamie Price looked disappointed. ''Fraid there's no one to help you with that case.' She paused. 'Maybe the two of us together …?'

'No. Really. Thank you but I can manage.'

Kay slung the strap of her handbag over her shoulder, grabbed the handle of her case and headed towards the staircase. Then, trying not to show what an effort it was, she made her escape. She decided she liked Mamie Price, but right now she was desperately tired, and rather than gossip with this pert little woman all she wanted to do was lie down and go to sleep.

The room had a washbasin with a mirror above and was attractively decorated with floral wallpaper. Kay looked at her wristwatch and saw that she had just over three hours before she had to meet Miss Davies at the restaurant. She stripped down to her underwear and tentatively lifted back the eiderdown and blankets on the bed. The sheets and pillow cases were clean and smelled of lavender. Before getting into bed, she set the alarm on the small travel clock Miss Bennet had given her as a parting gift and placed it on the bedside table.

Vaguely aware of an ache behind her eyes, she lay down and tried to sleep. But she found she couldn't relax, and the thoughts chased round and round in her head as she recalled the conversation she'd had with her mother the day before.

It was early morning and her mother had come in with a cup of tea. 'We'd better talk,' Thelma announced.

'Oh, Mum, now?' Kay struggled to sit up, gave in, and collapsed back amongst the pillows.

'Yes, now, Kay. You're off to London tonight and there are things we have to sort out.'

Resignedly, Kay sat up and took a sip of tea. Her mother turned and looked at the coat hanging from the top of the wardrobe door. 'Very nice,' she said. 'Did you enjoy your shopping trip?'

'Yes.'

'I wonder why you didn't think to take Julie. She would have liked a day in town.'

'Are you hinting that I should have bought Julie a coat?'

'Yes, I am. Or at least a nice costume. A little pleated skirt and a fitted jacket. That would do very nicely when she goes for job interviews, wouldn't it?'

'So Julie still intends to find a job when she leaves college, does she?'

Kay's tone was sharper than she intended and her mother snapped, 'What do you mean by that?'

'Exactly what I say. I've agreed to buy you a house and to give Julie two hundred pounds as you suggested.'

'Two hundred pounds is hardly a fortune, is it?'

'But maybe it's more than enough for her to buy her own clothes.'

'I can see it's no use arguing with you, Kay. Have you finished your tea?'

Her mother picked up the cup which Kay had placed on her bedside table and started to walk towards the door.

'Wait a moment,' Kay said. 'I'm going to London tonight. I don't think we should quarrel on my last day at home and I don't think you came in just to tell me I should have bought Julie a coat.'

Her mother looked thoughtful. 'No, I didn't.' Still holding the cup, she sat down at the bottom of the bed. 'And I don't want to quarrel either. I'm sure Lana is mighty pleased with herself, setting you and me against each other.'

Kay pulled her legs up and wrapped her arms around her knees. 'I hope you're wrong about that,' she said quietly.

'Why do you say so?'

'I don't like to think of her being spiteful.'

Her mother's lips thinned. 'No? Well, I won't disillusion you.'

Kay would have liked to have told her that her very words were disillusioning, but her mother hurried on. 'I came in to thank you for agreeing to buy me a house and to tell you that they've accepted my offer.'

Kay was stunned by how quickly her mother had gone ahead with the business of buying herself a new home. 'I didn't know you'd made an offer. In fact I didn't know you'd found a house you wanted.'

'I told you. I've been looking at those houses overlooking the dene.'

'The houses that cost about eight hundred pounds?' Julie asked wryly.

'That's right, but you'll be pleased to know that I found one that they were asking six hundred and fifty for. It's been on the market for a while. I offered six hundred flat and they've accepted it.' Thelma's eyes were shining.

'You made an offer?'

'I just told you that. And they accepted it.'

'Without consulting me?'

'There was no need. The house is just what I want.'

Kay wanted to say that that wasn't the point. The point was that it was her money that her mother was spending. And that her mother had taken it for granted that Kay would agree.

'It needs a bit of work,' her mother continued, 'but the two hundred we agreed on will take care of that and buy some nice new furniture and give me a little lump sum as well.'

'We agreed to that, did we?'

'Of course we did. Don't you remember?'

'I remember talking about it, but I don't remember agreeing to anything.'

'Really, Kay, when I asked you if you wanted to help your mother you said you did.'

Kay's mind flashed back to the conversation they'd had: *'Don't make it sound like charity, Kay. I should think you would want to help your mother without being asked.'*

'Of course I do.'

Kay realised there was no point in arguing further.

'So I'll go ahead and get a solicitor, shall I?' her mother asked. 'To see to the house and Julie's money.'

'And yours. Yes, go ahead.'

'You're doing the right thing, Kay.'

'Am I?'

'Of course you are. It was quite wrong of Lana to leave everything to you and nothing to Julie and me. Now that you're going to put things right—'

'By giving you half of my inheritance?'

'That's right. Now your conscience will be clear.'

'My conscience?'

'You would never have enjoyed your inheritance if it set you apart from your mother and your sister. Now, would you like me to bring you breakfast in bed and then help you with your packing? I shouldn't think you'll be staying in London very long, so you won't need to take too much.'

'And what happens when I come home?'

'What do you mean?'

'Where will I be living?'

'With me and Julie for as long as you need to. I've already told you that.'

'Oh, yes, I remember. Until Tony proposes to me.'

There was an awkward pause then her mother said, 'I'll go and start your breakfast.'

'Thank you, but you needn't bring it up. I'll come down. Then I can manage my own packing.'

Her mother hadn't tried to persuade her otherwise, which was probably why Kay had ended up with a bulging suitcase and not the faintest idea when she would be going home – or even if she wanted to.

Domino's was easy to find. Kay was relieved to see that Mr Butler's secretary was already there, sitting at a table near the window. A good-looking young man, wearing a black waistcoat over a white shirt, had just handed Moira a large menu.

She looked up and smiled at Kay. 'Do let Nico take your coat, Kay dear,' she said. 'It gets very warm in here, even when we sit near the door.'

Thoroughly flustered, Kay didn't know how to refuse, so she took her coat off and handed it to Nico. He hurried away with it and she sat down. She was aware that Moira was looking at her curiously.

Kay guessed why. 'I didn't really have time to shop for clothes,' she said.

'There's no need to be apologetic, dear. That skirt and blouse are perfectly respectable, if a little . . .'

'Dreary?' Kay said.

'Shall we say sensible? But as for the cardigan . . . did you knit it yourself?'

'I'm afraid to admit I did.'

Kay looked across the table and saw that Miss Davies was smiling. A moment ago she had almost started crying with embarrassment, but now she felt laughter bubbling up. 'I know. I should have left it at home,' she said.

'You should have thrown it away.'

'Oh, but that would be wasteful!'

'Then you should have given it to the Salvation Army, who would have found a nice old lady to give it to.'

By now both of them were laughing, and when the young waiter returned he looked at them curiously. 'You have found something to amuse you, Miss Davies?' he said.

'Yes, Nico, but you wouldn't understand. Now, we needn't bother with this menu. I'm going to order spaghetti Bolognese for both of us.' She handed the menu back. 'It's the speciality here,' she told Kay. 'I don't think you could find a better Bolognese anywhere in London.'

'This young lady is new to London?' Nico asked. He smiled at Kay.

'Yes, Nico, and stop flirting with her. She's too intelligent to be taken in by that alluring smile and those big brown eyes.'

Not at all offended, the young waiter laughed and hurried away.

'Was he really flirting with me?' Kay asked.

'Of course he was – he's Italian, isn't he? And you are a beautiful young woman, in spite of your utility outfit. Kay, my dear, I don't know what else you've brought with you to London in that bulging old suitcase, but I suspect that it might be a good idea for us to go shopping together.'

'Oh, no, please, I don't want to be a nuisance.'

'You won't be a nuisance, Kay. It will be a wonderful excuse to take time off from the office. Ah, here comes Nico.'

Nico was followed by a young woman carrying a small carafe of red wine and two glasses. Kay didn't remember Miss Davies ordering it, but as the waitress placed it on the table and filled the glasses she murmured, 'Your usual, Miss Davies.'

Kay had never had spaghetti Bolognese and she gazed in surprise at the large dish of white pasta topped with what looked like tomato flavoured mince. She sat back when Miss Davies said yes to finely grated cheese and then pepper from a giant pepper pot – for both of them.

'Haven't you had spaghetti before?' she asked Kay when Nico had gone.

'I've had spaghetti but it was nothing like this.'

'Tell me?'

'It came out of a tin. It was in a tomato sauce but there wasn't any meat. My mother served it on toast.' Kay sensed Miss Davies' amusement and added, 'It's very nice like that.'

'I know it is,' Moira said. 'But it's years since I had spaghetti on toast. Lana and I used to have it for a treat when we came home from the theatre.'

'You went to the theatre together?'

'That's where we met. Here in Wood Green at the Empire. The Wood Green Empire. We were both performing there.'

'You were on the stage?'

'Yes, dear, but I was never as successful as Lana.'

'May I ask what you did?'

'Only if you eat your spaghetti first.' Miss Davies smiled at her and Kay picked up her fork.

'Don't I get a knife?' she asked.

''Fraid not. But watch me – you'll soon get the hang of it. And drink up, dear.' Miss Davies picked up her glass of wine. 'Chin-chin!'

Kay sipped her wine and decided she liked it, but her main concern was to eat her spaghetti without making too much of a fool of herself. When they had finished, Miss Davies ordered Sundaes for them. This consisted of a tall glass dish full of layers of ice cream with chocolate, caramel and strawberry sauce. A lone wafer stick was stuck in the top at a jaunty angle.

'You promised to tell me what you did on the stage,' Kay said.

'I was a dancer. A very good dancer, but unfortunately I grew too tall to be a ballerina. I was too tall for the chorus line, too, so, not to be defeated I worked out my own solo dance routine. It was good – I have no false modesty – but never good enough to be top of the bill, like Lana was.'

'What did Lana – Miss Fontaine – do?'

'She could sing, she could dance, she could act – but don't you know all this? I mean, hasn't your mother told you anything about her?'

'Not much. I think they must have quarrelled. The last time she visited I was eight years old, and after that Lana's name was never mentioned in our house.'

'And yet she loved you enough to make you her heir, didn't she?'

Nico arrived with the coffee and the two women waited until he had gone before they resumed their conversation.

Kay stirred a spoonful of brown sugar into her cup and looked at it thoughtfully. Eventually she looked up at Moira. 'You and she were good friends. Did she never tell you what went wrong between my mother and herself?'

Miss Davies looked away for a moment, then said, 'She rarely spoke of those early days when she met your mother and father. Here you are, Kay, why don't you try one of these little biscuits? They're a sort of macaroon.'

Kay reached for one of the little round biscuits and remembered a conversation she'd had with her mother.

'She would take you up and make you believe you were important to her, and you would be only too pleased to help her out if needs be. But she never let anything or anyone – I want you to remember this, Kay – come in the way of her ambition.'

'Did you like her?' Kay didn't know what had prompted her to ask such a personal question and she felt herself blushing. 'I'm sorry, I shouldn't have . . .'

'No, it's all right. I don't mind answering. I liked her very much, even though I was fully aware of her faults. She was so . . . charismatic. If you became her friend you thought you were the luckiest person in the world. You would do anything for her, but you had to remember that Lana Fontaine would never let anything come in the way of her ambition.'

Kay gasped. Those were the very words her mother had used. 'But she was very talented, wasn't she?'

'Very. As well as being able to sing and dance, she had a beautiful speaking voice. She was a natural in either musicals or straight drama. I always believed she had enough talent to take her to the very top, but the more you got to know her, the more you realised there was something, deep inside, that was holding her back.'

'What was that?'

'I can't tell you.'

Can't, or won't? Kay thought, but she didn't like to press for an answer.

While she had been talking Miss Davies had taken a silver cigarette case from her bag. She opened it and offered it to Kay.

'No, thank you. I don't smoke.'

'Good girl. I wish I'd never started.' She extracted a cigarette and put it in a long, jewelled cigarette holder. After she had lit the cigarette, she closed her eyes and inhaled deeply. 'Ah, that's better.' When she opened her eyes she picked up the carafe. 'Pity to waste this,' she said. She made to fill up Kay's glass, but Kay put her hand over the top and shook her head. Miss Davies shrugged and smiled, then emptied the carafe into her own glass. Shaking her head wonderingly, she seemed to gather her thoughts. 'As I was saying . . . One day she just gave up.'

Kay must have missed the moment when Moira summoned Nico to the table, but suddenly he appeared with the bill placed on a silver salver. She saw Moira opening her handbag and said quickly, 'Oh, please let me pay.'

'Of course not,' Moira said. 'You are a valued client. Charles has told me to look after you.'

'You mean Mr Butler?'

'Yes. My boss. The man I am devoted to – although he doesn't seem to realise it.' She sighed and reached for the black fur shoulder cape that was draped over the back of her chair. 'Time for us to go. And I should tell you, I haven't been to the house since the day of Lana's funeral, so when we get here you'll have to forgive me if I blub like a baby.'

Chapter Six

'It's unsightly, isn't it?'

Moira closed the front door and came to stand behind Kay, who was staring up at a tall grandfather clock. The hands had stopped at twelve o'clock – midnight, Kay mused fancifully.

'I wouldn't say unsightly,' Kay said. 'Perhaps a little overpowering for the size of this hallway.'

'Do you like that sort of thing? Antiques? It's Victorian – carved walnut – too ornate for my liking. I'm sure it must be worth a pretty penny, but Lana could never bring herself to sell it, even though it doesn't suit the decor. It reminded her of the early days when, like two little Cinderellas, we had to be home before midnight.'

'You and Lana both lived here?'

'Why don't we go into the sitting room? I can light the gas fire in there, and I'll answer all your questions.'

When Moira knelt to light the fire Kay noticed once more how gracefully she moved. She remained kneeling until the elements flared into life, then she rose and sank gratefully into one of the brown leather armchairs. She had not started to 'blub' as she had threatened, but her finely drawn features showed signs of strain.

'Do sit down, dear,' she said, nodding towards the other armchair. 'What do you think?' She made a circling gesture with one arm which took in the whole room.

Kay looked around at the pale grey walls and the black and grey curtains. There was a large rug with geometric patterns in the same colours, and the upholstery of the sofa and armchairs was dark grey, with silver scatter cushions. A mirrored coffee table stood between the two armchairs, and on the wall above the marble fire surround there was a fan-shaped mirror. To one side of the fireplace, the tall floor lamp consisted of a bronze lady in sculptured robes, holding a large globe above her head with outstretched arms.

'Well?' Moira said.

'I think I like it.'

'Lana insisted everything should be streamlined and modern. Do you know what is meant by art deco?'

'I think so.'

Moira leaned back, stretching her long legs out in front of her and crossing them at the ankle. 'When Lana and I first rented rooms here, our landlady, Mrs O'Brien, lived in this room. She ate and slept in here so that she could rent all the other rooms to her theatricals, as she called them. What a mess it was when Lana took the house over! She had to start from scratch, as they say.'

'Stop! My head is spinning. Please will you explain?'

Moira laughed. 'Make yourself comfortable and I'll tell you a story.' She took out a cigarette and put it in the holder, then looked round and shook her head.

'What is it?' Kay asked.

'Lana won't allow smoking in the house. I mean wouldn't. She may be dead and gone, but it still feels wrong.' She extracted her cigarette from the holder and put it back in the cigarette case.

'You were saying?' Kay tried to hide her impatience.

'Sorry. When we met, what they call the roaring twenties were drawing to an end, but both of us still loved the fashions.

83

We were what was called flappers. Shingled hair, short skirts, and silk stockings whenever we could afford them. When we were broke we had to make do with rayon. Oh, and of course, long, beaded necklaces and jewelled cigarette holders. Unlike me, Lana never smoked, but she carried one just to look sophisticated.

'We were both appearing at the Empire and we had digs here. It was the first time in London for both of us, and even though Lana was nearer the top of the bill than I was, we became friends. I knew she was talented. And brave. She had only just recovered from – from some kind of illness, and yet she threw herself into rehearsals and worked until the weaker souls among us would have dropped.'

'And you had to be back here by midnight.'

'What? Oh, yes, the clock. Mrs O'Brien was very strict with the young ladies. She insisted that she kept a respectable house and that there would be no partying with dubious gentlemen for us. No going up to clubs in the West End and getting our pictures in the scandal sheets. We had to be home by midnight. Every night when we came home Lana and I would look up at the clock.

'With any luck we had seconds to go, and we would make a dash for the stairs and hurry up them, trying not to laugh out loud. But if we were a second late – I swear, just one second – the door of this room would open and Ma O'Brien, garbed in a gruesome old dressing gown, and her hair in curlers, would appear. The only thing missing was a rolling pin. She would demand to know where we thought we had been and what we'd been up to. That's why Lana stopped the clock at twelve – to remind us of those happy days.'

'So there's no wedding cake on the table?'

'What on earth are you talking about?'

'The clocks stopped; the wedding cake on the table . . .'

'Miss Havisham! *Great Expectations*! Clever girl. No, you won't find a mouldering wedding dress here. Although, to tell the truth, I'm not exactly sure what you will find. Everything in the house is yours. Even the clock; Lana bought it when Mrs O'Brien died.' Moira paused and closed her eyes for a moment. 'We were very happy here, you know,' she went on. 'Young and hopeful. Working till we dropped but enjoying every minute. Coming home after the show, washing our underwear and hanging it over the bath. Eating spaghetti on toast and drinking cheap wine when everyone else was asleep.

'That's why Lana kept her room here, even when she was on tour. Also, it saved having to pack up absolutely all her worldly goods and take them with her. And as the other tenants moved out, Lana took their rooms, too. By then she was appearing in the West End and in the movies, and she could well afford the rent. And as my career had come to an abrupt end, I looked after the place for her.'

'What happened?'

'I had a fall. Very embarrassing. The audience laughed. I think some of the dimmer ones thought it was part of the act. I fled in tears and never trod the boards again.'

'I'm sorry.'

'No need to be. I found a job with Mr Butler, and I've stayed in it ever since. I even live there. Mr Butler owns the whole property, shop, office and all. The tiny apartment up on the top floor is mine, rent free. But we digress. Eventually Lana had the whole house – bar this room. When the old girl died that problem was solved.'

'Why didn't she buy the house instead of renting it?'

'Kathleen, Mrs O'Brien's daughter, wouldn't sell. She and her husband own other houses round here. They know the future is in property, especially as there are so many people still homeless after the war. The rents are soaring. God help whoever takes this house on when Lana's tenancy is finished. Are you cold?'

'No. Why do you ask?'

'You were shivering.'

'You'll laugh.'

'Of course I won't.'

'When you were talking about you and Lana – when you were young – coming home from the theatre, sneaking up the stairs, washing your clothes and eating your supper . . .'

'Yes? Go on.'

'I could almost hear you – almost see you. Both of you. It's as if Lana still lives here.' Kay paused, waiting for Moira's response.

'I know what you mean. I can feel it myself. Lana had a very strong presence, both on the stage and in real life.' Moira stared speechlessly at the fire for a while and then she sighed and smiled at Kay. 'You know, when Lana made her will she discussed it with me and she told me she wanted you to come here, but I can't tell you why. Perhaps while you're here you'll find the answer yourself.'

Kay was bewildered by how quickly her life had changed. From working behind a shop counter and getting the grocery orders in a small northern seaside resort, she had been transported by fate to the capital city, where life seemed never to come to a standstill and where she had discovered you could be completely alone despite the hustle and bustle of the crowded pavements. Kay had decisions to make, and although Moira was kind, Kay felt the need to confide in someone from home. She considered her options. Her mother? Her sister? Tony? She discounted all three quickly and sat down to write to the only person she could open her heart to.

Dear Miss Bennet,

I don't think I fully understood when I made a joke about inheriting Lana Fontaine's 'goods and chattels' that she meant a whole houseful of furniture. Looking at the house from the outside, it is quite an ordinary, although solid-looking, tall terraced house in a tree-lined avenue. Respectable suburbia! Inside is not quite what you would expect. Although she didn't own the house, over the years my godmother had redecorated and refurnished in a very modern way. Miss Davies, the solicitor's secretary, told me the style was art deco.

But what am I to do with all the beds (there are five bedrooms), tables, chairs, curtains, carpets, let alone the contents of the cupboards, drawers and wardrobes? Do you sense the size of my problem? I would love to know what was in my godmother's mind when she made her will.

Why, oh why, did she burden me with this? I mean, she walked out of my life when I was eight years old. It's not as if she had no one else she could trust with the task. Moira Davies and my godmother were friends going back to the days when they were both in the theatre and appearing in the same show. You may wonder why Lana did not leave something to Moira. Well, it seems that over the years she showered her with gifts – including a beautiful Royal Albert tea set that is just like yours. She told her that, as there was no knowing which of them would take the final curtain call first, she wanted her to enjoy nice things while they were both alive.

So here I am at Brook Lodge doing nothing but panic. Miss Davies has suggested that it would be better for me to move into the house, and she has offered to sort this out with the landlady. She doesn't think that will be a problem. The guest house is clean and comfortable, but the food is uninspiring. I suppose I have been spoiled by my mother's cooking.

As far as I can see, there is only one other guest here at the moment. A girl of about my own age, called Shirley Walton. Tonight she suggested we should share a table for our evening meal, and while we were eating she told me that she has just come up to London to take up a job as a secretary at the BBC. She's staying here at the guest house because her mother is an old friend of Mrs Price, who, it turns out, is the owner of Brook Lodge. Shirley doesn't intend to stay here. Mrs Price is very kind to her and doesn't charge her the full amount, but even so she can't really afford it and would rather rent a room somewhere.

I think I found out most of this during the first course (brown Windsor soup), and by the end of the second course (boiled leg of mutton with carrots and potatoes), she had told me about her family, her schooldays at the local grammar school, and her broken romance. This was one of the reasons she had decided to apply for a job in London. She is not at all boastful, but I think she must be very clever.

For dessert we had steamed currant pudding and custard. Thankfully Shirley seemed to have run out of steam. Is there a joke there somewhere? After coffee, Shirley wanted us to go to the pictures but I was too tired. She was disappointed and that made me feel guilty, but if I had gone to the cinema I would probably have fallen asleep. Shirley is so excited about starting a new life in London, whereas I have come here to sort things out and then I will be going home again.

So my new friend has gone to the pictures by herself and here I am in the residents' lounge sitting as close as I can get to a lacklustre fire and writing to you on notepaper supplied by Brook Lodge. How strange life is. I was expecting to feel homesick and yet I am not. Instead I feel as though I am in limbo. But now I must go to bed and try to sleep, for, as Scarlett O'Hara would say, 'Tomorrow is another day.'

Yours sincerely,

Kay

25th October 1949

Dear Mum,

Thank you for your letter. I will be leaving Brook Lodge on Monday, the last day of the month, and moving into the house where Lana Fontaine lived. Miss Davies arranged this for me. The landlady could not really complain, as the rent is paid until the end of the year. She did, however, ask for an extra four pounds a month to cover the inconvenience. I have no idea how my moving in would inconvenience her, but Moira said it would be better to keep her happy.

Until then, for the next few days, I shall continue to go each day and carry on sorting through drawers and cupboards. I feel like a thief, although so far I have not found anything of great value. My friend Miss Bennet – she was my form teacher in my last year at school, remember? – thought there might be some valuable jewellery. She remembers seeing photographs of Lana in magazines where she absolutely 'dripped with diamonds'.

Well, Lana might have had some good jewellery then, but there is nothing now. I have two theories to explain this. Maybe the jewellery did not belong to her; maybe it was lent by the film studios. (I know they did this sort of thing when they wanted their stars to look glamorous at special events.) Or perhaps after she retired from acting she slowly sold off anything of value in order to go on living here. Moira thinks this may be so. She told me that after Lana stopped working, things – like a piece of Lalique glassware, or maybe a Tiffany lamp – began to disappear.

If this is the case, I'm sad that she had to sell things she might have held dear to her, but I'm not at all concerned for myself. The things that are left can tell me so much about her. The clothes in the wardrobes are the most revealing. They are stylish and elegant, and so evocative that they almost bring her to life for me. Moira, who is so fashionable herself, says they are almost a history of twentieth-century fashion.

Lana must have kept every garment she ever bought. Moira told me that although the majority of them are copies run up by a corner-shop dressmaker, there are also some genuine gowns designed by Elsa Schiaparelli and Madeleine Vionnet. Also some silk scarves by someone called Hermès. I am afraid these names mean nothing to me, even though Moira says they are quite famous.

There are some clothes that have never been worn. Moira says Lana just couldn't stop herself from buying new things. She thinks I should have any that I take a fancy to. What do you think? And would you like me to send some that I think would suit you and Julie?

Even more interesting than the clothes are the boxes of letters and photographs and theatre programmes. I'm afraid Lana wasn't at all methodical with paperwork, and it will be a nightmare trying to get them in order. I don't know why I feel compelled to do this. Perhaps it is just curiosity on my part – the chance to peer into someone else's life – or maybe it's a perfectly natural desire to find out more about the woman who was once your friend and who became my godmother, and yet who walked away from us without a backward glance.

I'm glad that your plans are going ahead smoothly, and yes, I'm happy for you to contact Mr Butler about the purchase of the new house and the money I've agreed to give you and Julie. I'm sorry that Miss Pearson and Miss Elkin took the news so badly, but I think you should take this as a tribute to the way you have looked after them. Staying here in Brook Lodge has made me realise how good a cook you are and how lucky I have been.

Mum, I'm really glad that you won't have to take in lodgers any more and I hope you and Julie will be happy in your new home.

Love,
Kay

Kay looked at what she had written before putting the letter in the envelope. Something about it made her stop and think. She had asked her mother if she should send some of Lana's clothes home for her and Julie. 'Send', not 'bring'. She had also said she hoped her mother and her sister would be happy in their new home. She had not suggested that she would be there with them.

In the letter she had written to Miss Bennet she had said that she felt as though she was in limbo – a state of uncertainty. And that was true. She didn't know whether she wanted to go home to the people and places she knew, and yet she could not imagine a life in London nor what she would do if she stayed.

Thoughtfully, she put the folded pages of her letter in the envelope and sealed it. There was no one at reception and Kay could hear tinny voices and recorded laughter coming from behind a closed door. Mrs Price must be listening to the wireless. There was no need to ring the bell and summon her to the hall. Kay left the letters on the desk as she had been told to do, and she also left five pence to cover the cost of two postage stamps. Then she went to bed.

Six days later Kay was in Moira's office, but this time, instead of relaxing in the armchair, she was facing Mr Butler's secretary across her desk. Moira held a letter in her hand and stared at Kay incredulously. 'This letter is from your mother's solicitor,' Moira said. 'Is it true? You've really agreed to buy a house for your mother as well as give a sum of money to both her and your sister?'

'Yes, it's true.'

'Why would you do this?'

'Well, my mother . . . my mother . . .'

'Talked you into it?'

Kay shook her head. 'It's not a matter of her talking me into it. It's just that when she pointed it out, it seemed unfair for me to have everything.'

'So you've given half of it away?'

'Yes.'

Kay shifted on the hard wooden seat uncomfortably. One of the legs was shorter than the other three, and every time she moved she felt as though she were going to tip over. She wondered if Moira had placed it there deliberately as a punishment for displeasing her.

In spite of the glass-shaded light above the desk, the room had grown progressively darker since she had arrived to collect the keys. What had started as a miserable drizzle was now a downpour. Fleetingly she wondered whether she might ask Moira if she could borrow an umbrella, but after one glance at the secretary's cross expression she decided not to.

'Kay,' Moira put the letter down and lit a cigarette. When she spoke it was difficult to judge her expression through the haze of smoke. 'Kay,' she repeated, 'your mother has chosen a very expensive house.'

'I know.'

'It seems to me that she is the one who is not being fair.'

Not wishing to meet Moira's eyes, Kay stared obdurately at the typewriter.

'It's not too late to change your mind,' Moira said.

Kay shook her head. 'I can't do that.'

She wished she had asked for the keys to the house as soon as she had arrived, and then, regardless of the rainstorm, she might have made her escape. The phone rang, saving her momentarily from Moira's wrath, but the caller was dealt with briskly, and when Moira replaced the receiver she picked up the letter and read through it again. 'You could at least tell your mother that she must choose a less expensive house,' she said, 'and as for giving Julie two hundred pounds, that's extravagant, to say the least.'

'She's my sister.'

'You were Lana's goddaughter. Julie was not.'

'My mother was Lana's friend.'

Moira leaned back and narrowed her eyes. 'But they didn't keep up the friendship, did they? Haven't you wondered why?'

'I just don't know. Lana used to visit us every now and then. She would bring presents – for Julie, too. Her visits were always exciting. Then suddenly the visits stopped. My mother would never talk about her. But I don't think that's significant. You see, my mother doesn't like talking about anything that happened in the past; not just Lana's visits.'

93

Moira picked up the letter and held it out towards Kay. 'Did it not occur to you, Kay, that this is not what Lana wanted?'

'What do you mean?'

'For goodness' sake, don't pretend to be stupid.'

Kay felt herself flushing. 'I'm not pretending, and I'm not stupid.'

'Good. Now that we've established that, are you instructing me to go ahead with these arrangements?'

'Yes, please.'

'Your saying please doesn't make me feel any better about it.'

'I'm sorry.'

'So you should be.' Moira opened a drawer in her desk and took out a bunch of keys. She sighed and handed them to Kay. 'Here you are. I was going to come with you, but to tell the truth I feel too exasperated.'

Kay took the keys and walked towards the door. Just as she was just about to open it, Moira said, 'Wait. I think you'd better borrow this umbrella.'

Clutching the coal scuttle, Kay braved the rain and dashed across the small garden to the coalhouse set in the back wall. Her spirits rose when she discovered it was almost full. She loaded up the scuttle and made her way back to the kitchen.

The apple-green enamelled range had a fireplace and grate on the left, and a large and small oven on the right. The oven doors had paler green inserts which matched the doors of the kitchen cabinets. The counter tops were stainless steel and the lino on the floor was pale green and grey. That would be hard to keep clean, Kay thought as she glanced at the footmarks she had just left there.

The fire was no problem – she dealt with it efficiently and was soon rewarded with a satisfying warmth – but she was relieved to see that the kitchen also boasted a gas cooker, as she had never had to cope with cooking on a range. When she had lit the fire she had seen a damper and pulled it out, guessing that there would be a back boiler, which meant there would soon be hot water.

Why am I thinking like this? she asked herself. *It's not as if I'm going to be here for very long.*

She had propped Moira's umbrella up in the sink to let it drain dry, and now she draped her coat over the back of a chair. She looked at it anxiously, hoping that she hadn't dirtied it when she was making the fire, and also that it would prove as durable as it was fashionable. She had never paid as much as fifty-five shillings for a coat before. She arranged it carefully so that none of it was touching the floor, and then made herself a cup of tea. Moira had made sure that the cupboards and the refrigerator contained the basics.

Sitting at the table with her tea and the biscuit tin, she wriggled out of her wet shoes and was surprised and cheered to find that the floor was quite warm. She was still feeling upset after the conversation with Moira, so she decided she would sit and compose herself before going upstairs to choose which bedroom she would have. Only then did she remember the two letters Mrs Price had given her when she checked out of Brook Lodge earlier that morning. Fishing them out of her bag, she looked at the envelopes and realised that she recognised the writing on both of them. She opened the letter from her mother first and discovered that Moira Davies wasn't the only person who was cross with her.

27th October 1949

Dear Kay,

I can't imagine why you would think I would want any of Lana Fontaine's cast-off clothes. No matter that

95

Miss Davies says they've never been worn, just looking at them would remind me of the time she hardly had enough rags to cover her back and I had to lend her something to wear if she was going out anywhere.

The show girls often had to get their own costumes together for a new act, and that meant opening their purses. Lana would come to me with that false, apologetic smile and say, 'Thelma, darling, about the rent this week . . .'

No, Kay, as far as the clothes are concerned, I think you should give them to the Salvation Army or take them along to a second-hand shop and see how much you can get for them. As for the photographs, why on earth are you bothering to go through them? What use will that sort of thing be to anyone now that Lana has gone? Take my advice and put them all out straight away. What you find there will be nothing to do with you.

And my, haven't you got pally with this secretary, Miss Davies? She's all over your letter. It's Moira this, and Moira that. I'm sure it must be very nice for you to have this clever new friend.

Well, at least I've got my new house to look forward to. Julie is very excited about living in that part of town. I wonder if we'll be able to move in in time for Christmas.

You'll be pleased to know that Mrs Fraser, who will be renting this house when we have moved, has agreed to have Miss Elkin and Miss Pearson. I've heard she is a respectable woman who used to cook at the British Restaurant here during the war. So they should be well fed.

Do you realise that in your letter you never mentioned when you would be coming home? Perhaps you would let me know.

Love,

Mum

Feeling thoroughly miserable again, Kay put her mother's letter back in the envelope, then, on the spur of the moment, she rose and tossed it in the fire. She had no idea what had prompted her to do so, but for some reason it made her feel better. She topped up her cup of tea before opening the second letter – the one from Tony.

27th October 1949

Dear Kay,

I'm still trying to come to terms with the fact that you slipped away to London without telling me exactly when you were going or when you would be coming back. And, so far, I haven't heard a word from you. Oh, I know you are sorting out your late godmother's house, but surely you could find time to write and tell me how you are getting on. Or if not, there is such a thing as a telephone, you know. I'm sure they must have one at the guest house.

Kay, have you any idea how embarrassing it was for me to have to go and ask your mother for your address? In fact it was worse than that. Your mother was out, and Julie answered the door. Now your sister has got it into her pretty little head that you and I have quarrelled; otherwise you would have written to me once you arrived in London. Have we quarrelled, Kay? I keep thinking back to the last time we went out together. I have to say, you seemed a little distant, but I don't think we quarrelled.

I'm sorry if this letter makes me appear to be thoroughly out of sorts with you, because I'm afraid there's more. Julie told me that you have given her two hundred pounds and also that you are buying a house for your mother. Your sister has no idea how much the house will cost, but knowing its location overlooking the dene, I'm sure it must be using up a large part of your inheritance.

Two thousand pounds must have seemed a large sum of money, but I wish you had asked my advice before giving any of it away. Now I'm guessing you will have about half of it left, and if you had only stopped to think, that was obviously not what your godmother would have wanted.

How are you getting on with sorting out the house? I would offer to come and help you, but in other people's eyes that might not seem proper. All I can say is, if in doubt, take the advice of Miss Fontaine's solicitor. He will be used to dealing with matters like this.

Please write and tell me when you will be coming home – if only to save me from Julie!

Love,

Tony

Kay gripped the letter tightly. She was shaking with rage. *How dare he?* she thought. *How dare he assume that he has the right to scold me about what I've done with my money and offer to give me advice about what I should do with the rest of it? And how patronising to say that two thousand pounds must have seemed a lot to me! Me, the poor, ignorant little shop girl who needs to take advice from a grown-up before making any more decisions – that's what he meant! And that feeble joke about going home to save him from Julie!*

When she had calmed down a bit, she did acknowledge guiltily that she ought to have written to him. Or telephoned. In fact, that thought had crossed her mind when she first checked in to Brook Lodge, but she had kept putting it off to another day.

This time she didn't even put the letter back in its envelope. She stood up and simply crumpled both letter and envelope and threw them on the fire. She watched them burn for a moment and then sat down and dropped her head into her hands. She was sitting like this when the doorbell rang.

'Hurry up, let me in out of this rain,' Moira said when Kay opened the door. 'Quick, let's go through to the kitchen.' She held up a shopping bag. 'I've got lunch.'

Kay watched as Moira reached into the bag and took out bread, cheese, cooked ham, a Victoria sponge and a bottle of wine.

'Nothing fancy, I'm afraid,' Moira said. 'I did the best I could with the coupons I've got left – and next month's, too. It pays to be friendly with the shop downstairs.' She paused and looked at Kay solemnly. 'I'm really sorry about the way I behaved earlier. Will you forgive me?'

'There's no need to apologise. I understand why you were annoyed.'

'Do you? Good. Then get the table set. We'll cement our friendship with this bottle of cheap but perfectly drinkable wine.'

Chapter Seven

Now

Kay placed the cardboard box on one of the chairs and stared at its contents, wondering if she should tip the lot out on to the dining room table, or lift the photographs out one by one. They were all different sizes, from tiny snapshots to studio portraits. Some of them looked like stills from the films Lana had been in. Kay decided to get out a few at a time.

For a moment, when she saw exactly how many there were, she wondered whether she should take her mother's advice and throw them all away without looking at them. After all, what could they mean to her? Two things drew her on. One: her godmother would not have left her these photographs unless she wanted her to look at them; and, two: she was suddenly filled with an overwhelming curiosity.

She put both hands into the box and took hold of a manageable amount. Inevitably their glossy surfaces made them slide about, and, equally inevitably, some of them fell to the floor. Kay put the other photographs on the table and then bent down to pick them up. Looking at the photograph that was uppermost in her hand, she recognised the façade of the Pavilion Theatre. She examined the snapshot more closely, focusing on two girls in stylish drop-waist shift dresses. They were waving at the camera with one hand whilst hanging on to their hats with the other. She had been a small girl when she last saw her godmother, so she wasn't quite sure whether the taller of the young women was Lana. But the other girl, no matter that it must have been taken more than twenty years ago, was unquestionably her own mother. She hardly needed to turn the photograph over to see the words: 'Northridge Bay, Summer 1925. My landlady's daughter, Thelma, and me.'

Kay sank slowly on to the adjacent chair.

Then

'Is that enough? Can I go now?' Violet Saunders lowered the camera and looked at Lana hopefully.

'No, just one more. And, Thelma, please try to smile.'

'I was smiling.'

'No, you weren't. I sneaked a look.'

'Lana, this breeze is cold and I can hardly hold my hat on. Can't we go home?'

'Yes, let's go home,' Violet entreated. With no spare flesh on her girlish frame, she had started to shiver. 'I'm coming out in goose pimples.'

'I'm not going back to the digs,' Lana said. 'Jack wants me to rehearse the new Chinese dance.' She looked at her watch. 'I said I'd meet him in the theatre in an hour from now.'

'An hour!' Violet began plaintively. 'What are we supposed to do for a whole hour?' Her big blue eyes looked as though they were filling with tears, although, in fact, it was the breeze that was making them water.

'I said I'd treat you to a Sunday special cream tea at Bertorelli's, didn't I?' Lana said.

'Did you?' Violet cheered up immediately.

'I'm not sure if you did, and I don't think I can,' Thelma said. 'I'll have to go back and help my mother.'

'Honestly, Thelma, don't you ever get a day off? You're a married woman, for goodness' sake. You must learn to assert yourself.'

'I would, but you know my mother hasn't been well lately. Now isn't the time to upset her.'

'OK, but let's have one more snapshot for my album.'

'Why do you want to keep an album?' Thelma asked. 'Most of the photographs you get people to take are very boring.'

'Thank you very much!' Violet said.

'Do you really think they're boring?' Lana looked genuinely surprised. 'But don't you see, one day when I'm famous, these photographs will be a record of my early years. Someone may even need them when they write a book about me.'

'Well, if that's the case.' Thelma smiled good-naturedly and posed for one last time.

Violet, whose camera it was, didn't like to remind Lana that they hadn't actually included her in any of the snapshots, and she rather hoped to be famous herself one day.

Despite Thelma's protests, they went to Bertorelli's, where Lana ordered three cream teas. She only picked at her own because, she told them, the Spanish dance she was about to rehearse was pretty strenuous.

A few moments after they had arrived Lana slipped away, quite forgetting to pay. Thelma, distracted because she was worrying about her mother, settled the bill without complaint. Violet looked at the remaining cream puff and decided against it. She tried to remember whether Lana had said a Chinese dance or a Spanish dance – perhaps the chorus would have to learn the same routine.

Jack Lockwood, waiting backstage at the Pavilion,

wondered if Lana would have persuaded Thelma and Violet to go for the teas he had given her the money for, and whether she would come to meet him. And if she did, would a plate of dainty sandwiches and a choice of cream cakes for his wife suppress his conscience long enough for him to be able to make love to Lana?

Now

How attractive they look, Kay thought, *and how happy.* They certainly seemed to have been great friends when this photograph was taken. Kay knew it was an unremarkable snapshot and yet the sense of place was overwhelming. If she closed her eyes she could almost smell the brine and hear the dragging of the waves across the shingle on the beach below, the laughter of children and the music of the merry-go-round in the amusement park.

Kay pushed the photograph to the other side of the table, hoping to find others that were similar. If she did, she might learn more, not just about Lana, but about her mother, too. Her mother, who never talked about the past, might be revealed to her in photographs. At that moment, Kay realised that she didn't know which of the two, her mother or her godmother, was the most important to her.

She spread the photographs out on the table and scanned them curiously. There were two of Lana posing by herself. One of them showed her gesturing towards one of the playbills at one side of the ornate entrance. The print was too small and the shot too out of focus for Kay to read the names on the playbill, but on the back of the photograph were the words: 'Lana dreams of being top of the bill!'

The next photograph had the same serrated edges as the

others, but it had been taken from the street outside her own house and the people sitting on the garden wall facing the camera were her mother, her father and Lana.

Kay recognised her father immediately. She had loved him so much, she could never forget him. How striking he looked with his dark hair swept back from his handsome face, and how stylish in his white trousers and striped blazer. He was sitting in the middle with an arm around each girl, and all three of them were smiling. Her mother was wearing the same dress she was wearing in the other photograph, but Lana was in wide-legged slacks and a blouse with a spotted pattern. Neither girl wore a hat.

She was just about to turn the snapshot over to see what was written on the back when her attention was caught by something in the bay window in the house behind them. The lace curtain had been pulled aside and a pale, featureless face was staring across the small garden towards the three people sitting on the wall. Kay had the strongest feeling that this person must be her grandmother. Grandma Thomas had died before Kay was born, and her mother had been looking after the guest house ever since. When Kay turned the snapshot over, Lana's flamboyant handwriting announced: 'We three plus the spectre at the feast!'

It was probably a joke, Kay thought, and yet there was something mean-spirited about those words. She pushed the snapshot across the table to join the first one and decided to make herself a cup of tea.

Then

'Thank you, Violet,' Jack said. 'Shall I take a shot of you three girls, now?'

'We haven't time,' Lana said, 'Poor old Mrs Bartlett will be sitting at the piano waiting for us.' She smiled as she said this, but Violet, who, despite her childlike looks, was keenly observant, sensed her underlying tension.

'Won't take a mo,' Jack said. 'It's only right that we should include Violet. After all, it's her camera. Give it here, Vi. Right. Now, the three of you sit on the wall. No, stand. Lana in the middle. That's right. Thelma, sweetheart, turn round. I don't want a shot of the back of your head.'

'Sorry. It's just that my mother . . .'

'That's better. Smile, please. Lovely! Here's your camera, Violet. Now then, Lana, make sure you bring your dancing shoes.'

'Oh, of course.'

Lana hurried into the house and soon came back carrying her dance bag – rather ostentatiously, Violet thought.

While she had been inside, Jack had caught hold of Thelma's hand and raised it to his lips. 'I can't wait until tonight,' Violet heard him murmur. 'Best bib and tucker, eh?'

Thelma had smiled distractedly and hurried into the house, barely pausing to acknowledge Lana's departure. A moment later the lace curtain in the bay window fell into place and Violet could hear Thelma coaxing her mother to go upstairs and rest.

'Have I missed it?' The voice was young and breathless.

Violet turned to see Eve, the other lodger at the guest house, hurrying up the street from the direction of the prom-enade. She was very slightly overweight and was breathing heavily with the effort.

'Missed what, exactly?'

Eve pulled a face. 'You know what I mean. Lunch. Have I missed lunch?'

Violet glanced at her watch pointedly. 'By about an hour. Really, Eve, it's not good enough treating Thelma like this.'

'Like what?'

'Being late for a perfectly scrumptious Sunday dinner. She's a wonderful cook, although I don't know how she manages it with everything else she has to do.'

'I didn't mean to be late, but the sun was shining and the sea was actually warm enough to paddle in.'

'You and the other carefree maidens of the chorus line, I suppose.'

'Don't tease. Do you think Thelma will have kept something hot for me?'

'Of course she has, although you don't deserve it. Come along in and I'll get it out of the oven while you go and wash your hands.'

'All right, Mother!'

The two girls smiled fondly at each other and Violet reminded Eve to shake her shoes free of sand before they entered the house.

'Bye the way,' Eve said. 'I saw Jack and Lana hurrying towards the theatre.'

'Yes, they've got a rehearsal with Mrs Bartlett.'

Eve looked puzzled. 'I thought the old girl said she couldn't work this Sunday?'

'Did she? Jack must have persuaded her to change her mind.'

'Why aren't you getting ready?'

Thelma looked up at Lana. The Sunday newspaper was spread out before her, but if anyone had asked her what she had been reading, she doubted she would have been able to tell them. She was in two minds about what she should do that night.

'You've finished the rehearsal?'

'Yes. Jack's clearing up, but he sent me home to tell you he won't be long. But don't change the subject. Why aren't you getting ready?'

'It's no use, Lana, I can't go,' Thelma said.

'Why not? I'm perfectly capable of looking after your mother for one evening, you know.'

'I know that, and I'm grateful for your offer, but if she wakes up she'll expect me to be there.'

'She won't wake up if you give her the sleeping draught before you go.'

'I don't like to do that.'

'Why not?' Lana was beginning to sound exasperated.

'Because it seems dishonest, somehow, to give my mother a sleeping draught so that I can have an evening out.'

'Why did Dr Davidson prescribe the draught in the first place?'

'He said my mother needed the sleep.'

'There you are then.'

Thelma smiled tiredly. 'You're very persuasive, Lana.'

'Listen to me, Thelma, my sweet.' Lana pulled a chair out and sat down facing her. 'You work from dawn to dusk looking after your lodgers, and now you have to take care of your sick mother, as well. You deserve an evening out, and I happen to know Jack has reserved a table at the Grand. He'll be so disappointed if you let him down.'

'Do you think so?'

'He's your husband. You shouldn't have to ask me that.'

'No, I shouldn't, should I? It's just that we don't seem to have time for each other lately. I'm busy here and Jack seems to be always at the theatre.'

'I hope you're not criticising him. The show at the Pavilion is better than it's ever been in the past, and it's all because Jack works so damned hard – working out new routines, cracking the whip with the less talented so that they can put on a halfway decent show, and encouraging those who have talent to become true stars.'

'Those who have talent? You mean yourself, don't you?'

Lana looked surprised, and then wary. 'Yes, I do. Is that conceited of me?'

Thelma shook her head and laughed. 'Conceited? You?'

Lana frowned and began to get up. 'Well, if you're going to be mean to me . . .'

Thelma reached across the table and took Lana's hand. 'Don't go. I'm sorry. I didn't mean to hurt you. I would never have spoken like that if I hadn't been so weary. Of course, you're the only one of the players who has the talent to be a real star, and who can blame Jack for wanting to encourage you? Forgive me?'

Lana stared at Thelma crossly for a moment and then she relaxed and smiled. 'Only if you go upstairs this very minute and start getting ready. And hurry up in the bathroom so that Jack can have all the time he needs.'

Thelma looked at Lana oddly for a moment and then rose and folded the newspaper. 'All right. I'll go.'

Lana smiled. 'I've put the dress on your bed.'

'Which dress?'

'The black beaded silk. It will look fabulous with the little silver jacket.'

'Those are your clothes.'

'I wouldn't have been able to buy them if you hadn't lent me the money.'

'That's true. But you're taller than I am.'

'Don't quibble. It will look just as good mid-calf on you as it does just brushing my knees. Now, off you go!'

'All right. Just one thing: my mother might like a boiled egg for her supper.'

'For God's sake, Thelma. It might be hard for you to believe this, but I can actually boil an egg!'

'Violet and Eve have had a meal, but if they want any supper there's some cooked ham in the larder for sandwiches. For you too, of course.'

'Thelma!'

'What?'

'Go!'

'All right!'

Thelma and Lana looked at each other and burst out laughing. Thelma hurried upstairs and she just managed to get out of the bathroom before Jack came home. Nevertheless, they were a little late, and Jack had to order a taxi.

'Has she settled?' Lana asked.

'Sleeping like a baby,' Violet said.

'Did she eat her egg?'

'Yes, and all the soldiers, too.' Violet showed Lana the tray she had just brought down from Mrs Thomas's room. 'I popped the sleeping draught in her tea and sat with her until she dropped off.'

'Poor baby,' Eve said, and both Lana and Violet looked at her questioningly.

'What are you talking about?' Lana asked, barely concealing her irritation with the youngest of the chorus girls.

'Well, for a start I don't know why people say sleeping like a baby. My sister's baby never sleeps. She cries all night. But Sally would never drop her.'

'I didn't drop Mrs Thomas. "Dropped off" is just a figure of speech,' Violet said.

'I know that.'

Both Violet and Eve were laughing now, and Lana looked increasingly exasperated. 'Pack it in, you two!'

'Sorry,' the two girls said in unison, but they looked at each other and went on giggling.

'I'm going to the sitting room to listen to the wireless,' Lana said. 'And then I won't have to listen to you two twittering on.'

Lana got up and hurried along to the sitting room, leaving Violet and Eve to wash the dishes, just as they had made the ham sandwiches and Mrs Thomas's boiled egg. She was thoroughly out of sorts. She couldn't understand why Jack had suggested that he ought to take Thelma out to dinner. But once he had, she had to go along with it and pretend that she felt just as guilty as he did. The awful thing was that she *did* feel guilty. She knew that Thelma didn't deserve such betrayal. And yet, she couldn't help thinking that perhaps she did. Hadn't she trapped Jack into marrying her by making sure that her mother found them in bed together?

The one consolation tonight was that she had encouraged Thelma to wear the outfit that Jack had told her she herself looked sensational in. She hoped that every time he looked across the table he would make unfavourable comparisons.

In the kitchen her fellow lodgers were clearing up.

'What on earth is wrong with Lana?' Eve was astonished.

'Don't you know?' Violet asked.

'No, I don't.'

So Violet told her.

Now

'Go on, Kay, try it on. It looks as though it's just your size.' Shirley held up a grey tailored dress with modestly padded shoulders and a pencil-slim skirt.

'Shirley, I haven't time. The van from the film studios will be here first thing in the morning. Crack of dawn,' Kay said.

'This outfit is so tasteful, and so efficient-looking. It would be perfect for the office, wouldn't it?'

Shirley took the dress from its hanger and held it up

against her body. She was tall and slim. Her straight brown hair fell almost to her shoulders and was curled under in a pageboy style. Kay thought the dress might have been made for her.

'I don't know how you can resist these gorgeous clothes,' Shirley said. 'This looks as though it's never been worn, doesn't it?'

'It has,' Kay told her. 'Lana wore it in a film, *The Second Mrs Jones*.'

'Really? How wonderful. But how do you know that?'

'There's a label with all the details attached to the hanger. Here look and see.'

Shirley took the hanger from Kay. 'So there is. Are all the clothes from her films, then?' She slipped the dress back on to the hanger.

'Those in the wardrobe in this room are.'

'You mean there are wardrobes full of clothes in other rooms?'

'They were. Full, I mean. Moira Davies, my solicitor's secretary, arranged for a woman from Rowell's, a posh second hand-shop, to come and take what she wanted of my godmother's everyday clothes. When they sell them I'll get a percentage. Luckily Mrs Rowell wanted everything. She sent a van round only an hour later. Miss Davies said that as soon as she had told Mrs Rowell that the clothes had belonged to Lana Fontaine it was a done deal.'

'So they're all gone?' Shirley said. She looked disappointed.

'Not all of them. My godmother had some clothes that she'd never worn. Miss Davies persuaded me to keep them. She said I might need them some day, although I can't imagine when that will be. I don't mix in the same sort of circles Lana Fontaine did.'

'Oh, Kay, don't say that! We're in London now. You never know what will happen.'

'What will happen is that I'll be up all night packing if we don't get started pronto.'

'Are you sure you don't want to keep any of them? I mean, as a memento? After all, she was your godmother.'

'What would I do with them? I have no need of bonnets or bustles, or ball gowns, have I?'

'Oh, clever!'

'What do you mean?'

'Bonnets, bustles, ball gowns. They all have the same first letter. That's alliteration, isn't it?'

'Maybe it is, but you offered to help me, not give me an English lesson.'

Shirley looked crestfallen. 'Was I showing off?'

'No, not showing off. Just being a nuisance.'

'Oh, Kay, don't be cross with me. It's just so exciting. I'd never been to London until I started this job, and here I am helping you sort out the costumes your godmother – a famous actress – wore in her films.'

Kay smiled at her. 'I'm not cross, Shirley. But you know, I've never been to London before, either, and I hadn't seen my godmother since I was a little girl, and I'm finding all this a little overwhelming.'

'I shouldn't have come today, should I? It's just that I was at a loss what to do with myself and Aunt Mamie suggested I should visit you. She thought you might be glad of some company on a Sunday afternoon.'

'I am. Really. If we work together we'll be in time to have supper and listen to a concert on the wireless.'

'Righto! So what do we do?'

'You can start by helping me to bring those cardboard wardrobe boxes up from the dining room and then we'll try to sort the clothes into some sort of order before putting them in.'

It was only after they'd carried the boxes upstairs and had

sunk, laughing, on to the bed that Shirley said, 'What sort of order did you mean?'

'Heavens, I'm not sure. I'm just repeating what the wardrobe mistress told me. I should have asked her what she meant.'

They looked at each other helplessly and then Shirley said, 'She could have meant historical order. Starting with that Maid Marian dress.'

Kay looked relieved. 'That'll be it!'

'But on second thoughts . . .'

'Tell me.'

'I think it's more likely to be the order of the films.'

'But how . . . ? Oh, of course, the labels on the hangers. I'll just check.' A moment later Kay groaned and sat down on the bed again. 'They're all over the place!'

'We'd better get started, then.'

'Do you mind sitting in the kitchen?' Kay asked.

'Of course I don't,' Shirley said. 'It's lovely and warm in here.'

'That's the idea. But it's not just that.'

'What else then?'

'You saw the sitting room when you arrived.'

Puzzled, Shirley said, 'What's the problem? It's fabulous. So stylish.'

'Yes, it is. But it's not very cosy, is it? Not the sort of room you could relax in your old clothes in.'

'I think I know what you mean. Your godmother was very sophisticated, very *à la mode*. The sitting room is just the place to entertain guests with cocktails and canapés, but not the place for the toast and Marmite and mugs of strong, sweet tea that we're enjoying now.'

They smiled at each other. 'I'm really glad you came round,' Kay said.

'Of course you are. Otherwise how would you have lugged those boxes down the stairs all by yourself?'

'You know that's not the reason.'

'Well, I certainly hope not. Any chance of another slice of toast?'

Kay slipped two slices of bread into the electric toaster. They fell into a companionable silence. When the toast popped up, Kay noticed that Shirley was frowning down at her wristwatch.

'What's the matter?' she asked.

'I hadn't realised how late it was,' Shirley replied. 'Aunt Mamie will be getting worried. Would you mind if I phoned her?'

'The telephone isn't connected.'

Shirley looked disappointed. 'I'd better go, then.'

'Otherwise you could have stayed the night. That is, if your aunt wouldn't mind.'

'She's not really my aunt, you know. I've just always called her that, and truth to tell, no matter how kind she's been to me, I think she'll be happier when I find somewhere else to stay.' Shirley sighed. 'But now . . .'

'I'll get your coat.'

Shirley smiled faintly. 'That's supposing we didn't pack it with all the other clothes.'

The boxes filled the hallway. They had to squeeze past to make their way to the mirrored coat stand. Kay handed Shirley her coat and she was just buttoning it up when she said, 'Oh, no.'

'What is it?'

'I thought we'd packed everything,' Shirley said, 'but there's something in a garment bag on top of that box.'

'Oh, that.' Kay smiled. 'That's for you.'

'For me?'

'Here you are.' Kate reached over and pulled the garment

bag towards them. 'Open the zip – just a little.'

Shirley did so. 'Oh, you mustn't, Kay. I can't accept this.'

'I don't see why not. You said yourself it would be perfect for the office, didn't you?'

'I did, but . . .'

'No buts. We can't have you looking anything less than tastefully efficient at the BBC.'

Shirley was obviously thrilled with her present. She draped it over her arm and they battled their way laughingly past the wardrobe boxes to the front door.

'Thanks for coming,' Kay said.

The air in the street was bitingly cold.

'Shut the door before you freeze to death!' Shirley said, and she hurried off along the frosty pavements.

Kay closed the door and made her way back to the kitchen to sit by the fire. *I must get the phone reconnected*, she thought, *and I'd better find out how to get in touch with the coalman. Then there's the milk. It would be much easier to have it delivered.*

A moment later she realised how foolish that was. She had cleared out the wardrobes and arranged for someone to come from the auction house. She had not yet sorted out the photographs and another box containing various documents, but she had already decided that if she ran out of time she would have them shipped home – although she knew her mother would not be pleased about that.

There was absolutely no point in ordering milk and coal and having the telephone connected. Unless . . .

A little later, lying in bed, she let herself very cautiously explore the path she should take. She was suddenly filled with excitement. She knew what she wanted to do, but how was she to make it possible?

Chapter Eight

Mid-November

'It's all arranged with your landlady, Kay. If I wasn't so worried I would suggest that we go out and celebrate.' Moira was frowning anxiously.

'Well, *there's* a mixed message,' Kay said. 'Tell me, what would we be celebrating and why are you worried?'

Moira put the cover on her typewriter and tidied some of the papers she hadn't dealt with into the 'In' tray. She looked up at Kay and sighed.

'We'd be celebrating the fact that you have decided to stay in London. From the little you've told me about your life at home, I think you've made the right decision. However, I can't help worrying about how you're going to manage financially. Kathleen has agreed that you can take over the tenancy of the house, but predictably she has put up the rent.'

'I still have most of the money Lana left me.'

'No, you haven't – you gave half of it away, remember?'

'All right, but I haven't spent very much. I must have about nine hundred pounds in the bank.'

'I know that seems a lot, Kay, but it won't last forever. You'll be paying twenty pounds a month rent for the house, and then you'll have all your living expenses. What will you do when the money runs out?'

'I'll get a job, of course. I won't wait until the money has gone – I'll get a job as soon as I can. Did you really think I would sit around doing nothing?'

'Of course I didn't. In fact, I guessed that's what you would say.'

'So why are you worried?'

'Because I'm not sure what sort of job you can expect to get. You're a good-looking young woman, you speak very well, but you have no experience of the sort of job you'll need to bring in a decent wage.'

'You mean some sort of office job?'

'Perhaps. However, you are now twenty-two, and since you left school all you have done is work in a grocery shop.'

'There are plenty of grocery shops in London.'

Moira smiled tiredly. 'Of course there are. In fact, I could probably put a word in for you at Carter's downstairs. Maybe it's just because I wanted better for you.'

'As I told a dear friend of mine, there's nothing wrong with working in a grocer's shop. I actually like it.'

'If you say so.'

'I do. And by the way, there's no need to worry about the rent,' Kay said.

'What do you mean?'

'Do you think my landlady would allow me to take in lodgers?'

Moira looked thoughtful. 'I don't see why not. Although she would probably see that as a reason to put your rent up yet again.' They looked at each other and laughed. 'But, Kay, would you really be happy taking strangers in?'

'I don't have to take in strangers. Remember I told you about Shirley, the girl who's staying at Brook Lodge?'

'Mrs Price's niece?'

'That's right. Well, Shirley only meant to stay there until she found a room to rent.'

'And she would like to move in with you?'

'She would, and even better than that, she's found another girl for me. Well, not exactly a girl. Jane Mullen is probably in her thirties. She's a widow, but she wasn't happily married. She's sold her house in Yorkshire and has come to London to make a new start.'

'My goodness. How do you know all this? Have you been grilling the poor woman?'

'Not at all. In fact, I haven't even met her yet.'

'Then how—'

'Mrs Price. Shirley says she has a way of getting people to talk. Shirley went home one night to find her aunt and Mrs Mullen in the residents' lounge. Mrs Mullen was crying and Mrs Price was comforting her. Apparently Mrs Price's husband deserted her not long after he was demobbed from the army. As for Shirley, she had always believed that she and the boy next door were made for each other, but found out that he was walking out with her best friend. Shirley, her aunt and Mrs Mullen ended up drinking a bottle of port wine between them and complaining about the lack of any decent men in the world.'

'They could be right about that,' Moira said, half seriously, and Kay noticed how she glanced towards the door that led to Mr Butler's office. Moira saw that Kay was watching her and she shrugged. 'It's a long story, and it's mostly my own fault,' she said.

Kay was intrigued. She had never met Mr Butler, and she sometimes wondered if she ever would. He was not in the office today. Moira had told her he'd had to go to the country to deal with the affairs of an old client.

'Well, it seems as though you've worked everything out,' Moira said. 'You know, I feel partly responsible for you, Kay. Lana was my friend and you are her goddaughter. When Lana made her will, she told me how fond of you she was

118

and said that if ever I believed it necessary, I should look out for you.'

Kay thought she knew what was coming.

'So, you see, I'd like to meet these two young women. Would you mind?'

Kay laughed. 'Of course not. I'll ask Shirley to arrange with Mrs Price for us all to have dinner at Brook Lodge one night soon. My treat. Will that suit you?'

'That's fine. But right now I'm going to phone Domino's and ask that good-looking rogue, Nico, to keep us a table for tonight.'

It was Saturday, and although Shirley had asked Kay to join her and Jane for lunch at Brook Lodge, Kay told them she needed some time on her own to get the house ready. But before she started work she sat down near the fire with the letters that had arrived that morning. She opened the envelope of the letter she wanted to read first. She had recognised the beautiful writing and knew that there would be nothing in the letter to upset her.

25th November 1949

My Dear Kay,

Although I will miss you, I am pleased that you have decided to stay in London. In spite of what Miss Davies has said, I am sure you will be able to find a good position, and you could always consider evening classes.

Meanwhile, how exciting to be setting up home with your two new friends. From what you told me about them in your letter, it sounds as if you will all get on very well with each other. Shirley's job as secretary to a drama producer at the BBC sounds very interesting. As you know, I love listening to *Saturday*

119

Night Theatre, and I don't mind admitting I listen to *Appointment with Fear,* not because I like to be frightened but because I'm partial to Valentine Dyall. Who wouldn't be? If your friend Shirley works on anything exciting, please let me know.

Your other prospective lodger, Jane Mullen, must consider herself very lucky to have found two friends like Shirley and you. From what you tell me, the poor woman has had a terrible time of it. Alone and frightened, with nobody to turn to – you wouldn't believe that now we are about to reach the middle of the twentieth century a father could be so unforgiving. He sounds like a character from a Victorian melodrama.

It's just as well you made your decision before you sent the furniture off to auction, isn't it? From the sound of it, you will have a comfortable and beautifully furnished home. I am sure you have made the right decision to put off sorting through Miss Fontaine's photographs and papers until after you have settled in to your new way of life. Once you get Christmas and New Year over, it will be a job for the long dark nights until Spring returns.

Kay, don't forget to enjoy yourself. Go to the theatre, to concerts and to the cinema with your friends. Buy yourself some fashionable clothes. Perhaps you will think me frivolous to suggest this, but I know you well enough to trust that you will not become a spendthrift. It's just that I always thought that a girl with your intelligence and personality deserved more than the rather humdrum life you were living here in Northridge Bay.

As for me, I can't remember whether I told you that the Sampsons' son, young Norrie, is now coming round to take the orders. He is very kind and has taken it upon himself to ask me if I need him to run any errands. He tells me that you are a great miss at the shop and that many of the customers ask about you.

My sister Sarah has written to say that she is looking forward to coming to me as usual at Christmas and that she will be taking me to a pantomime in Newcastle. I am to choose which of the four theatres we should go to!

Well, Kay, thank you for finding the time to write to me as often as you do. I hope you don't find my letters dull in comparison to the life you are leading now.

I wish you and your new venture well.

Yours sincerely,

Jane Bennet

Kay put the letter back into the envelope and poured herself another cup of tea. In spite of her good intentions, so far this morning she had done nothing at all, save light the fire in the kitchen, have a breakfast of tea and toast and marmalade, and then sit in the chintz-covered old chair that looked a little out of place in the streamlined kitchen, to read the letters which had been posted in Northridge Bay the day before.

She hadn't even bothered to get dressed, but she was cosy enough in her very unglamorous pyjamas and the lovely pink, fluffy wrap-around dressing gown she had found hanging on the back of one of the bedroom doors. It must have been Lana's, Kay thought, and in this instance, sophisticated film star Lana Fontaine had sacrificed glamour for sheer old-fashioned comfort.

Kay had slipped it on without thinking and found that she didn't feel at all uncomfortable about wearing a dead woman's robe. She couldn't understand why she had overlooked the dressing gown when she was clearing the house of Lana's clothes. *Perhaps she made me overlook it until she meant me to find it*, Kay thought, *and if so, she would want me to wear it.* Although imaginative, Kay had never been in the least superstitious, so she tried to suppress these irrational thoughts. But she didn't take the dressing gown off.

Now she pulled one of the wooden chairs over to use as a table. She put her cup of tea on it, and slipping her hand into her pocket, drew out the two letters she had not read yet. She looked at the envelopes critically, and reluctantly opened the slimmest one first.

It contained only one sheet of paper. It was from Tony.

25th November 1949

Dear Kay,

So you have decided to stay in London. Thank you at least for writing to tell me, so that I was able to inform Julie that I already knew. She actually came to my house to tell me the news. You make no mention in your letter of coming home to visit or of wanting to see me again, so I suppose I must assume that I have been given the brush-off.

I think I am supposed to thank you for all the lovely times we had together, but, looking back, I'm not sure if they were in any way special. And if you are expecting me to plead with you to come home or to hurry to London to persuade you in person, you will be disappointed.

However, at least I must recover my manners in time to wish you well.

Yours sincerely,
Tony

Kay lowered the letter and saw that her hands were shaking. She was overcome by a mixture of rage and regret. Tony was hurt, that was obvious, and yet he couldn't bring himself to admit to having any real feelings for her. That had been the problem all the time they had gone out together. He had shown every sign of being keen, and yet time and again he had drawn back just when she had believed he might be going to ask her to marry him.

She thought the second paragraph unnecessarily cruel, claiming that they had never had any especially enjoyable times together. Did he really believe that she wanted him to plead with her to come home? Her anger faded when she realised that Tony, never having admitted to himself what he felt about her, was probably baffled to find himself hurt. His pride was hurt because he wouldn't expect any girl to finish with him, and his feelings were hurt because, after all, he may have had some deeper feelings for her.

However, it was the last paragraph, the line about recovering his manners, that made her cry. It showed that his sense of humour was surfacing sufficiently to make him realise how discourteous his letter had been. *Oh, Tony*, she thought, as she began to laugh through her tears, *I can't stay angry with you, and even though you believe our times together weren't special for you, they were for me. But that still won't save your letter from going into the fire!*

Drying her eyes with a clean rose-fragranced handkerchief she found in the pocket of the dressing gown, Kay settled back into the comfort of the armchair. She sipped her tea and paused to wonder what she *had* expected of Tony. She realised she had been unfair. I should have told him outright that I didn't think our affair – if that's what it was – was leading anywhere. Was I secretly hoping that he would come and carry me home again? I don't think so. Maybe I have been as indecisive as he was.

Thank goodness I decided to stay in London, she thought. And thank Lana for making it possible. If I had stayed in Northridge Bay Tony and I might have wasted years of our lives drifting along never being able to commit to each other – and never quite knowing why.

Kay looked long at the next envelope before opening it. She had recognised the writing and had been surprised to see that it was from Julie; the last person she would have expected to write to her.

25th November 1949

Dear Kay,

Mum has asked me to answer your letter. She's too upset to write herself. She says that you are doing completely the wrong thing staying in Lana Fontaine's house. She thinks that if you must stay in London you should find somewhere else. If you sold all the clothes and the furnishings etc. you would have enough to set yourself up somewhere fresh. Somewhere that has nothing to do with the ties of the past. I thought that was a strange thing to say, but Mum was in a proper state about it all.

Well anyway, she's got the new house to look forward to. There's even a chance we could be in by Christmas. If we are, she says I can have a party. Just a discreet little affair for my friends from college. There's to be no loud music or dancing, because she wants the neighbours to think well of us. (In other words, she doesn't want them to think we're common!)

We'll not be too far from where the Chalmers live. I thought I might invite Tony to the party. After all, he's fancy free! I called round to tell him that you weren't coming back, you know, but he told me you'd already written to him, and he thought it was just as well, because he'd been worried for some time that you might be taking him too seriously.

He seemed pleased to see me when he came home. Oh, did I tell you that when I called round, Tony and Mr Chalmers hadn't got back from the office? So his mother invited me in. She's small and thin, like a little bird. You'd think a puff of wind would blow her away. She asked me if I'd like to have a drink with her while I waited. I thought she meant a cup of tea or coffee, so I said yes. The next thing I knew she'd opened this fancy drinks cabinet – inside was all lights and mirrors – and she was fiddling about with a cocktail shaker, just like in the pictures. I haven't a clue what the drink was, but she put an olive and a twist of lemon peel into each glass. I must say I liked it.

She seemed pleased to have someone to talk to, although she kept popping into the kitchen where someone called Mrs Slater was getting the meal ready for when the 'menfolk' came home. That's what she called them, the 'menfolk'. She said she was pleased that I had called, because she hated drinking alone. I said no to a second drink, but it didn't stop her. Then, when Tony and his father arrived, she got all silly and told Tony not to linger too long with the lovely young lady because the meal was almost ready.

Tony took me to the hall to talk, which I thought was a bit rude because there was nowhere to sit except the telephone table, so we both stayed on our feet. He made up for this oversight by being very charming. He actually said that he was pleased we were going to live nearby, and that Mum might like to call and introduce herself to his mother. Fancy that! It looks as though life is going to change once we've moved to the posh part of town.

I'm sorry you won't be home for Christmas, Kay. It won't be the same without my big sister. By the way, whichever house we're in, Mum has told Miss Pearson and Miss Elkin that they must spend Christmas Day with us. That's kind of her, isn't it? She's got a soft heart, really, although most of the time she manages to hide it very well.

If I could afford it I would come to London to visit you sometime over the Christmas holidays. I won't be going back to college until after the New Year. But, as I say, I can't afford it. Never mind, I'm sure that one day soon you will be inviting me to come and stay with you and we could see a show or two. What do you think?

Love,
Julie

Kay was pleased to have a letter from Julie, although she couldn't help thinking her sister might be gloating a little with the references to Tony and his mother. She smiled at the hints Julie was dropping about visiting London and she supposed that she probably would invite her to stay. But not yet. She also supposed that when she did, she would send Julie the train fare, even though her sister should have plenty of money of her own, considering the amount Kay had given her. She found that she was actually looking forward to seeing her sister in the not too distant future. She would certainly take her to a show, a musical perhaps – *Oklahoma* or *Kiss Me Kate*. However, Julie would have to wait until her Easter break from College. The week between Christmas and New Year was too soon.

Kay could hardly believe that Julie had actually called at the Chalmers' house. And yet why should she be surprised? Julie had been flirting unashamedly with Tony since she'd been sixteen. Going to tell him that Kay was staying in London was just an excuse to see him. And he would know that very well. She hoped that, in her dear friend Miss Bennet's words, Tony would not salve his hurt pride by 'playing with Julie's affections'. And then she smiled. Instinctively she knew that Julie could look after herself.

Folding the letter, Kay put it back in the envelope and sat for a while staring into the fire. She was truly sorry that her mother was upset; so much so that she had not been able to reply to her letter. Kay did not know what she could do. She wasn't going home. That decision was final. And she wasn't going to find somewhere else to live. That was a preposterous idea, and she really couldn't understand why her mother was so against her staying here. Her godmother and her mother must have quarrelled very badly indeed, Kay decided – so badly that her mother could neither forgive nor forget.

And what did she mean by 'the ties of the past'?

Kay sighed. *We're back to that quarrel again*, she thought, and then she remembered the photographs in the box which she had stored along with some others in the small bedroom on the top floor. Those snapshots she had seen had shown two attractive young women who looked as though they were good friends.

So if they had quarrelled, when had that been? Kay knew she had been eight when her glamorous godmother had stopped visiting them. She sat forward and, resting her elbows on her knees, put her chin on her clenched fists and gazed into the fire. She kept very still and listened to the rhythmic ticking of the clock. Then a voice, no two voices, came echoing across the years:

'*Please, don't be like that*,' someone said. Someone who sounded as if she were crying. '*Don't you know you're breaking my heart?*'

Another voice, an angry voice, replied, '*You can stop the melodrama. It won't work with me. Nothing you say will make me change my mind.*'

And then there was silence. Kay willed the voices to come back, but all she could hear was the clock ticking and the crackle of the coals in the fire.

Kay sighed and sat back in the chair. She didn't believe in ghosts, so she knew that the only explanation was that she had heard those voices when she was a child and was remembering them now.

Suddenly an unexpected ray of sunlight shone through the window and lightened not only the room but also the oppressive atmosphere. Kay stood up and shrugged her shoulders to ease the tension.

What should she do now? Another voice came through loud and clear. 'Buy yourself some fashionable clothes!' This was no ghost voice and neither was it a memory from her childhood. It was from Miss Bennet's letter. Kay could almost hear her dear friend urging her on.

'All right,' she said. 'That's exactly what I'll do.'

Chapter Nine

'So it seems as though it will be just Kay and me here for Christmas,' Jane Mullen said.

Kay, Shirley and Jane were sitting with mugs of cocoa at the kitchen table. This was the room they inhabited most, for although the sitting room was attractive and had the benefit of a sofa and armchairs, it never got quite as warm as the kitchen when the fire was going full blast.

'Don't, you're making me feel guilty,' Shirley said.

'There's no need to feel guilty,' Kay told her. 'We quite understand that your mother will want you to come home.'

'And that's another thing I feel guilty about.' Shirley sighed. 'I don't really want to go home. Fancy having to face that long train journey when I'd rather be here with you two. I mean, I love my family, they couldn't be nicer, it's just that since coming up to London I've felt as though I'm a proper grown-up person, not a kid any more.'

'Don't worry, that's quite normal,' Jane said. 'When you get older it will change again and you'll look forward to going h-home.' Jane suddenly faltered and grasped her mug with both hands. She stared down at the table, her drawn features expressing pure misery.

Kay and Shirley exchanged dismayed glances. They knew why Jane was upset, but neither of them liked to say anything. Privately Kay thought she would try to make sure that Jane had a wonderful time this Christmas, even if there were only the two of them.

'And there's another thing,' Shirley said. 'I mean, just wait until my mother sees my hair.'

Jane looked up and smiled wanly. 'What's wrong with your hair?'

'I should never have had this perm, that's what's wrong.' Shirley sighed. 'My mother doesn't even like me to wear a little bit of lipstick, never mind going curly.'

'She'll be so pleased to see you that she probably won't even mention it,' Jane said.

'You don't know my mother!'

They all laughed, but Kay could see what an effort it was for Jane, and she admired her for it. She looked at her two new friends and thought how different they were. Shirley was tall and graceful and had a confident demeanour. Jane was small and delicate with red–gold wavy hair and a light dusting of freckles over her pretty face. Shirley could be forthright, whereas Jane was reticent. They were so very different in character and yet, since moving in, they had got on well enough.

And what about me? Kay thought. *How do the two of them regard me? I know I can be determined, and yet I have never wanted to hurt anyone's feelings; which is why I stayed at home as long as I did, I suppose, even though I was not really happy there.*

'What about Miss Davies?' Shirley asked. 'Won't she come to see you on Christmas Day?'

'I'm not sure,' Kay said. 'I invited her to come and have lunch with us, but she said a friend might be calling to see her.'

'Well, at least I can help you put the decorations up before I go,' Shirley said.

'Which reminds me,' Kay said. 'I haven't bought any yet. A quick trip to Woolworths is called for.'

'There's no need. Unless you want new ones, that is.'

Both girls looked enquiringly at Jane.

'There's a whole boxful in that cupboard in my room. Didn't you know?'

'No, I didn't,' Kay said. 'Although I ought to have known. I mean, I thought I looked in all the cupboards before you moved in.'

'I'll go and get them, shall I?' Jane looked happier. 'We can sort through them and see what we've got. Clear the table, you two, so we can spread them out.' She hurried out of the room and Kay and Shirley smiled at each other.

'Well, that's cheered her up,' Shirley said. 'I felt dreadful just then, complaining about going home when poor Jane would love to be able to go and see her parents but that tyrant of a father has forbidden her ever to darken their doors again!'

'Don't worry,' Kay said. 'She seems to be very resilient.'

'It seems to me she's had to be.'

A short while later they looked down at the contents of the box which they had emptied on to the kitchen table. The garlands were a little disappointing. Stylish rather than festive, they were black and silver, with not a holly berry in sight. However, there were also three boxes of coloured glass baubles and bells, and another of icicles; the kind that glowed in the dark. Best of all there was a beautiful golden-haired angel. The three girls looked at each other and almost simultaneously they said, 'We'll have to have a tree!'

Lying in bed that night, Kay was full of plans of how to make her first Christmas away from home special. Of course she would miss her mother and her sister, but, just like Shirley, she would rather be here, with her friends.

A few days ago she had realised that she knew nothing about Moira's home life. She knew she lived in the flat above the office, but that was all. Moira had never mentioned whether she had a flatmate, but somehow Kay didn't think so. Kay was in Carter's, the grocery shop downstairs, at the time, and as soon as she had finished her shopping she went up to the solicitor's rooms.

The door was ajar and she could see there was no one in Moira's office, but she could hear voices coming from behind the door that led to Mr Butler's room. She stood there, hesitating, and almost laughed out loud when the thought crossed her mind that the man did exist after all. A moment later the door opened and Moira came into the office, then closed the door carefully behind her.

'Come in,' she called out. Followed by, 'Why are you smiling?'

Flustered, Kay replied, 'No reason – just pleased to see you.'

'Well, that's nice, but you haven't come here just to tell me that.'

Kay was taken aback by Moira's ill-humoured tone and she almost turned and fled. Then her friend said, 'Sorry, did I sound ratty? It's all these Christmas cards.'

Thoroughly puzzled, Kay just stared at her.

'Look at them.' Moira gestured towards her desk, which was covered with the cards in question and their envelopes. 'He's signed them all, but now he wants the envelopes addressed by hand. And, of course, that's my job. Well, after all, I am the paid help, aren't I?'

Kay was puzzled. 'Well, yes, you are.' Moira shot her a furious look. 'I mean, you are his secretary.'

Suddenly Moira laughed. 'Of course I am. I don't know what's wrong with me today. Perhaps it's because I can't stand all this fuss at Christmas. "Bah, humbug!" you know. But come in, do, and if I make us a cup of tea perhaps I could persuade you to help me.'

'Of course I will.'

When Kay was settled in a chair at the other side of the desk, she asked for a fountain pen and a list of addresses. 'Oh, no,' Moira said. 'The cards are for his clients, so that's confidential. I'd like you just to put them in their envelopes and I'll address them.'

About a quarter of an hour had passed before Moira looked up from her task and said, 'But why did you come here? I'm sorry, I should have asked.'

'I came to invite you to spend Christmas Day with us. I didn't know that you thought it all humbug.'

Moira laughed. 'I don't really, and I would like to come, but I can't promise. You see, he – my friend might call.'

'When will you know for sure?'

'I won't.' She sighed. 'You've probably guessed, so I might as well tell you.' She lowered her voice, 'I'm involved with a man who isn't free. He'll come if he can get away, but even then it won't be for long. There, that's all I can say,' she ended hurriedly with a nervous glance towards the other door. 'Now, let's finish these cards.'

Of course Moira's ill-humour that day hadn't been about the Christmas cards, Kay realised now, and she wondered how a woman as attractive and intelligent as Moira could be so devoted to a man who was probably married. When she left the office that day she had made Moira promise that she would come if she could.

With sleep still evading her, she thought of something that was puzzling her. *How could I have missed the decorations? I'm sure I looked in all the cupboards. I mustn't give way to superstition, but I can't help thinking Lana wanted me to stay here for Christmas, so she hid them until it was the right time to find them. And now that I have, I shall try to decorate the house as beautifully as she would have done.*

★ ★ ★

133

Jane had bought some ropes of tinsel, and she and Shirley helped Kay put up the garlands. But it wasn't until the day before Christmas Eve that Kay went out to buy a tree. Her mother had always waited until after she and Julie were in bed on Christmas Eve before putting up the tree. Then, the next morning, she would go downstairs before they got up to switch the lights on.

The shops were busier than ever, and Kay had to use a certain amount of charm to persuade the butcher to deliver the small turkey the next day. Then she dodged the traffic to cross over to the greengrocer's. The evocative smell of the Christmas trees met her halfway. Kay stared in dismay at the row of trees propped against the window of the shop. They were all too big for her to be able to carry home. And then she noticed a small, grubby boy with a bogie made from old pram wheels. He saw her looking at him and grinned.

'Tuppence,' he said.

This would solve Kay's problem – she would probably be able to load the buggy with some holly, too – but the boy looked much too small to be able to manage such a task. She stared at him doubtfully.

'One penny, then,' he said.

'Oh, no, it's not that,' Kay said. 'I was just wondering if you could manage.'

'Of course I can.' The boy looked indignant.

'Oh, go on, then,' Kay said and he shot into action.

He chose the biggest tree and, under Kay's instructions, a couple of bunches of holly.

'Yer might as well 'ave some mistletoe,' he said, and put it on top of everything else before Kay could stop him.

The shopkeeper had been watching through the window, and Kay went inside to pay him. 'I could deliver that lot for you,' he said. 'You should have asked.'

'Oh, no. He'd be so disappointed.'

'Good luck then. You'll need it.'

Luck deserted them before they had gone a hundred yards from the shop. The boy stopped suddenly to avoid a friendly dog and everything slithered off the bogie on to the pavement. Worse was to follow. The dog sniffed around the tree and cocked his leg.

'Gerroff, yer little tyke!' the boy yelled, and managed to shoo the dog away just in time.

Kay was helping him load up again when she realised they were being observed by a very tall man. The fact that he was also very handsome wasn't lost on her, but she almost flinched at his look of disapproval.

'How old is your son?' he asked.

'I'm ten,' the boy said before Kay could recover herself enough to answer.

'That's disgraceful,' the man said. 'Making the poor little lad carry that home for you.'

'He's not carrying it, he's pulling it, and he's not—'

'And the poor child looks as though he could do with being introduced to a bar of soap, never mind spending your money on frivolities like Christmas trees.'

'Well, thank you for your advice,' Kay said, 'but now my *son* and I are going home.'

'You'll not get far, you know,' the tall man said. 'That load will fall off again as soon as you meet another obstruction.'

Kay looked at the bogie in despair. 'I think you're right.'

'What you need is a length of rope.'

'And where would I get that?'

He shook his head. 'Can't help you there. I guess this will have to do.'

'What . . . ?'

Kay watched in astonishment as he took the belt from his gabardine overcoat and used it to tie the tree and the holly to the buggy.

'Now if you would carry the mistletoe, your lad and I will get this tree home for you. Come on, sonny. Off we go.'

'Can't,' the boy said.

'Why not?'

'Don't know where to go. She's not my mum.'

'Oh, I see.' The man looked grave again.

'What do you see?' Kay asked.

'It's slave labour.'

Kay stared at him for a moment, and when she saw his smile she burst out laughing. 'You've been teasing,' she said.

'Too good an opportunity to miss. Now, let's go.'

When they reached home he insisted on unloading the bogie and carrying everything in for Kay. 'Where . . . ?' he asked.

'Just leave the tree in the hall – near that clock.'

'Righto. I'm Tom, by the way, Tom Masters.'

'Kay. Kay Lockwood.'

'And I'm Billy Gibson, if you want to know,' the boy said. 'And what about me tuppence? Will you still pay me or does he get half?'

Tom Masters laughed. 'No, you'll get your full share. In fact, I think you deserve sixpence.' He took the coin from his own pocket. 'But if you're going to do this again, get yourself a length of rope.'

'I will. Ta.'

'Wait a minute. Do you live far away?'

'The next street to the shop.'

'Off you go then.' He watched the boy hurry away. 'He probably wants to see if he's in time for another customer before the shop closes.' He turned and smiled. 'I knew he wasn't your son, you know.'

Kay laughed. 'You had me fooled for a moment.'

'Well, then . . . I suppose I'd better go.'

136

'Wait . . . I mean, would you like a cup of tea? My friends are here. I mean, I'm not . . .'

'Alone in the house?'

'Now I'm embarrassed.'

'Don't be. Let's go and meet your friends.'

'You should have let me go to buy the tree,' Shirley said.

It was later that night. Tom Masters had only just left, and the three of them were discussing him.

Jane laughed. 'Have you considered that if it had been you struggling home with the tree he might have just let you get on with it?'

'What do you mean by that?' Shirley was affronted.

'No insult to you. It's just that it's obvious that he is mighty taken with our Kay.'

'Oh, no,' Kay said. 'He was just being a gentleman.'

'Yes, that's probably it,' Shirley said, and then she and Jane laughed at Kay's disappointed expression.

'Well, it's just as well I'm going home tomorrow,' Shirley said. 'Less competition.'

'Stop it, both of you,' Kay said. 'And we'd better get to bed if we're going to get up at the crack of dawn to see Shirley to the station.'

'I'll see her off,' Jane said. 'You'd better stay here, Kay.'

'Why?'

'Didn't our new friend say he was coming along to help you put up the tree?'

'Yes, he did, but we'll have plenty of time to get back.

'You, not we,' Jane said. 'I'm staying in town to do some shopping. And you never know. Tomorrow is Christmas Eve and the tube and the buses will be packed. Goodness knows how long it will take to get to the station and back.'

'And you don't want to miss him, do you?' Shirley added.

'I mean, if there's no one in when he calls he might take that as a sign that you're not interested.'

'Stop this, you two,' Kay said. 'Tom did his good deed for the day and I'm very grateful. That's all. You're making far too much of it.'

Kay hated the way the other two exchanged knowing glances. Nevertheless, when morning came, she didn't object when Shirley and Jane set off to the station without her.

Chapter Ten

The Year's End

The kitchen door opened and Kay, who was sitting reading by the fire, looked up in surprise. 'What are you doing here?'

Shirley grinned and put her small suitcase down, then began to take off her coat. 'I persuaded my mother that it wasn't fair to leave you on your own at New Year. I must have been convincing, because she took me to the station herself this morning.'

'But I'm not alone. Jane will be here.'

'I lied to my mother. Do you think God will forgive me?'

'Probably not.'

The two of them looked at each other and smiled.

Shirley draped her coat over the back of a chair and went to fill the kettle. 'I simply must have a cup of tea,' she said. 'A very inconsiderate gentleman in our compartment insisted on having one of the windows open. In this weather! No one complained. We just sat there getting sprayed with sooty rain. Very English.' She quickly looked round the kitchen. 'Where's Jane?'

'She went for a walk.'

'In the cold and the rain? She must be mad!'

'Not mad. I think every now and then she needs to be by herself.'

'Poor old Jane.'

'And who is taking my name in vain?'

Startled, both girls turned towards the door. Jane stood there carrying a shopping bag.

Shirley was the first to recover. 'Poor old Jane going out on a night like this. That's what I meant.'

Kay didn't know whether Jane believed this feeble explanation, but she put the shopping bag on a chair and said, 'Warm plates, please. Pop them in the range oven for a minute or two.' She took a newspaper-wrapped bundle from the bag and laid it on the table. 'Unless you want to eat your fish and chips straight from yesterday's news.'

Shirley moaned. 'Fish and chips! So I'll have to sit here and watch you two scoffing them!'

'No, you won't,' Jane said. 'The portions are huge. We can easily share everything between the three of us. So what's it to be? Plates or paper?'

'Definitely paper and no knives and forks needed!' Kay said. 'Shirley, get the salt and pepper and vinegar out. And Jane, I think you deserve this seat by the fire.'

While they were eating, Shirley regaled them with stories about her family Christmas in Cornwall. The aunts and the uncles, the cousins and the grandparents. Even though she was pleased to be back in London, it was obvious that she had enjoyed herself.

'And Mum didn't mention my perm once,' she said. 'Well, she didn't *mention* it but I caught her looking at it every now and then. If she had said anything I was all prepared to tell her that secretaries at the BBC are expected to be up to date and sophisticated; not to say positively glamorous.'

When she had finished, she crumpled up her newspaper wrapping and threw it on the fire. Jane was about to follow her example but Kay stopped her.

140

'Wait a minute,' she told Jane. 'We don't want to set the house on fire.'

At these words Jane's eyes widened in alarm, and despite the heat, Kay could have sworn she shivered. She would have liked to have asked her why she had reacted in this way but decided not to. She sensed Jane would not like it.

When they had filled their cups with hot, strong tea, Shirley suddenly clapped a hand over her mouth. 'Oh, no,' she said. 'Why did you let me rabbit on about Christmas at home like that? Showing off, my mother would call it, and my boss at the BBC would say I was like an actor hogging the limelight. Very much the old thespian, is Julian Fry.'

'What on earth are you talking about?' Jane asked. 'As far as I know you work in a sound studio. There won't be any limelight to hog.'

'I know. But he can't help talking that way. A lot of them can't. They cut their teeth in the theatre, you see.' She pretended to slap her forehead. 'There, you've done it again. Somebody shut me up and tell me what Christmas was like for you.'

Kay and Jane looked at each other and smiled. Then 'Quiet,' they said in unison.

'Quiet? You mean you didn't go anywhere, or do anything interesting?'

'We ate too much turkey,' Kay said, 'and after a couple of days of cold turkey and chips or turkey sandwiches, we threw the remains out for the birds.'

'They're little cannibals, aren't they?' Shirley said.

'We had a Christmas pudding,' Jane added. 'Bought, not home-made. And apparently this was the first time Kay had ever tasted the shop variety. Her mother always makes them and even managed to during the war.'

'My mother's a very good cook,' Kay said.

This was too much for Shirley. 'For goodness' sake. Here

you are in the most exciting city in the world and all you did was stuff yourselves with turkey and pudding.'

'Well, not quite all,' Kay said and Shirley raised her eyebrows hopefully. 'Jane bought a games compendium at Hamleys and we played a fierce game of Snakes and Ladders.'

'And Ludo,' Jane said. 'Don't forget the Ludo.'

Shirley stared at them for a moment and then said, 'You are teasing me, aren't you?'

'Just a little bit,' Kay replied.

'So come on, spill the beans!'

'We went into town and treated ourselves to afternoon tea,' Kay said.

'At Fortnum & Mason?'

'Lyons Corner House.'

Shirley shook her head in mock despair.

'Then we went to a show.'

'That's better,' Shirley said. '*Black Chiffon? The Lady's Not For Burning?*'

'Actually no. We went to see *Puss in Boots* at the Palladium.'

'Well, it is Christmas,' Shirley said and she smiled at them. 'I'm sure you deserve a little bit of frivolity rather than high drama. Go on.'

'That's it,' Kay said. 'Nothing further to report, ma'am.'

'I don't believe you,' Shirley said.

'Why ever not?'

'What about Tom?'

'What about who?'

'Tom Masters. Don't pretend you don't know who I mean.'

'What about him?'

'Didn't he call round to see you, bearing flowers and chocolates?'

'No, why should he?' Kay asked.

Jane must have sensed her discomfort, for she suddenly said, 'Why don't we change the subject? In fact, why don't we stop this idle gossiping and open my nice new bottle of gin?'

Shirley looked at her with interest. 'I've never had gin.'

'Well, now's the time to try.'

Jane took two bottles from her shopping bag, one of gin and one of lime juice. She held one of the bottles to her nose and sniffed. 'Mmm, smells a bit of fish and chips, but that will only be on the outside. Now, where are some decent glasses?'

'I'll get them,' Kay said.

She went to the dining room to get some glasses from the drinks cabinet, knowing full well that they would be talking about her.

Jane would be telling Shirley to stop talking about Tom, and Shirley's eyes would widen as she nodded sagely. When she returned to the kitchen, Jane made a show of pouring the drinks while she instructed Shirley to slice a lime – which had also come out of her seemingly magic shopping bag.

Kay had never tasted gin and lime – or gin in any form – either, and she wasn't sure if she liked it. She knew her mother treated herself to a gin and tonic now and then, but it always seemed to make her cry.

'By the way,' Shirley said, 'I noticed there were a couple of little parcels under the Christmas tree. Or rather, there were two before I added a couple on the way in.'

'We decided to wait to open the presents until you returned.'

'I'm here now,' Shirley said.

Kay hurried out to get the presents.

A moment later they were all laughing over their identical jars of carnation-scented bath crystals; definitely Woolworths' best. Then Shirley's laugh turned into a big yawn. 'I've got to go to bed. And don't wake me up too early. Tomorrow is New Year's Eve, and remember, Aunt Mamie has invited us to the party at Brook Lodge.'

Jane followed her up and Kay took over the armchair. She stared into the fire for a while then leaned back and closed her eyes, feeling the warmth of the glowing coals on her face. She sighed. She had been so sure that Tom Masters would call round to see her. Even though they had just met, they had behaved like old friends when they had put up the Christmas tree the day after they had met.

The next morning after seeing Shirley off, Jane had gone to the West End to shop as she had said she would. Alone in the house, Kay couldn't settle. She found herself waiting for the doorbell, and when it did ring she forced herself to take her time in answering it.

'I'm here to help with the tree as I promised,' Tom said. 'And it's all right. You don't have to feed me.' He held up a carrier bag that was bulging with intriguing-looking paper parcels. They went through to the kitchen, where he set the bag on the table but refused to divulge its contents. 'Right, let's start on the tree.'

Tom hung up his coat on the hallstand and Kay got the tree decorations from the dining room, where she had put them rather than take them upstairs again. She set the large box down on the chair near the telephone table and Tom looked inside.

'They're lovely,' he said. 'Some of those glass baubles must have been expensive.' He looked at her enquiringly.

'I didn't buy them,' Kay assured him. 'I inherited them, or rather, they came with the house.'

'Oh?'

'My godmother lived here. She rented it, but in her will she left all her personal possessions to me.'

'Lucky you.'

Tom smiled at her but she had the uneasy feeling that somehow he had made her give him that information. Not that it mattered, she told herself. Her moment of discomfort passed and they began to dress the tree, Tom placing decorations on the higher branches easily. Soon all that was left was the golden-haired angel.

'You'd better let me do that,' Tom said and he held out his hand.

'No,' Kay said. 'I'm going to put the angel on.'

'You're not quite tall enough. Unless you're going to stand on that chair.'

'I don't need the chair.'

'Do you want me to lift you up?' He looked as though he was keen on the idea.

'No.' Taking the angel, Kay ran up the stairs until she could lean over the bannister and position the angel in her rightful place. 'See?' she said.

Tom grinned. 'Well done. Now let's eat. I'm starving.'

They were laughing as they went into the kitchen and their happy mood continued as Tom emptied the carrier bag. He had brought crusty rolls, Brussels pâté, cheese, two slices of cheesecake and a bottle of red wine. Kay got plates and knives, then hurried through into the dining room to get some proper wine glasses. When she got back to the kitchen she saw that Tom had found the corkscrew in the knife drawer and was waiting to pour the wine.

As they enjoyed their feast they talked. Kay did most of the talking. Tom seemed to know how to draw people out, and, after hesitating at first, she soon found herself telling him a little about her background and why she had come to London. He seemed to be interested in her friends, too. She had to restrain herself from telling him too much about their private lives. He hadn't seemed to notice when she held back, and she decided he was simply being friendly.

When he said it was time for him to go as he had shopping to do, he seemed to be as disappointed as she was. It was only later that she realised she knew very little about him, except that he had been in the army during the war. She had no idea what his job was and she had decided to ask him next time he called. When he left he hadn't exactly said he would call again, or better still, ask her to go out with him, but she had been sure she would see him again very soon. She was wrong – or was she?

Once when she went to the High Street to do some shopping she thought she had glimpsed him hurrying towards her. She had her smile all ready, but a moment later he had vanished. Another time something had made her turn round just before she boarded the tube and she was sure the tall man surrounded by the surging crowd had been Tom. He must have seen her, but he didn't smile or wave, or attempt to catch up with her. *Perhaps I'm seeing things*, she thought, and the door swished shut before she had time to find out if the man she had seen was really Tom.

Before she fell asleep she berated herself for behaving like a schoolgirl with a crush. But that was exactly what it was – a serious crush. *Stupid woman*, she told herself. *He did his good deed when he helped you home with the Christmas tree, he enjoyed a bit of female attention from the three of us, and then he was probably disappointed the next day to find Jane and Shirley weren't here. So what should I do now? Forget about him, of course. There's nothing else I can do.*

Mamie's full-length maroon chiffon dress had a square neckline and shoulder pads. Kay thought it would have been fashionable during the war. Kay looked around at the other guests. Most of them were friends and neighbours of Mamie's, but there was a sprinkling of residents who looked surprised to be there. Probably most of them would rather have been at home than marooned in a guest house in Wood Green, for whatever reason, on New Year's Eve.

All of the women present were dressed a trifle formally. Most of the men were wearing lounge suits, although at least two of them wore dinner jackets. Shirley had warned Kay and Jane that they must be smart, and they had done their best. Shirley herself was wearing a jade-green figure-hugging dress of fine worsted jersey.

'This is to go with my new sophisticated look,' she had told Kay and Jane.

Kay wore a shiny full-skirted dress in red taffeta. When she had bought it the day she went shopping to cheer herself up, she had been shocked to find herself attracted to something so bold. Not having had much experience in buying expensive clothes, she had relied on the sales assistant to guide her. She was assured that red and blue were still the colours of the year. It had crossed her mind that there wasn't much of the year left, but by then the dress was being tissue-wrapped and packaged, ready for her to take home.

Shirley and Jane had told her she looked stunning. 'A proper Scarlett O'Hara,' Shirley said. 'Without the décolleté. That Peter Pan collar is just modest enough to take away the impression of a temptress.'

Thank goodness for that, Kay thought, and she wondered if Shirley knew how much she had changed in the short time she had been working for the BBC. Well, not exactly changed. Blossomed. That was the word.

'You two are certainly going to outshine me,' Jane had told them.

'Not at all,' Kay reassured her.

'What could be more fashionable than a little black cocktail dress?' Shirley added. 'And as for that necklace. Are they real?'

Jane laughed. 'Of course not. How could I afford diamonds? Just paste, I'm afraid.'

Mamie had gone to a great deal of trouble to make the buffet spread inviting. And Shirley found it hard to resist the temptations of the table.

'Shall we tell her?' Jane asked Kay laughingly.

'Tell her what?'

'That her beautiful, svelte figure will not stand many more of those canapés. They may be small but they're very rich.'

'I heard that,' Shirley said. 'And you're right. My New Year's resolution will be to exercise more restraint as far as food is concerned. Promise you.'

A moment later Shirley was led away by Mamie to be introduced to some friends of hers. 'My niece works for the BBC,' they heard her saying proudly.

Jane raised her eyebrows. 'Poor old Shirley.'

'Why so?'

'She'll be paraded round all these old dears who will want to know if she's met anyone famous.'

'Do you know, I don't think that bothers her,' Kay said.

'Being paraded round?'

'Not exactly, but I think she rather enjoys the kudos her job gives her. And why shouldn't she?'

'No reason at all. She's in a different league from you and me, isn't she? I mean a woman who made a mess of her marriage and a girl who worked in a grocery shop.'

For some reason this hurt. It was true that Kay had enjoyed working at Sampson's, but it was also true that she had resented having to leave school so that her younger sister could go to college. She had decided to make the best of things. 'A proper little Pollyanna', her old friend Miss Bennet had teased. Miss Bennet had also urged her to strive for something more.

Well, here she was in London. She was renting a lovely house in her own name and she had two lodgers. Or paying guests, as her mother would call them. But that was not all Miss Bennet would have wanted for her. Nor Moira Davies either. She decided that her resolution should be that she must find an interesting job.

'Why so thoughtful?' Jane asked her.

'Oh, you know, the end of the year, *tempus fugit* sort of thing.'

'I thought you looked sad.'

'No, not sad.' As she spoke she suddenly noticed that Jane looked very sad indeed. In fact her eyes were sparkling with unshed tears. 'Oh, Jane, what is it?'

'Memories. Just memories. Ignore me.'

'You two should be mingling, you know,' Shirley said as she approached them. Then she lowered her voice and said, 'Aunt Mamie's friends are sweet, but not one of them is less than fifty. And I can't tell you how many of them want to talk about the war. And now listen to them! They've started singing "Pack Up your Troubles", and that was from the First World War!'

'They're enjoying themselves,' Jane said. 'Don't be cruel.'

Shirley looked mortified. 'Was I being cruel? I didn't mean to be.'

The three girls looked over to the group that had formed around the piano. Kay thought, *Here we are, about to tip over into the second half of this disastrous century, and these people are drawn together by their memories, both good and bad.* It was very touching but she could understand why Shirley felt impatient with them. Like all young people should, she wanted to move on, not be drawn into the past.

'Do you know,' Shirley said, 'I reckon we've done our duty here, so why don't we vamoose up to Trafalgar Square?'

'Why?' Kay asked.

'That's where everyone goes. There'll be a big sing-song, and when Big Ben chimes midnight everybody will kiss everybody else.'

'That sounds like something to be avoided,' Kay said.

'Oh, for goodness' sake! How old are you? What I meant was that it will be like a big outdoor party.'

Surprisingly, Jane said she would like to go. Kay thought it odd when she said, 'It might be nice to get lost in the crowd for a while.'

'As long as we don't lose each other!' Shirley riposted. 'All right, Kay?'

'All right.'

Mamie didn't mind that they wanted to leave before midnight. 'Off you go and enjoy yourselves, but Jane, cover that necklace up with a scarf. There are villains about on a night like this.'

'It's only paste,' Jane told her.

'Really?' Mamie looked surprised. 'Even so, you don't want someone snatching it and hurting your neck, do you?'

Jane agreed to keep her coat buttoned up and Mamie insisted that they have another glass of sherry each to fend off the cold. Fortified thus, the three of them set off for Trafalgar Square.

It seemed as though the whole world was heading in the same direction. Trains and buses were full, and after a nightmare journey on the underground, Kay was hugely relieved when they arrived at Trafalgar Square. The pavements were overflowing, and now and then Kay imagined that she saw a man head and shoulders above the rest of the crowd. *I'm hallucinating again*, she thought. Either that or it was the second glass of sherry.

Groups of revellers linked arms and sang their hearts out.

'It's a long way to Tipperary,' a nearby group of youths began, but they didn't seem to know all the words.

'Come on, you girls, join in,' one of them invited. And Shirley, taken up with the jolly atmosphere, began to sing in earnest the very songs she had wished to escape from at Mamie's.

The fervour of the crowd increased until Big Ben began to chime. Everyone became quiet and waited in hushed expectancy. Then they began to count down. At the last stroke they all shouted 'Happy New Year!' and all three girls found themselves being kissed heartily – Jane and Shirley by the nearest slightly tipsy young man. But not Kay.

'Happy New Year, Kay,' the man who had taken her in his arms said. She looked up to see Tom smiling at her. And then he kissed her.

Part Two

Chapter Eleven

Northridge Bay, February 1950

Julie glanced at the collection of envelopes stuffed behind the clock on the mantelpiece. All of them had been opened, but as far as she knew none had been answered.

'Mum, are you ever going to write to Kay again?'

'I have written to her.'

'You sent a Christmas card, that's all. She writes to you every week. Sometimes twice.'

'There's no need. Waste of good postage stamps.'

'How can you? Anyone would think you didn't love her any more!'

Mother and daughter stared at each other. The sitting room was as quiet as a room can be when the world outside is covered in snow. Even the ticking of the clock and the crackle of the flames in the hearth seemed subdued.

Julie had just come back from college to find her mother sitting by the fire. She had looked up listlessly and then returned her gaze to the local newspaper.

'Of course I love her,' Thelma said at last. 'She chose to leave home. I didn't ask her to go. In fact I begged her not to.'

Julie had taken off her shoes in the hall and now she sank her feet into the luxurious new carpet. The pale green and pink flowered pattern was not what she would have chosen, but her mother loved it. As she loved the mock-Tudor furniture and heavy velvet curtains. All this was out of keeping with the modern style of the house, but her mother was happy with it. Therefore Julie couldn't understand why Kay, who had made it all possible, had been banished to a handful of unanswered letters behind the clock.

'You will be sending Kay a birthday card, won't you?'

Julie was surprised at the spasm of pain that crossed her mother's face. 'I suppose so.'

'I know!' Julie said, trying to get her mother to show some enthusiasm, 'why don't you and I go to visit her? I'm sure she'd be delighted, and she'll have room to put us up.'

'No!'

'Why not?'

'I vowed I'd never set foot in Lana Fontaine's house.'

Her mother's answer was so vehement that it left Julie too shocked to ask for an explanation. Nevertheless, she carried on. 'Well, if you don't want to go, would you object if I went?'

'Suit yourself,' her mother said. Then she added shrewdly, 'But what will Tony have to say?'

'Tony? What's he got to do with it?'

'Don't dissemble, Julie. I know you think you've got him hooked. Well, if I were you I wouldn't go off and leave him on his own. Particularly not to visit your sister who made a fool of him.'

Julie sighed. 'You're right. But it's not very nice of you to imply that I'm out to hook him.'

'Aren't you?'

At last there was a ghost of a smile on her mother's face, and Julie responded jauntily, 'Well, don't pretend that you wouldn't be happy to have Tony Chalmers as a son-in-law.'

'You're right. I'd be happy. But just be careful, Julie.'

'What do you mean? Why should I be careful?'

'When Tony was going out with Kay he couldn't be bothered with you. He thought you were a nuisance.'

'Mum!'

'It's true. So why is he showing this sudden interest?'

'He's come to his senses.'

'Don't fool yourself. It's my opinion that he wants to pay Kay back in some way. Show her that he cares so little that he has flown from her arms straight to those of her kid sister.'

'Oh, Mum, do you really think so?'

Thelma suddenly looked mortified. 'Julie, pet, try to forget that I said that. Put it down to my bad mood. Tony is very lucky to have a girl like you care about him. Even his mother thinks so.'

'Does she?' Julie had been on the point of tears, but now she cheered up immediately.

'Yes, she does. Whenever I call round for coffee she makes a point of asking how you are and saying what a fine-looking couple you and Tony make.'

'You're not kidding me, are you?'

'No, sweetheart. I wouldn't want to do anything to hurt you. My one true daughter.'

In spite of her pleasure at her mother's words, Julie's heart sank when she saw that they had come full circle and her mother was back to criticising Kay again. She had not realised how much she was going to miss her elder sister, and it was upsetting that her mother felt the way she did – especially as it was Kay's money that had bought them this lovely house and the furniture.

Now that her mother was in a slightly better mood, Julie risked asking her, 'So will you write to Kay? Pop a line or two inside her birthday card?'

'I suppose so.' Her mother folded the newspaper. 'We thought we couldn't have children, you know. Your father and I. Then Kay came along.'

'A blessing!'

Her mother laughed, but it wasn't a pretty sound. 'I suppose you could call her that.'

Unsure of where her mother's quixotic mood was going now, Julie said, 'And then there was me. Another little blessing!'

'A little miracle.' Her mother stood up. 'Are you going out with Tony tonight?'

'No. He and his father are going to their boring old club for a game of snooker.'

'If you're serious about this young man you'll have to get used to that.'

Julie sighed. 'I know.'

'So let's have tea together by the fire and listen to the wireless. With any luck we'll find a good dance band.'

Thelma hurried through to the kitchen to prepare two trays.

London

Kay stared down at the glittering brooch pinned to the satin lining of the small leather box. It was formed in the shape of a panther with sparkling green eyes. Kay knew it to be a copy of the brooch belonging to the Duchess of Windsor, and it must have cost a fortune. She looked up at Jane.

'I can't possibly accept this!'

Jane laughed. 'It's gold-plated, not gold, and those are crystals, not diamonds and emeralds.'

'But it looks so real!'

'The best fakes do. But in any case, I wouldn't call it a fake. It's an honest copy.'

Shirley, who had been watching this scene, said a trifle waspishly, 'You certainly know about jewellery, don't you, Jane?'

Jane flushed. 'I like pretty things. What's wrong with that?'

'Nothing! I'm sorry. Just jealous, I suppose. All I've got for Kay is a boring old book!'

'Thanks for letting me know,' Kay said as she picked up the wrapped present from the breakfast table.

Shirley laughed. 'Well, I'm sure you could tell by the shape of it.'

'And I'm sure it won't be boring. Not if you chose it,' Jane said. This earned her an apologetic smile.

Kay took a copy of *Brat Farrar* by Josephine Tey from the wrapping paper. 'How did you know I wanted this?' she asked.

'I didn't, but I know you like mystery and suspense, and it's by the same woman who wrote *The Franchise Affair*. You raved on about that.'

'Thank you, both of you,' Kay said.

'Righto, thanks accepted. Don't let's have a speech about how you don't deserve it, because you do. Now, I don't know about you two stay-at-homes, but I've got to get to work. But before I go, are we doing anything special tonight?'

'I've bought a nice cake for teatime,' Jane said, 'but that's it. Kay will be going out to dinner with Tom.'

'Actually, we all are,' Kay said. 'We're going to Domino's, Tom's treat.'

'All three of us?' Shirley said. 'The insurance business must be doing well.'

'The table's booked for eight o'clock, so hurry home in time to change, won't you?' Kay said.

'You bet!'

'Wait a moment,' Jane said. 'Are you sure we ought to accept this invitation? I mean, Tom might like to have Kay to himself.'

'That's true,' Shirley said and she looked at Kay doubtfully.

'No, really, you've got to come. He wants it to be like a birthday party. I've told you, the table's booked and the champagne's on ice!'

Shirley smiled happily. 'Righto! See you later.'

She hurried off to work. Jane still looked doubtful.

'I suppose she thought she was being tactful, but I'm not sure if that was the real reason that Jane didn't come with us to Domino's last night.'

Kay had popped in to Moira's office for a chat, and they were enjoying coffee and chocolate biscuits.

'Why do you think she called off?' Moira asked.

'I really can't be sure, but I have noticed that she avoids Tom's company if at all possible.'

'She doesn't like him?'

'How could anyone not like him?' Kay laughed.

'Well, we're not all love-struck, but I must admit on the occasions I've met him he seems very agreeable. If a little reserved at times.'

'I don't think it's a matter of not liking him,' Kay continued. 'She just seems a little wary of him.'

'I can't imagine why. But apart from Jane's absence, the evening went well?'

'Very well, and I'm seeing Tom again tonight. Just the two of us. We'll probably go to the flicks.'

Moira replaced the lid on the biscuit tin and put their empty coffee cups on a tray. 'Thanks for reporting in, Kay, but I must get back to work.'

'Reporting in? Oh, yes. Nothing to report, I'm afraid.'

'I'm sorry, dear. It must be disheartening, but here you are,' she handed Kay half a dozen filing cards. 'My friend in the agency picked these jobs out as likely. So off you go and write some letters or make some telephone calls, whatever is required.'

The house was quiet when Kay returned. At first she thought Jane must be out, but she found her sitting at the kitchen table poring over some newspapers. The room was cold.

'Jane, you've almost let the fire go out!'

'My God – you startled me, creeping about like that!'

'I wasn't creeping about. You were too absorbed in whatever you were reading to hear me. And you might have put some coal on the fire.'

It was the closest Kay had come to having a quarrel with either of the girls. She went to the fire to build it up, and by the time she was satisfied that it wasn't going to go out and had washed her hands, Jane had made one neat pile of the newspapers so that Kay could not see what had taken her attention. She smiled apologetically at Kay.

'I'm sorry about the fire, but that's – that's how my husband died, you know. In a house fire. A careless coal dropped on the hearth, rolled on to the rug. That's what must have happened.'

'My God, Jane, that's awful. Why have you never told us?'

'I couldn't. I don't like to think of it, but sometimes . . .'

'Of course. There's no need to say more. I'm sorry I snapped at you.' Kay decided to change the subject. 'But why all the newspapers? Surely you're not looking for jobs, too?'

'No, not jobs, although maybe I should consider that. You see, I get so bored doing nothing that I like to read the papers to see what's going on in the world.'

Kay wasn't sure whether she believed this. She had never seen Jane pore over the newspapers before today, although there was always the possibility that she read them in the public library. *I'm inventing explanations*, Kay thought vexedly, and decided to forget the subject and get on with her own job hunt.

'Try not to be too disheartened, Kay. The right job will come along eventually, I'm sure of it.'

Tom and Kay were huddled close under his umbrella as they queued outside the cinema.

'I'm beginning to think my old schoolmistress friend, Miss Bennet, was right and that I should take myself off to evening classes.'

'An excellent idea.'

'I could do shorthand and typing and then you could get me a job in your office.' She felt Tom draw back and looked up into his face. His expression was unreadable but she knew she had said the wrong thing. 'I was joking,' she said, although she acknowledged to herself that it was only half a joke.

'Oh, of course.'

Instinctively she drew away from him, only to be pulled back violently as a car went speeding by, splashing the queue of people with dirty rainwater.

'Bastard!' somebody yelled and a young woman started shouting, 'My coat, my new coat!'

'Are you all right?' Tom asked Kay.

'I'm soaked to the skin.'

Tom held her at arm's length and examined her closely. 'You can't go to the cinema like that. You'll end up with pneumonia. Come on, let's go home.'

Kay was aware that she was making squelching noises as she walked and she began to laugh.

'I'm glad you can see the funny side,' Tom told her. 'I suspect most women would be crying, not laughing.'

Then, as if things weren't bad enough, Kay slipped on a greasy paving stone and went over on her ankle. She screamed with pain.

'What is it?' Tom asked in alarm.

'My ankle – the weak one!'

Tom immediately supported her with his arm. 'Can you walk?'

'Just about.'

'All right. My place is nearer.'

Kay didn't argue with him. She knew where he lived – he had a flat just a few streets away from her own – but she had never been there. Thankfully the flat was on the ground floor, and when he had opened the door he actually picked her up and carried her over the threshold. As soon as they were inside, Tom lit the gas fire. He disappeared for a moment, then came back with his dressing gown.

'Not very glamorous, I'm afraid, but take off whatever needs drying and wrap yourself up in this. I'll put your damp clothes over the back of a chair. No clothes horse, I'm afraid.'

He went into what Kay assumed was the kitchen and she heard him filling the kettle. By the time the kettle had boiled, Tom had changed into a pair of dry slacks and a large, comfortable sweater. He laced their tea with whisky, and then it seemed the most natural thing in the world to sit in each other's arms on the threadbare old sofa in front of a popping gas fire. *If the insurance business is doing well*, Kay thought, *it doesn't reflect in the way Tom lives*. She yawned.

'Poor love,' Tom said. 'I think you'd better stay the night. I'll take the sofa,' he added hastily and Kay laughed.

'I'd better phone home; Shirley and Jane will worry.'

'What will you tell them?'

'I'll tell them that you'll take the sofa.'

163

It wasn't really very funny, but that set them both off laughing until, suddenly, Tom pulled her close and kissed her so passionately that it left them both breathless.

'You'd better make your phone call,' Tom said. 'I'll get the bed ready.'

The telephone was on a table in the tiny hallway. Apart from a notepad and pencil there were one or two letters which looked like advertising material. One brown envelope was different. Kay glanced at it idly and saw that it was addressed to Sgt Thomas Masters. So that had been his rank in the army, Kay thought. Like many ex-servicemen, Tom hardly ever talked about the war.

Kay was glad that it was Jane who answered the phone. Much as she liked Shirley, there were times when she couldn't cope with her forthright way of speaking and her sense of humour. Jane told her to look after herself, whereas Shirley would no doubt have pretended not to have believed the reason she was staying at Tom's for the night.

If the living room was sparsely furnished the bedroom was like a monk's cell. *If Tom lives any kind of life, it isn't here*, Kay thought, and immediately gave up that line of thought as too complex.

Fortified by the hot, sweet drink and comforted by a hot water bottle, it didn't take her long to get to sleep. She woke up in the morning with only a vague ache in her ankle and a keen sense of disappointment. True to his word, Tom had spent the night on the sofa.

Chapter Twelve

March

Kay crossed the impressive entrance hall of Broadcasting House and was self-consciously aware of the uneven click-clacking of her shoes on the marble floor. Shirley was waiting for her by the reception desk, and she took her through to a small lobby where there were two lifts. On the wall opposite the lift doors was a magnificent tapestry which had been presented to the BBC by the French Government for their freedom broadcasts during the war. Shirley told her it had been made by Aubusson.

Kay had been in town for a job interview in the haberdashery department at Liberty's. Because of her lack of experience she didn't feel very hopeful. And, in any case, Moira didn't approve. She was still insisting that Kay should hold out for 'something better'. Shirley had told her that, whatever the outcome of the interview, she was going to treat Kay to a lunch in Broadcasting House. The two girls took the lift down to the basement and followed a long corridor to the canteen.

'Well, here we are,' Shirley said as she gestured around a dingy, windowless space. 'Not very classy, but the food's good if basic. And it's cheap!'

They each took a tray and lined up behind an assortment

of BBC staff at the hot counter. Kay gazed at the serving dishes containing mince and dumplings, liver and onions and battered fish.

'Not bad for one and sixpence each,' Shirley said. 'And how about those super puddings for threepence?'

Both girls settled for the mince and dumplings with generous helpings of potatoes and mushy peas, and jam roly-poly pudding and custard. Then Shirley led the way past the plastic-topped tables, looking round as she went for anyone she knew. Now and then she waved and smiled, but they settled for a vacant table so that they could have a good old chinwag, as Shirley put it.

She had just started asking Kay about her job interview when she suddenly leaned across the table and said, 'There's my boss, Julian Fry. He's coming this way. Isn't he gorgeous?'

Kay looked up and saw a distinguished-looking older man walking towards them. He was casually dressed in corduroy trousers and a polo-necked sweater. His greying hair was a little too long but he had a certain style. But gorgeous? Not really. Nonetheless, it was obvious that Shirley was impressed, and when he asked if he could join them she flushed visibly. Kay realised straight away that he was agitated about something. He didn't even glance at Kay but demanded whether Shirley knew if that silly cow Lydia had turned up yet.

'Honestly,' he said, 'doesn't she realise she's lucky to get any part these days? And then just not turning up when the studio's booked and waiting!'

'I kept phoning her like you said, Mr Fry,' Shirley said. 'Her landlady said she didn't come home last night and she didn't know where she was.'

'Oh, Gawd,' Julian Fry drawled. 'Maybe I should send a taxi round her usual drinking holes. They may find her asleep behind the bar. That actually happened once, you know.'

'And if she can't be found?'

'She's for the drop. She's off my list for good this time.'

'But what about the play?'

'As you know, it's only a tiny part, a lady-in-waiting to the queen. I'll write it out; give her lines to the other girl. So, when you've finished your lunch you can type up the new scripts for me.'

'Oh.'

'Don't worry. I'll make as few changes as possible.'

'You said that once before!'

Kay was surprised that Shirley should answer him back, but she saw that they were both smiling. She had been fascinated listening in to the conversation, and she was almost sorry when Shirley's boss picked up his tray and made to leave them. Then, as if he had only noticed her for the first time, he looked at Kay and sat down again.

'You didn't tell me you had Vivien Leigh here as a stand-in,' he said, and he bestowed a brilliant smile on Kay.

'Actually, my name is Kay Lockwood and I don't think I resemble Vivien Leigh at all.'

Julian studied her closely. 'No, you don't. It's a first impression – the eyes, the hair – but you have a much more interesting face.'

Kay wasn't sure how to respond, so she said nothing, but she could feel herself flushing.

'Let me introduce my landlady,' Shirley filled the awkward silence.

Julian was immediately interested. 'You're the girl who lives in Lana Fontaine's house? Shirley told me. She was your godmother. How glamorous!'

'I don't know about glamorous,' Kay said. 'I mean, she was glamorous, yes, but the last time I saw her I was a small child. I simply remember her as warm and full of life.'

'So I don't suppose you have any idea why she suddenly stopped working, do you?'

'No, I don't.'

'But, tell me, how did your parents know Lana?'

'My father worked in the theatre.'

'Jack Lockwood?'

'You knew him?'

'Only that he was a friend of Lana's. I believe he used to visit her now and then.'

'I had no idea.'

Julian looked at her through narrowed eyes. 'No, I don't suppose you did.' He paused. 'Shirley, my sweet, your friend may not be Vivien Leigh, but she is an actor's daughter who happens to have a most melodious and expressive speaking voice. You can forget about ordering a taxi and I won't have to do a rewrite. We have a perfect lady-in-waiting. Miss Kay Lockwood.'

16th March 1950

My Dear Kay,

I have just switched my wireless off and I had to write straight away. That was you, wasn't it, playing a small part in the afternoon play? Your voice is so distinctive, surely I'm not mistaken? I wish you had warned me that you were going to be on. I might have missed the broadcast. Although you know how much I love my radio drama, so perhaps you wanted to surprise me and took a chance.

Please write and assure me that I am not going gaga in my old age. Tell me I am correct and also if you are going to be in any more plays.

Yours sincerely,

Margaret Bennet

Dear Miss Bennet,

No, you are not mistaken; it was me playing the part of one of Queen Victoria's ladies-in-waiting. I couldn't write and tell you because I didn't know until a few hours beforehand that I was going to be in the play. I was lunching with Shirley when I was dragooned into it by her eccentric boss, Julian Fry, a drama producer. One of the cast had not turned up. I say dragooned, but, in truth, I thought it would be a very interesting thing to do until I got to the studio and discovered that there would be no more rehearsals and that the play was going out live.

The rest of the cast were very welcoming, and at least I didn't have to learn any lines. We read from the scripts and I'd had time to do a quick read-through before we started. We were sitting round the microphone and as we came to the end of each page we bent down and put them very carefully on the floor, taking care not to rustle the paper. My character only appeared on three pages, so once I had been banished from court, I was able to relax and enjoy watching the professionals at work.

The sound effects were amusing. Most of them were on records and played in a control room called the cubicle, but a studio manager was in the studio with us and he produced what Shirley told me later were spot effects. For thunder he shook a sheet of metal and for horses' hoofs he knocked coconut shells together. Yes, really!

All the time I sensed Shirley watching me through the glass partition. I think she was nervous for me. Strangely, after an initial attack of butterflies, my nerves settled themselves and I began to enjoy the experience.

It may seem a strange thing to say, but I felt as though I was at home in that studio. I was disappointed when the red light went out and the final music was faded in. I could hardly believe that I was going to receive payment – the magnificent sum of three guineas. The studio manager gave me an envelope with a cheque inside.

Better still, Mr Fry wants me to work for him again. He is developing a serial set in a village. An old family, having suffered the vicissitudes of war, is struggling to hang on to the ancient family home. He wants me to play the daughter. Can you believe it? I thought I must be dreaming. But no, the very next day I went to a meeting with some other members of the cast and the scriptwriters. Mr Fry told me that he thinks I could probably fit in other drama work, too. I don't know when this will get going, but I'm confident enough to give up the search for a different sort of job.

Who would think life could change so much over lunch in the basement canteen of the BBC? I owe it all to Shirley, though I'm sorry to say that she has been a little worried. She thinks I will change. Become toffee-nosed. (Forgive the slang, but those were her words!) She says that in her short time in the drama department she has watched people get above themselves. I pray I won't.

I hope I haven't bored you with all this, but who else can I tell? Please tell me if you think I'm becoming self-obsessed!

Yours sincerely,
Kay

Dear Kay,

Of course I don't think you are becoming self-obsessed, but I am sad that you do not feel you can tell your mother and your sister of your good fortune. May I ask why?

Also, I hope that if you ever work with Valentine Dyall in one of *The Man in Black* stories you would tell me all about it.

Yours sincerely,

Margaret Bennet

Dear Miss Bennet,

Of course I will tell you if I ever work with Valentine Dyall, or any other of your favourite actors and actresses.

As for the other question, I don't know how to answer it. You know my mother didn't want me to come to London in the first place, and I have the feeling that my becoming an actress, even a radio actress, will upset her even more.

Yours sincerely,

Kay

Dear Kay,

This correspondence is becoming like a conversation. Perhaps we should telephone each other. If only long-distance calls were not so difficult.

You will have to tell your mother sooner rather than later. Someone might hear you on the wireless, and then how would your mother feel?

Yours sincerely,

Margaret Bennet

Kay folded Miss Bennet's latest missive and put it back in its envelope. She felt ashamed. Miss Bennet had said long-distance telephone calls could be difficult, but probably what she really meant was that they were expensive. *I can afford to phone her and I will*, Kay thought. *I could choose a time convenient to her and we could have a nice little chat. It would be like phoning home.* Kay sighed. She wished with all her heart that she could phone her mother, but she knew that such a call would only end up upsetting them both.

Moira was over the moon. 'Lana would be so pleased for you,' she said. 'Just think of the advice she would be able to give you.'

'Or my father.'

'I beg your pardon?'

'My father was an actor, too, you know.'

'Of course he was. And so handsome. I remember when I met him I thought he ought to be a film star.'

'You met my father?' Kay was astonished.

Moira looked flustered. 'Perhaps I should have told you before now, but he did come up to London once or twice to visit Lana. He joked that he was checking up on his protégée. After all, he said, he'd set her on her way to stardom. I think the reason I didn't tell you was because his visits always left Lana so unsettled. She once actually said to me that her days had never been truly happy since she left Northridge Bay.

'Of course that was nonsense. You can put it down to actor's temperament. She enjoyed all the trappings of being a successful actress. Until the day she said to me, "Moira, darling, I've had enough." She went on to ask me what was the point of it all. Of course I couldn't tell her.'

This conversation reminded Kay of the boxes of photographs and papers that she had put aside when she had decided to take in two lodgers. She knew that she wanted to look through them again, and perhaps even solve the mystery of why Lana had given up acting so suddenly. Shirley had offered to help. Perhaps she would take her up on that. But not yet . . .

Tom was equally pleased for her. He called round with an enormous bouquet of flowers. 'How shall we celebrate?' he asked. 'Dinner or the theatre? Or both?'

'Why don't we just go to the pictures?'

'I won't hear of it. I'll book a table at Stefano's. That's in Soho and within walking distance of theatreland. Leave it to me, will you?'

'Mmm. Tom?'

'Yes, Kay?'

'It will be just the two of us, won't it?'

'Of course. Why do you ask?'

'Well, it's very generous of you, but you do seem to like having Shirley and Jane around, don't you?'

'Do I?'

Kay nodded.

'Well, I suppose it's because I feel guilty whisking you out all the time and leaving your friends behind. They're new to London, too, aren't they?'

Kay didn't find this answer at all satisfactory, and she was mortified to hear how waspish she sounded when she said, 'You needn't be in the least worried about Shirley. She has new friends at the BBC. They seem to be a lively crowd and in fact Shirley will probably be late home again tonight.'

'And Jane?'

'Jane seems to be quite happy staying in the house and avoiding the limelight, as Shirley would say.'

'She's not here now.'

Kay smiled. 'Her one indulgence. She likes shopping in the West End. But she's usually home by teatime.'

Tom looked thoughtful. 'Does she buy nice things?'

'As a matter of fact, she does. A little bit of jewellery, fashionable clothes. But why are you so interested?'

'Simply because if she buys jewellery and smart clothes, where does she expect to wear them?'

Kay was perplexed. Not only because this had also occurred to her, but also because she felt uncomfortable with the way the conversation was going. Tom seemed to sense her unease, because suddenly he smiled and took her in his arms.

'But you're right, of course. It would probably be cruel to insist that she comes along with us when she would rather hide away here. Now, why don't you put these flowers in water while I make us a cup of tea?'

'Righto. But I'll have to find a vase big enough for this extravagant bouquet.' She smiled at him, 'I think I know where I can find one.'

Kay left Tom filling the kettle and went to the dining room, where she was sure she had seen a large vase on a shelf in an alcove at one side of the fireplace. She was right. The pale green three-sided vase was definitely tall enough. She was just about to reach for it when she spotted a square scrap of paper on the floor. She picked it up and turned it over to find it was an old photograph. It must have fallen down when she first emptied the box.

It was a photograph of her father standing outside the theatre. From the angle of his head, he looked as though he was talking to whoever was taking the snapshot, but Kay couldn't read his expression. Either the photograph had faded more than the others or the light had been dim. Perhaps it had been a rainy day.

'Tea's up!' she heard Tom call, so she dropped the photograph in the box, reached for the vase and hurried back to the kitchen.

Northridge Bay, 1926

Jack Lockwood stood in the entrance of the Pavilion Theatre and stared out at the rain-lashed lower promenade. The rain was bad enough, but it was high tide and a fierce wind sent the incoming waves crashing over the balustrade to soak anyone foolhardy enough to make their way to the matinée.

His troupe – the boys, the girls and the musicians – were hurrying past him to enter the theatre and dry off in the dressing rooms before getting ready for the show, but so far not a single customer had turned up, and Jack didn't blame them. He had almost decided to use the time to rehearse some new sketches and he was walking towards the entrance when a voice shouted, 'Smile please, Mr Lockwood!'

He turned round and saw Violet aiming her camera at him. He shook his head. 'It will be a waste of a shot. There's not enough light.'

'Go on, say "cheese",' she pleaded.

'All right. But why?'

'It's for Lana. You know she thinks someone will write her life story some day? Well, she wants me to take a picture of anything that looks interesting. And here you are, standing outside the theatre.'

Jack laughed. 'Go on then.'

Violet took her shot and Jack wondered whether Lana would offer to pay for the film or the developing. Probably not, he decided.

As the afternoon went on, the wind dropped a little, the swell of the sea became less turbulent and the rain eased off sufficiently to allow the more hardy holidaymakers to venture out.

It wasn't long before a gaggle of families could be seen descending the steps from the upper promenade and begin to squelch their way towards the theatre. Jack groaned and almost wished that he'd had to call the afternoon show off. The audience would be damp and restless, especially the children. He would have to instruct the cast to keep the pace brisk and the musicians to up the tempo. Also it might be a good idea to reward the audience with free hot drinks during the first interval – no – that would send the children scurrying to the toilets – the second interval would be better. Cheered a little since the decision had been made, he turned to Mrs Benson sitting in the ticket booth and gave the thumbs-up.

Then Jack remembered why he loved this life and how he wouldn't want to live any other way. Especially not to become a hotel manager, as Thelma wanted him to be. Thelma knew only too well that Jack had reached his zenith as the actor-manager of a series of seaside entertainments, and no doubt she wanted to make sure that they had a less precarious future to look forward to.

It was Thelma's dream to own her own house rather than rent one. Perhaps they could buy an established guest house and in time expand. He was sure that Thelma could run a hotel with her eyes closed, but it would be better to have a man nominally in charge. Jack would not be able to bear that, and he wished with all his heart that he and Thelma could have managed to conceive a child. Thelma would make a good mother, he was sure of that, and with the rearing of a child to occupy her she might let go of the idea of owning a hotel.

However, now the sun was shining and the orchestra had started to play a medley of popular tunes. Much cheered, Jack decided to give the children in the audience an extra treat. They could make a queue and go up on to the stage at one side where Eve, a motherly-looking girl, would give out the twists of paper containing sweets. And then the children could walk across the stage – always a thrill – and descend the other side.

Totally exhilarated, Jack hurried through the auditorium, smiling and welcoming those who were already taking their places. And then he remembered that he had another problem.

The taxi had barely driven off when a dark figure stepped out of the shadows and seized Lana by the shoulders.

'Where the hell have you been?'

She yelped with fright. 'Jack! How could you? I could have had a heart attack.'

'Hush, keep your voice down. You'll wake the neighbours.'

'Well, if I do, it's entirely your fault. Hiding behind the hedge and jumping out like that.'

'I wasn't hiding, I was waiting.'

'Well, you've no right to. Nor have you any right to ask me where I've been.'

'Yes, I have. You're in my troupe, remember. I'm not only the boss; I'm also responsible for the way you girls behave. We don't want any scandals. So answer my question.'

'Monty took me to a club he knows in Newcastle.'

'So it's Monty now, is it?'

'All right, Mr Montague waited for me after the show and told me he wanted me to consider signing up with his agency. He wants me to go to London with him. He says he can get me work. We went to the club, we discussed a few options, and I said I'd think about it. That's all.'

'I don't believe you.'

There was such venom in Jack's voice that Lana gasped. 'Why ever not?'

'It doesn't take until three o'clock in the morning to discuss a few options.'

'We danced, we had a drink or two. I had to be nice to the man.'

Jack's grip became tighter. 'How nice?'

Lana reached up and prised Jack's fingers from her shoulders. 'Stop that. You'll leave bruises. It wasn't like that. What kind of girl do you think I am?'

'I don't know, Lana. I don't know what to think.'

'And nor do I.'

'What do you mean?'

'I thought you'd be pleased for me. I mean, you're always going on about how I have the makings of a real star.'

'And that's what you want?'

'Of course it is. You've known that from the start.'

Now that her eyes had become accustomed to the flickering street lamp, Lana could see Jack's expression and was shocked to see how wretched he looked.

'Yes, you're right,' he said. 'That's what attracted me. You're not only beautiful, you're talented – exceptionally so – and hard working. You deserve this break.'

'So why are you so angry with me?'

'Do I have to tell you?' They stared at each other and Jack pulled her into his arms. This time tenderly.

'No, you don't have to tell me, Jack, and I'm sorry. But even if I stayed, what future would there be for us? You're married.'

'I could always . . .'

Lana put a hand to his lips. 'No you couldn't, because that would cause a scandal. And as you've already pointed out, we can't afford a scandal. My career would end before it began.'

'Your career.'

'Yes, my career.'

'Don't you love me at all, Lana?'

'Hush, Jack, that's not fair.' Suddenly she shivered and Jack held her even more tightly than before. 'We'd better go in,' she said. Then added, 'What about Thelma?'

'What do you mean?'

'Where does she think you are?'

'I told her I had some work to do at the theatre. She's used to me keeping peculiar hours.'

'And she believed you?'

'Why shouldn't she?'

'Oh, Jack, because she's not stupid and she's desperately in love with you. And that's another reason why I should leave the troupe as soon as possible. Now,' she tried to sound light-hearted, 'I need my beauty sleep. And so, my darling, do you.'

Once inside, Lana took off her shoes and crept up the stairs and along the quiet corridor to her room. It took her ages to get to sleep. Monty had promised her stardom; Jack was offering her love. But it was a love she could not accept. Not only because she felt sorry for poor old Thelma, but also because her career meant more to her than anything else. If Jack divorced Thelma and they got married, it was not the scandal that Lana was worried about, it was the fear that Jack would expect children. A family could put an end to her ambitions. Jack could hardly expect her to give up now. Not when the London stage was beckoning.

When Jack got into bed Thelma sighed and turned over, moving into the circle of his arms. Guiltily he pulled her close. Lana was right. It was inevitable that she would put her career above any love that she might feel for him. She would go to London. He must make the most of the time they had left together. Surely no one could blame him for that.

Chapter Thirteen

London, April 1950

It was a ridiculous concept, she knew that, but Kay had got it into her head to search through the boxes for her father – and she wasn't just thinking about whether there were any photographs of him. If there were, she imagined that she would find out more about him; what kind of man he had been. Two people had told her that Jack Lockwood used to come to this house to visit Lana. Not Jack, her mother and the children. Just Jack.

The fact that Moira knew about the visits was not so surprising, considering that she and Lana were old friends. But Julian Fry? He wasn't a particular friend of Lana's; in fact, Kay wasn't sure whether he had even met her, and yet he knew that Jack Lockwood would call to see Lana every now and then. So it must have been common knowledge.

Kay supposed that the visits could have been professional – something to do with the stage plays or even the films Lana had appeared in – but she was beginning to think that her mother might have had good cause to dislike Lana Fontaine.

So she searched through the two boxes that remained after her initial clear-out – one of photographs and one of papers. She thought she might find letters from him, but she soon discovered that there was only a collection of bills and receipts from gown shops. There were no letters, no Christmas cards, no birthday cards, nothing remotely personal. She threw each bill and receipt on the fire, something she would not have been able to do when she first went through these boxes.

I'm angry with her, Kay thought. *I'm angry because I suspect her of hurting my mother deeply. But if what I suspect is true then my father, my handsome, loving father, is equally guilty.*

All that was left in the box was a collection of theatre programmes. *Do I want them?* Kay wondered. She decided that she would offer them to Moira and then turned her attention to the remaining box containing photographs. She began searching through them feverishly, looking for photographs of her father and Lana together, but there were none, except for those she had already seen featuring her mother as well. *Why is this so important to me?* she wondered. *It's not just the obvious explanation.* And then, not daring to find the answer, she thrust the thought to the back of her mind.

'What are you doing up so late?' Kay turned round, startled, as Shirley walked into the kitchen. 'Oh, I see. You promised I could help you sort through those.'

'Did I?'

'Well, remember I'd be pleased to help. Tea or cocoa?'

'Cocoa, I think.'

'Shall I make some for Jane?'

'She went to bed early. Said she was tired.'

'Don't know why. All she ever does is go shopping. She shops as if she's come into a fortune and is determined to indulge herself – her wardrobe must be full to bursting. I wonder where all the money comes from. I know she said she sold her house in Yorkshire, but surely she can't just live off the proceeds for ever? She doesn't seem to need to get a job, and all she does is go out and spend, spend, spend. All right, I can see you disapprove. I'll stop being catty.'

'Please do. And Shirley, I'm going to take you up on your offer. I want to hand the box over to you. I'll buy some photograph albums and I'd like you to try to arrange the photographs chronologically. Only a few have dates on, so there'll have to be some guesswork. Would you like to do that?'

'Love to! I've got that kind of brain, you know.' Shirley concentrated on pouring the milk into a pan. 'That's settled then. By the way, Julian says he thinks you'll go far. He predicts great things for you.'

'And you value his opinion?'

'Of course I do.'

'It's not more than that, is it?'

'What do you mean?'

'You're not a little star-struck?'

'If you mean, am I in love with him, I have to admit that I might be. Is it obvious?'

'I'm afraid it is. And what about Julian? How does he feel about it?'

'I shouldn't think it's ever crossed his mind. After all, he's old enough to be my father.'

'Does that bother you?'

'Not in the least!' Shirley smiled. 'But can we change the subject before I succumb to embarrassment?' She spooned cocoa into two cups and then slowly added the hot milk, stirring all the while. When they were ready she put the cups on the table and sat down. 'And what do you think of Jane's phone calls?'

Kay raised her eyebrows. 'So it's all right to talk about Jane, is it?'

Shirley laughed. 'Naughty of me, I know, but yes. What do you think about her phone calls?'

'You've lost me.'

'She waits until we've gone out. Sometimes when I come

home she's just walking away from the telephone table. I could be wrong, but it looks like she's been making a call.'

'Yes, come to think of it, I've noticed that, too.'

'So who do you think she phones? She's supposed to be alone in the world, isn't she?'

'We could be wrong about the phone calls.'

'I don't think so. Why do you think she's being so secretive?'

'She's just a private person, and we shouldn't gossip like this.'

Shirley sighed. 'I suppose not. But I can't help thinking there's more to Jane than meets the eye.' She sipped her cocoa in silence for a while and then looked at Kay uneasily. 'And have you noticed the newspapers?'

'I thought we weren't going to talk about Jane.'

'I'm sorry, Kay, I've got a confession to make. I feel dreadful.'

'What have you done?'

'You must have noticed how she likes reading newspapers?'

'For goodness' sake! What's unusual about that?'

'Nothing – except that she's secretive about that, too. I mean, why should she try to hide it from us?'

'You said you have a confession to make.'

'I looked through the newspapers she threw out.'

'So?'

'There were bits torn out.'

'What are you getting at?'

'Well, she must be keeping those bits, mustn't she?'

'I suppose so.'

'I made notes of the dates and I checked in the cuttings library at work – I told you I have that kind of brain – and Jane seems to be keeping a record of a burglary, one that went horribly wrong. Somehow the thieves managed to start

183

a fire. They got away and they're still on the run. The police are after them.'

'The thieves started a fire?'

'The whole place burnt down.'

They stared at each other for a moment, remembering how frightened Jane was of fires and what she had told them about the death of her husband.

'Perhaps that's how her husband died,' Shirley said. 'He was a fireman, or maybe a policeman. And even if he was cruel to her, maybe she still loved him.'

'Oh, poor Jane,' Kay said.

'Do you think there's a connection?'

'There could be.'

'Then why doesn't she tell us? She must know how much we would support her.'

'Shirley, stop this. If Jane wants us to know she will tell us in her own good time.'

'I know. You're right. And if there is a connection we should be really sorry for her. It's just . . . I don't know how to say this. It's just that I've discovered that I find it really hard to like her.'

4th April

Dear Julie,

I suppose I must say congratulations. Does that sound grudging? I'm sorry, but I am worried that you haven't given enough thought to what you are about to do. You're so young to be getting married, and you've hardly done any living yet. By that I mean you went straight from school to college, and now you're going straight from college into married life. You've never had a job that might widen your horizons.

Kay put down her pen and stared at the letter she had started to write, then crumpled it and dropped it in the waste bin. She decided that the tone was indeed grudging, not to say hectoring, and she loved her younger sister and wanted her to be happy.

Julie's letter had arrived that morning, and every word expressed her joy. Kay couldn't help but be pleased for her, but nevertheless, she was filled with unease. In the past Tony had never regarded Julie as anything more than a nuisance. How could his feelings change so swiftly? She hoped her younger sister wasn't going to get her heart broken.

If only I could talk to Mum about this, Kay thought, but each time she had phoned home her mother had had some excuse for not being able to come to the phone. Kay glanced at her watch. Julie would be home from college. Kay took a chair through into the hallway and sat at the telephone table. At least she could talk to Julie.

Even with the light on, the hallway was dark. The rain had started early that morning and hadn't eased up. Kay dialled the operator and asked to make a long-distance call, giving her the name of the exchange and the number. She shivered, but it was too late to go and get a cardigan; the phone was already ringing. It was Julie who answered.

'Kay! You got my letter?'

'I did. Congratulations.'

'I'm so happy!'

'Then I'm happy for you.'

'You're not mad at me?'

'Why should I be?'

'Come off it, Kay. You and Tony were going out together for ages. Aren't you the teensiest bit peeved?'

'Not at all. I think Tony is a very lucky man. You're young, you're beautiful, you have a good brain – what more could he want?'

'So you're not angry?'

'Not in the slightest.'

'That's all right, then.'

Kay thought that Julie sounded peeved. She smiled when she realised that her sister actually wanted her to be jealous.

'Kay . . .' Julie sounded hesitant.

'What is it?'

'Mum asked me to tell you that she doesn't think you ought to come to the wedding.'

Kay was astonished. 'Why not?'

'Well . . . you see, everyone knows that you and Tony were just as good as engaged, and Mum thinks that would make people gossip even more.'

'Even more than what, Julie? I don't understand.'

Kay heard Julie catch her breath.

'Julie – is this something to do with why Mum wouldn't talk to me?'

'I suppose so.'

Kay had a premonition. 'Julie, when is the wedding?'

To her dismay Kay heard a muffled sob. Julie's voice was breaking when she answered. 'As soon as possible.'

'Oh, no!'

'I'm not going to have the kind of wedding every girl dreams of. We're getting married in the register office as soon as Tony can get the licence.'

'You're pregnant?'

A note of defiance crept into her sister's voice. 'Yes, I am.'

'Oh, Julie sweetheart, I'm so sorry.'

'There's no need to be,' Julie sounded angry. 'At least Tony is doing the right thing by me.'

Kay thought carefully about what she should say next. 'You don't have to get married, if you don't want to, you know.'

Her sister sounded shocked. 'Of course I do. What would people say if I had a child out of wedlock?'

'People needn't know.'

'What do you mean?'

'Come and live with me. I'd love to have you and the baby. We could make a happy home.'

'Mother would be heartbroken. And besides, I want to marry Tony. He's all I've ever dreamed about.'

'And Tony?'

'What do you mean?'

'Is it what he wants?'

'Of course he does. He loves me. He said so.'

Julie's answer didn't reassure Kay. 'Julie, I don't want to see you in a half-hearted arrangement with a man who would not have married you if you had not been pregnant.'

Kay heard Julie gasp. 'God, Kay, you can be cruel.'

'I don't mean to be. I want the best for you. If you have any doubts, any doubts at all, just pack your bags and come and live here. We can make a new life for you.'

'New life? Oh, yeah. And who would ever marry me if I had an illegitimate kid? It may be halfway through the twentieth century but times haven't changed that much. If Tony hadn't stepped up to the mark it would have been off to the naughty girls' hostel for me and you know it.'

'Julie—'

'No, listen, Kay. I love Tony and he loves me. You've got to believe it. His parents have been OK about it. They thought it was time he settled down. They're going to buy us a nice little house to start off with. After she got over the shock, Mum is actually looking forward to being a grandmother. And, by the way . . .'

'What?'

'There's no need to feel sorry for me. Even if you never managed to land him, Tony Chalmers is a damned good catch.' With that, Julie slammed her receiver down.

★ ★ ★

Tom opened the door and smiled with pleasure. 'You're early. How did it go?'

'Very well. I think.'

'You only think? Here, come on in before the rain washes you away.' Tom took Kay's umbrella and shook it, then propped it up behind the door. He drew her in, and as usual her heart began to race as she found herself standing close to him in the tiny hallway. 'Your coat, madam.'

Kay slipped out of her raincoat and handed it to him. 'Is it ever going to stop raining?'

'I don't know, but if this coat doesn't dry out by the time we've had supper then you may have to stay the night again.'

Tom led the way through into the sparsely furnished living room. It could have been cheerless but was saved by the lively popping elements of the gas fire and a vase full of bright yellow daffodils on the table.

'So tell me what happened.'

'Only after I've eaten the spaghetti Bolognese you promised me.'

Over supper Kay told Tom all about the radio play she had appeared in that day. It was a murder mystery starring a famous fictional lady detective. Kay had played the innocent girl accused of murder and who was saved from the gallows at the last minute.

'Actually it was very complicated,' she told him. 'I'm still not sure how Miss Marlow managed to work out what happened.'

'Me neither.'

'You listened?'

'Of course I did.'

'In the office?'

There was a slight pause before Tom said, 'I brought my work home today.' And then he hurried on, 'I have to admit,

188

it was a damned good story, even though they got the police procedures a little wrong.'

'How would you know that?'

'My work,' he said quickly. 'Insurance fraud and that kind of thing brings me in contact with the boys in blue. More spaghetti?'

'Yes, please. It's delicious. Where did you learn to cook like this?'

'In Italy. I was taken prisoner and escaped. I holed up with an Italian family for a while.'

Kay took a spoonful of parmesan and scattered it on her pasta. 'You never talk about the war.'

'A lot of men don't. Another glass of wine?'

'Yes, please.'

'So tell me, was the work what you expected?'

'Yes. The rehearsals went well and there were no mistakes. I still can't get over how lucky I've been to find this work.'

'If this afternoon's performance is anything to go by, you were cut out for it.'

'Tom, is it all right if I make a phone call?'

'Do you want to tell the girls you're staying here tonight?'

'Maybe. I'll decide later. But now I want to phone an old friend at home. It's long distance. I'll pay for the call.'

'There's no need for that. Is the old friend Miss Bennet?'

'You have a good memory.'

'It goes with my job. Go on, but don't stand too long in the hall. You'll catch cold. I'll brew up some coffee. Then we'll curl up in front of the fire.'

Kay's old friend was delighted to hear from her. 'Of course I listened, Kay,' Miss Bennet told her. 'And everyone here is talking about you. Who would have dreamed that when you went to London to sort out your inheritance your life was going to change so drastically? Kay, my dear, you're becoming quite the star.'

Chapter Fourteen

'Are you on your own?'

'Of course.' Nevertheless, Jane gripped the receiver tightly. She was always nervous when she used the phone in the house, but it was too tempting to stay indoors when the weather outside was foul.

'So where are they?'

'Shirley's at work and Kay's at some rehearsal for the new serial she's going to be in.'

'Your landlady's getting quite famous. I thought the idea was to find somewhere quiet and anonymous where you would be completely unnoticed.'

'That's OK. Nobody notices me. Except . . .'

He came back quickly. 'Except what?'

'Well, Kay's boyfriend goes out of his way to try and include the three of us in anything he plans.'

'Do you think there's anything in that?' Suddenly Maurice sounded wary. 'Is he keeping tabs on you?'

She thought for a moment. 'No, he's probably just being polite. But then there's Shirley.'

'Yeah, I know, you saw her looking through the newspapers you'd dumped. That was a really stupid thing to do.'

'How else can I find out what's happening?'

'Nothing's happening. They're chasing their tails.'

'But what if someone lets us down? There's a reward, isn't there?'

He laughed. 'Haven't you heard, there's honour among thieves? Besides, only one person knows and I've promised to cut him in.'

'What's the hold–up?'

'No one wants to touch them. It's still too hot. If you've been reading the papers you know that. If only the house had been empty, things might have died down by now, but as it is, it's murder. And that means the high jump for me and for you too if they catch you.'

Jane shivered with fright. She knew he was right but she wished he wouldn't keep reminding her of the fact. 'I miss you.' To her dismay, she was close to crying. 'Couldn't we at least wait it out together?'

'No way. The word is they're looking for a man and a woman. They haven't a clue who I am but they could be on to you. After all, anyone who called at the house would remember you. No one in the village ever saw me.'

'It said in the newspaper that a car was seen driving away at speed. I've never owned a car and I can't drive.'

'Who's to know that? Like I said, the more you keep out of it the safer we are.'

'I'm frightened you'll go without me!'

'I wouldn't do that. Believe me. We're in this together; we have been since the moment you let me into that house that night. I've already got the passports, and the minute I've got the money we'll be off. Now be a good girl and cheer up. Got to go. Bye.'

Her husband cut the line, leaving her wondering if she would ever feel safe and happy again. It wasn't meant to end like this. When she'd applied for the job as housekeeper at the manor house, they'd only envisaged a little pilfering until they'd milked the old woman dry. Then they would move on. That's the way they had been living since she first met Maurice when he'd left the army four years ago.

She was competent and respectable looking, he was good-looking and totally without morals. He'd been happy to live on whatever she could earn as a domestic servant, but always in houses where there was the opportunity for petty thievery. Maurice had developed a knowledge of antiques, but they always took the small stuff, items that wouldn't be missed by their elderly owners until Jane had moved on to another job with another change of name.

At first they hadn't planned to do anything different at the manor, but when they had discovered the jewellery, greed had overtaken them. One night when the old woman had been out visiting in the village, Jane had let Maurice in, in order to what he laughingly called 'case the joint'. At first they had been disappointed. There was some silverware and a collection of Dresden china, but not enough. Whatever they took would be missed.

It was only when they were sitting by the fire in the kitchen enjoying a glass of the old girl's best port wine, that she had told him that the mistress had quite a collection of pretty jewellery. She didn't think it could be valuable, because it wasn't locked away. 'It looks good but it can't be genuine,' she'd said, 'because she just leaves it on her dressing table or in her top drawer.'

'We might as well have a look,' Maurice said. He lit up a cigarette and told her to lead the way.

'Put that cigarette out,' she said. 'The old lady won't allow smoking in the house and she'll be able to smell it when she comes home.'

'So what? We'll be long gone. Even if the jewellery's worthless there's no point in you staying here. If there's nothing worth lifting then it's time we moved on.' Nevertheless, he tossed his cigarette on to the fire.

She went into the scullery and came back with an oil lamp. Maurice stared at it questioningly. 'There's no electricity upstairs,' she told him. 'We use lamps or candles.'

He laughed. 'This place is like something from the last century,' he said.

The old lady's bedroom confirmed his opinion: heavy brocade curtains, mahogany wardrobes and chests, and a four-poster bed. Curled up on the bed and fast asleep was a small dog. Maurice gestured towards it. 'Trouble?' he asked.

'Not if we're quiet. He's old; he sleeps most of the time.'

'Come on then. Let's get at it,' Maurice hissed impatiently.

As soon as he saw the jumble of necklaces and bracelets lying on the dressing table he knew that they'd struck lucky. 'It's old-fashioned,' he said quietly, 'but all of it is valuable. Some of the pieces are priceless.'

He stuffed everything into his pockets and then, taking the lamp, he went over to the bed.

Jane opened another drawer, but it contained nothing except a padded pink silk handkerchief case. She checked it, then looked across at Maurice. 'What are you doing?' she asked.

'Thought so,' he replied. He had opened the drawer in the bedside table. 'Look, she's left a couple of pairs of earrings here.'

He was just about to pick them up when the dog awoke. It yelped and began to growl. Then, without warning, it hurled itself at Maurice – who swiped it away so forcefully that it fell, stunned, to the floor.

Maurice staggered for a moment and dropped the lamp. The glass smashed and the oil spilled, spreading swiftly towards the curtains, and before he could do anything to save the situation they were alight.

He turned and yelled, 'Get out!'

'The dog!'

'Leave it!' He grabbed her arm and pulled her towards the door.

'My things . . .'

'Leave them. We've got to disappear before anyone sees the blaze.'

She had followed him blindly. Outside they'd run down the road to where he'd parked his car. As they drove away she realised he'd been right about the blaze being noticed. Figures had begun to hurry towards the house. They didn't find out till later that the old woman had gone in to get her dog and that neither of them had come out again.

Apart from the film stills and studio shots, Shirley thought Lana Fontaine's collection of photographs the most boring she had ever seen. It was as if away from her work she had no life worth recording – apart from the earliest snaps. Kay had told her that most of these had been taken when Lana was appearing at the Pavilion Theatre in Northridge Bay.

There were shots of Lana with other young women who looked like members of the same troupe, and also quite a lot of her and Kay's mother. They looked as though they had been the best of friends. At first, that is. For the happy smiles on the earlier photographs gradually gave way to a more reserved look, with the two of them standing a little further apart from each other.

And Kay's father was so handsome! Shirley wondered why he had never tried to get into films himself, but she supposed that with a wife and two children to support, he had thought that too risky. Some of the later photographs were of Jack Lockwood and his wife and two daughters. Kay's younger sister, Julie, had been a very attractive child. She was softly pretty, like her mother Thelma. Kay was not pretty; she was beautiful, with fine-drawn classical features. 'Good bone structure,' Shirley's mother would have said. Shirley thought Kay looked more like her father.

Lana was in some of these family snaps. Shirley remembered Kay telling her that her godmother used to visit every now and then when she and Julie were small children. Also that the visits stopped when their father died. Indeed, there were no more photographs of the Lockwood family after when Kay must have been about seven or eight years old.

Most of the personal photographs after that were of Lana and her friend Moira, mainly taken before Moira retired from the stage. Some of them were the usual larky snaps of two attractive young women, but Shirley could not help noticing that in some of them Lana was finding it an effort to smile.

But then she found an envelope containing a photograph that was quite different from the rest. The two people in it were surrounded by greedy pigeons, with a lion statue in the background. They'd visited Trafalgar Square, just as thousands of visitors to London do. Except these weren't holidaymakers; they were Lana Fontaine and Jack Lockwood. And the way they were smiling at each other was so intimate that it could only mean that they were lovers.

Shirley knew immediately that Lana had meant Kay to find this photograph, and she knew why. Apart from the fact that Lana and Jack were lovers, Lana had had another secret to keep, and she had done so until the day she died.

Then

'I can't believe you're leaving us like this,' Violet said as she pushed the hair out of her eyes. 'I mean, just waltzing into the theatre this morning and collecting your belongings without saying a word to anyone.'

'I told Jack last night.'

'That's short notice. You could at least stay until he found a replacement for you. And that will be difficult now – all the good people are already employed.'

Jack Lockwood's troupe had just finished a strenuous rehearsal, and most of the girls and boys had flopped down on the stage, trying to get their breath back. Lana had watched the rehearsal from the wings, and when Violet saw her she had hurried over to join her. 'So why did you come here this morning?' Violet asked.

'I'm not sure. I suppose I wanted to watch for one last time.'

'I don't understand you.'

'I've loved being here with all of you, but I don't want to be in the chorus line until kingdom come. I want to get some real acting experience. Maybe I'll go legit.'

'Straight acting, you mean?'

'Perhaps – or there's always musical theatre as a step towards it.'

Violet paused and suddenly her eyes widened. 'I get it. It's that agent, isn't it? He's found a job for you somewhere better than a little seaside show. But I thought he wanted you as a singer and dancer.'

'Yes, but in London! And he said that was just the beginning. He said he could see my career taking off in totally new directions.'

'So he's found you a job.'

'He hasn't.'

'Even so you're going to sign up with him?'

'You bet. Just as soon as he comes up with a contract.'

'And what about loyalty? Couldn't you wait until the season is over?'

'What would be the point? You know very well the show can go on without me. It's not as if I'm top of the bill.'

'So that's it!'

'What do you mean?'

'You want to have a leading role. I'm sure Jack would be only too happy to give you more solos.'

'This is pointless. We're going round in circles. I've made my mind up. My clothes are packed. I've said goodbye to Thelma and now all I have to do is call a taxi.'

'Why didn't you just go?'

'I've told you. I wanted to see you all for one last time.'

'Right. You've seen us. So bugger off!'

Violet stormed off across the stage to where Eve was sitting and flopped down beside her. Eve had been watching the exchange with wide eyes. She could only have caught snatches of the conversation, and now it looked as though she was questioning Violet eagerly.

No one came to say goodbye and Lana lingered backstage until she thought the theatre was empty, then she walked on to the stage. A strange echoing silence filled the theatre. Lana stood centre stage and looked out at the auditorium. In her imagination she could hear the orchestra strike up and the tap, tap, tap of the dancers' shoes as they performed the opening number. Then, in her mind's eye, she saw herself performing the first solo dance number Jack had given her. She was good – very good – and word had got around. Gossip travelled fast in the overheated world of the theatre. She had been thrilled when the influential agent, Monty Montague, had come all the way from London to see her.

He had wanted her to leave the show immediately, but until now loyalty to the troupe and more particularly to Jack had kept her there. She had promised Monty that as soon as the season was over she would pack her bags and head for London. He had said he would wait for her – but not too long. He told her she must contact him as soon as she was free.

And that had been her intention, until her pregnancy had

made it impossible to go on. She had had to conceal the sickness, and it was getting more and more difficult to hide the swell of her breasts. Because of them some of the dance routines were torture. She knew she would have to leave long before she had planned to.

Lana wrapped her arms around her body and she began to cry, huge, shivering sobs. 'What have I done?' she asked herself. 'I've ruined everything. How can I go to London now?'

Jack watched her from the wings, and when he could bear it no longer, he walked on to the stage and took her in his arms. 'Don't cry, Lana,' he said. 'I'll fix things for you.'

'How can you fix things? This pregnancy has ruined my life. My career . . . my ambitions . . .'

Jack smiled fondly. 'Don't be so dramatic, my love. In a few more months the baby will be born and you will be able to take up where you left off. Contact Montague if that's what you want.'

'That's what I want. But how can I do that with a baby in tow?'

Jack took a handkerchief from his pocket and dried her eyes. He kissed her gently. 'Don't cry, sweetheart. It's time we went to see Thelma.'

Now

'You knew, didn't you? You've known all along,' Shirley challenged Moira, who was finding it difficult to meet her unexpected visitor in the eye.

'Look, Shirley, I'm very busy.' Moira waved a hand over the stacks of papers that covered her desk. 'Could we talk about this some other time?'

'I'm not leaving until you've admitted that you knew from the start that Lana Fontaine was Kay's mother and you've told me what you're going to do about it.'

'What makes you think that I knew any such thing?'

'Are you denying that it's true?'

Moira sighed and sat back in her chair. She closed her eyes and then dropped her head into her hands. For a moment Shirley thought that she was crying, but when she looked up again her expression was of incredible weariness, not grief.

'I've kept Lana's secrets for so long,' she said, 'that I'd almost forgotten what the truth was.'

'So what are you going to do now?'

Moira looked alarmed. 'Do I have to do anything?'

'Of course you do. It isn't my place to tell Kay that while I was sorting through the old photographs I came to the conclusion that her father was having an affair with Lana and that the result was a baby – Kay, herself.'

'Do you think she might already suspect the truth?'

'Actually, I do. Otherwise, why was a collection of not very interesting old snapshots so important to her? But I don't think she knows the whole story.'

'What do you mean?'

'I think she has guessed about their affair but not that she was the result of it.'

'And you think I ought to tell her?'

'Don't you?'

'I just don't know.' Moira shook her head wearily. 'If only Lana had left clear instructions. But she didn't, and a long time ago I promised to keep her secret, I can't betray her now.'

'Why did it have to be a secret?'

'They promised Thelma.'

'Well, I think Lana wanted Kay to know; that's why she left her everything she owned. She wanted her to come to the house she'd lived in because it was her way of claiming her daughter. She must have known that Kay might work things out.'

'But that would be breaking her promise.'

'After she was dead and past caring.'

Moira uttered a moan of distress. 'Don't talk about her like that. You make her sound heartless.'

'Perhaps she was. I mean, why did she give Kay up in the first place?'

'She was unmarried.'

'If Jack loved her so much, he could have divorced his wife and married her.'

'She wouldn't allow him to. They couldn't afford any scandal.'

'You mean Lana couldn't afford the scandal, just when she had been promised work in London. Her career was about to take off, wasn't it? A truly loving mother.'

Moira flushed. 'All right, she put her career first, but she genuinely thought the baby would be better off with Thelma. And Kay would have her own father. And Lana did care, you know. She used to visit Kay whenever she could find the time.'

'Good of her. And what did Thelma think about that?'

'She didn't like it, but she couldn't refuse Jack anything. She even agreed when he pleaded with her to allow Lana to be Kay's godmother. But when Jack died, tragically young, Thelma cut off contact and forbade Lana to come anywhere near her daughter.'

'I don't blame her.'

'I thought that was spiteful.'

'Well, I think it was quite natural. But what I can't understand is why Thelma agreed to the arrangement in the first place.'

'She loved Jack. If she'd refused there was the chance that

Jack might leave her and go with Lana. I think she believed it was better to keep his child with her than risk losing him.'

'And she's never told Kay?'

'Obviously not.'

'Well, I think Kay deserves to know the truth and it's your place to tell her.'

'And what about Thelma?'

Shirley looked puzzled. 'What do you mean?'

'Do you think it would be fair to Thelma if Kay found out she wasn't her mother? She's brought her up since she was a baby. She must love her. Kay told me that Thelma didn't want her to come to Lana's house – surely you can imagine why?'

Shirley stared at Moira, momentarily speechless. 'You're right,' she said at last. 'Now what do we do?'

'I'll think about it. But until I've made up my mind, we must keep Lana's secret a little longer.'

Then

Thelma stared at Jack, unable to comprehend what he was asking of her. She wasn't really surprised when he had told her Lana was pregnant and that he was the father. She had suspected all along that something was going on. All those nights working at the theatre after the final curtain . . . Those extra rehearsals when everyone else had been given time off . . . They must have thought she was stupid. Or were they so in love that they just didn't care?

Finally the reality of what Jack was asking sank in. They wanted her to take the baby and bring it up as her own. Jack's baby. And Lana would go away and get on with her life and leave them be. At least, that's what she promised.

Suddenly Thelma was filled with fear. What if she said no? Would Jack leave her and go with the mother of his child?

Jack must have known what she was thinking, because he took her hand and said, 'We'll bring the child up together, Thelma. You and me and the baby will be a proper family.'

'How can we be? Everyone will know it's not my child.'

'I've thought about that. The baby isn't due until February. When the summer season ends, the theatre will close and we won't have any lodgers. If you were pregnant you probably wouldn't be showing by then. With some women you can't tell until the last minute.'

Thelma looked at him wonderingly. 'You've really thought this out, haven't you? So what do you expect me to do? Stay indoors and hide myself away?'

Jack hurried on. 'You can go for a long visit to your aunt in Harrogate. She's lonely, she's always asking you to stay for a while, and you love Harrogate, don't you? It will be like a holiday – and goodness knows you deserve one.'

'You expect me to stay away from home all those months?'

Jack looked uncomfortable but he nodded. 'Lana will bring the baby to you as soon as she can. When you come home it will be as the mother of the child.'

'Aren't you coming with me?'

'I'd love to but you know I can't. Once the theatre is closed I'll have to oversee the repairs and redecorations; that's in my contract. But I'll come and see you every week and, of course, I'll stay over Christmas and New Year.'

'And what am I supposed to tell Aunt Ellen when Lana turns up with a baby?'

'We'll tell her we're adopting it. There's no harm in that, is there? We'll say we're doing a good turn for a friend and ask her to keep it a secret. She's a good soul. I'm sure she will.'

Thelma saw the desperation in Jack's eyes and knew she was going to agree to the plan. She would do anything to keep him.

'All right, I'll do it,' she said. 'But meanwhile, Lana can't stay here. Find her some lodgings elsewhere and you must promise to keep away from her. And I don't want to see her again until she brings me the baby.'

Lana looked around her dingy bedsitting room in the lodging house in a shabby suburb of Newcastle and felt like weeping. Mrs Parsons, her landlady, had made it clear that she wasn't welcome downstairs, apart from taking her meals in the airless dining room, so Lana had to stay in this miserable, cramped space where the window overlooked the marshalling yards. The noise of the trains shunting up and down was constant, and the window was never free from soot, even after the window cleaner had been – his was a hopeless task. Lana spent many a sleepless night crying with fatigue and loneliness.

Jack had found out about Mrs Parsons. Or perhaps he had already known because some unfortunate chorus girl in the past had needed to stay here. He hadn't been quite clear about that. Mrs Parsons was a midwife who took in unmarried pregnant women and looked after them until the birth of their babies. She delivered the babies herself, but if a doctor was needed there was one nearby. All this was quite legal.

Lana couldn't complain about the food or the hygiene. As an expectant mother she was well looked after. At a price. Mrs Parsons had lost her husband in the Great War and she'd had to make her own living ever since. Lana suspected that as well as taking in expectant mothers she was also engaged in something not quite so lawful. A succession of young women, and sometimes not so young, appeared at the front door, to be ushered through into Mrs Parsons' private sitting room. Sometimes Lana heard one of them cry out in pain and sometimes she heard bitter sobbing. They never stayed the night.

Once, she had heard defiant screaming, and venturing to the top of the stairs, she had witnessed a girl who could have been no more than fourteen or fifteen rushing towards the front door. She was followed by an older woman, who made a grab for her, but the girl twisted out of her grasp, opened the door and fled.

The woman turned to face Mrs Parsons, who had followed, grim-faced. 'I'm sorry,' she said.

'So you should be,' Mrs Parsons replied. 'You'll still have to pay me for my time, and for God's sake don't let your daughter blab about this.'

'I won't. I'll send her away to my sister's farm until she's had the baby.'

'If I were you I wouldn't let her come back.'

'Perhaps I won't. After all, we'd never live down the shame of it.'

Chilled by this exchange, Lana had retreated to her room and wept silent tears for the unfortunate girl. She wondered what her future might be.

Today Lana huddled over the gas fire. She had to feed the meter herself, but she couldn't bear to think she was too poor to be able to keep warm. She had been profligate with her wages, had bought clothes which would probably be out of fashion before she could wear them again. She supposed she could always sell them. She wouldn't have been able to stay here if it were not for the fact that Jack helped out. And so he should, of course.

Her feelings for Jack swung wildly to and fro. She loved him; or at least, she had convinced herself that only if she'd been in love would she have allowed him to seduce her. And yet apparently she had not loved him enough to give up her dreams of success in the theatre and make some kind of life with him. And what kind of life would that be? He wasn't rich. He was handsome and talented, but in her heart she knew he didn't have that extra something that would make him a star.

It was a poor sort of life she would lead, and that was definitely not for her. No, once this nightmare was over she would head for London, leaving Thelma to bring up the child. Until that day came she would just have to get on with it.

Jack called to pay the rent once a week but he never got past the doorstep. Mrs Parsons would have no gentlemen in the house. She didn't want to 'get a name', she said. Nothing must happen under her roof. Of course, the neighbours must know what kind of lodgers she was taking in, but to allow the men responsible to cross the threshold would be a step too far.

Lana glanced at her wristwatch and cheered up when she saw it was nearly time for Jack to arrive. She turned off the fire and put on her warmest coat, then she went to sit halfway down the stairs. As soon as Jack arrived and had handed over the money she would hurry down and go out, defying Mrs Parsons' icy glare on the way. She would walk with him to the station, a journey that took a little over ten minutes. They would sit in the waiting room until his train came. There would be a fire in there and Jack would fetch two cups of tea from the refreshment bar. Then all too soon the train would arrive and he would have to go.

And then the highlight of her week would be over. Jack would go home to an empty house, and Lana would go back to her lonely room. The only thing that kept her going was Monty's promise that he would find her work as soon as she was fit enough. He was even willing to find her a convalescent home – and pay the bill. He said she was an investment. But until then the days dragged on. Sometimes, she thought, she hated this baby she was carrying.

He knew it was wrong, but Jack Lockwood didn't feel at all ashamed of the situation he had created. How many men could have such a loving wife as Thelma and such a desirable mistress as Lana Fontaine? Thelma was pretty in a soft, unchallenging way, and Lana, even now, while she was suffering a wretched pregnancy, was heartbreakingly beautiful. She still fired him with desire, and not being able to be alone with her was exquisite torture.

But what would happen when the baby came? Jack had not allowed himself to dwell on the fact that he had asked his wife to take his child by another woman. Had he been arrogant when he assumed that Thelma loved him so much that she would agree to the plan? He had not threatened to leave her if she didn't, but he was conceited enough to believe that the possibility would torment her and that she would keep the child in order to save her marriage.

Why had he married Thelma, the daughter of his landlady in a northern seaside town? She was very pretty and she obviously adored him. Had that been enough to make him propose? Well, of course it might have been different if her mother had not found them in bed together, but he was soft-hearted and he could not bear to cause Thelma any pain. That was partly the reason, but there was also the fact that if he refused to marry her he would probably have had to leave town just as he was beginning to make a name for himself and the Pavilion.

He had never thought very deeply about whether he loved Thelma. In fact he was cynical enough to doubt there was such a thing as romantic love. Until he met Lana. His complacent, cosy little life had been overturned and he knew that for the rest of his life, whether they could be together or not, he would belong to Lana body and soul.

★ ★ ★

Jack had insisted that Lana bring the baby after dark. It was February, and the Pavilion had closed at the end of the panto-mime season. Jack was planning the next show and auditioning hopefuls. There would be nobody in the guest house who knew Lana – nobody except Thelma and Jack himself. He had not come to Mrs Parsons' house to collect her; that had been taken out of his hands. Monty, her agent, had sent a car.

When they arrived at Jack and Thelma's house the chauffeur got out and hurried round to speak to Lana. 'Just sit there a mo, madam. I'll go and let them know.'

Lana watched him hurry up the path. The door opened almost before he had taken his finger off the bell. Thelma appeared in the doorway and stood quite still, with her arms folded across her body. There was no sign of Jack.

'Shall I carry the baby for you?' the chauffeur asked when he returned to the car.

'No,' Lana held her sleeping daughter more tightly to her breast, 'I'll carry her.'

'It's cold, madam. You'll have to be nippy.'

'She's well wrapped up and I can manage.' Lana got out of the car and turned her head to look over her shoulder. 'Would you bring those two parcels, please? I'm afraid they're quite large.'

'No problem. I'll follow you.'

'I'm not going to invite you in,' Thelma said. She didn't smile. 'It's best to do this quickly.'

Behind her the house gleamed with a warm light and there was a welcoming aroma of baking. But the welcome was not for Lana.

'Jack?' Lana asked.

'He's not coming to the door. He thought it best. Don't just stand there. It's cold. You'd better give me the baby.'

When Thelma took the child in her arms Lana felt that a precious cord had been severed.

'Are these to go inside, madam?' The chauffeur was standing behind Lana with the parcels.

'What are they?' Thelma asked.

'Feeding bottles, powdered milk, nappies, clothes,' Lana said.

'I've already bought all that kind of thing.' Thelma looked as if she was about to step back and close the door.

'Please take them.'

Thelma nodded her grudging assent and stood aside. The chauffeur placed the parcels on the floor in the hallway and then walked back to the car.

'You'd best go now,' Thelma said. She stepped back.

'Wait – please—'

'What is it?'

'Her name. I've called her Kay.'

Thelma pursed her lips.

'Jack chose the name,' Lana said.

'That's right,' Jack said. He had emerged from one of the rooms and he came to stand behind Thelma.

'Jack, I thought we'd decided it was best for you not to come to the door,' Thelma said. She looked vexed.

'I wondered what was keeping you. Is there a problem?'

Thelma shook her head. 'No problem.'

Jack put an arm around her shoulders. They both looked down at the baby, who had begun to stir and murmur softly.

Lana turned and fled.

The chauffeur helped her into the car and wrapped a fur rug around her. 'We have quite a way to go to the convalescent home. Try and get some sleep.'

Lana looked up into his face and saw he was smiling sympathetically. She wondered if had performed services like this before. She didn't feel as if she could ask him. He closed the door and she sank back into the luxurious leather seats.

The car sped through the darkened streets and out into the country. Lana closed her eyes but sleep evaded her. She considered the enormity of what she had just done. She convinced herself that Thelma would be a better mother for Kay than she could ever be. But the sight of Jack, Thelma and the baby, silhouetted in the doorway looking like a proper family, was an image that would haunt her for the rest of her life.

Chapter Fifteen

July 1950

Miss Bennet pursed her lips and frowned with displeasure at the heading of the article in the local paper: 'SUCCESS FOR SHOP GIRL!'

The piece had been written by one of the paper's enthusiastic young reporters, Jane Gill. Miss Bennet thought it trivialised Kay, who might have worked at a small town grocery shop but was far more than a 'Shop Girl'. Couldn't they at least have put 'SUCCESS FOR LOCAL GIRL'? Or 'LOCAL GIRL'S SUCCESS IN LONDON', perhaps. In her opinion, either of these would have been a better heading.

The piece was pretty much what you would expect in a local paper. Trying to avoid looking at the annoying heading, Miss Bennet picked up her new, more powerful magnifying glass. Squinting through it awkwardly, she settled down to read the article for the umpteenth time.

Many of you will remember Kay Lockwood, the cheerful young woman who cycled round town in all weathers collecting your orders for Sampson's high-class grocery store.

Miss Bennet smiled at the description of Sampson's as a 'high-class' establishment, although, to be fair, they did look after their customers in a respectful, old-fashioned way and always carried a few hard-to-obtain luxury items. Also, it could be no coincidence that the young reporter was Mrs Sampson's niece.

Well, incredible as it seems, Miss Lockwood has become a successful radio actress. Her younger sister Julie, who recently became Mrs Anthony Chalmers, has kindly told us how this came about. It started with an inheritance.

Avid film fans and theatre goers will surely remember the beautiful and talented actress Lana Fontaine. But did you know that before she became famous she appeared at the Pavilion Theatre here in Northridge Bay? It was here that she met the theatre's actor-manager, Jack Lockwood, and in fact she lodged at his house and became firm friends with his wife, Thelma. So much so that when the Lockwoods' first child, Kay, was born, Lana Fontaine asked if she could be godmother.

The Lockwoods' second child, Julie, remembers that in the years before Miss Fontaine became a major star of stage and screen – even going to Hollywood to make a series of films – she would visit Northridge Bay regularly, bringing presents for the children and reliving old times with Jack and Thelma.

Sadly fame and fortune swept her into a different life and she stopped coming to visit her old friends. But it seems she did not forget her godchild, Kay, and when the actress died last year, she left Kay everything she owned. Kay went to London to sort out Miss Fontaine's affairs, and a chance meeting with a radio drama producer led to her starting work as a radio actress working for the BBC. Her sister Julie says this is perfect work for her, as a childhood accident left Kay with a limp which might prove difficult for a stage actress.

I'm sure those of you who remember the way Kay used to pedal that old bicycle round the streets of Northridge collecting orders will be sure that not much could prevent her from living an otherwise full life.

Julie says that she and her mother had no idea that Kay was so talented, and thinks that Kay must have inherited her acting ability from their father, Jack, a gifted actor himself, who sadly died when the children were small.

Now Kay is about to play a leading role in a new radio serial, *Mulberry Court,* which will follow the fortunes of an old country family recovering from the war. You will find her name in the *Radio Times*. I'm sure her godmother, Lana Fontaine, would have been very proud of her.

Miss Bennet carefully tore the page from the newspaper, folded it and put it in an envelope. She would send it to Kay, who was far too intelligent to be offended by the 'shop girl' reference. In fact, with her keen intelligence and lack of false pride she was more likely to be amused.

She hurried through to the kitchen to make herself a cup of tea, then went back to the sitting room and switched on the radio. She checked the *Radio Times*, although she had done so several times already, then she settled down to listen to the first episode of *Mulberry Court*.

Thelma looked up from the newspaper, which was on the floor, open at the offending article about Kay, and glared at her daughter. Unable to sit comfortably because of her condition, Julie squirmed restlessly on the new sofa.

'Why did you do it, Julie?' Thelma asked. 'Why did you talk to the newspaper?'

'I didn't see any harm in it.'

'Did they tell you they'd asked me and that I had refused?'

'No, they didn't, and neither did you.'

'You should have known I don't like discussing personal matters.'

'Yes, I do know that. You've always been reticent about the past. But I also know that Kay is in the public eye now and people will want to know about her.'

'It's none of their business!'

'Oh, Mum, you'll have to accept that things have changed.'

Thelma turned her head and stared angrily into the fire.

After a moment Julie asked, 'Aren't you proud of Kay?'

'Proud?' Thelma looked at her daughter. 'Why should I be?'

'I can't believe you said that. She left school without her School Cert., she's had no training, and yet she has become a successful actress working on the radio.'

'And that's something to be proud of, is it?'

'Of course it is!' Julie said angrily. 'And our father would have been proud of her, too.'

'Why do you say that?'

'It's obvious. Dad was an actor, a showman; he loved working in the world of entertainment. I certainly haven't inherited his talent but it seems Kay has. You should be doubly proud. Unless . . .'

Thelma looked wary. 'Unless what?'

'Oh, Mum, I'm sorry. Is it too painful for you? Does all this bring back memories of Dad?'

Julie was surprised when she got a straight answer. 'Yes, it does.'

'I'm sorry. You never told me anything. You've never talked to Kay and me about the past.'

Thelma bent over and picked up the newspaper, then folded it and rose from her chair. 'Want a cup of tea, Julie, love?' she asked. Julie realised that their conversation was over. 'Or do you have to get home to make Tony's tea?'

'Tony's working late again. He says he'll eat something at the club.' Julie tried hard not to sound aggrieved. 'I thought I'd come here and have tea with you. Is that all right?'

'Of course it is.' Her mother looked pleased. 'I've got a tin of salmon. How about some sandwiches?'

'Lovely. And we can sit here by the fire and listen to Kay's play on the wireless.'

Her mother's smile vanished. 'If you want to listen to the play I'll make your sandwiches and bring them through, but if you don't mind I won't join you.' She left the room before Julie could answer her.

Thelma brought the new brass and glass tea trolley through, set with sandwiches, a home-made Victoria sponge and a pot of tea. She told Julie to make herself comfortable and left her on her own. *She could have switched the wireless on for me*, Julie thought and heaved herself clumsily to her feet.

She was just in time.

The cast was assembled in studio 6A. Holding their scripts, they sat around the microphone. As well as the performers there was a studio manager who was responsible for spot effects. He had his own script and his own microphone and a collection of props, such as a tea tray with cups and saucers so that he could produce the effects of a tea party. He was also wearing headphones so that he could take directions from the producer, Julian Fry, who was in the cubicle.

The cubicle was separated from the studio by a double-glazed panel so that Julian could observe what was happening with the cast. He was flanked by Shirley, the programme secretary, and another studio manager at the control desk who was responsible for the microphone balance. Yet another studio manager stood at two turntables to provide any music and sound effects which were on disc. And sitting quietly apart was the scriptwriter, who would be waiting anxiously to see how things went. *All in all there are nearly as many people in the cubicle as there are here in the studio*, Kay thought.

Everybody else was much more experienced than she was, and she found herself wondering if they were at all nervous. They couldn't possibly be. Looking at the actors who were to play the parts of her father, her mother, the family solicitor, the cook and a couple of villagers, she was in awe of their calm, professional manner.

Suddenly all the people in the cubicle looked as though they were concentrating. Kay knew that an announcer in a continuity suite in the sub-basement had started his introduction to the play. This would be followed by the opening music, played from a disc in the cubicle. In the studio the red light came on, and the play began.

When the closing music faded Miss Bennet sat back in her armchair and closed her eyes. She sighed with contentment. Kay had been wonderful. She had made her old schoolteacher completely believe in the character she was playing: a young woman from a privileged background who had driven an ambulance in the latter years of the war. Her fiancé had perished on D-Day, and she was now facing up to a changing world with courage and fortitude.

Thank goodness I encouraged Kay to go to London, Miss Bennet thought. *If she'd stayed here she might have wasted her life waiting for Tony Chalmers to propose to her. He was never right for her, and to give him his due I think he knew that. But I wonder if he ever regrets letting her go.*

Julie swung her legs down from the settee, where she had been lying propped up with cushions, and sprang to her feet. Then sank straight down again. She had moved too quickly, and for a moment she was overtaken with breathlessness while her head seemed to spin round. She placed one hand flat on her chest and waited for the world to right itself.

She was so excited, so overwhelmed by Kay's performance, that she wanted to run through the house to find her mother and berate her for not listening to her own daughter's triumph. For Julie, who really wasn't qualified to judge such things, nevertheless thought Kay's performance had been magnificent.

She only hoped her mother-in-law had been listening. Mrs Chalmers had promised she would, and if she had, Julie hoped she hadn't consumed too many gin and tonics. She was really looking forward to being able to talk about her talented older sister, and if her own mother would have nothing to do with it then Tony's mother would have to do.

When she felt steady enough to stand, she went through to the breakfast room, where she found her mother sitting at the table weeping her heart out.

Julie, God bless her, couldn't have been sweeter, Thelma thought. She had made tea and insisted that Thelma drink it, and refused to go home until she was sure that her mother had recovered sufficiently to be left on her own. Her younger daughter hadn't asked why she had been crying. She must have assumed that she was still upset about Kay being on the wireless. And that was partly true. What Julie didn't know was that Thelma had listened to the play after all. Only yesterday she had bought herself a small portable wireless to keep her company in the kitchen.

After leaving Julie in the sitting room with her sandwiches, she brought the wireless through to the breakfast room, put it on the table, sat down and stared at it. *Shall I listen or shan't I?* she agonised. She felt torn in two by conflicting emotions. Julie was wrong if she thought her reluctance to listen was because she didn't love Kay. It was much more than that. Soon she heard the echo of music coming from the sitting room. The play must have started. Unable to resist any longer, she switched her wireless on.

When the play was over she heard Julie coming and she switched it off and pushed it behind the curtain on the windowsill. Deeply moved, she could not bring herself to admit to Julie that she had listened to the play after all.

The red light went out. Kay glanced into the cubicle and saw that everyone was smiling. Julian Fry was shaking the scriptwriter's hand. A moment later he burst into the studio and said, 'Well done, everybody. I think this one's going to run and run.'

Shirley followed him in and came straight over to Kay. 'You were wonderful, darling!' she said.

'Darling'? Kay thought. How quickly Shirley had adopted the ways of the people she worked with. She listened to the cast congratulating each other in similar tones and wondered if it would happen to her. Suddenly she remembered her old friend, Miss Bennet, and decided that she must endeavour not to change. No matter how successful she might become, she must stay true to herself.

Shirley had moved on and Alex Walsh, the actor who played the part of Kay's father, approached her and said, 'Well done, my daughter. Your old father's proud of you.'

At this they both laughed, for Alex, whose character was

a man in his sixties, was in real life only a few years older than Kay, while Cynthia Russell, who played Kay's mother, was really old enough to be her grandmother. Everything depended on the voice. From the start Kay had been amused that the actress who played the cook with a lovely rural accent was in reality one of the most aristocratic-sounding people she had ever heard. There was so much to tell Miss Bennet, and Kay decided she must phone her as soon as she got home.

But what about her mother? Kay knew immediately that a call would not be welcome. Or Julie? Perhaps. Kay had her sister's phone number and Julie had been writing to her lately. But would she have listened to the play? Suddenly Kay felt bereft. Everyone else knew each other and they were already exchanging gossip as they prepared to leave.

'Wake up, Kay!' Shirley stood before her.

'Wake up?'

'You were miles away. I would have said you were thinking about your triumph except you looked so bloody miserable. What's wrong?'

Kay took a deep breath and dragged up a smile. She didn't want to tell Shirley that she desperately wanted someone to share her feelings with, because she didn't want to appear to be sorry for herself. However, what she did say was true enough. 'There's nothing wrong, it's just that I feel a bit deflated. While I was acting I was in a different world, and I was someone else entirely. It was exciting. Now it's over and I'm back down to earth.'

'Oh, of course. That's natural. I've learned it's the same for most of them.' Shirley waved a hand in the direction of the cast. 'You'll get used to it.'

'Anyone coming over to the club for a drink?' Julian said, and everyone said they would.

'Do you want to join them?' Shirley asked.

'I'm not sure.'

'Well, if you do, I'll take you over; it's only in the Langham. But first I want you to come with me back to the office. I sneaked a friend in there who bunked off work to listen to the play. Must go and turn the wireless off and tidy up, you know. Then we could all go to the club together.'

'But why?'

'Why what?'

'Why did your friend particularly want to listen to the play?'

Shirley made an airy gesture. 'Oh, you know. My interesting job. What I get up to. That sort of thing.'

Kay followed Shirley along carpeted corridors to Julian's office. She wondered if Julian knew about Shirley's friend.

'Here we are then.'

Shirley opened the door and preceded her into the room. Her friend was standing by the window looking out over the rooftops of London. He turned round slowly. Why had she thought Shirley's friend would be female?

'You were wonderful,' Tom said, and he took her in his arms.

At that moment Kay realised that the only person she wanted to share her triumph with was Tom.

Chapter Sixteen

Then

The play was over. Lana and the leading man remained in each other's arms as the curtains closed. Then they pulled apart and listened, breath held, to the frightening silence from the auditorium.

Lana looked at Don Bellamy nervously. 'Have I laid an egg?' she whispered. 'Have I ruined things for all of you?'

He shook his head but Lana could see the panic in his eyes. He managed a smile before he whispered, 'Wait and see.'

All this took mere seconds, but they were the longest seconds in Lana's life. Don had no sooner squeezed Lana's hand reassuringly than thunderous applause could be heard from the auditorium.

'They were simply holding their breath,' Don said, and laughing softly, he picked Lana up and twirled her round, setting her down again just as the curtains swished open and the other members of the cast came to join them on the stage.

The house lights came up and Lana looked out at the audience with tears in her eyes. Tears of joy.

'The audience are on their feet,' Don said. 'It's a standing ovation!'

Everyone took a bow and then the curtains closed, but the applause continued and they opened again. Lana lost track of the times this happened, but the shouts of 'Encore!' continued until all the other members of the cast had left the stage again and only she and Don were left taking bow after bow.

Finally the stage manager made a decision and the curtains remained closed. The audience groaned good-naturedly, and as the fire curtain was lowered they began to leave the theatre, talking to each other animatedly.

'Well done, darling,' Don said. 'I think we're headed for the West End.' He pulled her towards him and kissed her forehead, then he hurried off to join the others backstage.

Lana remained where she was, and just before vanishing into the wings, Don turned and called for her. 'Come along, Lana, enjoy your triumph.'

'All right,' she replied but she was reluctant to move. She stood centre stage and looked around at the set – the drawing room of a comfortable middle-class house. She walked over to the sofa and sat down. Then she sank back and closed her eyes. She felt as though her world was spinning. Tonight she had become part of the legitimate theatre. She had appeared in her first play. Not just appeared, she had taken the female lead. Monty had been sure she could do it and it seemed that he had been proved right. That was, if the audience's reaction was anything to go by.

The stage lights dimmed and Lana could hear the excited voices of the cast congratulating each other. *I ought to join them*, she thought, but suddenly her limbs could not support her. A strange lethargy overtook her and she let her mind float free as she began to relive certain moments of the play. She heard herself saying her lines, saw herself moving about the stage confidently. She heard the audience laughing when they were supposed to and their gasp of surprise when something unexpected happened.

She was reliving the performance all over again and she didn't want to leave the magical world that she and the others had created for all too short a time.

Then a voice brought her back to the real world. 'There you are,' someone said, and Lana opened her eyes and looked up at the shadowy figure standing over her. Her eyes adjusted to the light and she saw that it was Moira.

'Thank you for leaving my name with the stage door-keeper,' her friend said.

Lana didn't answer. She just smiled up at her friend beatifically.

'You were marvellous,' Moira said. 'I don't know why you ever thought you couldn't do it.'

'It was because this is my first straight play. No singing, no dancing. Just spoken drama. And I was so inexperienced compared with the others. Totally untested, in fact. And they all knew each other. I thought they resented me at first – they were worried that an unknown beginner would ruin their chances of success. The atmosphere thawed a little once we got into rehearsals, but I was still very much the new girl at school.'

'And tonight you've proved that you have every right to be here. And it's happened so quickly for you. But you know, when we first met less than two years ago, I knew straight away that not only would you soon be top of the bill, but that you'd leave the variety theatre altogether. You're perfect for stage drama, and maybe even films. You have such a lovely speaking voice. Lana, my love, you'll soon be moving in a very different theatrical world than I do.'

Lana reached up and took Moira's hand. She pulled her down to sit beside her and said, 'But whatever happens, we'll still be friends, won't we? We'll still be able to confide in each other when nobody else would do?'

'I hope so,' Moira said fervently. 'After all, we've had a lot of fun together, haven't we?'

'We certainly have. Through happy times and sad times. Times when we could afford to eat in fashionable restaurants and times when we were down to our last tin of spaghetti.'

A voice from the wings shouted, 'Lana, come and join us! The champagne's flowing!'

'You'd better go and mingle with the others,' Moira said. 'You don't want them to think that tonight's triumph has gone to your head, do you? Why are you sitting here instead of joining the party anyway?'

'I just wanted to wait until I connected with the real world again.'

'And have you connected yet?'

Lana laughed as she got to her feet. 'I'm not sure, but you're right – I should go and join them. Coming with me?'

Moira's eyes widened. 'You bet. And I'd like you to introduce me to Don Bellamy.'

'Will do. But I'm afraid he's spoken for. Very happily married to a rich society girl, in fact, and she's here to keep an eye on him.' Lana pulled Moira to her feet. 'I'm so glad you came,' she said.

'As if I'd have missed it.'

Lana smiled, but she could not meet her friend's eyes. She had spoken truthfully when she'd said that she was glad Moira had come tonight, but nevertheless there was someone else who she wished fervently could have been here. Jack. Without Jack to share her triumph, tonight's success was strangely hollow.

The bundles of newspapers had just arrived on the Newcastle train. Jack waited impatiently by the newsstand in the station until they had been sorted and spread out on the counter. Early travellers were already queuing at the ticket office and then hurrying over to buy their usual paper to read on the way to work.

Jack didn't have a usual paper. Thelma liked the local rag, as Jack called it, but unless there was something in it about the Pavilion he found it incredibly boring. This morning he chose a selection of the national newspapers, paid for them and hurried down through the town to the theatre.

There was a sea fret, and mist swirled mysteriously on the lower promenade. Jack's muffled footsteps echoed dully on the glistening paving stones. He let himself in through the stage door, and as soon as he reached his office he put the kettle on the gas ring and switched on the two-bar electric fire.

He made a mug of tea and stirred a spoonful of condensed milk into it. Then he sat staring at the newspapers he had placed on his desk. Last night had been the opening night of *Reluctant Lovers*, Lana's first straight play. He had wanted to be there but could not come up with a good enough excuse. Very occasionally he managed trips to London on theatre business, and he would see Lana. But this time there was nothing to take him there and he knew instinctively that if he invented something, Thelma would know he was lying.

He reached for the newspaper on top of the pile, *The Times*, and turned the pages, examining every inch. There was nothing. He hadn't really expected there to be. It was the same with the *Telegraph*. He must have been crazy to think that the old established broadsheets would bother to send anyone along to review an out-of-town play.

The *Sketch* was full of the doings of high society, as usual, and the *Daily Herald* took itself too seriously to bother with a new play when there was trade union business to report on. He was left with two papers. The *Daily Mirror* – nothing.

Then, finally, the *Express*. And there it was. Jack held his breath when he saw the heading: 'A STAR IS BORN!' He let his breath out slowly and began to read.

Last night an unknown actress trod the boards of the King's Theatre in Wimbledon and, as well as stealing everyone's hearts, won a standing ovation. The play itself, *Reluctant Lovers,* is a drawing-room comedy of the sort which is meant to cheer us up in these hard-pressed times. It is amusing enough, but without the two leading players, Don Bellamy and Lana Fontaine, it would be very ordinary.

Don Bellamy is something of a heart-throb, but as well as being good-looking, he has oodles of stage presence and is a master of timing. I wonder what he thought when he was told that an inexperienced actress, who it is rumoured has a background in Variety, was going to play opposite him. If he had any doubts he needn't have done. She is magnificent.

Lana Fontaine is beautiful and talented and has the most attractive speaking voice. Her timing is at least as skilful as Don Bellamy's. The way they played off each other enthused the rest of a lively and competent cast and lifted this little play to the ranks of a masterpiece. It will surely be going to the West End, where I predict we will see much more of Lana Fontaine.

Jack clipped the piece from the paper and put it in the top drawer of his desk, where he kept Lana's letters. She sent them to the theatre. Perhaps he would start a scrapbook to record her career. Perhaps he wouldn't. As Lana's fame grew it might prove to be too painful. He was glad for her, of course. She was well on the way to achieving her dreams.

But what were his dreams? Jack asked himself. He was

happy enough here at the Pavilion. He didn't think he'd ever believed he would be more than a provincial entertainer. He was king of the seaside follies. He had Thelma whom he had betrayed. She didn't deserve that. Her pretty face no longer shone with happiness and there were silver streaks in her lovely hair. She had allowed herself to put weight on; she was no longer the slender girl he had married. No matter what pain it cost her, she was a good mother to Kay, Lana's daughter, who brought him joy every time he looked at her. Joy and pain, because he couldn't be with his daughter's mother.

Jack sighed, gathered up the newspapers and put them in the wastepaper basket. He had told Thelma that he was going to the theatre early to work on some improvements while it was quiet. He could hardly have taken the newspapers home. Now he would go back to play the part of the family man.

Thelma was barely awake when Jack had slid out of bed and got dressed. He had moved around the room quietly so as not to awaken Kay. His daughter was sleeping in the cot which was pushed against the fireplace wall. Jack had blocked off the hearth to stop the draughts harming the baby. The bedroom they slept in was too small, but the other bedrooms were occupied by lodgers, all of them performers at the Pavilion.

Jack leaned over and kissed Thelma before he left. 'I'll be about an hour,' he said. 'I'll be back to help you with the breakfasts.'

The show this year hadn't been going too well, and Jack had told Thelma that he wanted to go to the theatre while it was quiet and work out some new routines. She had no reason to disbelieve him. And no matter how busy he was, she knew he would keep his promise and come back in time to help her.

Since Kay was born Jack had taken over as breakfast cook. No one else knew this, as it would hardly be appropriate for the show's director and star performer to wait on tables for his troupe of entertainers. Thelma had not had to ask him to help her. Since the advent of his baby daughter he had gone out of his way to try and make life easier for her. She supposed it was gratitude, and she didn't mind exploiting it now and then. But she would never have gone too far, for the truth was she loved him as desperately as the day she had first set eyes on him, and she lived in perpetual terror that one day he might leave her.

After breakfast Eileen, the young maid, arrived to clean and make beds as well as help Thelma to prepare the meals. For the past month or so, after she had washed the lunch dishes, she had taken Kay out in her pushchair while Thelma snatched a rest in bed.

When Thelma heard Jack close the front door behind him she got up and crept over to the little cot. Kay was still sleeping. She looked down at her as she did each morning and tried to convince herself that the little girl looked like her father. She had Jack's dark hair, but her eyes were blue whereas Jack's eyes were brown.

'She's got your lovely blue eyes, Mrs Lockwood,' Eileen had told her. 'And with those dark curls she's going to be a real beauty.'

Thelma had almost cried out in distress. She knew that whenever the child looked at her in years to come, she would be reminded of another pair of eyes. The dark-fringed, beautiful eyes of a woman who had looked at Jack and decided to make him her own. And as the child grew, the resemblance might become stronger. In moments of despair Thelma asked herself how she would cope, and also why on earth she had agreed to take the baby in the first place. The answer to that was because Jack had asked her to, and she loved him so much that she would do anything to please him.

Also, she had come to believe that she was going to remain childless, but if she brought up Jack's baby it would make them into a proper family. Jack's loyalty would not be divided between two households. He adored his daughter. He loved being a father. Maybe it was the actor in him, but he treated Thelma as if she really were Kay's mother.

The child opened her eyes and looked unseeingly around her. Then she focused on Thelma and smiled. She was an easy baby who gurgled with laughter when Jack took her in his arms. She took her bottle and slept when she should. There had been very few sleepless nights.

Before Thelma reached down to pick Kay up, she gripped the rail of the cot and closed her eyes. She had waited because she could not be sure of Jack's reaction. He loved this child so much. Did he have room in his heart for another one? However, she didn't think she could disguise her condition for much longer. Tonight she would tell Jack that they would no longer be able to manage in this tiny room. Something wonderful had happened. A small miracle. Very soon they would be a real family. There would be no more pretence. She would have a child of her own. She prayed that he would be as delighted as she was.

Now

Tom thought Shirley looked more excited than Kay did. In fact, Kay looked rather preoccupied. He guessed that she might be trying to come to terms with her undoubted success in the radio play. He saw how she had to drag herself back from whichever world she had been inhabiting when Shirley took her arm and said, 'Kay, have you been listening to me?'

'Um . . . sorry, what did you say?'

The two girls smiled at each other and Tom thought how lucky they were to have such a sincere friendship. Kay was talented but still a newcomer to the world she now found herself in. Happily Shirley would be there to guide her.

Shirley had suggested that they go over to the BBC club. 'We'll have a drink and we'll make sure you have a chat and a smile with as many of them as possible. It's already obvious that you're going to be the star of this show, so you don't want to give the impression that you're big-headed and stand-offish, do you? You've got to cultivate an image.'

Kay was bemused. 'An image?'

'You know what I mean.'

'Yes, I think I do, but you know, Shirley, I would find it very hard to be anyone but myself.'

Shirley frowned, but Tom was drawn to Kay all the more for her unpretentious and candid nature.

'People change, you know,' Shirley said anxiously.

'What do you mean?'

'Success changes you. It happens to the nicest people.'

Kay smiled. 'I promise you I'll make every effort not to let that happen to me. I won't change.'

Shirley's frown disappeared and she gave Kay a hug. 'Of course you won't. Now let's go to the club.'

'Wait a moment,' Kay said. 'Tom and I aren't members.'

'That's all right. I'll sign you in, but you know, if you're going to become a member of the BBC Repertory Company you'll be able to join the club yourself.'

'Am I? What's the Repertory Company?'

'So Julian hasn't mentioned it yet? The Rep is a bunch of actors who are always on call. They're an interesting lot; several of them are survivors of the group that dodged the air raids during the war by camping out in the concert hall at

Broadcasting House. They couldn't afford to have programmes like *Paul Temple* or *The Man in Black* delayed by an
air-raid siren. And another thing, do you think you ought to
get an agent?'

Momentarily thrown by Shirley's lightning change of
subject, Kay paused to think before asking, 'Do you think I
need one?'

'I think you do. After all, you're going to be in demand.
And I think you should start keeping a scrapbook.'

'What do you mean?'

'You know – for newspaper cuttings.'

'Shirley, I haven't a clue what you're talking about.'

'It will be a sort of portfolio for you. Every time you're
mentioned in the newspapers or a magazine we'll clip it and
put it in the scrapbook. And of course we'll keep a record of
when you're mentioned in the *Radio Times*. And your agent
will want some good photographs of you for publicity.'

'Shirley, stop! My head's spinning. I promise you we'll
talk about this later, but now, why don't you take us over to
the Langham for this drink you've promised us?'

Shirley smiled. 'Righto. Is that OK with you, Tom? Will
it interfere with your plans?'

'No, we've plenty of time. I booked a table at Veeraswamy's
for seven o'clock. It's only a short walk down Regent Street.
Or I could hail a taxi and we could arrive in style.'

'Good,' Shirley said. 'Kay and I will have time to freshen
up in the cloakroom at the club.'

Kay looked bemused. 'What are you two talking about?'

'I thought we should celebrate,' Tom said. 'I hope you
like Indian food.'

'I've never had any,' Kay said.

Tom grinned. 'I'll start you off on something fairly mild,
but in time I hope you'll come to appreciate Indian cuisine
as much as I do. By the way, Shirley, did you phone Jane?'

'I did. She doesn't want to join us. She said she was tired and wanted an early night, although I can't imagine what she has done to make her tired – except go shopping, of course.'

That's a pity, Tom thought. *Someone else will have to stay on duty longer than I planned. I can hardly back out of the restaurant treat now. I'll have to make a phone call – there's bound to be a public phone at the club.* He wondered whether he would be able to claim the cost of tonight's jaunt on expenses and immediately felt ashamed of himself for making light of the situation.

He'd had an incredible stroke of luck when he'd observed Kay's difficulties with the Christmas tree. It had got him into the house. But that was months ago, and the trouble was that as the investigation dragged on, he had got closer and closer to Kay. He had not expected to fall in love, and the more he loved her, the guiltier he felt.

Kay had enjoyed the Indian food but the menu had left her bewildered. Even Shirley had to admit that she was baffled. Tom took over and ordered a meal that he said would introduce them gently to the dishes on offer. Kay and Shirley had been delighted with the exotic flavours, and while they were enjoying their meal, Tom had told them a little of the history of the fashionable restaurant.

Veeraswamy's had been opened in 1926 by the great-grandson of an English General and an Indian princess. It became popular with the rich and famous: kings and princes, actors and film stars.

'Really?' Shirley asked him. 'Do you think there's anyone famous here tonight?'

'There most certainly is.'

'Who? Where?' Shirley glanced round excitedly.

Tom laughed. 'Right here at our own table.'

Shirley frowned and then her face cleared and she laughed. 'Of course. Our very own star. Kay Lockwood.'

They had all enjoyed the meal and Tom had insisted on a taxi to take them home. He had come in for a cup of tea – it was his opinion that coffee didn't go with curry – but he had not lingered. Shirley had wanted to talk, but Kay had pleaded exhaustion and gone to bed. She had a lot to think about.

She had seen the menu at the restaurant and thought the prices a little high. When she said so, Tom had smiled and told her that he only came here as an occasional treat. Now, lying sleepless, Kay wondered whether he dined there alone or whether he took someone with him. She could hardly have asked him.

And then there was Shirley's idea of keeping a scrapbook. Kay thought about it and accepted that it was a good idea, but apart from publicity shots she wouldn't need many photographs. Not like Lana. Her godmother had kept enough photographs to fill half a dozen albums. Shirley had sorted them out for her – she must wonder why Kay had put them away and apparently never looked at them since. Kay had flicked through them alone in her room. There had been an envelope inside one of them containing one photograph . . .

She knew that for her peace of mind she should leave things be, but she couldn't help herself. She sat up in bed, switched on the bedside light and leaned across to open the drawer in her bedside table. She picked up the envelope and opened it. She sat perfectly still for a moment then took out the photograph. She forced herself to look at it. A cheerful snapshot taken by a street photographer. Two happy people smiling at each other. An everyday sort of holiday shot, and yet it told her so much more.

She ought to have been prepared for her reaction. It was always the same. She found herself shaking with anger at the story the picture told. The questions it answered. And yet she couldn't bring herself to tear it up.

Her peace of mind torn apart by conflicting emotions, she thrust it back in the envelope and pushed the envelope to the back of the drawer. Then pushed the very thought of it to the back of her mind.

Then

Lana and Moira didn't make the curfew. They got back to their lodgings at one in the morning. True to form, Mrs O'Brien appeared in the doorway of her room.

'What time do you think this is?' she demanded. 'Been up West, have you?'

'Actually, no,' Lana said. She drew herself up to her full height and smiled down on the angry little woman. 'We've been to Wimbledon.'

Moira suppressed a giggle at the conflicting emotions displayed on their landlady's pugnacious face. Nobody had ever stood up to her before, and she was both astounded and angry. But also puzzled.

'Wimbledon?' she asked. 'What have you been doing there?'

'Miss Fontaine has been taking the lead in a stage play,' Moira told her.

'Oh yeah? *Miss* Fontaine isn't an actress. She's a chorus girl like you are.'

'As a matter of fact, she's not a chorus girl,' Moira said. 'She's a solo song and dance act. At least she was until tonight. Here you are. See for yourself.'

Moira handed over an early edition of the *Express*. During the party the stage manager had gone out and bought all the papers, several copies of each, and Moira had made sure to bring the relevant paper home. She watched while their landlady squinted down at the play review.

'So this is really you?' she asked, looking up at Lana.

'Unless there's another young woman with the same name, it is,' Lana replied.

'Well,' Mrs O'Brien said. 'Who would have thought you had it in you?'

Lana, who still hadn't come properly back down to earth, decided not to take offence. 'Thank you for the compliment,' she said sweetly. 'And while you're here, I wonder if we could discuss my renting the empty room next to mine?'

'Why would you want to do that? It's not half as nice as your room.'

'Oh, I don't want to move from my room. I want to rent both of them.'

Mrs O'Brien shook her head. 'I don't understand.'

Lana smiled condescendingly. 'Well, you see, now that I'm going to be famous, I'll need somewhere to make into a sort of dressing room. Somewhere to keep all my new clothes.'

Their landlady looked doubtful, but she didn't want to miss the chance of letting the room without having to advertise it. 'All right,' she said, 'but I'll have to put the rent up.'

Lana didn't ask why. She and Moira fled upstairs, managing to hold in their laughter until they reached the makeshift kitchen on the first-floor landing.

'Hungry?' Lana asked.

'Starving.'

'How about spaghetti on toast?'

'Perfect,' Moira said. 'A perfect way to celebrate your success.'

Chapter Seventeen

September 1950

'Are you on your own?'

'Of course I am. Kay's boyfriend is taking her and Shirley to some fashionable restaurant to celebrate Kay's new part on the wireless. He invited me, but I told him I wanted an early night. And you needn't keep asking if I'm alone when I phone you. There's no need – I'm not stupid.'

'You should stick to the phone box.'

'I've told you, the house is empty. No one will know.'

Jane thought uneasily of the times she had almost been caught using the phone. When she had heard a key in the lock she had said goodbye, put the receiver down and moved away quickly, trying to make it look as though she had just come downstairs. She hoped she had fooled them.

Maurice wasn't convinced. 'When the phone bill comes in they'll see you've been making calls. They can trace them.'

'Why would they want to?'

'I mean the police could trace them.'

'Why on earth would they? As far as anyone is concerned I'm just a lodger in Kay Lockwood's house.'

'So if Kay asks you who you've been phoning, what will you say?'

'She wouldn't do that. She's too well mannered. But in any case I'll think of something.'

'It had better be convincing.'

'I told them my father threw me out. I'll say I've been phoning my brother to get him to patch things up.'

'Have you told the girls that you've got a brother?'

'I can't remember. I might have done when I was staying at Brook Lodge.'

'If you're not careful you'll trip up over your lies. Just stick to the phone box in future.'

Jane suddenly felt rebellious. 'Well, you know what the answer to all this is, don't you?'

'Tell me.'

'You have to make sure that you find a fence and get rid of the goods before the phone bill comes in.' Jane didn't usually answer him back but to her surprise he laughed. 'What have I said?' she asked.

'*Find a fence and get rid of the goods.* You sound like a gangster's moll in a B movie.'

Jane found herself shouting. 'That's just what I am, isn't it? You're a gangster. So I must be your moll!'

Maurice sounded worried. 'Don't talk like that, baby. I shouldn't have said that. You're my wife and I love you. And I can't wait until we can be together again. You mustn't lose your nerve. It won't be much longer.'

'Well, why don't you tell me where you are?'

'I can't do that. The person who's helping me told me not to, and he's not the sort of bloke you can cross.'

'So, how will I know where to find you?'

'I'll tell you what to do when the time comes. But listen, why don't you have a bag packed so you can make a quick getaway?'

'Just one bag?'

'We'll have to travel light.'

Jane sighed. 'I'll have to leave some of my clothes behind.'

'You haven't got that many clothes, have you? I told you to buy only what was necessary.'

'I know, but it will still be hard to choose.'

Maurice laughed. 'That's my girl. Just think, it won't be long before you'll be able to buy anything you want. Maybe even in Paris. Now we'd better hang up.'

Maurice cut the connection and reluctantly Jane put the phone down. She went into the kitchen to make a cup of tea. She wasn't hungry. She was too overwrought to eat. She had lied to Maurice, or at least she hadn't told him the full truth. When they had parted he had given her a bundle of notes to keep her going and told her to get herself some clothes – not too flashy, she mustn't draw attention to herself.

She had done that, but what he didn't know was that she already had a considerable amount of money of her own. On the night of the fire, when Maurice had been examining the bedside drawer in the old girl's bedroom, she had opened a drawer and seen a bulging handkerchief case. She had looked inside and found that it was full of money. Some instinct had made her stuff the notes down the neck of her dress.

She still didn't know why she had done this. Perhaps it was because, much as she loved him, she had never trusted Maurice entirely. Even then it had crossed her mind that he might take the jewels and abandon her. This money would be her nest egg. It would take care of her just in case she had to fend for herself.

The trouble was, she had never had so much money in her life and she craved luxury. So she went shopping. With nothing else to do to fill her days, she bought clothes and jewels without any thought of how she was going to explain them to Maurice.

As she sipped her tea she realised that she would have to leave the most fashionable clothes behind. But she would take the jewellery. Most of it was paste, and Maurice would recognise it as such. The one or two genuine articles she would have to hide from him – just in case of a rainy day.

Maurice replaced the receiver and sat back frowning. As far as he knew, they were going to get away with it. But Jane was getting edgy and there was no knowing what she might do. In her present mood she could make careless mistakes. He hoped he wasn't going to have a problem with her.

On the way to London they had abandoned the car and caught the train. That first night in London they had stayed in a cheap lodging house near King's Cross. When Maurice had signed the book he'd given her the new name of Jane. The next morning he had said he was going to see an old friend who owed him a favour, but he didn't say who it was or where he would find him. He'd told her to wait there and stay in their room. Jane had been tired and frightened, and still overwhelmed by what had happened. She hadn't argued with him. Neither of them had imagined that getting rid of the jewellery was not going to be easy.

Kostas was an old friend from Maurice's army days. He owned a restaurant in Soho, but that was just a front. Maurice knew that the man who had been a fearless private soldier during the war had returned to his previous way of life and was a force to be feared by the rest of the criminal fraternity.

He took Maurice to a sparsely furnished room on the third floor – and then dashed his hopes. He wouldn't touch Maurice's hoard. He looked at the jewellery and shook his head. 'Too hot, my friend,' he said. 'Your victim is bound to have listed them in her will. If I took them from you they'd have to disappear for a year or two. Maybe longer. You'll have to find someone who can afford to wait.'

'Who's to say the jewellery didn't burn with the house?'

'Look at it. This old-fashioned stuff could only have belonged to an old woman. If these items suddenly appeared on the market someone would be bound to put two and two together.'

'What the hell am I going to do?'

'Don't worry. I'll find you someone. Maybe one of the Maltese brothers can afford to invest in them. I'll do this for you because you saved my life at El Alamein, but then we'll be quits, and I never want to see you again.

'Meanwhile I'll find you somewhere to stay – a nice little flat in one of my properties. It's fully furnished and I'll stock it up with food and drink, good stuff, from the kitchen downstairs. All you'll have to do is heat it up, and if this goes on for too long someone will bring you more after the restaurant closes at midnight. You can't go out. And the jewels stay with me. That way you won't be tempted to go off and try to make it on your own.'

'Wouldn't that save you a lot of bother?'

'Maybe so, but it would deprive me of my cut.'

'You're taking a cut?'

'Of course. What did you expect?'

Maurice was silent. He knew how foolish it had been to think that Kostas would help him just for old times' sake.

His old army buddy continued. 'Did you tell the girl where you were coming today?'

'Not a word.'

'My name?'

'There was no need for her to know.'

'Good. She can't stay with you. She knows nothing about me, and that's the way it's going to stay.'

'Where can she go?'

'Get tonight's paper. Look for an anonymous small hotel somewhere far enough away from here. Somewhere boring. Will she do as she's told?'

'Yes. No problem.'

'You'd better be right. If she causes trouble I'll have to deal with her.'

At Kostas's words, Maurice knew what it meant to say your blood ran cold. 'She won't cause trouble,' he said.

'Can't you just ditch her?' Kostas asked.

'No.'

'Sentimental reasons?' Kostas sneered.

'Something like that.'

'You've gone soft, Maurice. I hope you don't regret this. Convince her that it's best for you to split up. Remind her that they're looking for a man and a woman, and if they find you they'll hang the pair of you and I won't help you. Give her enough cash to keep her happy, and before you say goodnight take her here.' Kostas gave him a business card.

Maurice looked at it. 'A photographer?'

'Say I sent you. He'll take your photographs and make you some passports.'

'Passports?'

'I'm assuming that you won't want to stay in good old Blighty?'

'Too right. I wasn't thinking straight.'

'He'll send the passports to me. Tell your girl you'll get in touch with her when it's time to scarper. Then come back here. Alone.'

Even though Kostas had said he would help because Maurice had saved his life, he had been completely unsentimental. Maurice had agreed to do everything he was told – and he did until Jane had strayed from the plan.

The silly bitch had made friends with Shirley, a young woman staying at Brook Lodge, and she had decided to move in with her and another girl who had a house nearby. He remembered their heated conversation.

'For God's sake, why do that?' he'd said.

'Because I'm lonely,' she'd replied. 'And that's your fault.'

'Don't do it, Jane. You know I told you to lay low.'

'You didn't tell me how long it would be.'

'I'm doing my best, and meanwhile it's safer to stay where you are.'

'And spend whole days on my own!'

'That's right. You shouldn't get too close to anyone.'

'I don't care what you say, Maurice, I'm going to move in with Kay and Shirley.'

Jane sounded as if she was on the edge of hysteria, and if she fell to pieces it could be dangerous for both of them. He gave in. 'Give me the phone number.'

'I don't know if there's a phone. Apparently the house has been empty. You'll have to stop being so secretive and give me your number.'

'I can't do that.'

Kostas had been reluctant, but he had given him permission to use the phone to keep in touch with Jane. The girl was a loose cannon, and who knew what she might do if she lost patience with the situation. But he had forbidden him to give Jane the number, and Maurice had agreed.

'Would they know if I phoned you?' Jane asked.

Maurice paused. Kostas phoned him now and then to tell him what progress he was making, but apart from that, he had been left severely alone. Apart from the bloke who brought him food and drink in the early hours of the morning, no one came to the third-floor flat. The other flats were empty.

He wondered what he should do. He didn't know whether he believed Jane when she said she didn't know if there was a phone in the house. Maybe this was a way for her to exert some power over him. Whatever the case, it was obvious that she was not going to budge.

'All right,' he said at last. He'd given her the number and had told her not to let anyone else have it.'

'As if I would,' Jane had said. 'Do you think I'm stupid?'

Maurice had never thought Jane was stupid. He'd never thought her beautiful either. She certainly wasn't plain, but she would never stand out in a crowd. She was entirely different from the sort of boldly dressed woman he usually went out with. He'd been drawn to women who were attractive in a flashy sort of way, demanding, spoilt, and, let's face it, more than a little common.

Jane was different. Jane – or Irene, as she had been called when they first met – worked in a café near the station. Maurice had just got off the train and headed straight there, having left the place where he had been staying that morning then making for a town where he had a few useful contacts. He'd left in a hurry and hadn't had time to eat. In spite of feeling crumpled after an uncomfortable journey in a crowded train, he knew he was good-looking, and he smiled to himself when, out of the corner of his eye, he saw female heads turn as he walked to the back of the room, but he kept his own head down.

The table he chose was near the swing door that led to the kitchen, and the smell of frying surrounded him, but Maurice didn't want to sit near the window or anywhere where he would be in full view of passers-by. You never knew who you were going to bump into in these unsettled times after the war, when society still seemed topsy-turvy and it was easy to make a dishonest living if you kept moving on.

The menu, stained with tomato sauce, was propped up between the vinegar and a bowl of sugar.

Maurice studied it. The food on offer was fairly basic, and when the waitress came over with her notepad and pencil he ordered double egg and chips with black pudding, a couple of slices of bread and butter and a pot of tea. All for half a crown.

She looked at him curiously, called him 'Sir' and seemed to come back with his order in next to no time. Later, when she brought the bill, he gave her a bigger than usual tip – a whole shilling, in fact. He didn't understand why, but he found himself drawn to her. Perhaps it was because of her quiet efficiency, or perhaps it was because from the very start she looked at him with open adoration.

Everything seemed to develop at breakneck speed. He got into the habit of dropping in to the café for his midday meal, and then, one day when he had been particularly busy chasing up a consignment of black market tea, he didn't get there until almost closing time. By the time he'd finished his meal, he was the only customer left and the young waitress had finished wiping down the other tables. It seemed the natural thing to do to wait for her outside, and to his own amazement he asked her to go to the pictures.

After that she became his regular date. He was fond of her. She adored him, but nevertheless she hung on to her virginity until he put a wedding ring on her finger. By then he'd realised she knew a little too much about him, so he'd given in and bought the ring. They got married at the registry office with two passers-by acting as witnesses.

The girl had no family, which was just as well. Concerned parents might have asked awkward questions – might even have discovered that he was already married. His conscience was easy about that. He hadn't seen Joan since before the war, not that she would care, and she might even have perished in a bombing raid. It was easy to forget that they had once been man and wife.

He often wondered why his new wife was so willing to adopt his dishonest way of life. He decided that it was partly because she loved him, but also, after years of boring work in the café, that she enjoyed the excitement of it. At heart she was as dishonest as he was.

He knew Kostas had been right to suggest that he dump her, and he hadn't been altogether honest when he had let his old pal believe that he loved her. Perhaps he did. But not as much as wanting to save his own skin. He was stuck with her. She was growing more and more agitated, and in her present state there was no knowing what she might do. She had his phone number, and she might even help the cops to find him.

He had told her that if they were caught they would both hang. But this wouldn't be the case if she turned King's evidence. She could tell them everything they wanted to know in return for a lenient sentence. She could also claim that she only acted as she did because her husband had forced her to. He knew he only had to say the word and Kostas would 'deal with her'. As yet it hadn't come to that.

Chapter Eighteen

'So you haven't told her yet?'

Moira was filing some papers. She pushed the drawer shut and turned round, waiting for Shirley's answer.

'No. I thought we decided to leave well alone.'

'Did we? I don't think we decided anything. Or maybe I hoped that, since you are her friend, you would make the decision.'

'And I hoped that since you were Lana's friend and you've known the truth all along . . .'

They stared at each other for a moment and then Moira changed the subject abruptly. 'Are you staying long enough for a cup of tea?'

'I wouldn't mind. Shall I fill the kettle?'

'Not here. I've had enough of this place for today. I'll lock up and we'll go upstairs to my flat.'

Shirley was surprised. She had got into the habit of dropping in to the solicitor's office to see Moira now and then, not just because they were worried about Kay, but also because a friendship had grown between them. Both of them were efficient secretaries, and even though Moira Davies was old enough to be Shirley's mother, they got on well together. But she had never been invited up to Moira's flat before.

She followed Moira up the lino-covered staircase, where the smell of polish mingled with the tempting aromas coming from the shop on the ground floor. Then she waited on the tiny landing while her hostess fished her keys out of her handbag.

'I always lock up,' Moira said over her shoulder. 'It's unlikely that anyone would venture up here, but there are some dubious characters around these days.'

Moira opened the door and Shirley followed her in, then stopped and looked around her. 'This is lovely!' she said.

There was no hallway. The door opened straight into the living-cum-dining room, which was a total contrast to the austere office below. The walls were a neutral beige, the curtains slightly darker; the rust-coloured sofa and armchairs were of the latest Danish design and were scattered with cushions in bright primary colours. A large rug had geometric patterns in the same colours. The whole effect was cheerfully fashionable.

Moira saw Shirley's surprised expression and smiled at her. 'What were you expecting? An old maid's bower? All flowers and chintz?'

Shirley shook her head. 'I'm not sure what I expected.'

'Or perhaps stippled walls and utility furniture, suitable for the unremarkable life I lead?'

'I imagined no such thing.'

'Why don't you sit down?' Moira said. 'And if you're not in a hurry, I can do better than a cup of tea.'

Without waiting for an answer, she dumped her handbag on one of the chairs, opened a door and walked through into what looked like a kitchen.

'Can I help?' Shirley asked.

'No, that's all right.'

A moment later Moira reappeared, carrying a bottle of red wine and two glasses. 'Are you expected home for an evening meal with Kay and Jane?' she asked.

'No. Kay is going out with Tom, and Jane has usually had something to eat by the time Kay and I get home.'

'Why doesn't she wait and eat with you?'

'She used to, but she's kept herself to herself lately. I can't say exactly why, but she seems to be anxious about something.'

'Perhaps she's fretting. After all, she has a tragic past, hasn't she?'

'I suppose so,' Shirley said, but she didn't sound convinced.

'So won't you stay and eat with me?'

'I'd love to. I shouldn't say this, but being in the house with Jane at the moment makes me nervous. It's as if she's waiting for something to happen.'

'What kind of thing?'

'I have no idea, but whatever it is isn't good.'

'What does Kay think about it?'

'I don't think she's noticed. I mean, she's so taken up with her new job. And Tom, of course.'

'Ah, Tom. Do you think that's serious?'

'On Kay's part, yes.'

'But not Tom's?'

'He seems keen, but sometimes I get the impression that he's holding something back.'

'Perhaps he's just being cautious,' Moira said. 'After all, it happened very suddenly. One day he helps her home with the Christmas tree and the next day he becomes a regular caller. He's older than Kay and he's been through the war. He'll want to be absolutely certain of the relationship.'

'You're probably right.'

'I am. And now let's eat.'

Moira vanished into the kitchen and soon the table was laid with a selection of cheeses, pâté and crusty rolls.

'It's handy having the shop downstairs,' she said. 'It means I'm never caught out if . . . if visitors call.' Then, 'Oh, the hell with it,' she said suddenly. 'You've probably guessed that the only visitor who's likely to call after the day's work is done is Charles.'

'Charles?'

'My boss. Charles Butler.'

'No, I hadn't guessed that,' Shirley said. 'In fact – please don't laugh – Kay and I wondered if Mr Butler even existed. Whenever we call, the door to his office is shut, and so it remains.'

Moira laughed. 'I can assure you he exists, but he comes to the office less and less these days. He's taking on less work, and much of what he does take on he leaves to me. He wants to retire, you see.' Moira's smile vanished. 'And when he does, God knows what I'll do.'

'Surely you'll be able to find another job?'

'I suppose so, but it's not the job. Charles owns this building. If he sells the property rather than renting it out, I'll probably have to leave.'

'Is he likely to sell it?'

'Mr Carter, who runs the shop, has let him know that they will make a good offer. With property prices the way they are at the moment, Charles would be able to have a very comfortable retirement.'

'But surely they wouldn't be allowed to put you out? I mean, the flat is furnished. You're what's called a sitting tenant, aren't you?'

Moira shook her head. 'That would only apply if I'd ever paid any rent.'

'I don't understand.'

'You've surely guessed by now that Charles Butler is more than my boss.'

Shirley was discomfited. 'I suppose I have.'

'When I had to give up the stage because of my fall, I had no idea what I should do. My mother wanted me to go home, but I couldn't bear the thought of leaving London. The trouble was I wasn't trained to do anything except sing and dance.

'Lana found fame and fortune very quickly. She was always generous. She saved my life. Or rather, she paid my rent, fed me and sent me to a secretarial school.' Moira gave a tired smile. 'I discovered I had a brain. I beat four other applicants to this job with Charles, and it didn't stop there. The job became a learning process, and I probably know as much about the law as he does.'

She paused and sighed. 'The trouble was, as you've no doubt guessed, I fell in love with him and he with me. Or that's what I believed. He was already married, of course – that's something Lana and I dealt with in different ways.'

'I don't understand.'

'Lana knew from the start that Jack was married, but wisely she became completely independent of him, whereas I allowed Charles to set me up in this flat. Which suited him very well, by the way. Not just because we were lovers, but because, if we worked late, I could make him a nice meal. My only defence is that I was head–over–heels in love with him.'

Moira sighed again, then made an effort to rally round. 'But forgive me. I'm embarrassing you. It's at times like this that I miss Lana woefully. She was my best and only real friend, and we spent many a night comforting each other over a bottle of wine. Speaking of which, it's time I filled our glasses up and we tucked in to the cheeses and this delicious pâté.'

The mood after that was subdued and the conversation desultory. When Shirley decided it was time to go, Moira asked her to stay a little longer and tell her about Lana's collection of photographs. 'I've hardly seen any of them, you know. Lana was my dearest friend. I would have liked some to keep.'

'Perhaps you could ask Kay to let you have some. But I'm sad to say that most of the snaps are totally boring. I can't imagine why Lana hung on to them.'

Moira smiled. 'I can tell you why. She thought that one day someone would write her biography. She told me when I asked her why she was so obsessed with the camera.'

'Do you think anyone will? Write her biography, I mean?'

Moira shook her head. 'Lana stopped working sooner than she should have done. Memories are short, and it grieves me to think that she may already be forgotten. No one has ever shown any interest, but if I lose my job, I might have a go myself. I have enough savings to publish the book myself if none of the publishers want it. It would be something I could do for my old friend. One day I might ask Kay if I might have the albums, or at least borrow them.'

'There are three of them, and remember, there's one photograph that I didn't mount – the one in the envelope. I slipped that inside one of the albums.'

'You wanted Kay to find it?'

'I'm sure that Lana wanted her to. And I think I know why. She wanted to lead Kay to the truth. But I don't think Kay has even looked at any of the photographs. She was just grateful that I had tidied them up for her.'

'I think she's taken up with her new job. It must be pretty exciting suddenly finding a new career and being so successful.'

'She takes it very calmly, you know,' Shirley said. 'She's admitted to having nerves before a broadcast, but that's normal; most of them do. But she hasn't let any of this go to her head. I mean, who would have dreamed that her life would change so dramatically? From shop assistant in a tired seaside resort to successful radio actress living in London. It's as if she was in limbo before this happened and now she's found her proper place in the world.' Shirley smiled. 'Am I being fanciful?'

'Perhaps, but I know what you mean.'

'I can't imagine what would have happened to her if Lana Fontaine hadn't made her her heir,' Shirley said.

'There was no danger of that happening. But Kay might have decided not to come to London. She could have asked me to sort everything out for her,' Moira said.

'Well, thank goodness she did come.'

'Now it's my turn to be fanciful.' Moira paused.

'Go on.'

'There was no danger of Kay not coming to London. Lana was determined that she would.'

Shirley's eyes widened. 'There's something about the way you said that that makes me shiver.'

'Thelma prevented Lana from seeing Kay when she was alive, so Lana was determined to claim her daughter when she was dead.'

'What are you suggesting? That Lana's ghost is still hovering around?'

'Not exactly. It's just that her yearning for her daughter became so strong that it lingers in her house, and Kay can't help being influenced by it.'

Shirley stared at Moira for a moment and then laughed nervously. 'Maybe you're right, or maybe it's the wine talking.'

'Or maybe I just miss my old friend so much that some part of me wants to believe she's still around.'

As Shirley opened the door and stepped into the hall she heard the click of the telephone receiver being put back on the cradle. Jane turned to face Shirley looking nervous and guilty.

'Speaking clock,' she said. 'I phoned the speaking clock – my watch had stopped.'

Shirley shrugged. She didn't point out that both the clock just a few feet away and the clock in the lounge were ticking away. Any further conversation was halted when the phone rang.

'Go on, answer it,' Shirley said as she turned to close the door.

Jane did so and Shirley heard her say, 'I'm sorry, she isn't in.' Then she glanced round and asked Shirley, 'Do you know what time Kay will be home? Her sister wants to speak to her.'

Shirley shook her head. 'I don't.'

'I'll tell her you called,' Jane said into the phone, 'but she might be late.' She replaced the receiver and looked thoughtful. 'She sounded upset. I hope there isn't any trouble at home.'

'You'd better leave a message for Kay,' Shirley said.

'She asked me to tell Kay to phone her no matter how late it was, but what if she doesn't come home tonight? Sometimes she stays at Tom's place.'

'I don't think she will, tonight. She's got an early rehearsal in the morning. In any case there's nothing we can do about it. No matter how late she is, her sister will just have to wait until she gets back.'

Shirley realised how unfeeling that sounded, but she couldn't help being influenced by the little she had learned about Kay's life before she came to London. Kay had never criticised either her sister or her mother, but the facts were enough to portray them as acquisitive and selfish.

Jane scribbled a note on the pad next to the phone then looked at Shirley questioningly. 'Do you fancy a drink? I've got a nice new bottle of port wine.'

Shirley was surprised. It was so unlike Jane to ask for company. She glanced at her face, and despite the reservations she had about her fellow lodger, she actually felt sorry for her. There was definitely something worrying her. She would rather have gone straight to bed, but Jane looked so wretched that she summoned up a smile and said, 'OK. But nothing alcoholic. Go and put the kettle on.'

Not long after the girl had gone into the house it began to rain. The man sitting in the car a few yards down the street cursed as his view became obstructed by the water flowing down the windscreen. He couldn't turn on the windscreen wipers since he didn't want to switch on the engine, so he sighed resignedly and wound down the side window. Luckily the wind wasn't blowing his way.

Nevertheless, he pulled the brim of his hat down and turned up his coat collar. Then he lit a cigarette, flipped the dead match out of the window and leaned back. He could still see the front door. Two little chickens home to roost, he thought, and Tom would take care of the other one.

Not that Kay Lockwood was a suspect; she had only been the means of getting inside the house. The Christmas tree incident had been fortuitous. The girl who worked at the BBC wasn't their target either. It was the girl who had signed herself into the guest house as Jane Mullen that they were interested in. She was the reason that he would have to sit here all night just in case she set off to make contact with her partner in crime.

So far she had led the other members of the surveillance team quite a dance with all her shopping trips. All that had proved was that she had plenty of cash – probably more than she should have had if she was the young woman who had worked as a servant in the old manor house. The place had burned down, taking the life of the poor old woman who had employed her. No matter that the old girl had gone into the house to try and save her dog, Jane Mullen and her accomplice would be charged with murder.

The reason they weren't moving in on the girl was that they wanted both of them. They had almost got them. The story was all over the papers, and the owner of the hotel where they had stayed when they first arrived in London had thought his new guests might be the couple that were on the run. He had phoned the police, but they had missed catching the man. They had a pretty good idea that he had vanished into the underworld. He almost certainly had stolen goods. A former maid of the poor old lady had come forward to say that there had been some expensive jewellery in the house. Jane's accomplice would want to get rid of his booty, and when he did, he would contact the girl and they would meet up. That was when the police would move in and arrest both of them. So they'd decided to watch the girl. So far it had been a waiting game.

The man yawned. He had been unlucky to draw the night shift. He would have to sit here in a rapidly cooling car until his relief turned up the next morning. Whereas Tom Masters, lucky devil, would probably be tucked up warm and cosy with the unsuspecting young woman in the flat he had rented nearby. It was all in the course of duty, but the man wondered if Sergeant Masters' conscience ever troubled him.

Chapter Nineteen

The rain stopped almost as suddenly as it had begun, and the street lamps dropped pools of shimmering light on to the wet pavements. Early fallen leaves lay damply in the gutter. The man tossed his cigarette stub out of the car window and lit another one. This had been a long case and boredom made him weary; smoking helped to keep him awake. Several cigarettes later he saw two figures hurrying along the street in his direction. The man was a good head taller than the woman and he had an arm round her waist, maybe to support her because she had a slight limp. He recognised them straight away as Tom Masters and Kay Lockwood.

They hurried up the short path to the house. Kay opened the door and the light in the hallway illuminated them as Tom took her in his arms and kissed her. *All in the name of duty*, the watcher thought, and he smiled cynically. The embrace didn't last long. Kay went in and closed the door and Tom stayed there for a moment, watching the house, then he turned and began walking towards the car.

'Anything to report?' he asked as he leaned towards the open window.

'Nothing. She's been home all the time I've been here.'

'Right. I'll be getting along, but not before you've cleared this mess up.'

'What mess?'

'All these cigarette stubs. They're a sure sign that someone has been waiting here.'

'So what? I doubt if she would notice them.'

'Maybe not, but you can't take the risk. She's keeping up a good pretence and I don't think she's anybody's fool.'

'Righto, Sarge. My mistake.'

He got out of the car, picked up the soggy cigarette ends and, for the want of anywhere else to put them, stuffed them in his coat pocket. Before he got back in the car he watched Tom Masters walk away. He would have liked to ask the sergeant if he'd had an enjoyable evening, but he didn't quite have the nerve.

Truth to tell he admired the man. This investigation had dragged on and Sergeant Masters had had to juggle this job with his other assignments. Since the war ended, there had been an upsurge of criminal gangs in London, some of them led by vicious thugs who thought nothing of murdering anyone who was foolish enough to oppose them. The sergeant thought that this job might have a connection with one of the gangs, because it had become certain that the thieving pair – well, the man at least – must have powerful friends who had enabled him to go to ground.

As well as bearing the responsibility of this job, it was rumoured that Tom Masters also had personal problems. But he kept his own counsel and never let them interfere with his work. If he pulled this job off he was sure to be promoted. And if he could find some personal happiness along the way, then good luck to him.

The house was quiet. Kay stood very still in the hall, overwhelmed by the tumultuous feelings his kiss had aroused. A sixth sense told her that Tom was still standing outside. Would he ring the bell and ask to come in? Was he as reluctant to say goodnight as she was? When she heard his footsteps walking away the feeling of disappointment was overpowering.

Eventually she sighed and took her coat off. When she hung it on the hallstand she noticed the note propped up on the telephone table.

Kay,
> Your sister wants you to phone her. She says it doesn't matter if it's late.
> Jane

The lack of information was worrying. Before picking up the receiver, Kay crossed the hall and went into the kitchen. She switched on the light and saw that two cups and saucers had been left to drain on the bench. The fire was still glowing and the room was warm, which suggested that Shirley and Jane had only just gone to bed.

Kay wondered if she should go up and ask them if they could tell her anything about Julie's call so that she would be prepared for bad news. For a moment she stood there, unsure what she should do, and then decided she might as well get it over with. She waited only long enough to kick off her shoes, then dialled the operator and asked to make a long-distance call.

While she waited it occurred to her that Tony might answer the phone, and she wasn't sure how she would deal with that. But it was Julie who answered.

'Kay, is that you?'

She sounded so distressed that Kay immediately thought the worst. 'Is Mum all right?' she asked.

'What?'

'Has something happened to Mum? Is that why you phoned me?'

'No . . . no. Mum's fine.'

'Then what's the matter? Julie – you're OK, aren't you?'

'If you mean has anything happened to the baby, no. I'm disgustingly healthy, but thanks for asking!'

Kay heard a muffled sob.

'Please tell me what the matter is.'

'Oh, Kay, I'm just so miserable and I don't know what to do.' Julie began to cry in earnest.

'Julie, please stop crying. It can't be good for the baby to have you so upset like this. If you can tell me what the matter is I may be able to help you.'

Julie stopped crying abruptly. 'No one can help me.' She sounded like a heartbroken child.

Kay was beginning to lose her patience. 'If I can't help you, why did you phone me?'

There was silence for a moment and then Julie said, 'I'm sorry. I just needed to talk to someone and I don't want anyone else to know. It's Tony, you see. He hasn't come home again.'

'Hasn't come home? Home from where? Where does he go? And what do you mean by "again"?'

'He goes to his wretched club in Newcastle. He stays there as late as possible – until the last train. If the club was residential I think he'd stay there all night. Then when eventually he does come home he sleeps in the spare room. He says it's because he doesn't want to wake me, but the truth is I'm not asleep. I've just been lying there waiting for him. Oh, Kay, the nights are drawing in and I hate being in this house all by myself.'

'Why don't you tell him that?'

'Pride, I suppose. If I did say anything it would be like admitting that there's something wrong. It would be out in the open. Do you know what I mean?'

'I think I do. But Julie, love, you won't solve anything if you don't talk to him about it.'

'I don't think it can be solved. You see, I don't think he loves me any more. In fact I don't think he ever did love me.'

Her sister sounded like a little lost child who needed a comforting hug. Kay was acutely aware of the distance between them.

'Julie, you must be wrong. Why would Tony marry you if he didn't love you?'

Her sister gave a bitter laugh. 'Because I was pregnant, remember? This is a small town and his parents are important people. They didn't want a scandal, so he did the right thing. And what's worse, he only went out with me in the first place to get back at you.'

Kay didn't know what to say, because she suspected that this might be true.

Sounding very subdued, Julie said, 'And in a way, so did I.'

'What do you mean? How could your marrying Tony be getting back at me?'

There was a pause and then Julie said, 'I was always jealous of you.'

'I can't believe that. You're beautiful and you're clever and you could probably have had any boy you wanted.'

'But I wanted Tony, and the way he ignored me only made me more determined to win him from you. When you went off to London I saw my chance. And I had to hurry up about it in case you came back and you and he got together again. Tony's pride was hurt. He didn't understand how you could go off and leave him. I . . . well, I sort of made him feel better.'

Kay was appalled. 'Julie . . . are you telling me that you got pregnant on purpose?'

'Yes, I am. And I think he's guessed as much. Oh, Kay, what am I going to do?'

'Have you talked it over with Mum?'

'I wouldn't dare. I know just what she would say.'

'What would she say?'

'You've made your bed and now you'll have to lie in it.'

'You're wrong, Julie. Mum would never say that to you.'

'What makes you so sure of that?'

'Because she loves you very much. She always has. In fact, if you want to know the truth, I was always a little jealous of the way she preferred you.'

Kay's sister gave a sad little laugh. 'You jealous of me? Are you serious?'

'I am.'

'Then what a pair we are!'

'Julie, why don't you come to London?'

'You mean for a holiday?' Julie sounded uncertain.

'No, I don't mean a holiday. The offer's still on. Come and live with me.'

'And leave Tony?'

'Yes.'

'You mean get a divorce?'

'It might not come to that.'

'What do you mean?'

'If you come here Tony might come to his senses. He might wake up to the fact that he's been behaving badly. He might remember that he loves you.'

'He won't do that.'

'Why not?'

'Because, like I told you, he never did love me. I set out to get him and I'm ashamed to admit that. So the way he's treating me is no more than I deserve.'

'Julie, don't talk like that.'

'Why not? It's true.'

'Then if you're so unhappy, you should make a clean break. I'd love to have you and your baby here.'

There was a brief silence then Julie said, 'That's impossible, Kay. Mum would never forgive me.'

'She'd miss you, yes, but she could come and stay whenever she wanted.'

'I'm not talking about her missing me. This is a small town. You can imagine the gossip. If I left my husband I would become notorious, tarnished somehow. It would be a scandal. Mum would never live it down. I can't do that to her.'

Kay sighed. 'Of course you can't. I didn't think of the consequences. So what are we going to do?'

'Perhaps I could come for a visit.'

'Whenever you like.'

'And if I could phone you now and then . . .'

'Of course you can. Not that I've been much help.'

'Just being able to talk about it helps a little,' Julie said. 'And, Kay, I'm so sorry.'

'What are you sorry for?'

'For going after Tony the way I did. If I'd kept out of the way you and Tony might have got together again.'

'No, Julie. That's one thing you needn't feel guilty about. Even if I hadn't come to London, Tony and I would have parted sooner or later. That relationship was going nowhere.'

The sisters said goodnight and Julie, tired and weary after the emotional phone call, went to bed. Even though her problem had not been solved, she felt comforted just being able to talk to Kay. She realised now how much she missed her sister, and on looking back over their lives, she saw quite clearly how their mother had neglected Kay. Kay had been sent to work in a shop so that she could go to college. Until recently it had never crossed her mind that Kay might have dreams of a better kind of future; dreams she had never spoken about.

No matter what their mother said, Kay had been quite right to go to London and make a better life for herself.

Mum should be proud of her, Julie thought. *I know I am.*

And then, even though Tony had still not come home, instead of lying miserably awake, she fell into an exhausted sleep.

Kay was wide awake. Her admission to Julie that her relationship with Tony had been going nowhere had made her think about her relationship with Tom. She couldn't remember the moment she had fallen in love with him. Perhaps it was the very first time she saw him, when he had tied the Christmas tree to the small boy's buggy with the belt from his coat. There was such a thing as love at first sight, wasn't there?

Tom was kind and considerate, and when he took her in his arms and kissed her he left her weak with desire. He behaved as though he loved her, but he had never told her that he did. Neither had they made love. When she stayed at his spartan little flat he slept on the sofa.

Kay suddenly felt utterly depressed. She had wasted years of her life in a futile relationship with one man, only to have fallen in love with another who seemed unwilling to commit himself. Perhaps she should stop seeing Tom, she thought. Perhaps she should walk away while she still had some pride left.

Tony knew very well that Julie lay awake while she waited for him to come home. He crept upstairs without putting any lights on and held his breath as he made his way to the spare bedroom, not knowing that tonight his caution was unnecessary. He felt guilty. He knew he wasn't being fair to his young wife and was causing her much pain.

She was so lovely. Many a man would not be able to

understand why he could not be happy with her. Even now, when her body was changing with her pregnancy, her skin was soft and flawless and her hair lustrous. But her appealing young face had lost its air of joyful confidence and was marred by hurt and anxiety. And this was his fault.

He knew what she must be thinking. She must believe that he had fallen out of love with her, when the truth was he had never really loved her. Not in the romantic way that she craved – and deserved. On his part the attraction had been entirely physical.

He had been puzzled and upset when Kay had abandoned him without warning: upset because their relationship had seemed so comfortably secure, and puzzled because he could not understand why Kay had found it so easy to end it. He had needed reassurance, and Julie's obvious adulation had soothed his hurt pride.

Ought he to have proposed to Kay years ago? He was still not sure why he hadn't. She was attractive and intelligent but perhaps not sufficiently compliant. In her own quiet way, Kay had never been afraid to disagree with him or express her opinions. At the time, that had seemed reason enough to hold back. Now he wasn't so sure.

He had to admit that one of the reasons he had been drawn to Julie was that she would make a much more amenable wife. She would not question his opinions. Although she was probably as intelligent as her sister, she was less interesting. But now she was expecting his child, and if he allowed their marriage to fall apart he would probably never live down the scandal. It might be the twentieth century, but divorce was still frowned upon.

His previously good reputation would be forgotten; he would no longer be regarded as the perfect gentleman. And he didn't think his status as a war hero would help him. The world had moved on, and the heroic actions of better men than he had been consigned to history. If Julie became unhappy enough to leave him he would be known as an irresponsible, ungentlemanly cad who had ill-treated his young, innocent wife.

Tony had enjoyed being well thought of and was unwilling to risk the loss of his reputation. He would have to pull himself together, as his father had told him when he had confided in him. He must also try to be kinder to Julie, and to suppress the real reason for his despondency: his unrelenting and mystifying yearning for Kay.

At this time of night, away from the main road, the streets were quiet, and Tom heard a phone begin to ring when he was still some distance from his flat. The nearer he drew, the more convinced he was that it was his. He began to hurry. Like most people, he believed that a phone call at night meant there was some kind of emergency. In his case it could be something to do with work; there might have been a breakthrough, some dramatic development. But if the call was not from the station, there was only one other person who would call him. Kay. However, he doubted that it would be her. He might be imagining it, but he thought she had been a little distant lately. Well, not exactly distant, but quiet and perhaps a little reserved. It shouldn't have mattered to him, but it did. Uncharacteristically, he found himself fumbling when he put his key in the lock. He was expecting the caller to lose patience and ring off any moment, so he slammed the door behind him, strode across the tiny hall and grabbed the receiver. 'Yes?' When he heard who it was he said, 'I told you never to call me here.'

'Then why did you give me the number?'

'For emergencies. You know that.'

'Well, this is an emergency. Just listen to me, will you?' She sounded hysterical, but then she often did.

264

Tom sighed and resigned himself to standing in the draughty hall. 'Go on then, tell me what's so urgent.' After a few minutes he cut in to the agitated flow. 'For God's sake, Dora, he's eighteen years old; he's entitled to go out for a drink.'

'I know that, but you know what he's like. Easily led. His so-called friends could get him into trouble.'

'They're not bad lads – high-spirited, perhaps, but they've never been in trouble,' Tom said wearily.

'So far.'

'And Ricky's not easily led. He's just quieter and more thoughtful than the others. He wouldn't do anything stupid.'

'Then where is he?'

'What do you mean?'

'The pubs are closed. Why isn't he home yet?'

Tom looked at his watch and sighed in exasperation. 'Twenty minutes, Dora. The pubs closed twenty minutes ago. He'll be on his way.'

'It doesn't take twenty minutes to get home from the local.'

'Maybe he didn't go to the local. Maybe the lads wanted to try somewhere new.'

'Or maybe they've gone into town to one of those jazz clubs,' Dora said. 'The ones in cellars. They can get drink there – and worse.'

'You mean drugs?'

'Yes. You're a policeman. You know very well what I mean. I don't know what London's coming to.'

Tom had been expecting that. Dora thought that ever since the war, the world they had known was descending rapidly into hell.

'Dora, what's happening isn't new. Believe me, it's always been easy to get drugs or to drink after hours. Do you really think Ricky would be so stupid as to indulge in anything so dangerous? You've done a good job with him. You coped

265

when the two of you were on your own during the war. You brought him up to be a fine young man. Sometimes I think that you don't know your own son.'

There was a short silence and Tom thought that was the end of it, but Dora changed tack. 'You promised you'd come home at least once a week.'

'I said I would if it were possible.'

'Well, you haven't.'

'I'm working on a case. More than one, but this one's important. I'm leading the team; I have to be accessible – ready for action.'

'Oh, yeah, Mr Big, aren't you? Well, it's taking you long enough, isn't it? The next thing you'll be telling me is that you won't be home for Christmas.'

'Of course I will. I'm pretty sure we'll be wrapping it up very soon.'

Tom was lying. He wasn't sure at all. This investigation had been going on for nearly a year, and there had been no hint of Jane making a run for it. There was simply nothing anybody could do but wait.

It was worrying. The Yard had had to commit quite large resources to this assignment. There had been some scaling down, but the police would never give up on a case of murder. Tom had to manage his time carefully between this and other cases. It was fortunate that he had a good team. Not one of the men had ever complained about the long hours spent keeping the house under observation. Tom smiled wryly. He imagined that some of their wives were getting as fed up as Dora was.

'I suppose you think it's funny that you keep us guessing whether you'll be here to carve the turkey and set light to the Christmas pudding!'

'Dora – stop this! We're getting nowhere.'

He expected tears but was saved when he heard a noise in

the background. 'Where have you been?' Dora asked. 'I've been so worried.'

It seemed that Ricky had come home. Tom heard his voice, and although he couldn't make out the words it sounded as though he was soothing his mother. After a moment or two she actually laughed. She would be all right now. Ricky understood Dora and could always make her see reason. Tom felt guilty about leaving him to cope with the situation, but Dora didn't even say goodnight to him before putting the phone down. Thankful that the latest crisis was over, Tom followed suit.

He hung up his coat and went through to the unwelcoming living room. No matter that he fed the meter with sufficient pennies to have the fire on as long as he liked, the place never felt really warm – unless Kay was there. He went through to the tiny kitchen and put the kettle on. When he had made himself a cup of tea he added a shot of whisky and then sat down on the sagging sofa and tried to relax.

He examined his conscience and knew that he had not been entirely fair to Dora. She had come to rely on him so much. Even though his job was demanding and could mean long hours, until now he hadn't begrudged her his time and attention. Now all his thoughts were filled with Kay. And they shouldn't be. What he had done was totally unfair.

The incident with the Christmas tree had been a giant stroke of luck as far as work was concerned. Early on in the investigation he had planned to find some way into Kay Lockwood's house by making friends with her or Shirley, the girl who worked for the BBC. A casual friend. That was all he was supposed to be. Just sufficiently familiar with the girls so that he could call and visit now and then. It wasn't the plan to attach himself to just one of them. That was why he had decided to arrange meals out or even trips to the cinema for all three girls.

But it hadn't worked out that way and it wasn't entirely his fault. From the beginning Shirley and Jane had got it into their heads that he was smitten with Kay. Perhaps he had been, although he hadn't realised it until it was too late. As for the other two, Shirley had welcomed him as a friend but Jane Mullen remained a little detached. She kept herself to herself, and she was obviously wary of any stranger, but he didn't think she had guessed that, for a very different reason, she was the one he was interested in.

Part Three

Chapter Twenty

Northridge Bay, 1931

The shower of rain had been short but fierce, and the wind blowing in from the sea had caught up the wet leaves and plastered them on the window panes. Sunday lunch had been as good as ever and everyone felt sleepy. The girls from the show went up to bed for a rest and Jack, after helping Thelma with the dishes, suggested that she should have a nap, too.

She smiled wearily at him. 'What about these two?' She gestured towards the children, who were sitting with their toys on the breakfast room floor.

'It won't be long before that one is in dreamland.' Jack smiled and nodded his head in the direction of his younger daughter. Julie had abandoned the building blocks and was sucking her thumb and clutching her panda bear to her chest with the other hand. 'I'll carry her up,' he said.

He returned a moment later and Thelma looked at him questioningly.

'She's fast asleep,' he said.

'But what about Kay?'

They both looked at their elder daughter. She looked back and smiled brightly.

'I'll sing her off to sleep. It usually works.' Jack bent down and swept her into his arms. Straight away she snuggled into his embrace and looked up at him with adoration as he began to sing her favourite lullaby.

Thelma loved listening to Jack's pleasant tenor voice but, weary from looking after the house, the lodgers and her two small children, she couldn't suppress a yawn. Soon Kay's eyes were closing and Jack turned to leave the room. He stopped in the doorway, looked over his shoulder and mouthed, 'Come up.'

In spite of her exhaustion, Thelma felt a surge of desire, and while Jack settled Kay in the nursery with her sister, she slipped into their bedroom and undressed before getting into bed. The silence was peaceful. It was almost as if the house itself had gone to sleep. Thelma stretched her hot limbs in the pleasantly cool sheets. She smiled in anticipation of the pleasure that was to come.

But when Jack came to join her he didn't seem to be in any hurry to make love to her. He sat on the bed and took one of her hands. 'Tired, sweetheart?' he asked.

'Not *too* tired.' Thelma felt herself flushing at how suggestive she sounded. She had never learned how to initiate lovemaking but had always waited for Jack to lead the way. Over the years he had done so more and more infrequently, and Thelma didn't know either the words or the actions that would tell him she desired him. This was the nearest she had come to letting him know that she wanted him to make love to her, and when he shook his head she felt hot with shame.

'I mustn't be selfish, darling,' Jack said. 'You work so hard and you deserve a rest.'

Thelma wanted to scream at him that she deserved much more than that, but she turned her head into the pillow to hide the hot tears that were coursing down her cheeks.

'Shall I sing you to sleep?' Jack asked, and without waiting for a reply, he let go of her hand and pulled the bedclothes up around her shoulders. He began to sing the same lullaby that he sang to the children.

Thelma forced herself to lie still and breathe gently as though she were on the verge of sleeping. After a while he stopped singing and leaned over to kiss her on the forehead.

'When I come back I'll bring you a cup of tea,' he whispered.

'Come back?'

'I've got to go to the theatre and work on some new dance routines.'

'Oh, of course. Dance routines.' She knew she sounded sarcastic and she steeled herself as she waited for Jack's reaction.

But all he said was, 'That's right. Now let yourself relax and go to sleep.'

Thelma kept her eyes tight shut and held her breath until she heard the door close behind him. Then she pulled the bedclothes over her head so that she would not disturb the children, and began to cry in earnest.

Jack was angry. Angry with Thelma, who was entirely innocent, and angry with himself, because he knew he was behaving badly. He knew very well that he had been neglecting Thelma, and until now she had never complained. She hadn't exactly complained today, but she had made it plain enough that she wanted him to make love to her. If only he could have done so out of kindness. He winced at the words. But every time he had forced himself to make love to his wife he felt that he was betraying the woman he truly loved: Lana.

The lower promenade was glistening because of the recent rain, and puddles had formed where the paving was uneven. Here and there lay an ice cream wrapper, empty crisp packets, or a twist of paper that had contained boiled sweets, and the waste bins were overflowing. Jack kicked a deflated beach ball angrily. Anyone coming to the theatre would have to walk past this mess, but every time he complained to the council they promised to empty the bins more frequently and then forgot all about it.

In his office Jack switched on the electric fire and put the kettle on. When his tea was ready he added a more than generous shot of whisky to his cup. The theatre was cold and damp smelling, but Jack couldn't lay the blame for this on the council, or at anyone's door but his own. When he had signed the yearly contract it had been made clear to him that for as long as he was the tenant he would be responsible for the upkeep of the building.

He would have to do something about it, he supposed, just as he would have to breathe some life into this year's show – even at this stage of the season. Audiences had been falling off, and despite his malaise, he had too much pride to accept any more disappointing reviews.

Today he had not been lying to Thelma. He really did intend to work on some new routines and inject some new life into the show. In the past he had used it as an excuse to get out of the house, and he had long suspected that Thelma knew that. He had not missed the sarcasm she had injected into the words 'dance routines', but he had chosen to ignore it. The theatre was the only place where he could telephone Lana.

'Jack! What kept you?' Lana sounded fretful.

'I had to get the children to sleep.'

'Why?'

'Thelma looked exhausted. She needed a nap.'

'I see. Good of you to be so concerned,' Lana said dryly.

'Don't be jealous, darling. Thelma works hard; she deserves some consideration.'

'Of course she does. And I am jealous, I admit it. I can't bear thinking about all the cosy little scenes you and Thelma and your daughter must have together.'

'I have two daughters.'

'Yes, but only one of them is mine.'

Lana was sounding more and more overwrought and Jack's anger returned. He tried hard to control it. 'There was a time when you could have settled for cosy little scenes as you call them, but you wanted your career more than you wanted me.'

There was a brief silence followed by a stifled sob. Then she said, 'It doesn't help for me to admit that. I've thought about this many times, and I've begun to wonder why you didn't act more forcefully. Oh, Jack, why didn't you make me stay with you?'

'We both know that nothing I said or did would have persuaded you. Not when success on the London stage was beckoning you.'

This time the silence was longer. 'I've made us both miserable, haven't I?'

'You would have been even more miserable if you had given up your ambitions, wouldn't you?'

'I suppose so.'

'And it isn't all bad, is it? Look how successful you've been.'

'But what about you, Jack?'

'I have Kay. Every time I look at her I'm reminded of you.'

Lana sighed. 'I know you're trying to be kind, but that makes me even more jealous. You can see Kay every day. I only have snatched visits in between engagements. And when I do come Thelma hovers over us all the time.'

'I don't deny that, but at least she has never stopped you coming.'

'And now you have another daughter. You and Thelma together. That must make you close. Jack . . . Are you there?'

'Yes, I'm here, but I might as well not be.'

'What do you mean?'

'I look forward all week to Sunday when I can slip away and phone you, and today you seem to be determined to quarrel.'

'I don't want to quarrel. I just want you to know how I feel.'

'Well, you've told me, and I can't do anything about any of it. So we might as well say goodbye.'

'Goodbye? No . . . Jack!'

Jack realised what she was thinking. 'I only mean that we should end this call, and hopefully by next week you will be more like the Lana I love so desperately.'

'Desperately? Do you really love me desperately?'

She sounded eager for reassurance and Jack laughed softly. 'You know I do.'

'Then why won't you leave Thelma and Julie and bring Kay to me? I'm sure you could find work in London. A man of your talents.'

'Maybe so, but I'd never be as successful as you and I don't fancy playing second fiddle.'

'You see? You don't love me, do you? Otherwise you wouldn't mind playing second fiddle, as you call it. Or any damn fiddle.' Lana's voice rose and there was a sound halfway between a laugh and a sob.

'Lana, let me keep my pride. And in any case, I can't leave my daughter. I love Julie as much as I love Kay.' He held his breath but there was no reaction from Lana, so he carried on, 'And I can't leave Thelma now. You know I can't. Thelma isn't like you. She wouldn't survive on her own.'

'Poor old Thelma!'

Jack paused. 'Do you want to end this call?'

'No, and I'm sorry for giving you a hard time.' Lana sounded genuinely contrite. 'Especially when I have such good news to tell you. Or perhaps it's because of my news.'

Relieved to hear her more like herself, Jack laughed. 'What is your news, darling? Have you won a leading role? Perhaps in Terence Rattigan's new play?'

'Oh, that? As a matter of fact, the lead was offered to me but I turned it down.'

'You turned down the lead in what could be the most exciting play of the century so far? Why on earth did you do that?'

'Because I've had another offer.'

'And that is?'

'A part in a movie!'

'Forgive me, but what's so special about that? You've been in several movies.'

'I know. But not in Hollywood.'

'*Hollywood?*'

'Yes. Why do you sound so surprised?'

'I'm not surprised. I'm stunned.'

'Aren't you pleased for me?'

'Of course I am. I'm thrilled for you. I'm just surprised that a moment ago you wanted me to bring Kay and live with you. How could I afford to live in America?'

'Oh, you wouldn't have had to worry about that. The money I'm being offered is amazing. More than I was paid for my six British movies put together.'

'Congratulations. No one deserves this more than you do.' Jack put the receiver down and ended the call.

Sitting in his poky, now overheated, little office he stared at the telephone and counted the seconds before it would ring. He knew it would, but when it did he didn't answer. He was shocked by his reaction. Shocked that Lana's good luck could affect him so devastatingly. If she went to Hollywood, and if she did well, it might be years before he saw her again. He didn't know if he could bear that.

He stared into his cup of tea and then picked it up. It was cold. *Is my heart breaking?* he thought whimsically. Some lines from Shakespeare's *As You Like It* came to mind: 'Men have died from time to time, And worms have eaten them, But not for love.'

No, he wasn't going to die, but the prospect of Lana being at the other side of the Atlantic for God knows how long was like a living death. He sighed. At least he had Kay – the little girl who was so like her mother that every time he looked at her his heart would break all over again.

'Jack? Jack! Jack, you beast, are you still there?'

When Lana realised what Jack had done, she put her own receiver down and started dialling. After a while she crashed her receiver down and tried again. And again. And again.

Moira, who had been an unwilling listener to the conversation, rose from her chair, took the receiver from Lana and put it down. 'I'm going to make you a cup of tea,' she said, 'and I think we should sit in the kitchen. It's more cosy in there.'

'Tea! Cosy! I despair of you, Moira,' Lana said tetchily. 'Here we are in the most fashionable sitting room you've ever seen, a room I employed an interior designer to create for me, and you want to sit in the kitchen!'

'Yes, I do,' Moira said. 'There's an autumn chill in the air, and despite your new electric fire, this fashionable room is cold. I'm going to sit in the kitchen. Are you coming?'

'Don't bully me.'

Moira smiled at her. 'I'm not bullying you, Lana. You're obviously in a foul mood and I think you need to sit somewhere warm and comfortable and tell me all about it.'

Moira didn't wait for an answer. She led the way to the kitchen where she put the kettle on and began to get cups and saucers out.

Lana followed and said grumpily, 'You heard the telephone conversation. What more is there to say?'

'I heard one side of it.'

'But surely you could guess what Jack was saying from my responses?'

'I suppose I could. Here, drink this tea. You're shivering. Take your cup and sit in the chair by the fire.'

Lana did as she was told but she remained unsmiling. 'So what more do you want me to tell you?'

'First I'll tell you. I don't think you were fair to Jack.'

'Oh, so you're going to take his side.'

'It's not a matter of sides. If it were, I would take your side no matter how unreasonable you were being.'

'So you think I'm being unreasonable?'

'I do. But Jack is being unreasonable, too.'

Lana sighed and sipped her tea. 'So tell me what I should do?'

'You know what you're going to do. You're going to go to Hollywood and become an even bigger star than you are already. I know you pretty well, Lana, and nothing will come in the way of your ambition, so it's totally unfair of you to expect Jack to leave Thelma and his younger daughter and bring Kay to you. What kind of life would he have being second fiddle, as he put it, to a movie star? And it would be unfair to Kay as well.'

'Surely not. She would love being in Hollywood, and just think of the life I could give her.'

'I am thinking. And I've read the stories in the movie magazines about children of the stars and the trouble they get up to because their parents think that all they need to do is spoil them with more money than is good for them, when

279

what they want – what they need – is more time with their parents.'

'But Kay would have Jack. He would make sure she wasn't spoiled. He would look after her.'

'And look after you, too, I suppose? What would that do to his pride?'

'Oh, but he might find work there. Even become a movie star himself. He's handsome, he can act. He can sing and dance. I'm sure he'd be perfect in musical films.'

'And then who would look after Kay?' Moira sipped her tea and looked up to find Lana staring at her balefully.

'Sometimes I hate you,' she said.

Moira smiled wryly. 'Why? Because I tell you things you're intelligent enough to work out for yourself?'

Lana stared at her for a moment and then took a deep breath, leaned back in her chair and breathed out slowly.

'Watch out!' Moira said. 'You're going to spill what's left of your tea.'

Lana opened her eyes and shook her head. 'No, I'm not, and you're going to pour me another cup and then tell me why you think Jack is selfish, too.'

Moira filled Lana's cup, gave it to her, then pulled her chair over to the other side of the hearth. She knelt down, took a shovelful of coal from the scuttle and built up the fire. When she was settled she said, 'Jack is being selfish because I think he was trying to make you feel guilty about going to Hollywood.'

'How so? He said I deserved the success. He congratulated me.'

'Then he put the phone down and wouldn't answer when you called back.'

'Yes, you're right. The beast!'

'Also, when you started your affair, you knew very well

280

that Jack was a married man. And married men don't always keep their promises.'

Lana groaned.

'He must have known of your ambitions and yet he made you pregnant.'

Lana's laugh was bitter. 'Well, that was my fault, too. And he offered to look after us, you know. Me and the child.'

'How? Was he going to hide you away in some little backstreet house and come and visit you only when he could get away from his real family?'

'Don't say that!'

'Why not? It's true, isn't it?'

'Right again!' Lana stared into the fire moodily. 'But there's something you should know.'

'What is it?'

'Never once did Jack mention abortion. And if he had I wouldn't have considered it.'

Moira looked at her and smiled gently. 'Yes, I believe you. And if you hadn't had Kay, the two of you might have parted as soon as you got the offer from Monty. You might have been sad for a while – and so might he – but you went ahead and had the baby; the baby you both love. I know you love her, even though you were willing to give her to Jack's wife to bring up.'

Lana looked defensive. 'I did that because in the circumstances I was convinced that my daughter would have a better life. A proper home with a good woman and her own father instead of being hidden away in some little backstreet, as you put it.'

'That sounds very noble, Lana, but it also meant that you could carry on with your life in show business, didn't it?'

Lana stared at Moira unbelievingly. 'You really have got it in for me tonight, haven't you?'

'I'm sorry if I sound cruel. You're talented and spirited

and generous and kind, and I consider myself the luckiest woman in the world to have you as my friend. And it's because we're friends that I want to tell you something that you may not have considered.'

'What's that?'

'First of all, I'd be inhuman if I didn't feel sorry for you – and Jack – because I don't believe you had a shady little affair.'

'Thanks!'

'I believe you truly loved each other.'

'And still do,' Lana said vehemently.

'But have you ever considered that you weren't free to do so?'

'Of course I have! Is that what you wanted to tell me?'

'No, I wanted to point out that both you and Jack must never forget that the most important person in this sad little tale is Kay.'

Lana stared at her friend despondently. 'I know that,' she said.

'Leave her, Lana, leave her in peace.'

'Is it so wrong that I want to see her?'

'No, but you must consider what's best for her. She has her father, she has Thelma, who must be a good woman to have agreed to take your daughter, and she has a happy home.'

'So the deceit must go on?'

'I believe it must.'

Lana stood up abruptly. 'It's late. I'm sorry I've kept you. You should get back to your flat.'

Moira took this curt dismissal well and Lana went to bed. *One day*, she thought, *one day I want Kay to know the truth. Somehow I shall bring her to me.*

Chapter Twenty-One

1 October 1950

Dear Miss Bennet,

Every time I put the phone down after one of our chats I have felt guilty that I haven't told you what has been happening. But to tell the truth, I thought I would wake up one morning and find it has all been a dream. Now that I'm certain it isn't, I can tell you. I'd better explain.

Recently I was given some advice by Julian Fry. I think I told you, Julian is the producer of *Mulberry Court*. As the show only goes out once a week, I have been able to take on other engagements, and often Julian has found these for me. Do you remember the piece I did for *Woman's Hour,* when I and another actress pretended to be housewives advising each other how to plan the weekly shopping and how to make best use of your ration book? Well, having worked in a grocery shop for years, I was able to make a few suggestions – much to the scriptwriter's annoyance! However, the producer was pleased, and that led to my doing a recipe spot now and then. Me, giving cooking advice? Hilarious! But the producer said I sounded like an experienced housewife. How could she know it was all an act?

By now Julian said I ought to have an agent, who would not only find work but would also negotiate my fees. Julian suggested I approach Hilton Gray, a well-known agent who has a good reputation. He said I would have to have an audition, and he helped me get some pieces prepared. I won't bore you with the details. I'll only tell you that I now have an agent to represent me. As far as the audition was concerned, Mr Gray told me to forget it. He'd heard me in *Mulberry Court* and he said if I hadn't come to him he would have asked Julian to introduce us.

All this is exciting enough, but it's not the reason I'm writing to you. Mr Gray is quite old but he is very energetic. Like Julian, he dresses in a rather flamboyant way and he has an encyclopaedic knowledge of show business. He does very well for his clients. Not very long after he had taken me on, he called me to his office and said he had the perfect part for me, but he wouldn't say any more over the phone.

I had no idea why he was being so secretive. As I set out for his office in Oxford Street, I felt I was a character in a spy story. When, eventually, I was sitting facing him across his impressive antique desk, he looked so solemn that I thought I must have misheard him on the phone, and that he was going to tell me that he didn't want to represent me after all.

'I've got a great part for you,' he said at last. 'In a film.'

The world stood still, as they say.

'It's the second lead,' he continued. 'And it's perfect for you.' He paused and, looking a little vexed, he said, 'Why aren't you thrilled? Most young actresses would be.'

'Haven't you noticed that I limp quite badly?' I asked him.

'Of course I have,' he said, 'but in this case it doesn't matter.'

I stared at him for a moment, and then I'm afraid I said, 'Oh, I see, I'm to play the part of a cripple!'

'Yes, you are,' he said, quite brutally. 'What's wrong with that?'

I couldn't think of a thing to say.

'Are you ashamed of having a limp?' he asked.

'Of course not!' I replied.

'So?'

'So what?' I knew I was being rude and I honestly didn't know why I was so upset. But Mr Gray did.

'You've had much success on the radio,' he said. 'But despite your talent, nobody from the theatrical world has approached you.'

'I didn't expect them to,' I said. 'After all, no one would accept a heroine who limps across the stage.'

'You're right,' Mr Gray said, 'but that would depend on the character, wouldn't it?'

He sounded so matter-of-fact that I began to calm down. I actually managed to smile when I said, 'I don't think there are many parts written for leading ladies who limp.'

'There aren't, although there may be some for minor characters.'

I stared at him.

'Go on, say it,' he said. 'There's no harm in valuing yourself.'

'What do you mean?' I asked.

'You're much too talented to play a minor character,

unless it was a cameo appearance, of course.'

'I'm hardly well known enough yet to play a cameo role,' I said.

Mr Gray smiled. 'I notice you used the word *yet*.'

I was embarrassed. 'I'm sorry. Did I sound conceited?'

His smile broadened, 'It's not a crime to be confident of your talent, Kay. And I suspect that underneath that cool, rather reserved exterior you are as ambitious as your godmother was.'

'If you mean Lana Fontaine, how did you know she was my godmother?'

'Julian told me,' Mr Gray said. 'But we should get back to work. In the part I have secured for you the character is in a wheelchair. That's why they had to have someone with a good voice.'

'No!'

He raised his eyebrows. 'Why not? Are you too proud to play the part of a young woman who cannot walk?'

His words shocked me. 'Of course not. It's just that I shouldn't like to be typecast. I shouldn't like people to think that I only got the part because I have a limp.'

'But that wouldn't be true. You're perfect for the part because the character is young and determined and beautiful. And if this goes well you will be offered more parts. The cinema is different from the stage, in that the script can cut out walking shots, and I'm sure the director will be only too pleased to have close-ups of your expressive face.'

Do you know, Miss Bennet, I had never considered that I might have an expressive face. Until that moment I had believed that my future was in radio, where it doesn't matter what you look like and the voice is all important.

So you've probably guessed by now that I agreed to take the part. It was hard work fitting in the filming with my radio work, because I don't want to leave *Mulberry Court*. Shirley said that they could always find another actress to take over the part – every now and then they have to do that in radio serials. Well, all I can say that I'll have to wait and see. At this stage there are no more film parts lined up. Mr Gray says he's sure there will be.

What you might not have guessed is that the film is 'in the can', as they say. The director's final 'cut and print' echoed round the studio two weeks ago, and *A Dream Of Love* is ready to be shown in cinemas throughout the country.

Shirley and Jane know about this, and so does my friend Tom. And I have written to Julie. But I haven't told my mother because she doesn't seem to be interested in anything I do. Whether or not Julie will tell her is up to her.

I hope you will go and see the film, because I've saved the best part until last. Guess who is playing a cameo role? Valentine Dyall! I am as much a fan as you are, and I asked him for two autographed photographs. He very kindly obliged. One photograph is for me, of course, and the other is already in the post for you.

I hope you are well.

Yours sincerely,

Kay

That evening, when she guessed Kay would be home from work, Miss Bennet dialled a long-distance number. The phone was answered immediately.

'Julian, is that you?'

The young woman with the forthright manner was not Kay. Miss Bennet guessed who she was speaking to.

'Shirley? This is Miss Bennet.'

'Kay's friend? I'll get her for you.'

The young woman, although perfectly courteous, had sounded disappointed, and Miss Bennet wondered whether Julian Fry was more to Shirley than just her boss. She thought she might ask Kay about this, at the risk of being thought a nosy old woman. But not tonight.

'Miss Bennet? Did you get my letter?'

'Yes, dear, that's why I'm calling. I'm glad you wrote and told me all your news, but by the time I got your letter I already knew that you were in a film.'

There was a small silence before Kay replied. 'How did you know? No, I've guessed. It's in the local paper. It comes out today!'

'It's on the entertainments page, just above next week's listings. There's a big headline saying, "Kay Lockwood Takes To The Silver Screen". I reached for my magnifying glass immediately! The headline was followed by a description of the film, ending: "*A Dream Of Love* is starting at the Coliseum next Monday".'

'I should have written to tell you sooner.'

'You should also have written to your mother and not allowed her to find out by reading the local paper, or indeed seeing the poster on the billboards. Forgive me for saying so, dear, but I think what you have done is spiteful, and whatever the situation is between you and your mother, this will only have made things worse.'

'My mother has behaved quite hurtfully, you know.'

'Maybe so, but couldn't you be grown-up enough to try and make things better between you?'

'Oh dear, are you cross with me?'

'Not cross, Kay, but a little disappointed. What were you thinking of? You must have known that she would find out sooner or later.'

'What can I do?'

'I suggest that you phone your mother and apologise for not letting her know.'

'What shall I say?'

'No excuses. Tell her the truth. And may I suggest that you telephone her immediately?'

'I feel as though I'm back at school.'

'Oh dear. Do I sound like an old schoolmarm?'

'No. You sound like an old friend.'

'Thank goodness for that. I want you to know, Kay, that I think of you as much more than a former pupil. In fact I couldn't be more fond of you.'

Kay had tears in her eyes as they said goodbye.

Miss Bennet had made her feel ashamed, but at the same time Kay couldn't help thinking that it was her mother's attitude that was the problem. Nevertheless, she settled herself more comfortably on the chair next to the telephone table and was just about to dial her mother's number when the phone rang. Thinking it would probably be for Shirley, who seemed to be expecting a call, she picked up the receiver, prepared to go and get her friend. But the person at the other end was Julie.

'I've been trying to get through for ages,' her sister said.

Kay smiled. 'You're exaggerating. I wasn't on the phone for very long.'

Julie's tone lightened. 'Oh, I know, but it's very frustrating when you phone someone and the number is engaged. Especially when you have so much to say.'

'Well, you're through now, so say whatever you want to say.'

'I think you might have written to me sooner. We found out that you'd made a film from the local paper before the post was delivered.'

'We?'

'Tony always reads the papers over breakfast. He prefers to do that rather than speak to me. He reads the local rag first, in case there's any news in it that would affect the wretched business. Anyway, there's a piece on the entertainments page, just above the cinema listings, all about you being in a film. Local girl makes good kind of thing.'

Julie sounded petulant and Kay knew she would have to tread carefully. 'What did Tony say?'

'Not very much, actually. He frowned and handed the paper over to me and said, "Did you know about this?"'

'I glanced at the paper and shook my head, and he gave a sort of shrug and buried himself in *The Times*. Before I could get on with my poached eggs, the phone rang. It was Tony's mother. She'd read the paper and she was so excited. She wants to get up a group to go to the cinema on Monday, then go back to her house afterwards and have a party.'

'But that's good of her, isn't it?'

'Oh, it's any excuse for a chance to have a drink or two.'

'Julie, that's unkind.'

Julie sounded defensive. 'Yes, I know, but she's turning into a dipso and it's all because she's so lonely. Tony's father is either at work or his wretched club, and she's left to entertain herself with the contents of the cocktail cabinet. Her friends all dropped off long ago.' Julie sighed. 'Apart from Mum. The poor love still thinks it's an honour to be invited there. Thank goodness she doesn't like alcohol, or there'd be two lonely old dipsos.'

Kay was shocked. 'You mustn't speak about our mother like that. Nor Mrs Chalmers. I know you're pregnant, but couldn't you go along and keep your mother-in-law company now and then?'

'When Mr Chalmers and Tony are working late or at their club, do you mean? Then there'd be two of us!'

Kay felt desperately sorry for her younger sister, but she didn't see what she could do. 'Do you go to visit Mum when Tony's out? Now that you've left home she must be lonely too, you know.'

'What? And let her know what a sad state my marriage is in?'

'I don't know what to say. Whenever you've phoned me lately you've never sounded as miserable as this.'

Kay heard Julie draw in her breath and then she said, 'Oh, Kay, I'm so sorry!'

'You're sorry? Why?'

'For moaning on like this when I should be congratulating you. But I must say, I still think you ought to have let me know that you've become a film star.'

Kay laughed. 'Yes, I ought to have told you what was happening, but I was afraid the whole thing would be a flop. And as for being a film star, I've only taken a supporting part in one film and I don't even know if I'll be offered a part in any others. My agent will do his best for me, but he says I'm so individualistic that I mustn't expect instant success in movies. The right roles will only come along now and then.'

'I'm sorry to hear it.'

'No, Julie, you needn't be. I love doing radio work and I'd be happy to do that forever.'

'If you say so.'

'I do.'

'So why didn't you tell Mum about this?'

Kay was shocked at how swiftly Julie had changed the subject. 'Would Mum have been interested?' she asked.

'I honestly don't know, but it was spiteful of you to let her find out in her beloved *Seaside Chronicle*.'

This was the second time within the hour that Kay had been accused of acting spitefully. She had to accept that it might be true.

'I'll phone her now.'

'That's good. And Kay, don't worry about me. I'll be all right when the baby comes. Mum is looking forward to being a grandmother, and so, God help us, is Mrs Chalmers. I won't be lonely then, and as for Tony, I have the feeling that he'll be a marvellous father – just wait and see.'

The sisters said goodbye and Kay hoped and prayed that Julie was right, and that her errant husband would change his ways and become the kind of husband that Julie deserved.

Kay sat very still and tried to compose herself before phoning her mother. She dialled the number very reluctantly and found herself hoping that her mother was out. She wasn't. Kay was expecting a hostile answer, and was surprised when her mother said, 'Hello, Kay, pet.'

'Mum . . .'

'I know why you're phoning and I'm not angry.'

'I wanted to apologise for not telling you.'

'It's me that should apologise for making you feel that I wouldn't care. That was it, wasn't it? I haven't replied to your letters, and if you phoned I was abrupt, to say the least.'

'Yes, but I still should have phoned you.'

'Well, don't worry, Kay. I do care and I'm thrilled for you. As for the way I've behaved, I hope you'll understand one day, but at the moment I don't want to talk about it. Do you mind?'

Kay, who very much wanted to talk about her mother's behaviour, nevertheless said, 'No, that's all right.'

Then both of them found they had nothing more to say apart from, 'Take care' and 'Goodnight'.

Kay sat staring into space for a while and Shirley came into the hall. 'Have you finished?' she asked. Kay was surprised at how hostile she sounded.

'Yes. Sorry. Did you want to make a call?'

'No, I'm expecting one.'

Kay rose and turned towards the door. Shirley's face was drawn and her fists clenched. 'Why don't we have a cup of tea?' Kay asked.

'Oh yes, a cup of tea solves everything, doesn't it?'

'Shirley? What's wrong?'

Shirley clenched her hands more tightly, then let her breath out with a long sigh.

Thinking her friend to be more relaxed, Kay smiled and said, 'Right, who's going to put the kettle on?'

'I will.'

Kay thought Shirley had never looked so dejected. She followed her into the kitchen, where Jane was sitting by the fire reading a magazine article about fashion. She looked up and raised her eyebrows at the sight of Shirley's miserable expression. 'What's up?' she asked. 'Hasn't he called yet?'

Shirley bristled. 'What do you mean by that?'

'Well, the way you've been popping in and out of the hall and jumping up nervously every time the phone rang, I assumed you were waiting for a call, and that the caller would almost certainly be a man.'

'You have no right to assume anything,' Shirley said, 'particularly not about phone calls!'

'What are you talking about?' Jane looked nervous.

'I'm talking about the way you sneak away from the phone and try and pretend you haven't been making a call every time anyone comes in.'

Jane stood up and her magazine dropped unheeded to the floor. 'That's not true!'

'Isn't it?'

The two girls glared at each other.

'Stop this at once!' Kay said. But they continued to stare at each other. 'If you continue to behave like this I'll give you both notice to leave. I can't have you behaving like sulky children and causing such an unhappy atmosphere.'

Jane gave way first. 'I'm sorry, Kay.' She picked up her magazine and tossed it on the chair before making an effort to smile. 'Did I hear a cup of tea mentioned before? I'll make it, shall I? Why don't you two sit down?'

Shirley glanced at her watch and looked more miserable than ever. 'Count me out,' she said. 'I'm going for a walk.'

She left the room, and a moment later they heard the front door slam.

Summoned by the doorbell, Moira hurried down both flights of stairs. When she opened the door she was surprised to see Shirley.

'I'm sorry to call so late,' her surprise visitor said.

Moira glanced at her watch. 'It's only eight o'clock. That's not late.'

'Yes, but to bring you all the way downstairs . . .'

'Good for the figure. Now, come in and let's go up to the flat. Now that I have someone to share it with, I'll open a bottle of wine.'

When they were settled with a glass of wine and a plateful of salmon and cucumber sandwiches, Moira asked, 'Man trouble?'

Shirley's eyes were wide with surprise. 'Why do you assume that?'

'Mainly because you look so glum, but also because I can't think of another reason why you would drop by unexpectedly.'

'It could be about Kay.'

'I suppose it could, but I spoke to her earlier today and she didn't mention any problems, except that she was undecided about what to wear on Monday night.'

'What's happening on Monday night?'

'My goodness, whoever he is he *has* got you in a state. Monday night is the premiere of Kay's film.'

Shirley looked guilty. 'Oh my God, the premiere! I forgot all about it!'

'You'll still be coming with the rest of us, won't you?'

'Yes, of course. Even if he's changed his mind.' Shirley took a sip of wine and then choked back a sob.

'"He" being your boss, Julian Fry?'

'Yes.'

'And I take it from the way you're behaving tonight that he's actually more than your boss?'

'That's right . . . well, he is to me. I'm not sure what I am to him.'

Moira smiled sympathetically. 'I think I know what you mean. You've very unwisely fallen in love with your boss, and you don't know whether he's in love with you?'

'I thought he was, but now I just don't know. Maybe I've been kidding myself.'

'Are you lovers?'

Shirley blushed furiously. 'No, we're not. But . . .'

'But you want to be?'

Shirley nodded speechlessly.

'Has he been stringing you along?'

'What do you mean?'

'Leading you to believe that you mean more to him than just his secretary?'

Shirley dropped her head and covered her face with her hands. She groaned. 'I thought I was – more to him, I mean – but now I can't think why. I can't think of anything specific. He never actually said anything. Do you know what I mean?'

'I'm afraid I do.' Moira sighed. 'I fell in love with my boss, and I thought he loved me. Is that why you came here tonight? Because you needed advice from someone who was just as foolish?'

Shirley raised her head and wiped away a tear with her fingers. 'I hope you don't mind.'

Moira's smile was kind. 'If you want to have a friendly chat, I'm ready to listen. But first of all let's have another glass of wine.'

They sat in companionable silence while they sipped their wine. *She'll talk when she's ready*, Moira thought.

Shirley's first words surprised her. 'I thought I was the sensible one.'

'What do you mean?'

'The sensible member of the household. Jane sneaks about the house as though she's hiding something and only goes out to buy jewellery, or more clothes. And Kay, for all her cool confidence, has allowed herself to fall in love with Tom, even though he shows no sign of being serious about her.'

'Yes, that's strange, isn't it?' Moira said. 'They are obviously more than fond of each other, but I get the sense that, for some reason, Tom is unwilling to commit himself.'

Shirley shook her head and stared miserably ahead.

Moira sensed that she wanted to get back to discussing her own problem but didn't know how to start.

'You were saying that you thought you were the serious one,' Moira prompted.

'No – the sensible one. I guess I thought I was a little bit superior to the other two. I could watch what was happening to them and make judgements and think myself above that sort of thing.'

'By "that sort of thing" you mean falling in love?'

'Mmm.' Shirley nodded. 'When my boyfriend dumped me I can honestly say I wasn't heartbroken. I applied for a job at the BBC, and when I was accepted I left home and never gave another thought to him. I thought I was made of sterner stuff than Kay and Jane. Of course, I felt sorry for Jane. According to her, the man she loved was a violent bully and yet she still loved him. If we can believe that.'

'Why do you say that?'

'Because over the months she's told us different versions of her past – just little things, but enough to make me wonder.'

'And what about Kay?'

'Oh yes. No matter how nice Tom is, I would have given him his marching orders rather than be strung along like that.'

'You think that's what he's doing? Stringing her along for some reason?'

'Don't you?'

'I don't know. I admit I'm puzzled. But now what about you and your problem?'

Shirley sighed. 'Julian.'

Moira waited for her to continue.

'From the moment I first met him,' Shirley said, 'I admired him enormously. I hung on his every word. It took me a while, but eventually I realised I was in love with him.'

'And what were his feelings for you?'

Shirley stared at Moira miserably. 'I thought he had fallen in love with me, but now I'm not so sure.'

'What made you think he'd fallen for you?'

'A woman usually knows when a man's interested, doesn't she? I mean, interested in *that* way?'

'Unless she's very innocent.'

'Well, I'm not exactly worldly-wise, but sometimes the way he looked at me sent shivers down my spine.'

'Did he say anything?'

Shirley shook her head. 'Not exactly. But he liked being with me, I'm sure about that. After a show, when we all went for a drink in the club, he would sit beside me, and often we would be the last two there. Then he started taking me for a meal now and then – and I don't mean in the BBC canteen!'

'So what has changed?'

'He doesn't make a point of sitting with me any more and we haven't been out for a meal for weeks – well, a couple of weeks. I don't know what I've done to deserve this. Sometimes I think he goes out of his way to avoid me. Today I plucked up courage and said that I wanted to talk to him.'

'And?'

'He looked positively shifty! He said he had to go because he had some shopping to do for dinner tonight, but he would try and phone me before serving up.'

'I'm assuming you're here because he didn't phone.'

'Yes . . . well, no. I mean, Kay was on the phone for ages, so he might have tried to get through and found the phone engaged.'

'If that's the case he'll tell you so tomorrow.'

'I know. At least I think he will. It's just not knowing that makes me so wretched.'

Moira picked up the bottle of wine and looked questioningly at Shirley, who shook her head. She topped up her own glass. 'I can understand that, and I know how wretched you must feel. But Shirley, there's a question I must ask you.'

'What's that?'

'Is Julian married?'

Shirley looked visibly shaken.

'Well?'

'I don't know.'

'The possibility never crossed your mind?'

'Please don't scold.'

'I'm not scolding, dear, I'm just amazed that a girl who is as intelligent as you are has got involved with an older man who might very well have a wife, and maybe even children.'

Shirley began to cry in earnest, and Moira put down her glass and put an arm around her. 'I've been there myself,' she said, 'And in my case the man in question was indeed married with children, but by the time I found out I was hopelessly in love – and I still am. So no happy wedding day and no children for me. For God's sake, Shirley, don't let that happen to you. So, you say he hasn't made love to you?'

'No. And now I don't even know if he wants to.'

'Good. Count that as a blessing. Harden your heart. And you can come and talk to me any time you feel yourself weakening. Would you like to stay here tonight?'

'No. Thank you for letting me talk like this, but I'd better go. I left the house in a bit of a temper. I should put things right with Kay.'

The night air was damp and the streets looked dreary. Shirley hurried home, not just to apologise to Kay and Jane, but also in the hopes of finding that Julian had phoned after all.

Chapter Twenty-Two

The large, sleek car drew up outside the cinema and the crowd seemed to hold its breath. It was a cold evening, and Moira drew her fox-fur coat more tightly round her as, along with everyone else, she waited for the car doors to be opened. The coat had been a present from Charles many years ago, and the 'swing' style was no longer truly fashionable, but wearing it gave her a sense of occasion.

She must be the best-dressed woman in the crowd, she thought. She had a ticket for the event but she had chosen to be out here, along with a small bunch of friends, in order to soak up the atmosphere so she could tell Kay about it later. The crowd had gathered to watch the cast of the film arriving and then stayed on to see the most important guest of the evening.

Jane hadn't waited long. Moira had noticed how she blinked and turned her head away every time a camera flashed. Saying she had a headache, she had gone into the cinema to find the place allotted to her. For a moment it looked as though Tom would follow her, but he changed his mind and started talking to Shirley, who looked as miserable as sin because Julian hadn't turned up.

When Kay arrived, escorted by her agent, some people in the crowd looked puzzled. They didn't know who she was but they cheered anyway, because that was the thing to do. Valentine Dyall, although not the star, got a loyal cheer, almost as big as the cheer reserved for the two stars of the film, Yvette Todd and Michael Grainger.

But now, as the rear passenger door was opened by a smartly dressed man, there was a glimpse of cream satin and a flash of diamonds, and the crowd went berserk as Princess Margaret stepped out into the cold damp night and illuminated the air around her with the most dazzling smile. The bodice of her dress was encrusted with diamonds and an ermine stole was draped round her shoulders. For a moment the sight of such extravagant beauty lifted all who saw her out of the years of hardship and austerity, into a time of promise and luxury and hope.

After the Princess had entered the cinema, Tom escorted Moira and Shirley to the side door reserved for the less important guests, and they were in time to settle themselves before the orchestra played the national anthem and the film began.

Tom had booked a table at Stefano's and he escorted Moira, Shirley and Jane there when the show ended. Jane didn't look as though she was enjoying herself, and Shirley seemed like she had forgotten how to smile – until she entered the restaurant and saw Julian sitting waiting for them in the bar area.

Moira nudged Shirley and whispered, 'Act normally. Don't ask him why he missed the show and don't let him know you're upset.'

'I am not upset!' Shirley's reply, though whispered, was savage.

Moira smiled. 'Well, that's all right then.'

Shirley pulled herself together in order to introduce Moira and Jane to Julian before a tall, striking-looking woman took their coats. She showed them to a table which had a reserved card propped up against a vase of flowers. Tom ordered a bottle of wine and told them to help themselves, because he was going to collect Kay.

'Are you going to tear her away from the Ritz?' Julian asked.

'I assure you she'll come willingly.'

'But this is a chance for her to mingle with important people.'

'That's what I told her, but she said she would rather be with her friends. So, Julian, if you don't mind, would you look after Moira, Jane and Shirley? Please drink up the wine and tell the waitress that we'll order as soon as another guest arrives.'

Julian poured the wine and passed the glasses around. 'I'm terribly sorry,' he said.

'What for?' Shirley asked sharply, and Moira gave her a warning glance.

'I'm sorry to have missed the premiere.'

'So why did you?' Shirley asked, and felt Moira kick her under the table. 'Ouch!' she said involuntarily, and Julian gave a puzzled frown.

When nobody said anything he went on, 'I was just about to leave the house when David turned up.'

'David?' Shirley asked, and turned and glared at Moira as if to say, *I don't care*.

'My son. He's come home on leave. He's doing his National Service in Korea. I couldn't walk out the moment he arrived, could I?'

There was a shocked silence until Moira said, 'Of course you couldn't.'

'Anyway,' Julian continued, 'all David wanted to do was sleep, so I told him what the situation was and he insisted I should go. Now you'll have to tell me all about it – the film, I mean. Do you think Kay pulled it off?'

'She was superb,' Moira told him. 'I'm not sure if the leading lady will be altogether pleased.'

'No, it's always difficult for ageing actresses to see new talent coming up.'

'For goodness' sake, Yvette Todd is not exactly ageing! She can't be forty yet and she's radiantly beautiful.'

'I know. I'm generalising,' Julian said. 'Miss Todd has nothing to fear – yet. But the film industry can be cruel. As soon as an actress, no matter how talented, shows the tiniest signs of ageing, she could be passed over for the romantic lead and offered "character" parts. Or, God help us, the part of the heroine's mother.'

Suddenly Moira went silent. She was remembering something that had happened years ago. Something she had promised never to divulge.

Tom took a taxi to the Ritz and told the driver to wait. As soon as he entered, a uniformed doorman approached and asked if he could help.

'Could you find Miss Lockwood – she's with the film party – and tell her that Tom Masters is waiting?'

A short while later, Kay came hurrying towards him and he caught his breath. In a sleeveless crimson evening gown, with what he guessed was a mink stole tossed over her shoulders and her dark hair swept up on to the crown of her head, she was stunningly beautiful. Her limp was hardly noticeable, but at the last moment she stumbled and he caught her in his arms. She looked up at him and laughed. 'I did that on purpose,' she said.

Unable to control his instincts, he drew her closer and kissed her more passionately than he had ever done before. It was Kay who drew away. 'Tom,' she whispered shakily.

'I'm sorry,' he said.

Kay's vulnerable expression turned to one of fury. 'Why

are you sorry? You must know what my feelings are, and unless I'm terribly mistaken, I believe you feel the same way. So for God's sake why are you sorry?'

'I can't tell you why.'

'Can't or won't?'

They stared at each other, Kay furious, Tom in utter misery. Eventually Kay sighed and looked resigned. 'Let's go and join my friends.'

'The taxi's waiting.'

Julian couldn't understand why the little gathering was so subdued. Kay deserved better than this. Tom looked strained, Moira distracted; Jane was a bundle of nerves, and Shirley seemed positively icy. Well, at least he thought he knew the reason for that, and it was entirely his fault.

From the moment he'd met her he had thought her delightful – young, attractive and totally life-enhancing. What a foolish old man he'd been not to realise sooner that he was falling in love with her, when he had no right to. Thank the Lord nothing had been said. He knew he'd done the right thing by drawing back and avoiding being alone with her, but he was acutely aware of her misery.

Thank goodness David had arrived home a couple of days early. Julian had been dreading sitting next to Shirley in the intimate darkness of the cinema. Once there, she would have thought it strange if he had put distance between them. But there was no way he would have missed the celebration at Stefano's. That would have been hurtful to Kay, the girl he liked to tell people that he had discovered.

To ease the boredom of his months of enforced captivity, Maurice had persuaded Kostas to send one of his henchmen along with newspapers and the occasional magazine, so he had been able to follow the case. There had been so little in the papers of late, so that Maurice was beginning to think the police had given up. This had cheered him up enormously, and he was even happier when Kostas had told him a couple of days ago that he thought he had found a buyer for the jewellery. And the price Kostas had quoted, even when he had taken his commission, was enough to set Maurice and Jane up for life in some foreign clime.

This morning he made himself a cup of coffee, put it on the table and flipped through the paper fairly casually. Then something caught his eye and he stopped and swore. Apparently a film premiere had taken place the night before, and there were a couple of photographs that took up nearly the whole page. One was of Princess Margaret being greeted by some bloke who must have been the cinema manager, and another showed the film stars Yvette Todd and Michael Grainger walking towards the cinema and half turning to wave to the crowd.

It wasn't Yvette Todd who had caught Maurice's attention, lovely as she was. It was a face in the crowd. A face Maurice knew only too well: Jane. *The silly cow!* Maurice thought. *What the hell is she doing going to the West End and showing herself off so publicly?* It would just take someone from the village where she had been working to recognise her and the game would be up. He couldn't tell Kostas about this. He knew very well that Kostas would not hesitate to have Jane 'taken care of'.

Maurice wondered what he should do. Should he take the money and scarper without her? He'd already considered that option and decided it was too dangerous to leave her behind. If he abandoned her she would talk – turn King's evidence to save her skin. No, he was stuck with her. She managed to phone him every day – sometimes twice. As soon as he had the money he would give her directions and they would clear off, away from London. Using the false passports Kostas had arranged for them, they could put this country far behind them. That day couldn't come soon enough.

Dora loved the Royal family. She kept a scrapbook of photographs of them, and today she reached for the scissors and the Gloy as soon as she saw the picture of Princess Margaret at the film premiere. It was only when the photograph was pasted into the scrapbook and the occasion and the date was written next to it that she turned her attention to the other photograph. She wasn't really interested in film stars, but she examined Yvette Todd's evening gown and hairstyle before glancing casually at the crowd of fans.

'The bastard!' she said out loud. 'He's got no time to come home but he can go out at night with some woman or other!'

Dora examined the women closest to Tom and couldn't decide which one was his fancy piece. For fancy piece there must be. She was sure of that. Dora felt her anger rising. If she confronted Tom about this, he would only say that it was something to do with his work, and he might get so fed up with her that he would never come home again. Ricky had warned her about that. Dora dropped her head into her hands and began to weep. She was sobbing so loudly that she didn't hear the key in the lock and the front door open.

When Tom walked into the room, he saw the newspaper spread open on the table and his heart sank. This was what he had been afraid of. This was why he had come, even though he should have been on duty and he'd had to get someone else to take over watching Jane.

'Dora, love,' he said, and she lifted her head to reveal tear-streaked cheeks.

'I haven't got long,' Tom said. 'Why don't I go and get

us a couple of hot pies from the baker's? We'll have lunch together.'

'All right. That would be nice,' she said dully.

'Set the table then.' Tom smiled at her, but he was already wondering how soon he could get away.

Thelma sat with the newspaper on her knee. She had just got back from the newsagent's and she wanted to warm up a little before looking through the paper. That was what she told herself, but in reality she was delaying the pleasure of reading about Kay. Julie had phoned her just after breakfast to tell her that Kay had been mentioned in a review in the *Express*. She had thanked her younger daughter but had given no hint that she would go out and buy a copy.

She gazed into the fire and remembered how Jack used to sneak off to the theatre, no matter what the weather, to read the newspapers if there was anything in them about Lana. Thelma suspected that he wrote letters to Lana, too, and that Lana was writing to him and having the letters delivered to the theatre. He always told her that he had some work to do, such as working out new dance routines, and as she never objected, he must have assumed that she believed him. During the winter break he could very well have been putting next year's programme together, but as far as Thelma could see, there was no reason to go and sit in the damp, draughty theatre instead of by a warm fire in their comfortable home.

She never confronted him about this. She was too frightened to do so. If she did, she would have to admit to herself that she knew he still loved Lana, and she did not want to hear Jack tell any more lies.

There came a time when he returned home with his breath smelling of alcohol. He never appeared to be drunk, so Thelma guessed he was taking just sufficient to stave off the cold. This made her want to cry.

Every time Lana came to visit, acting like Lady Bountiful with the latest and most expensive toys for the children, Thelma saw the way Jack looked at the mother of his first child and how he was subdued and despondent on the day she breezed off again. And, of course, Thelma never believed that Jack's occasional trips to London were anything to do with theatre business. Paradoxically she didn't blame Jack. All the blame fell on Lana. Like many women in Thelma's position, she came to see the other woman as the temptress who was intent on taking away everything that made her happy.

In later years Thelma came to blame herself for Jack's death. If she had confronted him, if she had told him that she knew his solitary trips to the theatre were a charade and said, 'For God's sake, read your newspapers and write your letters in the comfort of your own home,' he might never have caught flu and succumbed so quickly to pneumonia. When he first became ill he had assured her that it was just a bad cough.

Why hadn't she tried harder to stop him leaving the house on that fatal day? He'd laughed as he took his scarf from the hallstand, wound it round his neck and said, 'Don't worry, Thelma, I'm not a kid,' before being overtaken by a wracking cough. He left the house, not realising that Thelma knew very well he was going to the news-stand in the station. She looked out of the front parlour window and saw his tall figure leaning into the sleet as he walked up the road and away from her. He was never to come home again.

Late that evening, worried out of her mind, Thelma took the spare keys and went to the theatre. The wind was blowing in from the sea and it was bitterly cold. Each breath she took hurt her throat and brought tears to her eyes.

Inside the theatre it wasn't much better. She called out for

Jack, but there was no response. She was filled with dread. When she entered his office she found him slumped over the desk. She tried to rouse him, but it soon became obvious that he was dead. She reached for the phone and dialled 999.

While she waited for the ambulance she looked at the folder full of newspaper clippings. There was also a copy of today's *Daily Express* spread out on the desk, open at the entertainments page. She cast her eye over an article about a glamorous party, where Lana Fontaine had been seen dancing with the new heartthrob Robert Spencer. When questioned, Lana said that although they enjoyed working together there was no romance in real life. Thelma wondered if Jack had believed that and, if not, what torments he had suffered.

Thelma looked at the folder and remembered how Lana had always said that one day someone would document her life. She remembered all the photographs that Lana had insisted should be taken and wondered what had happened to them. Sitting down at the desk, she clipped the article from the paper and put it into the folder. She didn't know why she had done this, except that Jack would have wanted it. And closing the folder somehow symbolised 'the end'. Thelma kept the folder – again, she didn't know why, but it was if Jack were telling her that it would be important one day. She never opened it again.

She didn't keep the bundle of Lana's letters that she found in the bottom drawer of the desk. Jack had tied them up with a ribbon, as if he were some romantic schoolgirl. Thelma laughed through her tears at that. She didn't read them. Even in this situation she was too principled to pry – and in any case, she knew it would cause her grief. When Jack had been taken to the hospital mortuary she took the letters to the waste bin behind the theatre and tossed them in. She looked at them mingling with ice-cream wrappers, empty crisp packets and abandoned programmes; then she closed the lid and walked away.

Thelma locked up the theatre and went home. She wondered if the icy wind would freeze the tears that streamed down her cheeks.

'Please, don't be like that,' Lana said. 'Don't you know you're breaking my heart?'

Thelma could barely control her anger. 'You can stop the melodrama. It won't work with me. Nothing you say will make me change my mind. And keep your voice down. The children are in the next room.' Thelma walked over and closed the door.

Lana spoke quietly but she sounded just as desperate. 'She's my daughter. You have no right to stop me seeing her.'

'You gave up your rights when you handed her over to me.'

'Jack wouldn't have wanted this.'

'Jack's gone. We buried him last week.'

'I know. And why didn't you write to me until it was all over?'

'Because I didn't want any dramatics at the graveside.'

'Thelma . . . please . . .'

'It's no good, Lana. You chose your career rather than bring up your daughter. Kay is mine now. I never want you to come near her again.'

The coals shifted and settled in the grate. Thelma sighed and closed her eyes for a moment. Eventually, she wiped her eyes and willed the past to fade. She opened the paper, turning the pages until she found the review of the film premiere. She ignored the photographs, because Kay wasn't in them, but she read the review with interest. There wasn't much about Kay – only a small paragraph about the new star who had turned in an emotional and powerful performance, even though she had been confined to a wheelchair.

Thelma went through to the kitchen and took a shoebox from a cupboard in the dresser. Sitting at the kitchen table, she carefully cut out the review then put it in the box, along with the other pieces she had clipped from newspapers.

Nobody knew she was keeping this scrapbook. Julie would have been delighted, because she would have taken it as a sign that her mother was not only resigned to Kay's new life but that she actively approved of it. Thelma wasn't sure yet if that was true. She did know that Jack would have been proud of Kay, and Lana, too.

She closed the box and returned it to the cupboard. She sighed. Even though Lana was long dead, her ghost seemed to be winning the battle.

Part Four

Chapter Twenty-Three

The morning after the film premiere Kay and her two lodgers were quiet at the breakfast table. Shirley had gone out early to scan the newspapers at the newsagent's and had come back with the *Express*. She read the review out loud, then turned to Kay. 'Well done, old thing!'

'Yes, well done,' Jane echoed faintly. She reached for the newspaper and looked at the photographs.

'And I'd like to say,' Shirley continued, 'that I'm sorry I was such a selfish bitch last night. It's no excuse, but I was in a right old mood with myself.'

'I noticed. What was wrong?'

'Just something to do with work. But I shouldn't have let it spoil your triumph.'

Kay smiled wanly. 'Don't exaggerate. It was a good review but hardly a triumph. And I was just as moody. And as for you, Jane . . .'

'Mmm?' Jane looked up from the paper. 'What about me?' she asked, and Shirley could have sworn her fellow lodger looked nervous.

'You never said a word other than "please" and "thank you" all night.'

'I'm sorry. I suppose I was a bit overwhelmed. I'm not used to mixing with theatricals.'

Shirley burst out laughing. 'Theatricals! I suppose you mean Julian? And I can tell you, you had him puzzled. We all had. He tried desperately to jolly us all along, didn't he? Moira tried her best, too, but Tom was as unsociable as the rest of us.'

'Let's leave it alone,' Kay said.

'You're right. Let's just write it off as one of those things. And you and I had better get a move on if we're going to be in time for rehearsals for the next exciting episode of *Mulberry Court*.'

They managed to find seats on the bus, but even though the mood had lifted Kay and Shirley were still quieter than usual on the way to Broadcasting House. Eventually Shirley said, 'It's man trouble, isn't it, Kay? Come on, you can tell Aunty Shirley.'

Kay smiled. 'Only if you'll admit that that's what's bothering you, too.'

'It is, and I think you and I should have a good old chinwag over lunch. Share our troubles and all that. Agreed?'

'Agreed,' Kay said. 'And we could also speculate on what's bothering Jane. As far as we know, she hasn't got a man in her life at the moment, so what else is making her miserable?'

'I'm not sure if she's miserable about anything,' Shirley said. 'I think she's downright scared.'

Once Kay and Shirley had gone, Jane looked down at the paper and studied one of the photographs anew. She began to tremble. There was no question that it was her in the crowd, and the picture was so clear that anyone who knew her would recognise her immediately. She glanced at her watch. The diamond-tipped hands told her it was time to phone Maurice. She went through to the hallway and perched nervously on the chair by the telephone table, then dialled the usual number.

She held her breath as she waited for Maurice to pick up

the phone. She could only hope that he hadn't seen the newspaper. Her hopes were dashed the minute she got through.

'What the hell were you thinking of?' were his first words. 'Getting yourself photographed like that?'

Jane began to shake, and not just because the hallway was cold. 'I was in the crowd . . . I didn't think.'

'That's your problem, you silly cow. You never think, and that's because you haven't got anything to think with. If you had, you wouldn't have been in the West End in the first place. Why on earth were you there?'

'I was at the film premiere.'

Maurice swore. 'I guessed that. Just tell me why.'

'It was Kay's first film. They would have thought it funny if I hadn't gone.'

'You could have had a headache.'

'No, Maurice. I've used that excuse too many times when they've wanted me to go out with them. I think they're beginning to get suspicious. Especially that nosy bitch Shirley.'

There was a pause, and when he spoke he didn't sound quite so angry. 'Then it's probably time we moved on, isn't it?'

'I don't understand. How can we?'

'Because I've got the money. First thing this morning Kos—' He broke off then started again, 'My pal came round with it.'

Jane was silent. When she spoke there were tears streaming down her face. 'You mean it? You're not kidding?'

'Of course I'm not kidding. We're off, kiddo, and you'll never have to worry about your landlady and her pal again.'

'When are we going?'

'We're going today.'

'*Today!*'

'There's no sense in hanging around, so go and stuff some essentials in your handbag.'

'What about my clothes?'

'You won't need them. We've got enough moolah to buy anything you need as soon as we reach Paris.'

'But Maurice . . .'

'No "buts". We're travelling light. Understand?'

'Yes, I understand.'

'And leave the place tidy. We don't want your landlady suspecting anything until we've left these shores behind us.'

'Where shall I meet you?'

'Listen carefully. Don't write anything down.'

When her call ended Jane raced upstairs. Her heart pounding with elation, she began taking clothes out of her wardrobe. Maurice really couldn't expect her to leave all the new clothes she'd bought. She stared at them in bewilderment, wondering what to take and what to leave. She reached for her suitcase.

Ten minutes later, Jane frowned as she squashed the lid down. She glanced at the rest of her clothes heaped up on the bed then reached for a hanger. She started putting them back in the wardrobe and then paused and laughed. *What the hell*, she thought. *Why am I worrying about leaving the place untidy? By the time they get home from work I'll be long gone.*

Then she paused. If she left it like this they would just worry about her. They were daft enough, too. They might even call the police. Jane rummaged in her handbag and found a receipt from the jeweller's. Hastily she scribbled a note on the back and left it on the dressing table. Then she put on her best coat, picked up her suitcase and headed off to a new life.

The man in the car reached for the handset of his two-way radio and flicked the switch. 'Sergeant Masters, please.' There was a pause. 'That you, Tom? She's just come out carrying a suitcase. Looks like she might be off.'

'Could be. Word is that a huge amount of French francs changed hands this morning.'

'Francs? She'll be heading to Victoria, then?'

'Looks like it. Keep on her tail and keep in touch. I'll send back-up. This could be it.'

Kay picked up her lunch tray and followed Shirley to the furthest corner of the basement canteen.

'Why are we doing this?' she asked.

'Doing what?'

'Hiding away like this?'

'We don't want anyone to join us, do we? Not while we pour out all our troubles.'

Kay settled in her seat and frowned uneasily. She was no longer sure that she wanted to 'pour out her troubles'. After all, nothing Shirley could say would help; but before she'd had a chance to tell Shirley that she'd changed her mind, the other girl said, 'It's about Tom, isn't it?'

Kay sighed. 'There's no other man in my life at the moment, is there?'

'And you're in love with him?'

'Perhaps.'

'Oh, come on, Kay, it's obvious that you're crazy about him.'

Kay stared at Shirley, tight-lipped and silent.

Shirley continued, 'Do you think he's messing you about?'

'In what way?'

'Well, he seems keen, but he's obviously not taking the relationship any further. One reason for that could be that he's married. Have you considered that?'

Kay stared at her friend in consternation. 'No . . . actually, I haven't.'

'Why not?'

'It never occurred to me. He seems . . . too honourable. Or am I naïve as well as stupid?' Kay felt her temper rising.

'Naïve, probably. But what other explanation could there be? I mean, he seems as keen as mustard, he calls by the house as often as he can and he's always taking you out.'

'And my friends too!'

'Yes, I've noticed that. It's almost as if he's fallen for you but he can't allow himself to get too close.'

'Do you think we could stop this conversation?'

'I've upset you.'

'Of course you bloody have.' Kay attacked her shepherd's pie furiously.

Shirley looked crestfallen. 'I thought it would help to confide in each other.'

'Well, it doesn't.'

Shirley was silent, and when Kay looked at her she saw to her dismay that she was crying. 'I'm sorry,' she said through her tears.

'No, I'm the one who's sorry,' Kay said.

'You see, I thought we could console each other.'

'I know you did.'

'I thought we had the same problem. I'm in love with Julian. Original, isn't it, to fall in love with your boss? And I thought he was in love with me – or at least was interested – and then suddenly he turned all cold and distant. Then last night we learned he had a grown-up son. So that's it. He's married.'

'Miss Walton, could I have a word with you?' Kay and Shirley looked up to see Julian standing over them. He was carrying his lunch tray but he didn't look in the slightest interested in it. 'In my office.' He dumped the tray on the table. 'I was going to join you for lunch,' he said, 'but I think there's something we need to talk about. Now.'

Kay had never felt so sorry for anyone as she watched Shirley follow Julian out of the canteen. She stared down at the abandoned food and completely inconsequentially thought what a waste it was. She took up a forkful of her mince and potato and realised that her hand was shaking. She put the fork down again, and to her horror she began to cry. Why had she never considered the fact that Tom might be married?

She took her handkerchief from her handbag and scrubbed the tears from her cheeks before anyone from the surrounding tables noticed her. Then she resolutely ate every scrap of her lunch and drank her coffee. In a few minutes she was due in the studio. Nothing must come in the way of the next episode of *Mulberry Court*.

After the broadcast Kay declined her fictional parents' invitation to join them in the club.

'Are you OK?' Alex asked.

'You are looking a bit peaky, darling,' Cynthia added.

'I'm tired, that's all. I need to go home and put my feet up.'

Alex joked good-naturedly about her new career as a film star, but Cynthia told her to ignore him and make sure she had an early night.

After everybody had gone and the studio had been cleared, Kay looked around for Shirley and couldn't find her. Norman, one of the studio managers, came up with a note. It was short and sweet: 'Don't wait. Will tell all later, Shirley.'

Drat the girl, Kay thought. *Doesn't she realise that I'll worry about her?* Feeling utterly despondent, Kay went home alone.

The house was quiet. And cold. Kay hurried through to the kitchen and discovered that Jane had let the fire go out. And she had also neglected to clear the breakfast table and wash the dishes. Jane didn't have to wash the dishes; it was just that she always did. Kay wondered if she was all right. She went upstairs and knocked on Jane's door. After waiting a few moments she opened the door, went in and then stopped and stared at the open door of the wardrobe, the half-closed drawers and the pile of clothes on the bed.

Kay was utterly bewildered. It was like a scene from the *Marie Celeste*. What could have happened to the girl? At that moment she heard the key in the lock and hurried downstairs as the front door was opening.

'Jane,' she called. 'Are you all right?'

But it wasn't Jane who walked into the hall; it was Shirley.

'I'm not Jane and why shouldn't she be all right?' Shirley said.

'You'd better come up.'

Shirley followed Kay upstairs and stared at the state of Jane's room. 'What on earth . . . ?' she said.

'It's not like her, is it?' Kay said. 'I mean, she's always so careful with her clothes.'

Shirley was staring upwards. 'Can you remember, did she keep a suitcase on top of the wardrobe?'

'I think she did.'

'Well, it's gone. She's left us.'

Kay shook her head. 'But why like this?'

'Haven't a clue.'

Kay watched uneasily as Shirley, less reluctant than she was to pry, moved around the room turning over clothes or shoving them aside. So it was she who found the note on the dressing table. 'Listen to this,' she said. '"Sorry to leave so unexpectedly. Family crisis. I'll send you any rent I owe you. I'll be back for my clothes."'

Shirley looked up from the scrap of paper. 'What do you think of that?'

Kay was bewildered. 'I thought she'd quarrelled with her

family. I thought her father forbade her to come anywhere near them.'

'Or so she told us. You know, I don't believe a word of it. She won't be back for her clothes and you can say goodbye to the rent. She's run off.'

'Why would she do that?'

'I don't know, but I wouldn't mind betting it's something to do with the telephone calls she denies making. We won't see her again.'

'If that's the case, what will I do with this lot?' Kay stared at the heap of clothes.

'I would give it until her rent's due, and if you haven't heard from her after that, I'd sell everything or give the lot to the Salvation Army. Meanwhile, I'll help you tidy up, and then I suggest we go downstairs and put the kettle on.'

Kay was thankful that Shirley could take everything so matter-of-factly and was pleased to accept her offer of help. Back in the kitchen she made up the fire and Shirley made a pot of tea. It was only when they were sitting at the kitchen table that Kay remembered how upset Shirley had been last time she had seen her. She didn't like to ask what had happened, so she was relieved when Shirley brought the subject up herself.

'About Julian,' she said and then she stared into space.

'Was he . . . was he angry with you?' Kay asked.

'Just a little. He didn't like the fact that I was talking about him to you.'

'Oh dear.'

'I told him it was his own fault.'

'You didn't!'

'I did, because it was true. Oh, I know he's my boss, and even when I spoke to him like that I thought I was risking the sack. But it was his fault that I was miserable and I thought he ought to know that.'

'What did he say?'

'He was taken aback, but he apologised.'

'Thank goodness for that. Why are you smiling?'

'Because the next thing he did was to take me in his arms and kiss me.'

'What did you do?'

'What do you think I did? I kissed him back, of course!'

Kay was shocked. 'But how could you? I mean, he's married, isn't he?'

Shirley's smile faded. 'Julian's a widower. His wife died ten years ago. He's brought David up on his own.'

'Then what was the problem?' Kay asked. 'Why did he blow hot and cold the way he did?'

'Because of the age difference. Julian thought it wouldn't be fair to me. I told him I didn't care. I reminded him that Charlie Chaplin is thirty-six years older than his wife Oona, so what's a mere twenty-five years' difference?'

Shirley paused to fill up her cup, leaving Kay in suspense. 'Don't be infuriating,' Kay said. 'What happened next?'

Shirley grinned. 'I asked him to marry me, of course.'

'You didn't!'

'I think you said that earlier.'

'What did he say?'

'He said yes.'

'Shirley, that's wonderful! I'm so happy for you!'

And Kay realised it was true. No matter how miserable she was about her own situation, she wanted her friend to be happy.

'Then he immediately apologised.'

'Why?'

'Because I'll have to leave Broadcasting House. You see, the BBC doesn't like married couples to work together, nor even work in the same building, so I'll have to go to Bush House and find a job in the World Service. I told him I didn't mind. I'll be more upset at leaving you.'

'How do you mean, leaving me?'

'When I get married.

'Oh, of course.'

'I'm really sorry, Kay. I'll help you find a respectable replacement if you like. Two, if Jane never appears again.'

'That's all right. I'm not sure if I want to take in any more lodgers. Now that I have so much work coming in, I no longer need the rent.'

'What about company?'

'I'll still have you as a friend, presumably?'

'Of course.'

'And there's Moira.' Kay collected the cups and saucers and took them to the sink. *And what about Tom?* she thought. *Can I count him as a friend?* Forcing herself to smile, she turned to face Shirley. 'You know, I don't feel like cooking tonight. How about fish and chips?'

'You bet.'

'I'll go, you warm the plates.'

Kay got no further than the front door. When she opened it she found Moira standing there with her hand raised, ready to ring the bell. Kay's welcoming smile died when she saw how distraught Moira was. 'What is it?' she asked.

'Here,' Moira said and she thrust a copy of the evening paper into Kay's hands. 'You'd better read this.'

Chapter Twenty-Four

CAUGHT AT LAST!

Murdering jewel thieves arrested in Victoria station as they were about to board the boat-train.

Remember the two killers who set fire to a manor house in Yorkshire, thus ending the life of the blameless old lady who lived there? One of them is thought to be a young woman who now calls herself Jane Mullen, but is suspected of having had several aliases, and is wanted for a string of petty crimes. She worked as housekeeper for Lady Charlesworth, and one night when her employer was visiting friends in the nearby village, she allowed her partner-in-crime, Maurice Snape, to enter the house. It is assumed that the pair of them stole Lady Charlesworth's jewels and who knows what else, because as they fled with their loot they set fire to the place. No one knows why, but maybe it was to cover their tracks.

The heartless thieves must have known that Lady Charlesworth's little dog was in the house but they left it to suffer a painful death. Even worse, Lady Charlesworth saw the fire from the village and hurried home in an attempt to rescue her beloved pet. She died in the fire. In the opinion of this newspaper, this makes the heartless pair murderers who should hang for their crimes.

After they fled, Snape and Mullen dropped out of sight, and it seemed as though they were going to get away with it. However, the police had traced Mullen almost as soon as she arrived in London. Unfortunately there was no sign of Snape. Scotland Yard decided to play a waiting game. They chose to let Mullen think she'd got away with it and kept watch on her in the hopes that eventually she would lead them to Snape, who had probably vanished into the London underworld, and would be trying to dispose of the loot. When he succeeded in this, the pair of them would almost certainly flee abroad.

A team of detectives, led by Sergeant Tom Masters, played a waiting game until today, when it looked as though Mullen was about to fly the nest. She was followed to Victoria station, and as soon as she met up with Snape, the pair of them were apprehended.

Apparently Mullen immediately offered to give King's evidence in order to save her own neck – which proves there is no honour among thieves.

Sergeant Masters, who had been working under-cover, refused to reveal where Mullen had been hiding out in order to protect the innocent.

Kay and Shirley sat next to each other at the kitchen table as they read the article. Shirley finished first. She sat back and waited until Kay looked up. For once, Shirley had nothing to say.

'Did neither of you have any idea?' Moira asked. She had joined them at the table but had kept quiet until they had finished reading.

'How on earth could we have guessed that Jane was a thief who was on the run?' Shirley said.

Kay kept silent.

'Although I did think there was something fishy about her,' Shirley continued. 'But a thief and a murderess?' She shook her head.

'I don't think she meant to murder anyone,' Kay said.

'Are you making excuses for her?'

'No, Shirley, I'm not. But remember how the fire made her so nervous?'

'Or guilty.'

'Yes, I suppose so.'

'I feel as though I've let you down,' Moira said.

'Why do you say that?' Kay asked.

'When you decided to take lodgers I should have asked the girl for references.'

'Huh!' Shirley said. 'She would probably have forged them.'

'I suppose so. Kay, what are you going to do now?'

'I'm going to try to forget what a fool I've been.'

'You weren't a fool,' Shirley said. 'Jane was very plausible.'

'I didn't mean Jane, I meant Tom. All these months I've welcomed him into this house, and I thought at the very least he wanted to be my friend, when all the time he was using me in order keep watch on Jane. You read what the paper said. Sergeant Masters was "working undercover". Well, now that he's done his job I don't want to see him again for as long as I live.'

'We can write you out of one or even two episodes, Kay, but you'll have to be back for the Christmas special.'

'Thanks, Julian. I won't let you down.'

'I can understand why you want a break. Shirley told me you're pretty upset about Tom Masters pretending to be your friend when all the time he was keeping tabs on Jane. And it must be pretty distressing to discover what kind of woman you had living with you – a thief and a murderess!'

Kay's smile was strained. 'Shirley says I should write a book about it, and if I don't, she will. She'll change all the names and the location, of course. She said it wouldn't do for the star of *Mulberry Court* to get the wrong kind of publicity.'

'And Tom would never reveal anything, of course. You've got to give him credit for that.'

'If you say so.'

Kay was silent and Julian took the hint. 'OK, I'll change the subject. So where are you going? Somewhere warm or some very expensive hotel?'

'Neither. I'm off to a seaside resort on the windy north-east coast.'

Julian raised his eyebrows.

'I'm going home.'

Tom hadn't expected to be welcomed with open arms, but neither had he expected to be kept on the doorstep.

'Kay isn't in,' Shirley said.

He turned his collar up in an effort to get some protection from the damp sleet. 'Well, can't you at least invite me in for a cup of tea?'

'I don't think so. You'll need a warrant to get into this house.'

'OK,' he said. 'Would you at least tell Kay that I want to see her?'

'Why?'

'To explain things, of course.'

'I'll tell her, but I don't think she'll listen. She doesn't want to see you ever again. That's what she said.'

'Here,' he took a card from his pocket, 'this is my phone number.'

'She already has it.'

'No, not the flat. I've given that up now.'

'Oh, of course. That was all part of the deception, wasn't it?'

'I didn't mean to deceive Kay.'

'Didn't you? You certainly didn't tell her the truth, did you?'

'You know I couldn't.'

'In other words, you didn't trust her.'

'It wasn't a matter of trust. I had no idea if Maurice Snape knew where Jane was staying. Any false move might have put Kay's life in danger. And I would never have forgiven myself if that had happened.'

'And what about *my* life?'

Tom saw Shirley's faint smile and was encouraged. 'Yours too, of course. Listen, Shirley, give Kay my card. That's my direct line at the Yard. Tell her to phone me.'

'It's no use, Tom. Kay's going away for a while.'

'Where's she going?'

Shirley laughed. 'As if I'd tell you. Now, if you don't mind, it's bloody freezing and I'm going to close the door.'

'Shirley . . .'

The door slammed in his face.

Shirley remained where she was. For a puzzling few seconds she was undecided whether she should open the door again and call him back. *Get a grip, girl*, she told herself. She set off resolutely for the kitchen but it was a moment or two before she could banish the image of the pure misery on Tom's face.

'Who was that?' Moira was sitting by the fire.

'Tom.'

'You didn't invite him in?'

'Are you crazy?'

'Don't you feel the slightest bit sorry for him?'

'No, I don't. Not after what he did.'

'He was doing his duty.'

'He led Kay on.'

'I suppose he did, but it was only because he couldn't tell her the truth. I've seen them together, and you know what I think? I think he's genuinely in love with her.'

'Then why didn't he tell her that?'

'He couldn't, could he? Not while he was undercover.'

Shirley scowled. 'You're talking as if you actually like the guy.'

'I do. And furthermore, Shirley, don't you think you sometimes make your mind up about people too quickly? And once you've done so, you're determined not to admit that you might be wrong?'

'Is that what you think about me, Moira?'

'I'm sorry, Shirley, but I'm afraid it is.'

They were silent for a moment. Shirley stared into the fire but the only picture she could see was Tom's unhappy face. She looked at Moira and smiled wryly. 'It sounds like a cheap novel, doesn't it? Cops and robbers, a maiden betrayed, and a broken-hearted policeman. I shall have to buy myself a typewriter.'

Moira smiled, her criticism of Shirley forgotten. Or at least put aside. 'Are you really going to write a book?'

'Yes, I think I am. Once the wedding is over.'

Something was wrong with the heating, and by the time the train reached Newcastle Kay was shivering with cold. She dragged her case from the overhead rack and stepped out on to the platform. Someone was calling her name, and she turned to see Tony hurrying along the platform towards her, smiling broadly.

'Kay!' he said and gave her an enthusiastic hug. 'Let me take your case. My, that's not very heavy.'

'I'm not staying long. I have to be back at work in time for the Christmas special of *Mulberry Court*.'

'Julie will be disappointed. But let's get to the car. The wind blowing down this platform has come straight from Siberia.'

Tony cupped her elbow and hurried her out of the station. 'I wasn't expecting anyone to meet the train,' Kay said. 'I told Julie I would get a taxi.'

'You might have known your sister wouldn't stand for that. In fact, she would have been here herself if Kathleen hadn't arrived a little sooner than expected.'

'*What?* You mean she's had her baby?'

They had reached the car and Tony opened the back door and almost threw Kay's case in, then he turned and hugged Kay enthusiastically. 'Yes, Kathleen Chalmers, your new niece, was born two days ago. Oh, Kay, she's beautiful!'

'That's marvellous!' Kay said. 'Congratulations! But why didn't you phone me?'

'Julie wanted it to be a nice surprise.'

Kay couldn't help thinking it would have been more of a nice surprise if she hadn't found out about Kathleen until she walked in and saw Julie and her daughter together. She wondered uneasily if Tony had wanted to break the news himself because he imagined that she still had feelings for him and might have been upset, or whether he was just too excited to wait. She was prepared to believe it was the latter.

'It's a wonderful surprise,' Kay said. 'I can't wait to see my new niece.'

On the way home Tony could hardly stop talking, and every now and then Kay glanced sideways at his smiling face. On one such occasion Tony glanced round and saw her surprised expression. His smile vanished.

332

'Listen, Kay,' he said. 'I know I haven't treated Julie as well as I should have, and I'm guessing that she's confided in you. And I don't blame her. But, you know, I was pretty shaken up when you ditched me, and it was all too easy to settle for someone who had never hidden her admiration of me.'

'Is that what you wanted? Admiration?'

Tony looked embarrassed. 'Only because my pride was dented, and Julie is very beautiful, of course.'

'Do you love her?'

'I didn't think I did at first. In fact, I thought that I might have made a mistake.'

'Oh Tony, don't say that!'

'No, it's all right, Kay. The moment I saw Julie holding Kathleen in her arms I was overcome with love for both of them. My wife and my daughter. I saw the way Julie looked down at the baby she was cradling. She's so sweet and so loving. I was ashamed that I'd never seen that before. Julie is right for me in a way you never were.'

Kay caught her breath. Despite the fact that she knew he was right, she couldn't help remembering the happy times they'd had together.

Tony looked at her ruefully. 'I'm sorry. Is that hurtful? I don't mean to be. It's just that we were never really right for each other, were we? If we had been, you would never have gone off to London the way you did. And now it's all for the best, isn't it? I'm in love with my wife, we have a beautiful child, and you have your career. You made the right choice, Kay, and I hope you'll be as happy as we are.'

After leaving Kay's coat and suitcase in the hall, Tony deposited her in the bedroom with Julie, then, picking up a list from the bedside table, he dashed off to do some shopping. *How domesticated*, Kay thought, but his delight at new fatherhood seemed genuine.

Julie was sitting up in bed cradling her daughter in her arms. The baby was asleep, but Julie looked as though she didn't want to relinquish her. Kay was at a loss. She would have liked to hug her sister but she didn't want to wake Kathleen.

Looking pink and rosy and delightfully dishevelled, Julie reluctantly held her daughter up towards Kay. 'Here you are. Would you mind putting your niece in her crib?'

'Oh, but . . .'

'Don't worry. She won't break. And she won't wake up, not after the feed she's just had.'

Kay took the swaddled bundle and held her close. She was taken unawares by a surge of emotion. 'She's lovely,' she said.

Julie laughed softly. 'It's conventional to say that, but in this case it's perfectly true.' The sisters exchanged smiles, then, 'Go on. Put her down,' Julie said. 'And sit down on the bed and we can talk. Why are you looking worried?'

'Are you sure it's all right for me to stay here?' Kay said.

'Of course it is. That was the plan, wasn't it?'

'But that was before the baby arrived. You've got your hands full now.' Kay thought Julie had never looked so happy, but she also looked tired, and she proved the point by yawning deeply before she answered.

'There's no need to worry about that. Mum and Tony's mother are here all the time. Apart from feeding Kathleen, I don't have much to do.'

'Will Mum be coming this evening?'

'No, luckily.'

'Why luckily?'

'Because she doesn't know you're here yet.'

'Oh, Julie, why not?'

'Well, the plan was we should go round together, wasn't it? But then things started happening and, forgive me, Kay, everything else went out of my mind.' Julie paused and looked at Kay seriously. 'So, if you don't mind, I think you should go round after we've had tea. We'll be eating about five.'

Kay thought how authoritative Julie sounded and wondered if that was what motherhood did to you. She found herself asking Julie's advice: 'What shall I say to her?'

'Well, you could say Tony phoned you to tell you about the baby.'

'That would be a lie. And, by the way, why didn't he?'

Julie frowned. 'Partly because I wanted it to be a lovely surprise for you and partly because I was worried you'd change your mind.'

Kay glanced at her sleeping niece. 'Of course I wouldn't have changed my mind!' she said indignantly.

'Oh, I don't mean because of the baby. I mean you might not have wanted to face Mum on your own.'

'You make me sound a craven coward.'

'I'm not saying you're frightened of her. But things have been so bad between you – oh, I know it's been Mum's fault, not yours – that it would have been better for me to be a sort of referee to see that the pair of you behaved yourselves.'

Kay took her sister's hand. 'You're very wise, Julie. But you're also very tired. No, don't deny it. I think you should sleep for a while. I'll go downstairs, and perhaps I can help make the meal.'

'There'll be no need for that. I think I just heard Tony come back and he'll have brought his mother. You know, I think the birth of a grandchild might be just what she needs.' Julie yawned. 'I'll explain later. But go and have a chat with her. She knew you were coming and she's thrilled.'

'Why thrilled?'

'Because in her eyes you're rich and famous.'

'I'm not rich!'

'Maybe not, but you can't deny you're famous. Now off you go and let me get some sleep before Kathleen wakes up and demands to be fed again.'

A heavy mist had rolled in from the sea, muffling the sound of Kay's footsteps. She could hear waves lapping eerily on the nearby shore and drawing back across the shingle. The street lights had halos and the hazy light was barely enough to show the way. However, Kay knew these streets well; she still sometimes cycled around them in her dreams. She soon found her way to the house she was heading for.

'Kay! How wonderful to see you!' Miss Bennet said. 'Come in quickly and we'll go and sit by the fire.'

When Kay and her old friend were settled each side of the hearth, Miss Bennet said, 'If only I'd known you were coming I would have bought something nice for tea.'

'Please don't worry about that. I've just had a lovely tea at Julie's house. That's where I'm staying.'

'Not with your mother?'

'No. She doesn't know I'm here.'

Miss Bennet frowned. 'And why is that?'

'I needed a break and I phoned Julie. Of course, she invited me to stay, and the plan was we should go and face my mother together.'

'Why would you need to do that?'

'She was very much against my going to London and things have been difficult between us.'

'I think you should go and see her straight away, even without Julie to back you up. I realise your sister will be too taken up with your new niece.'

Kay was surprised. 'You know about the baby?'

Miss Bennet smiled. 'This is a small town, remember. The gossip gets around. Especially as Tony Chalmers is still very much a local hero. So how is your sister?'

'Blooming. Motherhood suits her.'

'Kay, I'd love to talk longer, to ask you about your work and the interesting people that you meet, but I really think you should go and see your mother before it gets too late.'

'I know . . . I'll be on my way. But I hope I can come and see you again before I go back to London.'

'Of course you can. How long are you staying?'

'Just over a week. I have to be back for the *Mulberry Court* Christmas special.'

'That sounds exciting.'

Kay laughed. 'I suppose it will be. There's going to be a guest star. Someone famous.'

'Oh, do tell me who.'

'I can't. Not even the cast have been told in case they let the cat out of the bag. We won't know until he or she comes along for rehearsal.'

'Well, we can speculate together on who it might be. But now, off you go and see your mother.'

Kay was reluctant to leave her old friend. She had been hoping that she could confide in her and maybe receive some sensible advice. But that would have to wait. The familiar streets were now wreathed in heavy fog. Kay almost set out in the direction of the house she had lived in all her life, then she remembered and reoriented herself. She trod a less familiar path to the house she had bought for her mother with the money left to her by Lana Fontaine.

It seemed strange not having a key. Kay rang the bell and waited at the unfamiliar door until her mother answered it.

'Kay. You should have told me you were coming.' The first words that her mother spoke to her were critical. 'Well, I suppose you'd better come in.'

Thelma stood back as Kay entered the house, then said, 'Well, what do you think?'

'About what?'

'About the house, of course.'

'From what I can see of it – this hallway – it's lovely.'

Her mother frowned slightly.

'I mean, it's fashionable,' Kay said. 'Like something in a magazine.'

Thelma smiled. 'It is, isn't it? Come on, I'll show you round. Wait a minute, where's your case?'

'At Julie's.'

'You went there first?'

'Julie invited me to stay.'

'Before or after she had the baby?'

'Before.'

'Well, I think you should change your plans now. Julie has enough on her plate. I think you should stay here.'

Kay was astonished. She hadn't expected her mother to make her welcome.

Thelma continued, 'After I've shown you round, we'll have a cup of tea, then we can go to Julie's together to get your things.'

Before Kay could respond, her mother ushered her upstairs to see the bedrooms and the bathroom and then downstairs again, showing her into every room. Kay was touched to see her mother's pride in her new home, and even though she thought some of the rooms were over-furnished she told her mother everything was beautiful.

While they were drinking tea in the sitting room, Thelma suggested that they phone Julie's house and ask Tony if he would bring Kay's case along. 'Better than us going out again on a chilly night like this, isn't it?'

'Oh, but Julie . . .'

'Julie won't mind. Not when she's so taken up with her new baby. I'll tell her that you and I have a lot to talk about.'

Kay's spirits sank at the idea but she could hardly object.

After Tony had been and gone her mother seemed rather subdued, and Kay wondered whether she had forgotten that they were supposed to be having a talk. Eventually Thelma sighed and said, 'Kay, have you anything to ask me?'

Kay was taken aback. There were so many things she wanted to know that she couldn't think where to start. Then she remembered something she had heard as a child; a conversation that had echoed down the years and come back to her recently.

'There is something. I'm sure I heard you and Lana quarrelling when I was a child. You were angry with each other. I wasn't in the same room as you, but I heard Lana say you were breaking her heart, then I think you said that nothing she could say could make you change your mind. Then I heard the sound of a door closing. I'm sure it's important, but I don't know why.'

Her mother sighed deeply. 'I lied to you, Kay, because I was angry and frightened. I told you that Lana just walked away from you after your father died without a backward glance. The truth is, I told her never to come to see you again. I absolutely forbade it.'

'Why?'

'I told you. Because I was frightened. I thought that with your father gone and because Lana was becoming rich and successful, she might take you away from me.' Thelma paused and for a moment Kay thought she looked frightened now. 'Kay, there's something you should know. Something I should have told you long ago. Lana was—'

'My mother.' Kay paused, remembering the shock and pain she had suffered when she had realised the truth. 'It's all right, I've already guessed that. I began to wonder as soon as I went to live in her house. There were boxfuls of photographs. It should have occurred to me long before it did that I looked like Lana, but it was only when I found a photograph of her and Dad together – it was the only photo in an envelope in a boxful of loose photographs, as if Lana were telling me that it was special. Lana and Dad looked so very happy, they looked like lovers – oh, Mum, I'm sorry to tell you this, but when I looked at that photograph everything fell into place as I'm sure she meant it to.'

Thelma was weeping. 'I didn't want Lana to take you away from me. I loved you as if you were my own child. When she left you everything in her will, I thought she was claiming you at last – that you would go to London, perhaps discover the truth, and then never come back to me.

'I know I haven't always been easy to live with,' she continued. 'It's as though what happened in the past soured me, took away my kindlier instincts. I hope you can forgive me for the many times I've been harsh or petty, because, whatever I've done, I've always loved you.'

Kay rose from her chair and knelt at Thelma's knees. 'And I love you, Mum. Anything I've discovered about Lana doesn't change that. You know, I don't think you needed to be frightened that she would take me away from you. She might have liked to visit me, but if she'd taken me it would have hindered her career. That was always more important to her than her daughter. As far as I'm concerned, you are my mother and always will be.'

'I'm sorry the weather's been so awful while you've been here, Kay,' Thelma said. 'I would have liked us to go for a walk along the prom. It may be cold and windy here on the coast, but the air is fresh. I've heard on the news all about that dreadful smog in London.'

'Just imagine what it must be like for babies,' Julie said. 'I've heard some children have died.'

'Older people, too,' Thelma added. 'Aren't you frightened to go out, Kay?'

'I've never had to go out when there's been a real pea-souper,' Kay said. 'If it's the slightest bit foggy when I have to get to work, Julian, that's the producer, insists we get a taxi. And he orders taxis to take us home, too. He's even suggested that if the fog is too bad, the cast should camp out in Broadcasting House, like some of them did during the war. But so far we haven't had to do that.'

'But what about your other assignments?'

'Just the same, Mum. If I had to go anywhere I would take a taxi, and allow a couple of hours to get there on time. It doesn't happen every day, you know,' Kay said reassuringly, when she saw her mother's anxious expression.

Thelma smiled tentatively and Kay blinked unexpected tears away; she was touched that her mother really seemed to care for her wellbeing.

The three of them were in the sitting room of Thelma's new house. Or rather, the four of them. Julie had been feeding the baby and now Kathleen lay contentedly in her mother's arms, on the verge of sleep. Kay watched as her little niece kept closing her eyes and a moment later opening them as if she was just too interested in what was going on around her and she didn't want to miss anything.

'By the way, Kay, what do you think of my fire?'

Startled by her mother's change of subject, Kay glanced at Julie for enlightenment and saw her sister smile as she nodded towards the hearth.

'Oh, the fire,' Kay said. 'I noticed it straight away. I love the way it flickers as though the imitation coals are burning.'

Thelma frowned. 'Is it so obvious that the coals are imitation? I thought they looked real.'

'Oh, they do,' Kay crossed her fingers as she replied. 'At first glance it looks very real, but then you see the two bars and you realise you've been fooled.'

Kay sensed that Julie was trying hard not to laugh, but

341

Thelma seemed pleased with her answer. She announced that she was going to make a pot of tea and bring it in on the tea trolley with some home-made cake.

The room was quiet. The only sound was the rain beating on the window. Kay and Julie looked at each other and smiled. Kathleen had gone to sleep. She puckered her rosebud mouth now and again as if she were still sucking.

'Do you want to hold her?' Julie said softly. 'Don't look so frightened. Come and sit beside me on the sofa and I'll put her in your arms. That's right.'

Kay looked down at her niece sleeping so sweetly, and for a moment was overwhelmed with love for her.

'You look good, like that,' Julie teased gently. 'Maybe one day in the not-too-distant future you'll find someone to love and—'

'Don't, Julie,' Kay said quickly, and she couldn't disguise the catch in her throat.

Julie looked contrite. 'Kay – I'm sorry.'

'It's all right. Don't worry.'

Kay managed a smile. *Julie probably thinks I'm pining for Tony,* she thought, *and regretting that I left him. Well, let her think that. It's preferable to telling her about Tom and having to admit to how easily I was deceived.*

They were silent for a while as Kay cradled the baby, somehow taking comfort from holding the warm little bundle in her arms.

'Kay?' Julie said hesitantly.

'Yes?'

'I want to ask a favour of you,' she paused. 'No, it's not just a favour. It's something very important.'

'What is it?'

Julie hesitated.

'I hope you know that I'll do anything I can,' Kay said. 'Just ask.'

'Then will you consent to be Kathleen's godmother?'

'You want *me* to do it?'

'Of course. Tony and I both think there couldn't be anyone better.'

'But what does Mum think?'

'She's all for it. She's started making plans for the christening already. She thinks we should wait a few months until the worst of the winter weather is over. Please say you will.'

Before Kay had time to answer, Thelma came back into the room with the tea trolley. She looked at them enquiringly. 'Well, Julie, have you asked her?'

'Yes, Mum, she has,' Kay said.

'And?'

'And there's nothing I'd like better.'

Chapter Twenty-Five

'You mean you'd already guessed that Lana was your mother?' Moira said.

'There was so much that I'd found hard to explain,' Kay said. 'Then I worked it out as soon as I saw the photograph – the one in the envelope that you didn't think to mention, Shirley. Well, when I saw the way they were completely at ease in each other's company and the way they were looking at each other, there was no doubt in my mind that they were lovers.'

Kay, Moira and Shirley were having supper in the kitchen. There was a blazing fire and the curtains were drawn against the snowy chill of a winter's evening.

'And I'd like to know why you two decided not to mention that you knew the truth of it,' Kay continued. 'In fact, you knew all along, didn't you, Moira? I believe Lana must have told you not long after you became friends. I think she needed someone to confide in.'

'We didn't say anything because we didn't want you to be hurt,' Shirley said.

'If only you knew!' Kay told them. She paused and then spoke less vehemently, 'My first reaction was to be angry. I felt that a trick had been played on me. Can you imagine what it must feel like to know that you have been lied to all your life?'

Moira looked uneasy. 'Lana believed that Thelma would be a better mother for you than she could ever be.'

'Really?'

Moira remained silent.

Kay sighed. 'That may be true. She would never have given up her career to care for a small child, would she?'

'All I can say is that I believe she came to regret what she'd done,' Moira said.

Kay shook her head. 'I'd like to believe that, but I find it difficult. Perhaps in time . . .'

Nobody spoke, and Kay looked at Moira and Shirley. Their faces were filled with consternation. She paused a moment or two longer, then she said, 'Don't worry. I'll survive, and I'm not really annoyed with you. I realise you wanted to be kind.'

'Of course we did,' Shirley said.

Kay smiled. 'Then how about making me a cup of tea?'

Shirley got up and cleared the used dishes from the table; Moira put the kettle on. A little later, when they were drinking their tea, Moira asked, 'What about Thelma, Kay? Were you able to put things right with her?'

'I hope I have. I think I understand her better. She didn't deserve to be treated the way she was. I loved my father, but now I have to accept how flawed he was. He and Lana, both.'

'They loved each other,' Moira said.

'Was that an excuse to go on with their affair after I was born, and when his wife was bringing up their child?'

Moira looked uneasy.

'Other people knew or guessed,' Kay said. 'For example, the first time I met him, Julian told me how Jack used to come up to London to see Lana. It seems it was common knowledge.'

'Try not to be too harsh on them,' Moira said.

Shirley added, 'You mustn't allow yourself to get bitter.'

Kay smiled. 'I'm not bitter. What would be the point all these years later? And no matter what the truth is, it's Thelma I shall think of as my mother.'

'I don't blame you,' Shirley said.

Moira looked troubled. 'Lana loved you, Kay. She talked to me about you all the time. She was heartbroken when Thelma refused to let her see you.'

'Moira, don't let's quarrel over this,' Kay said. 'You're loyal to your friend and I respect you for that. That's why I'm going to give you this keepsake.' She rose from the table and took a folder from the countertop. 'My mother gave me this. It's a scrapbook my father kept of all Lana's successes. I don't know why Mum kept it – probably because it was important to my father, and maybe she always intended to give it to me one day. But I think it would mean more to you than it does to me.'

Moira took the folder and flicked through it. Suddenly she looked sad. 'Thank you, Kay. I still miss her, you know. And although you've made your decision, if ever there's anything you want to know about Lana, just ask me. I'll tell you if I can.'

Kay looked thoughtful. 'Actually, there is something. It was a question Mum couldn't answer.'

'What is it?'

'Why did Lana suddenly give up her career? Do you know why she stopped working when she was at the height of her powers?'

'Oh, dear,' Moira said. 'I promised not to tell anyone.'

'Oh, go on,' Shirley said. 'Lana is long gone and I'm sure she wouldn't mind Kay knowing.'

Moira smiled. 'I'm not so sure about that, but I'll tell you anyway. It was simply vanity. She was offered a part that several older actresses were very keen to have, in a new Hollywood movie.'

'I think I know what you're going to say,' Kay said.

'The film was a comedy about family life. It was a terrific part – a leading part – but Lana turned it down.'

'She was asked to play the mother, wasn't she?' Kay said.

Moira sighed. 'Yes. Lana told me that she didn't ever want to play the part of an older woman; she wanted to be remembered as young and beautiful. The actress who eventually played the part won an Oscar, and Lana missed out on that chance because of sheer vanity. Ironically, she wasn't that old, in fact she was barely middle-aged, but Hollywood likes its heroines to be very young.'

'So she ended up with no career and no family,' Shirley said. 'She must have regretted giving Kay up the way she did.'

'She did. Many a time I had to remind her of her promise to stay away from her, but I think she dreamed of having Kay come here one day, and as it is, she only achieved that once she was dead.'

Kay looked thoughtful. 'I suppose I'd better tell you that once Shirley is married, I shall probably leave here.'

'Oh, but Lana hoped that once you'd seen the place you would stay,' Moira said.

'I'm sure she did, but sometimes her presence – her ghostly presence – is overbearing. I want a place without history – at least not that kind of history. I intend to buy a place of my own. I can afford that now. Somewhere where my mother and my sister and her family, and my old friend, Miss Bennet, can visit me. I would never ask Mum to stay here.'

Moira looked tearful. 'You'll forget all about her. Lana, I mean.'

'No, don't worry, I won't do that. After all, if she hadn't

347

made me her heir I wouldn't have come to London. I wouldn't have had the job that I enjoy so much, and Mum and I would never have come to an understanding. Even Julie and I are on much better terms. So, no, I won't forget Lana. I have much to thank her for, but like any other daughter, it's time I flew the nest.'

Dora placed a plate of corned beef hash on the table before Tom and he thanked her without looking up.

'For God's sake, Tom, have you forgotten how to smile?' she said.

'Sorry, just thinking about something.'

'What are you thinking about? The successful end to the case you were working on? How you're going to be promoted? Not likely. It's more like you made a total balls-up of everything and the Commissioner had put you back on the beat.'

'Pack it in, Dora. And – er, thanks for this, you know it's my favourite.'

Tom forgave himself the lie when Dora beamed with satisfaction, but then he caught Ricky's eye and saw his huge grin. *I hope the lad doesn't give me away*, he thought. *I can't stand much more of Dora's nagging.*

'I'm sorry you're going to have to work on Christmas morning,' Miss Bennet said when Kay phoned her, 'but I'm delighted that there's going to be a Christmas special. Are you allowed to tell me anything about it?'

'A little. The programme will begin in the village church and then will go on to show how the various households spend Christmas Day. I'm afraid I can't say more than that.'

'Oh.' Miss Bennet sounded disappointed. 'You told me there was going to be a surprise guest – somebody famous.'

'Yes, I did, didn't I? But we've all been told not to tell anyone. Not even our nearest and dearest.'

Kay heard her old friend sigh before saying, 'Well, I suppose I mustn't encourage you to break the rules.'

Kay smiled. 'No, but if you were to guess who it is I might not deny it.'

'Oh, go on, give me a clue.'

'He's a film star.'

'It's a man, then.'

'It is indeed, and in one of his films he played the part of a highwayman and he became involved with a very wicked lady.'

'*The Wicked Lady*! . . . James Mason! The guest star is James Mason. How wonderful!'

Kay laughed out loud. 'You could be right, but please keep it secret, even from your sister.'

'Of course I will. But now that I know, will you tell me what part he'll be playing?'

'He's playing himself. That's fact. The fiction is that he's an old friend of the vicar, and that's as much as I'm going to say. You'll have to listen to find out more.'

'Of course I'll listen. I'll pour my sister and myself a glass of sherry each and we'll sit by the fire while the turkey's cooking and listen to *Mulberry Court*. As if I'd miss it! And that reminds me, what will you be doing when the programme is over? Will you have lunch with your friends?'

Kay did not know what to say. She had not told Miss Bennet, or indeed her family, about the dramatic events concerning Jane, and she wasn't sure what Shirley's plans were.

'I may have lunch in the BBC canteen with some of the rest of the cast.'

'Oh, no! A canteen lunch. How miserable!'

'No, it won't be miserable. There'll be turkey and all the

trimmings, followed by a proper Christmas pudding, coffee and mince pies. And the cast of *Mulberry Court* are a friendly lot.'

'Well, if you say so, but how I wish you could come home for Christmas. I miss you, you know.'

Wanting to change the subject, Kay decided to tell Miss Bennet of her plans to buy a house, 'And I hope you'll come and stay,' she added.

'How wonderful, of course I will! Whenever you ask me.'

Tom, pretending to read yesterday's newspaper, could smell the turkey cooking. Dora, already in festive mood, was wearing a paper hat, drinking from a glass of port wine, and singing carols as she set the table.

Tom looked up. 'Anything I can do to help?' he asked.

'No, you just sit there and carry on being miserable,' Dora said. 'Ricky's going to give a hand with the vegetables while I listen to *Mulberry Court*.' She switched on the radio and cursed when it tuned in to the wrong station. 'Flipping Radio Luxembourg,' she said. 'Ricky, can you just come and get me the BBC?'

Ricky put down his copy of *True Crime*, retuned the wireless and went into the kitchen looking fed up but resigned. While they waited for the signature tune, Dora said, 'I'm sorry if I've been nagging you lately, Tom, but the truth is you've got me worried. Is there something the matter with you? Are you ill? If so, you should have told me.'

'No, Dora, I'm not ill.'

'Then what the blazes is the matter with you?' She stopped and her eyes widened. 'Flippin' 'eck, you're not in love, are you? That's what Ricky thinks. You've found yourself a girl and you're worried about what will happen to Ricky and me. I thought he was joking in his usual way, but it strikes me it might be true. Well, stop worrying at once. You've been very good to us since your brother died, and I've realised lately what a selfish cow I've been. Other war widows have coped much better than I have. It's time I pulled my socks up. Even my own son has told me so.'

'Ricky's a good lad,' Tom said.

'I know, I'm lucky to have him.'

'And he's lucky to have you. You've done a good job there, Dora.'

Dora looked serious for a moment. 'With your help, Tom. I'll never be able to thank you enough.' She paused and listened to the wireless. A familiar signature tune was playing. 'That's it! *Mulberry Court* is starting,' she said. 'But listen to me, if you've found a girl, just go and get her. And now let's listen to my favourite programme.'

Just go and get her, Tom thought. *If only it were as easy as that*. No matter how much he loved her, he doubted if Kay would ever speak to him again. He stared miserably ahead. He hadn't even heard the doorbell when Ricky came back into the room with an envelope.

'Was that the postman? I hope you gave him his Christmas tip. It's in an envelope on the hallstand.'

'No, it wasn't the postman, but I don't think he'll be long. They knock off at twelve today.'

'So who was it and what is it?' his mother asked him.

'One of Uncle Tom's pals from work.'

Ricky gave Tom the envelope. 'He hadn't time to come in,' he said. 'But he said it was addressed to you at the Yard and it's got urgent on it. He didn't want to spoil your Christmas dinner for you, but he thought he'd cop it if it was important and he ignored it.'

Dora looked vexed. 'Don't say you've got to go to work, Tom! They might leave you alone on Christmas Day.' She looked at him anxiously while he opened the envelope.

'It's all right. It's just a Christmas card.'

'Who from?'

'Nobody you know.'

Tom read the message inside the card and put it back in the envelope. When neither Dora nor Ricky were watching him he slipped it into his jacket pocket. This card would not be displayed on the mantelpiece with the others.

Kay and Shirley had got up earlier than usual on Christmas morning. Kay washed and dressed, and went downstairs to find Shirley waiting for her in the hall. Neither had slept well and they laughed when they saw each other's weary faces. Each was holding a small, gaily wrapped parcel.

'Happy Christmas!' they said in unison.

'As we haven't got a tree to put presents under this year, I'm giving this to you now,' Shirley said.

Kay sighed. 'I didn't feel like buying a tree just for me.' Then, worried that Shirley might think she was feeling sorry for herself, she smiled brightly. 'And this is for you.'

They exchanged the intriguing-looking parcels and put them on the kitchen table. Kay saw to the fire while Shirley filled the kettle and lit the stove, then they sat down to open the presents. Kay had bought Shirley a cream-coloured cashmere scarf, and Shirley's gift to Kay was a pack of three pairs of seamed silk stockings. They looked at their gifts, thanked each other smilingly, and then fell silent.

'What's the matter, Kay?' Shirley asked eventually. 'You look so far away, so despondent.'

'I've been thinking about Jane. I wonder what sort of day she'll be having in prison.'

'Don't say you're feeling sorry for her.'

'Not exactly sorry for her. Just a little sad, if you know what I mean?'

'I think I do. Such a waste of a life. Especially as she'll probably spend many more Christmases in prison.'

'I can't bear to think about it,' Kay said.

'Me neither.' Shirley paused and then seemed to pull herself together. 'I must be getting soft in my old age.'

'What do you mean?'

'Well, you can't say Jane didn't deserve her sentence, can you? But now we've got a big day ahead of us, and we'd better have some breakfast.' Shirley got up to make the tea, and Kay cut slices of bread to put in the toaster. Both were on edge, and tea and toast and marmalade was all they could manage.

Kay saw Shirley's hand suddenly begin to shake as she spooned sugar into her tea. 'I thought you didn't take sugar,' she said.

'I don't. I haven't taken sugar since I was fourteen and gave it up for Lent, but I lay awake for hours last night and I'm dog-tired. I need the energy to get through today.'

'It's not just fatigue. You're worried about something, aren't you?' Kay said.

Shirley looked as if she was about to deny it, but then she admitted, 'It's the thought of Julian and me spending the next couple of days with the family. My folks aren't too pleased that I'm going to marry a much older man, and this is going to be like a royal summons where they'll look him over and decide whether he's a suitable husband for their darling daughter.'

'Don't worry,' Kay said. 'I'm sure Julian will charm them.'

'You don't know my mother!' They both laughed. Then Shirley's expression changed to one of determination. 'It had to be done,' she said. 'This will be the only chance of a get-together before the wedding.' She glanced at her wristwatch. 'We'd better go. Are you ready?'

'I've just got to put my make-up on.' Kay smiled. 'I know *Mulberry Court* is a radio show so the listeners can't see me, but as you keep reminding me, wherever I go I have to look like a professional and successful actress.'

'Too right,' Shirley said. 'I'll wash the dishes while you make yourself glamorous, OK?'

'Thanks.'

Shirley washed the dishes quickly, put the cinder guard in place and then took an envelope from her handbag. She looked at it for a long moment, thinking back to her last conversation with Moira, then propped the envelope up against the sugar bowl. She left the kitchen, closed the door behind her and took her coat from the coat stand. Her weekend case had been packed the night before and was waiting near the door.

She heard a car drawing up outside and opened the front door, holding it ajar. 'Hurry up, Kay,' she called. 'The taxi's here.'

Kay hurried downstairs and pulled on her coat, and the two of them stepped out into the frosty air. Soon they were on the way to Broadcasting House and the Christmas Day broadcast of *Mulberry Court*.

When the last line of the script had been uttered, the studio manager closed the studio mike and played a recording of Christmas carols rather than the usual signature tune. The cast listened to the music on the studio speaker, and as soon as the red light went out, there were smiles and a babble of happy conversation. Julian hurried in and thanked their celebrity guest profusely.

Kay smiled as she looked around, but she felt rather detached from it all.

Shirley left the cubicle and came into the studio to have a

private word with Kay. 'You are going to stay for lunch as planned, aren't you?' she asked.

'I suppose so. I don't really want to go home and make a sandwich.'

'It's a pity Moira decided to go to her mother's. We could have invited her to join us here for lunch and then you could have kept each other company.'

'No, she's doing the right thing. If she'd stayed in town she would only have sat in her flat waiting to see if Charles would drop in for five minutes.'

'How do you think he manages that?' Shirley said. 'I mean, where does Mrs Butler think her husband goes?'

'Apparently their grown-up daughter comes over with the children, so while they're cooking the turkey, good old Charles tells them he'll leave them to gossip and he supposedly pops down to the local for a drink or two.'

'What a prize the man is! I hope Moira's seeing sense at last,' Shirley said. 'And I'm glad she's decided to take over the house when you buy your own place. But look, everybody else has gone – it's time we got down to the canteen. I happen to know that Julian is treating us to champagne.'

Despite the lack of tablecloths, Kay thought the tables looked suitably festive with small bowls of holly, Christmas crackers and the champagne flutes that Julian had apparently found in the back of a cupboard in the canteen kitchen. Kay sat with Cynthia and Alex, her fictional parents, and Norman, one of the studio managers. Shirley sat with Julian on 'high table', and to Kay's fond amusement, she made a point of flashing her engagement ring. Everybody was in high good humour and Kay found she was enjoying herself – until it was time for Shirley and Julian to take their leave and drive down to Cornwall.

Shirley came over to Kay's table. 'Walk with me to the door, Kay. Julian's gone to put our cases in the car.'

They went out and waited near the main entrance, and Shirley said solemnly, 'So much has happened since last Christmas, hasn't it?'

'Mmm.' Kay had to fight to suppress a sudden feeling of desolation.

They hugged each other, then Shirley said, 'I feel guilty about leaving you alone on Christmas Day.'

'Shirley – you've got to go! Here's Julian and he's pointing at his watch.'

'Right. I'll phone you when we get there. No matter how late.'

Shirley left Kay reluctantly, but she was soon smiling again when everyone seemed to appear from nowhere to give the happy couple a boisterously good–natured send–off.

The phone started ringing as soon as Kay put the key in the lock. 'Where have you been?' Julie said. 'I've been phoning and phoning.'

'I told you I wasn't coming straight home.'

'Oh yes, you've had a posh lunch at the BBC.'

Kay laughed. 'It wasn't exactly posh. I think you may have the wrong idea about the BBC.'

'Well, anyway, everyone here wishes you a happy Christmas, and both Mum and my mother-in-law are still swooning over James Mason.'

'Are they both at your house?'

'Everyone's here.'

'Oh, Julie, are you doing too much?'

'Not at all. I'm being waited on hand and foot. And now I'm being ordered to go up and have a rest. So, God bless you, and I'll hand you over to Mum.'

Her mother sounded subdued. 'I hope you don't mind, Kay, but I've told Julie.'

'What have you told her?'

'The truth. The fact that you are half-sisters.'

'I don't mind. What did she say?'

'She'd more or less guessed, since Lana had made you her heir, but she said that it made no difference, and as far as she was concerned, you would always be her full sister.'

'I feel the same way. And, Mum, there's something you should know.'

'What's that?'

'Don't sound so anxious! It's just that I'm leaving this house. I'm going to buy a place of my own – a place with no memories.'

Thelma remained silent for a moment and then she said, 'Are you doing this for me?'

'And for me.'

'I'm glad, Kay.'

'Happy Christmas, Mum.'

'Happy Christmas.'

When Kay ended the call she felt unutterably alone. Her family was so far away; Shirley was on the way to Cornwall to plan her wedding; and Jane, poor Jane, in turning King's evidence, was going to lose not only her freedom, but also the man she loved.

The house seemed cold and uninviting. She had not had the heart to put up any Christmas decorations, even though Shirley had said that she should. She went through to the kitchen and found an envelope propped up on the table. The Christmas card inside it had a message in Shirley's neat handwriting:

Kay,
    I was wrong about Tom and so were you. I've tried to put things right. Please stop trying to punish yourself.

Your first instincts were right. Whatever happens next, just listen to your heart.

Love,
Shirley

Kay stared at the cryptic message and knew immediately what Shirley meant. But was it too late? She felt like weeping.

Tom hitched up his burden and rang the bell. When Kay answered the door, she looked both astonished and unwelcoming. She stared at the object he was carrying.

'I was told that you didn't have a Christmas tree,' Tom said.

Kay's eyes widened. 'Where on earth did you get that?'

'At the corner shop.'

'Today?'

'Mr Patel never closes. This was his last tree. His son brought me round in his van.'

'I see.' Kay's expression was unreadable.

Tom almost gave up hope. Shirley's note had told him that Kay was going to be alone and that she hadn't put decorations up or even bought a Christmas tree. 'Buy a bunch of holly,' the note said. 'Steal it from someone's garden if you have to, but just get round there and convince her that you love her!'

Well, he'd done better than that. He'd found a Christmas tree. But now, looking at Kay's face, he wondered if this had been a mistake. It was probably reminding her of the day they'd first met and of how he'd tricked his way into her house. He glanced at the tree. Its branches were drooping, just like his spirits.

Just as he thought despairingly that he might as well go home, she spoke. 'Did you travel in the back of the van with the tree?'

'No. Why do you ask that?'

'You're covered in pine needles.'

'They started dropping the minute Raj drove away.'

At last she smiled and Tom began to hope again.

'You'd better give it a shake before you bring it into the house, then.'

Kay looked up at the leaden sky. The first flakes of snow had begun to fall. She stood aside to let him enter.

I'll Be Seeing You

Benita Brown

Orphaned Linda Bellwood has grown up looking wistfully through the windows of Fernwood Hall on to the lives of the glamorous Hyltons, knowing theirs is a world she can never be part of. But when she is hired as companion to the old Mrs Hylton, she becomes inextricably linked with the house and its inhabitants.

Linda soon finds herself drawn in as confidante to the beautiful, spoilt daughter Cordelia as her dramas are played out. It's Florian, the youngest son, whom she has the strongest connection to, however, and when their friendship blossoms into something more, she feels as if her dreams really have come true. But Linda begins to realise that the life she thought she always wanted is not as it seems, and it will take a chance encounter with a young artist to open her eyes to the meaning of true happiness . . .

As the tragedy and uncertainty of the Second World War takes hold, so a young woman must learn to let go of the past in this enthralling, romantic and heartbreaking novel.

Acclaim for Benita Brown's novels:

'A wonderfully evocative tale' *Lancashire Evening Post*

'A delightfully interwoven story of passion, love and loss' *Sunderland Echo*

'You won't be able to put it down' *Yours* magazine

978 0 7553 8468 6

headline

Memories of You

Benita Brown

When the close-knit Norton siblings are tragically orphaned, they are forced to separate. Helen, taken in by her selfish Aunt Jane, is treated like an unpaid servant, while her twin brothers Joe and Danny find themselves in a cold, unwelcoming orphanage. And little Elsie is adopted by the wealthy Partingtons, who spoil and encourage her to forget her past.

Growing up and blossoming, Helen finally escapes to London and finds work in a buzzing Soho café, discovering a new, exciting world there; one which introduces her to charismatic reporter Matthew Renshaw. She never gives up hope of a reunion with her brothers and sister. But time has changed them all in ways she could never have imagined, and just as her dream seems within reach, Helen is faced with a heartbreaking choice . . .

As the thirties lead into the Second World War, four siblings face an uncertain future in this captivating novel of love, loss and the enduring strength of family.

Acclaim for Benita Brown's novels:

'A wonderfully evocative tale' *Lancashire Evening Post*

'A story of hope and determination . . . a really good read' *Historical Novels Review*

'You won't be able to put it down' *Yours* magazine

978 0 7553 5292 0

headline